THEY THOUGHT NOTHING COULD EVER COME BETWEEN THEM....

Kristin bent down, cupped her hands, and took water from the shining place where Eric's reflection gleamed up at her.

"Eric Starbane," she said. "I have your image in my hands. I want to have you forever. Will you give me that wish?"

"With joy and with all my heart," he said.

Kristin raised her hands and drank. Then she turned to the pool and let her image show upon the sun-dazzled water.

Eric did not hesitate. He bent down and lifted water in his strong sunburned hands. "Now I have your image," he said. "And with your image, you. May I take it, forever to keep?"

Kristin nodded, almost overcome. "Yes. Take me. Drink me. I am yours. Anywhere and for all time."

BUT FATE WOULD PUT THEIR LOVE TO THE ULTIMATE TEST.

Books by Vanessa Royall

FLAMES OF DESIRE
COME FAITH, COME FIRE
FIREBRAND'S WOMAN

WILD WIND WESTWARD

Vanessa Royall

A DELL BOOK

Published by
Dell Publishing Co., Inc.
1 Dag Hammarskjold Plaza
New York, New York 10017

Copyright © 1982 by M. T. Hinkemeyer

All rights reserved. No part of this book
may be reproduced or transmitted in any form
or by any means, electronic or mechanical, including
photocopying, recording or by any information
storage and retrieval system, without the written
permission of the Publisher, except where
permitted by law.

Dell ® TM 681510, Dell Publishing Co., Inc.

ISBN: 0-440-19363-X

Printed in the United States of America
First printing—March 1982

*To
Al, Joan, Jim, and Suze.*

During the nineteenth century the towns grew; Norway filled up with landless men, storekeepers, sheriffs, moneylenders, bailiffs, notaries in black with stiff collars and briefcases full of foreclosures under their arms. Industries were coming in. The townsmen were beginning to get profits out of the country and to finagle the farmers out of the freedom of their narrow farms.

The meanspirited submitted as tenants, daylaborers; but the strong men went out of the country as their fathers had gone out of the country centuries before when Harald the Fairhaired and Saint Olaf hacked to pieces the liberties of the Northern men, who had been each man lord of his own creek, only in the old days it was Iceland, Greenland, Vineland the Northmen sailed to; now it was America.

From: *U.S.A.*
John Dos Passos

CONTENTS
Wild Wind Westward

PROLOGUE

PART ONE
NORWAY, 1860 — 19

PART TWO
NEW YORK, OSLO, LONDON, 1860–63 — 93

PART THREE
NEW YORK, PENNSYLVANIA, 1863–65 — 181

PART FOUR
MINNESOTA, 1865–1872 — 395

PROLOGUE

Adolphus Rolfson and his son, Gustav, rested their wet and blown horses on a high meadow overlooking the little village of Lesja, in Norway. The village nestled in a lush valley that followed the S-shaped curve of the Rauma River. Father and son had come a long way to this valley and this village, from Oslo in the south, because the time was right, they were ready to make their strike, and they wanted to savor the sweet sensation of victory over these stubborn, independent mountaineers.

Victory had been a long time coming, too. But now, in June of 1860, all the machinations were prepared, all the bribes had been delivered, and everything lay in readiness for a stunning series of land acquisitions that would make the name Rolfson a power throughout Scandinavia. And that was only the beginning! Europe, and the world, were poised upon the brink of an era of industry and business hitherto undreamed. To those bold enough to seize the day, to take command of the new forces moving in the world, would go fortunes compared to which the legendary gold of Midas would seem a couple of copper coins at the bottom of a jar.

Adolphus Rolfson had no doubt that he was one of those selected by destiny to build commercial empires. These he would pass along to his handsome, charming, arrogant son—a fine, hard boy, and how he could stare a man down—until, in not too long a time, the name Rolfson would be emblazoned on properties all over the globe. Today the village of Lesja; tomorrow the world. Adolphus was going to achieve his dream, by God, and too bad for anyone who got in his way.

"See that mountain range to the north of the Rauma Valley," he said to his son, pointing. "Once we get our hands on those pastures and the timberlands beyond, there'll be no stopping us." He shifted slightly in his saddle, which was made of the finest English leather, leaned over, and, as if accentuating the vehemence of his ambition with a small, crude gesture, shot a gleaming brown swath of tobacco juice down upon the rocks of the trail.

Gustav looked away momentarily. He respected the old man, and had worshiped him once, but the habit of tobacco-chewing was not one designed to ingratiate those who occupied the high places he intended to enter. Gustav himself appreciated a fine cigar. But he also knew that his irascible father supported his every ambition, and had, in fact, gone to considerable expense to eradicate from him some of the sharp, crude habits of a rougher time. Not all of those habits, however.

"I'm pleased you asked me to accompany you on this trip," Gustav said to his father. "Perhaps I'll find pleasure in one of these mountain wenches."

"Find your pleasure in the business of foreclosures first," growled the older man, but then he smiled to himself. He had never been able to conceal, not even behind a hard-bitten severity that was far more than façade, the indulgent delight he took in his only son. And he knew already, from previous, solitary trips to Lesja, trips during which he had set up the great trap he was now about to spring, that the village held a young woman to whom his son would be immediately attracted: Kristin Arnesdatter, just eighteen, eldest child of the poor farmer Arne Vendahl.

"You are amused, father?"

"What's that?"

"I saw you smile."

"Anticipation. Simple anticipation, boy. For you as well as myself. Now the horses are somewhat rested. Let us ride down into the village and keep our appointment with solicitor Thorsen. He will have all the proper legal papers ready to serve upon the . . . villagers."

He had almost said "victims."

The two men touched with steel spurs the still-glistening flanks of the bays they rode, and began their descent along the stony trail into the village. It was rocky country, indeed, seldom offering more than subsistence to the people who farmed it, unless the something more was freedom and independence. But Adolphus had no use for freedom and independence, not someone else's anyway, and he found the hard earth quite charming. He had known for some time, since his hired German surveyors had completed their work, that just beneath these mountains and pastures and hard, rocky hills lay iron and copper and nickel, metals for which the factory barons of Europe would pay vast ransoms of gold.

June was a gorgeous month here in the north. The long, dark winter was forgotten; the body-breaking cold, the soul-numbing burden of eternal midnight were cast aside. The sun reached its zenith, and on Summer Solstice, longest day of the year, the people celebrated with spirits and dancing and song, just as the residents of a Mediterranean town might observe the feast of a special saint. But the citizens of little Lesja might not party so happily this year, thought Adolphus, with grim satisfaction, as he and his son galloped into the village, scattering chickens and a few pigs and blond, blue-eyed children who scrambled away from the pounding horses. The children showed no fear—strong mountain youngsters seldom did—but they regarded with a watchfulness close to suspicion these two riders, the wide old husky one and the tall lean hard one, knowing by instinct that the strangers were related. Knowing by instinct and also by an unusual feature shared by father and son: a hard flat bony bridge of nose, which seemed to set their small eyes farther apart, like those of wolves.

The Rolfsons reined in their horses before one of the grandest houses in Lesja, a narrow, two-story, four-chimney structure of the finest mountain pine, with wide stone steps and a balcony outside the fashionable French doors on the second floor. Adolphus, who had spent his youth sleeping with animals for the heat of their bodies in a ramshackle building that was half barn, half house, thought the French doors grand indeed, but young Gustav did not care, even remotely, for anything that suggested the French. He admired the English; he had even learned the language.

A sign above the main door of the house said:

LARS THORSEN, SOLICITOR IN THE LAW

and Lars Thorsen himself appeared in the doorway beneath his sign, bustling down the wide steps and yelling for a stablehand, who came on the run from a barn behind the house.

"Here! Here!" cried Thorsen, grabbing the reins and handing them to the servant. "See to these horses! See to these horses!" He spoke to the stableboy as if the young man had never cared for a horse before, and, even if he had, would certainly find a way to mishandle the task this time. Solicitor Thorsen spoke to all subordinates in this scornful, and yet somewhat patronizing manner. He was a stocky, balding, red-bearded tyrant to anyone he considered inferior to him. But to those above him, or to those from whom he conspired to gain something—occasionally approbation but more often money or power—he could appear to be a fawning, bowing lackey, managing in spite of his bulky body to convey fussy obsequiousness.

He looked, to the Rolfsons, like an old red-haired hound, all too amenable, all too eager to please.

And that was very good.

"Let's go inside directly," snapped old Adolphus, swinging stiffly from his horse. Too old to be in the saddle so long a time. "I want an immediate accounting of the situation."

Something about Thorsen's manner caught the eye of young Gustav, who had trained himself to watch for weak-

WILD WIND WESTWARD

ness, and to strike when he saw it. "What's wrong?" he demanded of the solicitor, who, after a couple of gulps and swallows, managed only: "Nothing. No, nothing. All right. Let's go inside," leaving in the street a group of children watching the fine horses. From the windows of the village houses their parents were watching the closed door of the solicitor's expensive residence. The mountaineers, these old, hard, honest country farmers, knew. They knew. They knew that the law was at work behind that closed door, and they also knew that the law at work behind a door, especially Thorsen's, would not be of benefit to them, who waited outside. For the one hundredth time fathers tried to recall the exact wording of the notes they had signed. (Solicitor Thorsen was to have returned copies, but none had been forthcoming.) For the two hundredth time wives glanced worriedly at their husbands, but did not speak out. What good would it have done? What waited, waited.

Inside the house Lars Thorsen couldn't stop asking the Rolfsons to sit down, have a seat, take their ease. He kept on asking until Gustav interrupted.

"We *are* seated, solicitor, and have been for some time, as you can well see. Now, answer the question I asked outside. What's wrong?"

"Nothing's wrong," Thorsen replied in a quavering voice, perspiring freely and dropping into a sturdy straightbacked chair that had a thick cushion to receive the weight of his wide behind.

Old Adolphus leaned forward from his place on the couch upholstered with reindeer hide. His slitty eyes were icy, and his voice was even colder.

"If you fouled this plan for us, Thorsen, the Sonnendahl Fjord will never give up your bones."

"Sonnendahl Fjord," repeated a croaking Thorsen.

"What about it?" demanded Gustav, leaning forward, too, just like his father, and fixing the solicitor in a frigid unrelenting gaze.

"That's . . . that's where the trouble is."

"You had better explain. And damned quickly."

"Yes. Yes. I meant to. It's just that . . ."

Vanessa Royall

Gustav stood up and smacked the heel of his hand against the pistol he wore at his belt.

"Yes, please," gabbled Thorsen, turning to Adolphus. "You know how it was, sir, when you came here last year posing as a banker and giving notes to tide the farmers over during the bad harvest?"

The old man nodded, and made a grimace that was not unlike a smile. He had given loans to everyone, small loans, asking in repayment terms nothing more than ten percent of the loan payable to him each year for ten years, plus an equal payment of ten percent of the original loan for two more years, as interest. He had, for this, been regarded almost as a savior, just last year when the harvest failed and the cattle stood gaunt and milkless in the pastures. In the original loan documents repayment had been scheduled every September. But the original documents had been altered.

"Did Thorvaldsen fail to forge the new documents?" he demanded.

"No," bleated Thorsen. "His alterations are expertly done."

"Did Amundsen turn down the bribe?" he shouted, referring to a local judge who had been handpicked to supervise the court orders of foreclosure.

"No, no."

"Well, if the altered documents show a repayment date in June, and everything is in order, then I should get the land. We know that all of these farmers signed over their land as collateral, confident that, even with a scattering of bad harvests, they could easily manage to repay small loans in twelve years."

He sat back against the cushions of the reindeer-hided couch and regarded Thorsen contemptuously.

"I'm . . . deeply involved in all . . . this," blithered the solicitor uncertainly, "I just want to make sure of one thing."

"What's that?"

"The job you promised me? In Oslo, with your shipping company? Is it still on?"

"Are you going to serve these foreclosure notices here in Lesja or not?" interjected Gustav, staring at the solicitor with his hard blue eyes.

"Yes, but . . ."

"But? *But?* It seems damned late for a 'but.' "

"But I'm *afraid*!" Thorsen managed, in what sounded like a suppressed sob. Then realizing how pathetic he must sound, went on: "You see, at Sonnendahl Fjord today—"

"What the hell has this got to do with Sonnendahl Fjord? There's nothing we want at Sonnendahl Fjord!" shouted Rolfson senior. The fjord was miles to the northeast. Leave it to the fishermen, the dreamers, the lovers of beauty.

"Eric Starbane is at the fjord today. Or he was. He is on his way back to the village now."

Yes, Starbane, thought Adolphus. The Starbane farmstead, which, according to centuries-old custom, also gave its name to everyone in the family for as long as they owned the land, was small and tidy. Its soil was relatively rich, as well. But, as the German surveyors had reported, the Starbane land rested upon what was most likely the richest deposit of nickel from the North Sea to the Ural mountains of Russia.

"I thought Gunnar Starbane owned that land?"

"He did. But he died. That's the problem. Unlike most of these people, Eric can read, he can think, and he *will* fight. I would not put it past him to take this whole matter beyond Amundsen, who, crooked as he is, could still find ways to cow the others."

"We can handle him," said Gustav brashly.

"Wait," cautioned the old man, raising his hand. "Don't boast until you have seen your enemy. So," he said to Thorsen. "You've had a spy on him?"

"It is a matter of great delicacy."

"There is no such matter in business, solicitor!"

Thorsen debated with himself for a while, deciding whether or not to reveal his secret, and thus face burdens known only to him, or to chance a loss of the job in Oslo that Rolfson had promised, a fine job in an exciting city, far from the morose drudgery of these mountains. (He had always seen himself as a great man, immersed in high affairs.)

"I am in love with a girl . . . a woman of the village," he said, rather sheepishly, as if it were a weakness to be in love.

Adolphus laughed. He guessed the truth immediately.

"And she loves Starbane instead, am I correct?"

Thorsen nodded, flushed, hangdog, downcast.

"And she went today with him to the fjord?" goaded Gustav, snickering. He had never been rejected by a woman. He proceeded forcefully at the first flicker of rejection. Who cared? They might yield, they might fight, they might scream. But they were all the same, were they not?

Old Adolphus, though, had an immediate suspicion. "What is the girl's name?" he asked.

"Kristin. Arnesdatter. A Vendahl."

The old man nodded, thinking of the present he had meant for his son, thinking of the golden hair spilling down over her shoulders, over the breasts full and high behind her white peasant's blouse, thinking of the swell and curve of her hips, which were as good as or better than the finest he had known in his day, a day, thank God, upon which the sun had not yet entirely set.

"And did your spy tell you what the two of them, Eric and Kristin, were doing up near Sonnendahl Fjord?" he asked the red-faced, red-bearded lawyer.

Thorsen nodded awhile, and sputtered awhile more, but he finally managed to spit it out. "They were making love," he said, then added, as if it were a thing of incomprehensible wonder, "They were making love on the cliffs above the fjord. Right there in the open air. In front of God and . . ."

"And your spy?"

More nodding.

Adolphus thought it over for a minute. "We'll serve the first foreclosure papers on Eric Gunnarson," he decided. "If he's really a troublemaker, we'll deal harshly with him, and then the rest of these farmers will toe the line."

WILD WIND WESTWARD

"Gunnarson?" asked Gustav. "I thought his name was Starbane."

"It won't be after his land is mine." The old man leered. "That is the custom. Loss of land means loss of name. He will be nothing but some dead man's son."

"And someone's lover," added Thorsen, uncomfortably.

PART ONE

NORWAY
1860

I

Poised upon the moment of first loving by a man, Kristin Arnesdatter remembered all the words. Her mother's words. Her father's words. Quaint Pastor Pringsheim's words. Even the words of her friends at school. Kristin remembered everything they had ever said about being loved by a man: the obvious danger of it, the presumed ecstasy of it. And she knew beyond knowing, knew with her body more than with her soul or mind, or even heart, that all their words were false. That none of these people knew anything about love at all. She knew only the truth forged in the smithy of this body, her own, which was now so gloriously alive, more alive than it had ever been: *Each love is different, and if one does not create love for oneself, it will not be.*

"Never be naked with a man," Pastor Pringsheim had said, "never be naked with a man before you pronounce holy vows at the altar in the church of our forefathers. Loving with the body prior to the saying of vows will taint your relationship forever, and only disaster will come of it."

"You are a beautiful girl," Arne Vendahl had said to his daughter, "and you are my delight. But beauty is both a blessing and a burden. The men will come to you like bees to honey. It is their nature, as it is meant to be. But remember, we are poor. It should be easier for you to love a rich man than a poor one. Do you understand? Help your family even as you help yourself."

Kristin's schoolfriends had whispered about other aspects of romantic possibility. "You know my sister Lisa?" asked saucy little Loni Haakonsdatter, tying and untying

Vanessa Royall

the ends of her long, honey-colored braids. "The one that got married last year to Harald Fardahl from Glittertinden? Well, she told me a little bit about it. She said it hurts a little at first, but after a couple of times it feels so delicious you never want it to end."

But Kristin's mother, who lay ill now with what the doctors called "a wasting of the blood," had been quite prosaic in her advice. "Look at me, girl," she sighed one day, lying in the bed she seldom left anymore. "This is the bed in which I conceived nine children. In which they were born and in which two of them died. The ones who are still alive have barely enough to eat, even in the years of good harvest. And now I am dying in this very same bed. Remember me when your body asks you to satisfy its craving."

"What craving?" Kristin had asked, turning away to hide her blush. She already had a very good idea what it was: that feeling of being tender yet empty, which she experienced late at night, trying to sleep, thinking of men.

"You will certainly know it when it comes," sighed her mother, "you will certainly know."

And now, lying with Eric on the grassy cliffs above Sonnendahl Fjord, lost in his kiss this bright and blazing day, Kristin knew. Eric had ridden to the Vendahl farmhouse just after breakfast, looking like a blond Nordic cavalier, even though he had only a brown plowhorse for a steed. Dismounting, he had waved to Kristin, who was busy scrubbing the younger children's clothes by the stream behind the house, and sought out Arne. Kristin's father looked up from the blasting forge, at which he was reshaping battered horseshoes. Nodding at the young man in the wry, resigned manner assumed by fathers of beautiful girls, he plunged the red hot metal in a bucket of water, waited until the hiss and steam subsided, then greeted Eric. Kristin stopped scrubbing and strained to hear.

"Sir," Eric said, "about that matter of which we spoke. I should like to see Kristin today."

WILD WIND WESTWARD

Kristin saw her father lift his hand, a small wave, a gesture of assent. "Here is no place for talk," he said.

"We will not go far, I assure you."

Again, her father made the small wave with his hand, and returned to his forge. Kristin's mind was racing. *That matter of which we spoke? We will not go far?* But Eric was already walking toward her. She stood and brushed her skirts, hating the water and mud that sullied her appearance.

But he seemed not to notice at all, thank God. "Kristin," he said, "I have your father's permission to speak with you. Not here. Let's go for a ride, to someplace quiet."

Quickly she had raced to the house and slipped into her best blouse, soft and white, with mountain flowers embroidered in colored thread at collar and cuff, and she also put on her Sunday skirt of deep blue. She had spent much time sewing it herself, and was always pleased to wear it, knowing how well it showed the trimness of her waist and enhanced the fullness of her breasts.

"What are you doing?" called her mother weakly from the bedroom.

"Dressing. Eric Starbane is here. He . . ." She hesitated, feeling that something significant and important was about to happen. "He has come to speak to me," Kristin pronounced, feeling quite significant herself. "Father has given his permission."

But, in the bedroom, Kristin's mother had only sighed. *She would do more than sigh if she were here now*, thought Kristin, lying with Eric in the grass. They had ridden without many words through the pass west of Lesja, and up into the hills overlooking the fjord. Sheer walls of rock dropped down and down to the great gorge-like inlet, where the cold blue water lay still and lovely and deep as a jewel, as sapphire. The lighter, diamond blue of the Atlantic shimmered under the golden sun, and the warm grass upon which Kristin and Eric lay was green as jade.

They had been kissing and embracing for some time

Vanessa Royall

now, and she felt desire hot and racing in her body. This she had felt with Eric before, in stolen moments in darkness at village dances, or in the grove of pine behind her house, to which she would steal at midnight, meeting him there. But today, for the first time, he had caressed with his strong, gentle hand, the place where her need was deepest, and she herself had for the first time touched with wonder the great length of his own desire. Now, still embracing, they broke away from another long kiss, and looked deeply into each other's eyes. The plowhorse stomped and grazed a short distance away; a small waterfall gurgled and sang as it dropped to the fjord; the ocean wind was fine and sweet. Save for their own needful breathing, there were no other sounds.

"I love you so much, Kristin," he said.

I know, she thought. *How could I not know?* "I love you as well," she said. "No, better."

"But that could not be."

He looked at her in a way she had seen before, reverently, but with something left unsaid. But this time he did not keep the words to himself.

"I want you now," he said, holding her with his eyes and his arms.

Could this have been what he wished to talk to her about today? About which he had previously spoken to her father? She doubted it, but then it made no difference. All of the old cautionary words came to her, flocking like blackbirds along the red branches of conscience, and her whole girlhood flashed past, too, like a high-speed dream, like a seamless ribbon of flowing life.

"I want you, Kristin," he asked again. "Everything."

She pulled her eyes from his, leaned forward, and placed her forehead at the place where his strong neck met his wonderfully muscled shoulder, and it was there that Eric Starbane felt her tender nod of acceptance and assent.

And so it began for them, their lives, their one commingled life, which they could not have foreseen, not even in dreams. Nor did they care, then, to foresee it, because

WILD WIND WESTWARD

the only thing that mattered was the moment of love, and another moment, and yet another, until all the separate, discrete elements of time blended as one, and time did not matter either. Kristin raised her head from his shoulder, and his lips found hers, a kiss of promise and wonder, far more powerful than any kiss they had shared before.

The fastenings of her blouse were loosened even before she was aware of the June sun warm on her bare breasts, fastenings loosened as if by his breath, or by his kiss, which now encompassed tender, throbbing nipples, moved slowly, ardently, from nipples to neck to mouth, and then to nipples again, and down along the gentle golden swell of her fine belly. Like an implacable hunter, Eric tracked her with his kiss, loosening the blue skirt at the waist, and drawing it down, inch by inch, trailed by his kiss. Never before in her life had Kristin imagined—never had she felt—the piercing sensation that was not yet pleasure but rather anticipation of the pleasure that would come. This sensation went on and on and on, as he drew the sleek blue skirt from her strong slender legs, and tossed it onto the grass, where it lay like a wild shroud, like a sacred cloth that had previously concealed a holy vessel, but which, now, became a relic of its own, sanctified no more by what it had guarded than by what it had revealed. Kristin gasped and cried out as Eric kissed down the long length of her legs, first one, then the other, inch by inch, until, when she was naked for him, he began to track upward with lips and tongue.

She closed her eyes, but the sun beat down upon her, and from behind eyelids the June light fashioned flickering patterns of shapes and colors unknown even to the penumbra of the gods. *No more, no more, I cannot stand it,* cried her mind, but her body ruled, held sway, and it demanded everything and more, and more and more of everything.

Eric ripped off his white cotton shirt as he kissed upward toward the center of Kristin's being and, as he slowly moved on, divested himself also of the rough woven trousers he had worn. By the time he had kissed and caressed around the quivering depth of his beloved, by the time he had passed his kisses once more up over her belly and breasts, by the time he tasted her mouth again, he was naked as she.

"Marry me," he demanded, the hardness of him throbbing upon her belly. "Marry me, now."

"I do," she cried. "I do. I will, I will. Whatever it is that you say, and what it is that we do, do now!"

And they did. There was no pain, none at all, but rather a form of completion, a slipping into herself of something that must always have been meant for her, must even have been a lost part of herself. As Kristin felt Eric moving into her, she felt only rapture and promise. The time that had previously been stilled by their long kisses now shuddered in captured tumult, too entranced by what it must witness and bear even to quiver and beat. The feeling of Eric inside her was magnificent beyond thought and when he seemed to withdraw she sobbed, only to cry out in ecstasy as he moved all the way into her again.

She wrapped her strong legs around him which were golden from the sun and taut and powerful from climbing in the mountain pastures. She wrapped her arms about the hard, rippling width of his powerful shoulders, pressed down his golden head to her own, so that he might kiss her with his lips even as he rode her with his body, even as he kissed and retreated and kissed and retreated and kissed and retreated with the essence of himself. Without knowing when or how it had begun, she felt herself moving with him, completely with him, matching with her own twists and thrusts everything that he did. It was as if they were cavorting in dance upon the village green on the feast of Summer Solstice, so perfectly did their bodies mesh. Yet it was not only their bodies that were totally commingled. Souls, hearts, minds, too, everything together began to mount a height Kristin had never scaled, as if she were climbing in a glorious dream. Far back within the caverns of her mind she felt a blood-red pounding, as if something enchanting but unknown were knocking upon the door of her very being, asking, no, *demanding* entrance

WILD WIND WESTWARD

to her very self, to all that she was or would be. Eric was kissing her with his mouth, his body pounding hers and the wild red pounding at the door of her soul could not be refused. "Yes!" she cried, and then gasped, "*Yes!*" and "*yes!*" and "*yes!*"

Time, held in abeyance so long while Kristin and Eric had made their love, now lurched forward, so that by the time they regained breath—or, more accurately, forced themselves to breathe evenly again—hours seemed to have flown by. Now, truly, did Kristin remember all the words that had seemed so insignificant and meaningless before. Pastor Pringsheim's admonitions seemed not all that absurd, and the image of her own mother, nine children, the bed of life and death, would have been difficult to dismiss, had it not been for Eric's constant, prolonged caresses of tender gratitude, even after his own pleasure was fulfilled.

"How do you feel?" he asked, kissing her neck.

Kristin had to think a moment, to sort it out. "Like a woman," she said. "Just as I thought a woman ought to feel, after taking her man. I feel as if I were your wife."

"You are," he said, kissing her again. "That is what I wished to ask you today."

"You have asked. I have certainly accepted."

They laughed, delighted with their closeness and with each other.

Kristin's face tightened suddenly with another kind of bodily knowledge.

"What is it?"

"I'm hungry!" she realized. "I'm famished!" The keenness of the pangs, in fact, startled even her, who was often hungry in a house of too many mouths and too little food.

"Does this happen to you every time?" asked Eric, with an expression amused and worried at the same time.

She kissed him for answer. "*Every* time!" she teased. "Of course, every *time*! What is it that you think? Do you not already know you are my first? And only," she added.

"And only," Eric said.

Kristin did not ask him, but she knew he must have had many women before her, else how could he so skillfully have given her such great pleasure? But she did not ask. She was jealous, but she did not want to know. He seemed to sense the nature of her thoughts, and said, "Let's go over and bathe in the stream. It will feel splendid."

The grazing plowhorse seemed slightly startled by their sudden emergence from the grass, or perhaps by the movement of animals in the pine forest above the cliff, but settled to a desultory chomping of grass as his master and his master's mistress walked naked, arm and arm, toward the cold, translucent, rocky stream that ran from the mountains to the lip of the stony gorge, where it became a tumbling funnel of waterfall down into Sonnendahl Fjord.

Eric took her hand, and they walked a short distance upstream, until he found what he wanted: a deep, clear pool of icy mountain water held by a ragged, rocky inlet off to the side of the current. "Let's dive," he said, and before she fully realized what was happening, he took her with him, hand-in-hand, off the ledge, through the brilliant air, and they plunged into the peerless, freezing pool. The shock, painful and exhilarating, quickly passed, and upon opening her eyes she saw Eric diving beside her, the two of them, sleek and splendid, going down, down, captured and held by this strange, silent room of water and light. He held her hand still as they descended, dreamlike, to the savage, rock-strewn floor of the watery chamber. Kristin felt as if her chest were about to explode, and at the same moment Eric pointed upward, swinging the both of them into a graceful curve. They shot upward, faster, ever faster, and burst up to the surface and into the roaring light.

"That was wonderful," she told him, as they sunned themselves on the ledge beside the stream. "But not as wonderful as making love."

"No. Not as wonderful." The plowhorse nickered nervously, and Eric glanced around to make certain the beast was not too near the edge of the fjord. "When should we have the wedding?" he asked, turning back to Kristin.

"I thought we already had it," she said, stretching like a cat on the warm rocks, giving him a slow smile. It was so wonderful to be with him this way, to know she would be with him now forever.

"I mean the vows in Pastor Pringsheim's church," he said. "We have to do that part, for the sake of your parents. And," he added, with a laugh, "for the sake of everyone who will want to celebrate with us at the wedding dance."

Kristin knew this, too, of course. The mountain life was not an easy one, and those few happy occasions—Summer Solstice, the harvest festival, Christmas, weddings—were more than sufficient cause for eager revelry. Besides which, the union of Eric Starbane, handsome son of a fine old family whose bloodlines could be traced back to fabled Viking Eric the Red, and the exquisitely beautiful Kristin, had not gone unmentioned by the women of the town. It was sad, truth to tell, that Eric's parents were gone, and that he had no other kin in Oppland County or, as far as anyone knew, in all Norway. But that meant—the chattering women also noted—Kristin and Eric would have the fine old stone Starbane farmhouse to themselves, at least until the children came.

"We should do something, though," Kristin decided. "To make today even more special than it already is."

"How could that be?"

"I know. But there should be a . . . a ceremony, or something. . . ,"

And then she thought of it. "Stand up," she commanded, and he did, smiling in puzzled, playful expectation. Kristin stood too, and their two bare, golden bodies, young blond god and goddess, were shimmering images in the gently rippling pool.

Then Kristin bent down, cupped her hands, and from the shining place where Eric's reflection gleamed up at her, she took water. "Eric Starbane," she said, turning to him, all serious now, and touched by the meaning of what she was about to do, "I have your image in my hands. I want to have you forever. Will you give me that?"

Eric, watching her, lost his smile, knowing that his beloved was performing a ritual that, impulsive though it was, would nevertheless be something both of them could never forget.

"I grant your wish with joy and with all my heart," he said.

Kristin raised her cupped hands to her mouth and drank the cold water in which Eric's image had been. Then she turned again to the pool, and let her image show upon the sun-dazzled water.

Eric did not hesitate. He bent down and lifted water from her reflection, holding it in his large strong sunburned hands. He turned to her.

"Now I have your image, Kristin," he said, not at all surprised to hear a tremor of deep emotion in his voice. "Now I have your image, and with your image, you. May I take it inside me, forever to keep?"

Kristin nodded, nodded again, almost overcome, almost unable to speak. But to say the words was important to all ceremonies, and she said, "Yes. Take me. Drink me. I am yours. Anywhere, and for all time." And then, without knowing exactly why, almost as if a premonition, a chill wind, had blown down from the mountains and into her secret heart, Kristin added, "For all time, no matter what happens or how things appear. . . ."

Eric's arms went around her, and she was lost in his kiss, feeling the swell against her of his renewed desire, feeling herself flow again, and falling, falling, ready to yield, either here on the rocks, or on the grass again, or anywhere. . . .

But the old plowhorse whinnied in sudden alarm. Eric and Kristin, startled, turned to see the usually phlegmatic beast watching the hills above the fjord. They looked up to the hills as well, to see a horse and rider burst from beneath the shelter of thick pines, and race away down the trail that led to Lesja.

Kristin looked at Eric. She felt a flicker of fear. He seemed surprised, but not alarmed. She relaxed.

"I thought we were alone," he said.

They both knew, now, too late, why the plowhorse had

seemed restless a few times earlier in the afternoon. Lost in each other, they had not realized it then.

"I think someone's been up there all the while," she said, shivering, and wrapping her arms about her breasts. They walked quickly back to where their clothes lay fluttering upon the grass; the breeze off the Atlantic felt a bit more chilly than it had before. Kristin dressed hurriedly, her skin forming gooseflesh. Eric did not rush, though. His expression was concentrated, dark with thought.

"Did you . . . did you recognize the—?"

He nodded, fastening his belt.

"Who?"

He looked at her for a long moment. "It will just worry you," he said. "Perhaps it means nothing."

Kristin stepped close to him, and touched his arm with her hand. "We are together now," she said. "What matters to you also matters to me, and the other way as well. Please tell me."

He hesitated, but then spoke. "I did not see the rider clearly, but I recognized the horse. A black stallion, with a white patch on its shoulder. I saw it last year at the harvest festival. It belongs to Subsheriff Johanson, from Dovre, downriver."

Kristin's eyes widened in astonishment. Subsheriff Johanson had jurisdiction in the area of Lesja, but he seldom appeared, preferring to spend his time drinking beer and playing cards with Judge Amundsen and political cronies in Dovre. Johanson was also known to be friendly with solicitor Thorsen, in the village. She mentioned that fact to Eric.

"Well, he certainly was not with Thorsen today," Eric remarked, worried. He walked toward the plowhorse, clucking to gentle it, grasping the reins. He put an arm around Kristin's waist and swung her high up on the back of the huge animal; then, leaping up himself, he mounted behind her.

"What does it mean?" she asked. "He saw us making love, surely. He can make much trouble."

Eric knew that. Lovemaking before marriage might well be called sinful by Pastor Pringsheim and the church. It was also a crime. Yet the subsheriff, one of dozens of petty officials who had begun to harass citizens in recent years, had not ridden down to disturb them, to arrest them, or even to make his presence known. Instead, he—and perhaps other concealed observers, too—had watched surreptitiously from the forest, then had fled. What did it mean?

"Whatever is happening cannot be of any good," Eric decided, kicking the big horse with his heels, guiding it back onto the trail toward Lesja. "I am afraid we shall learn soon enough what is going on."

They said little on the ride back toward the village. In the quiet of his mind Eric cursed himself for having jeopardized his beloved. Such rashness: making love to her under the sun, the sky. It had seemed so wonderful, though, so natural. And it was, it had been. He knew that. But it had been rash nonetheless, and he cursed himself for it. Hours ago, everything seemed perfect. They would be married, and go to live on the farm which had been property of the family Starbane since Eric the Viking had turned away from the Western Sea, and had come home to Norway and peace. The farm was his. The only burden was a small loan his father had taken from the businessman Rolfson, of Oslo. But the first payment was not due until September, and after the harvest Eric knew he could easily make the payment, although, God knew, he had no money just now. He and Kristin would live on the farm free and in love, and have children and make love and grow old together. There were times when he thought it might be exciting to go off to Oslo, or Europe, or somewhere else, and maybe he would one day if he could afford it. But such a journey would be only a holiday. He would have to come back because he was a Starbane, and his land was freely his, and he was free upon it. Without the land and the name, he would be a commoner, just someone's son, available for hire by any man who met his price. Such men were dangerous. Look at Subsheriff Johanson, that snake, or solicitor Thorsen, a fawning, unprincipled sycophant, or Judge Amundsen in Dovre. Eric had heard that the judge's legal decisions tended to depend on whether plaintiff or defendant bribed him the more generously.

Eric could not bring himself to believe such a low thing. He was a fair and honest young man, and it was the responsibility of an honest man to give the benefit of the doubt. In addition he was a landowner, a free man with an ancient name, and no one and nothing could take that away from him.

He would ride back to the village, find out what was happening, and face whatever had to be faced.

Kristin, riding in front of him, was grateful for Eric's strong arms around her. She felt a little frightened, but also angry. *Be calm*, she kept telling herself, *be calm. Wait and see.* It was something she had been trying to teach herself for years: *patience*. Riding back home this day, she did not yet know how much need she would have of that virtue.

We are different, she reflected, thinking of Eric and herself. *And that is good.*

Two years younger than he, Kristin had known him, it seemed, forever. Lesja was a small village. Everybody knew everybody else, from the oldest widow in the town to the shepherd in the remotest mountain hut. Herself spirited and occasionally impulsive, Kristin had admired Eric's calm courage ever since she could remember. He did not flinch. He knew what was right, and stood for it. Many times, in younger years on the schoolyard, Eric had protected the littler children from bullies, even when the bullies were bigger than he was. He had beaten them then, and it would take a rash man to fight him now. At twenty Eric was over six feet two inches, and always a winner in the log-tossing contests on festival days. Eric turned away from no challenge, and never had. Kristin remembered the time Pastor Pringsheim had called all the church-school pupils before him.

"The altar candles are missing," he had accused, swinging the hard hickory cane with which he flogged those who, for one reason or another, had offended his rectitude or tolerance or simpleminded piety. One by one he asked each child, boy and girl, "You took the altar candles, did you not?" And every child answered in the negative. "Well, well," Pastor Pringsheim decided, not without satisfaction, "since no one is admitting the foul deed, you are all guilty, and everyone shall be soundly thrashed." Having said that, he grabbed whimpering little Gunnar Verondahl, dragged him to the front of the church, and forced him down upon the communion railing. He raised the cane to strike a mighty whack.

"Pastor, wait," Eric had said.

"So," said the minister, turning toward Eric, his cane still raised to strike, "the true miscreant wishes to confess?"

"No," said Eric.

Outraged and confounded, Pringsheim released little Gunnar and stepped over to Eric. "Then what is it?"

"If I may say so, sir, I do not think any of us took the candles."

"What? *What?* Why on earth do you say that?"

"Because you have asked everyone, and we have all denied it."

The pastor could not believe his ears. "And just because everyone has denied the deed, you think they are telling the truth?"

"Yes, I do," answered Eric, never flinching, never once letting his eyes move from the pastor's. "And beating us will not get your candles back."

"Then I shall beat you for impertinence!" cried Pringsheim, enraged, reaching to grab Eric's shoulder.

"You may," said the boy. "But that will not get your candles back either, if, indeed, someone has truly taken them."

Pringsheim had stood there for a long time, looking at this bold but entirely well-mannered young man, unable to deny the forthright fearlessness in Eric's eyes. The pastor passed from a feeling that he must flog Eric to save his

WILD WIND WESTWARD

own honor before the other children to a knowledge that if he thrashed anyone he would have little honor in the eyes of any. He did not apologize; that would not have been correct to one of his office. But he did say, "I have decided to postpone punishment on the chance that I am mistaken. We shall now search for the missing candles, on the slight possibility that they have been misplaced."

Half an hour later the offending candles were located in a sacristy drawer, where, it turned out, an eager but inexperienced deacon had placed them, rather than in their usual depository next to the coal bin. The mystery was solved, and Pastor Pringsheim did not flog so hastily after that episode.

The boy who had stood up to Pringsheim had become a man now, and Kristin rode with him back into the village. It was late afternoon when they returned, jouncing upon the stolid old plowhorse into the Vendahl yard. Arne was waiting for them in front of the house. At first Kristin thought her father looked furious, and tried to fashion some explanation for the sight—she was sure—Subsheriff Johanson had recounted. But, riding closer, she realized her father was tremendously afraid of something, almost in a state of panic.

Eric noticed it, too.

"Eric," he said, approaching and addressing the younger man before either he or Kristin had gotten down from the horse. "Have you heard the news?"

Eric realized instinctively that Vendahl was not referring to anything that had taken place between himself and Kristin. He also guessed that Subsheriff Johanson had had motives other than spying upon lovers to explain his presence in the hills this afternoon. Possibly there was some connection between Johanson's stealth and Arne Vendahl's fear. "We have been out riding," he told the older man. "I have heard nothing."

He jumped from the horse, and helped Kristin down, holding her by the waist. Arne was already telling his story, his voice ragged, his throat constricted by fear and incredulity.

Vanessa Royall

"Adolphus Rolfson and his son rode into the village shortly after you and Kristin departed," he said. "You remember Rolfson, yes? The man from Oslo who was so helpful in providing loans to tide us over last year's bad harvest?"

"I remember him," Eric said. He also remembered how he had argued with his own father, Gunnar, who was then alive. "Father, we do not truly need this loan. It would be convenient to have the money, but we have weathered worse years in the past. Do not sign the note."

But everyone else in the village was taking a loan, ten-year repayment terms were unheard of, and it seemed a pity not to take what this fine Rolfson man so eagerly offered. Eric had felt queasy about the affair. It had all been so *easy*. It had been unbelievable. And he knew now that he was going to find out it *had* been unbelievable.

"Rolfson and the boy went immediately to solicitor Thorsen's, where, after some time in conversation, Thorsen appeared on the steps of the *stavkirche* and ordered Pringsheim to ring the bell."

The church, an ancient structure fashioned entirely of wooden slats, or *stavs*, the staves themselves delicately, intricately joined, was an awesome, even fantastic reminder of Norse ingenuity. Raised almost a thousand years ago, it still stood strong against the mountains, and served the villagers not only as a place of worship, but also as a gathering place in the event that important news had to be promulgated, or important issues discussed. And so the solicitor had used the Pringsheim church bell to summon the citizenry.

"*Fellow townsmen*, he called us," recounted Kristin's father angrily. "He explained to us that Rolfson had come for the first payment on his loan, and also that he stood ready to foreclose upon anyone who could not make that payment, exactly as the terms of the loans provided."

"But that is impossible," said Eric. "I myself read the note my father signed, and, like all of the other loan papers, it specified that payment was to be in September, after the harvest. It is now only June, and we have used whatever money we had left to buy seed for the spring planting! How can it be that . . . ?"

"I know only what transpired," answered poor Arne, lifting his hands, palms open, a gesture of hopelessness, or supplication.

"You did not see your own note? The one you signed?"

"I can't *read*," Kristin's father pleaded.

That was true, and Eric knew it. He had simply forgotten the fact due to his tension in the face of the present threat. Eric and Kristin's generation was the first in Lesja even to have a semblance of regular schooling. The elders, unless they had been fortunate enough to have skilled parents, had seldom learned to read, even a little, although most had had sufficient pride to learn how to sign their names. It was highly embarrassing to have to make an X on one's confirmation document, or wedding paper, or upon the baptismal certificates of one's children. But being able to sign one's name did not bring with it the ability to decipher and interpret loan agreements. Such a task was left to solicitor Thorsen, who knew about such things.

"Something is very wrong," Eric decided. "Thorsen has to be mistaken, or perhaps Rolfson is. I read and reread the paper my father signed, knowing it would be my responsibility in the event of his death. And, now, it *is* my responsibility. And the paper clearly called for repayments in September."

"But Eric," called Arne, in a voice that was like a strangled whine, "Thorsen gave the notes to Pastor Pringsheim, and, upon reading them, he, too, was astounded to find that payment is indeed due *now*."

"Then they must be false papers!" declared Kristin, who had been listening to the men with increasing disquiet. "Something has been done to the papers."

"But I saw my own signature on the paper," said Arne, with an aspect of dazed resignation. "My own signature, which it took me so long to learn."

"Then it apparently took someone else less time to learn

Vanessa Royall

it even more perfectly," snapped Kristin, who sensed already, somehow, that a monstrous evil was afoot in these pure mountains.

Both men turned to her. Their responses differed. Eric, who knew and loved Kristin's spirited nature, her manner of deciding *this is what I think so I will tell you,* also knew she might be a bit hasty in her judgments. She had not yet learned the sanguine effect of a little patience. Eric himself was willing to withhold judgment until he personally inspected the notepaper at Thorsen's office.

Arne Vendahl's response to his daughter's outburst was less subtle. First, he cast a worried glance in Eric's direction, lest such a desirable suitor might have been put off by a young woman's temerity. Second, he admonished his offspring, "You will hold your tongue. This is a matter for men!"

"I do not see that it is being so well handled," she shot back. "We stand here worrying and talking while Thorsen and that man from Oslo make their plans."

Her father, who might once have swatted her behind for such a tone, such words, now seemed to realize that Kristin was right. And so did Eric.

"What did Thorsen say he would do?" he asked.

"Present the documents of foreclosure, and call upon the law to begin eviction proceedings."

It was a moment before Eric found breath to speak. "All of us?" he asked.

"All who signed and cannot pay the notes."

"We *all* signed and *none* of us can pay."

"That is the whole of it." Arne sighed. He could see no way out.

"What kind of devil is this Rolfson creature anyway?" snapped Kristin, incensed to the marrow of her young soul. "I am going to see him. Where is he staying? Where—?"

Her father was too dispirited to act, but Eric grasped her forearm, firmly but gently, in his hand. "It's not a time for rashness," he said.

WILD WIND WESTWARD

"Oh, it's not, is it?" she returned, her eyes afire and voice rich with a need to strike back at the tormentors. "What do you suggest, then?"

"I shall go over to Thorsen's right now and speak to him. I shall ask to see the note my father signed. I know his signature. It is clear that Thorsen, or Rolfson, or someone has made a terrible mistake."

Eric wanted to believe that, and yet, even as he spoke, he made a devastating connection: Subsheriff Johanson was empowered by law to enforce foreclosures and evictions. That would explain his presence in the Lesja region. "When are they due to begin the foreclosures?" he asked.

"Even today . . ." Arne Vendahl began, but then a boy could be seen racing from the village in the direction of the farm.

"That's Piet!" cried Kristin, recognizing one of her brothers.

"Yes," said Arne. "I told him to stay near Thorsen's, and to bring news if anything happened there. I wanted to be here to watch out for my property."

"What would you be willing to do in defense of it?" demanded Eric, his tone sharp but not cold. "Would you fight?"

Arne raised his hands again, this time in a gesture of helplessness. "The signature is the signature," he said. "The paper is the paper. What would a judge say? And I have seven children."

Seven children. Kristin understood her mother's words now, the business of being tied to the bed; she understood her father's plight. But understanding did not help to solve it.

Little Piet raced up to them, panting, but gleeful with the knowledge of his responsibility as a messenger. "They've . . . they've sent for . . . their horses . . ." he gasped, gulping for air after his run from the village.

"Who?"

"The solicitor . . . and the men from Oslo. And sheriff Johanson, with his men from Dovre."

39

"Men from Dovre?"

"Four of them. They have *guns*." He was excited to have seen the guns.

"Where do they intend to go?" his father inquired.

"To *his* place," Piet said, pointing at Eric. "They are riding first to the Starbane farm. What does it mean?"

But Eric did not answer. He was already on his horse, kicking the big beast into the semblance of a gallop. He felt the horse solid and powerful between his thighs. But he also felt the earth, his world, his freedom and future, falling and falling away.

II

A crowd of worried villagers had formed in the small but well-kept Starbane yard by the time Eric rode up, and reined in the panting plowhorse. They were watching the eight men who stood, conversing quietly, on the steps of the old stone farmhouse. Eight men: Thorsen; the two Rolfsons; Subsheriff Johanson, a big, burly man; and his four henchmen, all as mean looking and hefty as he. Still, they seemed slightly intimidated by the group of silent, watchful mountaineers. They were also waiting for Eric. The law stated that notice of foreclosure must be laid in the living hand of the man whose name was written upon the document itself.

"Is that the man?" asked Gustav Rolfson of the sheriff, as Eric dismounted and started toward his house.

"Yes. Gunnar Starbane's son."

Gustav was surprised, and not pleasantly so. Knowing himself to be handsome, strong, even suave, should such a quality prove useful, he had always thought of country people as rather doltish, when they were not downright spavined or ugly. But now, seeing Eric, he was forced to revise his casually held prejudice. Eric Starbane was no bigger than Gustav, but he looked somehow stronger, more intact, more *there*. Gustav felt a tremor that carried with it things that required a moment to decipher, things with which he was largely unfamiliar: the feelings of being challenged, threatened, jeopardized. Yet how could that be? Starbane had no chance against the Rolfson wishes. None at all. But Eric Starbane did not seem to know this as he strode purposefully toward his house, sweeping the eight men with his piercing, dark-blue eyes, obviously holding in check a strength—and an anger—formidable indeed.

"Well, Eric Gunnarson," drawled Gustav, addressing him in the common way.

Eric halted, at the base of the steps to his own house, entrance to which the men blocked. He fixed Gustav Rolfson with a sure, straight stare. "Starbane," he said.

"Well, for a little while more," admitted Gustav, in a slow, mocking voice. "But those who do not pay their loans on time cannot retain the land from which they take their name."

"The loan my father signed is due in September," Eric said.

Once again, Gustav was made uneasy by this young farmer. He seemed too unafraid, too independent. Perhaps it was simply a form of country naiveté, but Gustav had the instinctive feeling that such was not the case. Yet, what did it matter? There was work to be done.

Old Adolphus realized, too, that delay in presenting the official papers would give time for a larger crowd to gather. That might mean trouble. Also, he wanted to get on to the other farms. Even now it was late; the foreclosures would have to carry on tomorrow.

"Give it to him," he told Thorsen.

The solicitor, sweating, keeping his eyes off Eric, took from a leather satchel an envelope sealed with the stamp of crafty Judge Amundsen, of Dovre. He handed it to Subsheriff Johanson.

Eric, and all the watching villagers, saw the transmittal. While they well knew that acts ordered by law were to be enforced by the Oppland sheriff or his designates, they also knew that Thorsen, who had drawn up the loan papers in the first place, was now acting on the side of those who would foreclose the loans. And from this crowd of mountain farmers, honest, trusting, unsophisticated, there came a quick, sudden rumble of anger, like that first, faint sound of far-off thunder, which can be heard even before the dark clouds of the storm scud threateningly into view.

WILD WIND WESTWARD

Joining that crowd now were Kristin, her father, Piet, and several of her older siblings.

Eric, who had noted that Johanson, even while holding the envelope of foreclosure, seemed a bit unsure of himself, now saw the subsheriff give Kristin a long, knowing look.

Lord, thought Eric, he is going to use *that* against us. I cannot let him humiliate Kristin by telling what he witnessed at the fjord.

Until this very moment Eric had not thought he would believe a man capable of so low a thing. Yet he knew that Johanson had seen the lovemaking. And so the subsheriff—who had undoubtedly told Thorsen about it—would use what he had seen to his purposes. Almost everyone in Lesja, moreover, knew how the graceless, domineering, red-bearded solicitor yearned for Kristin, panting after her even to the point of absurdity. Underestimate neither a scorned woman nor a humiliated man.

"Give him the papers," old Adolphus growled again, inspecting a huge gold watch that he'd yanked from his waistcoat pocket. Time was running.

Eric saw young Gustav Rolfson's eyes move over the crowd. He saw Rolfson's gaze stop, resting on someone. That quickly, he knew. Turning, he saw. Gustav Rolfson was staring at Kristin Arnesdatter, born a Vendahl. Knowing the look of his own desire, it was not difficult for Eric to decipher that same look in another man. A raging wave of possessiveness took hold of him, but he pushed it back. Now was not the time to become emotional. And, anyway, Kristin would never, not in a thousand years, accept this arrogant citified scion who stood on the ancient steps of the Starbane house.

Johanson stepped forward, holding the envelope out toward Eric. Johanson was grinning. "Got all your clothes on now, I see," he hissed, too quietly for anyone to hear.

"Say one word about it and you die," Eric promised, in a cold, deadly whisper he could not, at first, believe had been his own. It was as if a mysterious current, buried deeply within himself, had suddenly pressed into quick channels, come up into the light of day.

Johanson paused. He did not know Eric Starbane, but had heard of him, had sometimes observed him from a distance at the festivals, as Eric, time and time again, won contests of strength and endurance. The envelope in Johanson's hand seemed quite a lot heavier than it had only moments before.

And the low mutter of the villagers was rising, dropping, rising again into a sustained and unmistakable suspiration of anger.

Eric fought down an impulse to swing out at Johanson, fought down an equally strong but less explicable desire to vault up the steps and smash the leering grin of arrogance from Gustav Rolfson's handsome face. Keeping his wits, he recalled something his father had told him once, upon returning from a trip to Oslo, where he had seen Parliament. "They talk and talk, they ask questions and talk some more," old Gunnar had said, with a shake of his head. "But the more they talk, the less happens."

Perhaps that rueful yet amused observation offered a useful lesson. "Wait!" Eric said, so that everyone could hear. "By whose authority are these foreclosures tendered?"

The townspeople were not surprised by Eric's words. They knew his intelligence as well as they knew his strength. But on the farmhouse steps, the Rolfsons and solicitor Thorsen looked at one another. They had not expected defiance in this way. They had counted upon a physical display from young Starbane. That was why the four deputies were present.

"This is one foreclosure, yours," explained Johanson, jittery, too, now.

"But it is only the first, is it not? After which all of my neighbors, gathered here in my yard, can expect to receive theirs?"

Old Adolphus cursed beneath his breath. Gustav, who fought to keep his eyes off Kristin so that he could follow the conflict, felt again a twinge of insecurity in the face of

WILD WIND WESTWARD

Eric's courage. Were he in the same position, Gustav was doubtful that he would be so steadfast. Well, what did it matter? he asked himself. He was not in Eric's position.

Subsheriff Johanson was licking his lips. "I'll tell everyone about the girl," he threatened again, hissing maliciously.

"I do hope your wife can afford a fine stone for your grave," Eric said, "you spying piece of offal."

Johanson, slow witted but cunning, now thought he saw a way to induce Eric's acceptance of the envelope. "Thorsen put me up to the spying," he said. "It's his business. I'm just doing my job. Here. Take this damn thing." He winked. "Take it and maybe I can get Judge Amundsen, down in Dovre, to find a job for you."

"I don't want a job. I already have my farm."

"Look, son. Be reasonable."

But Eric did not have the opportunity, just then, to respond, because the silvery glint of harness bells announced the arrival at the Starbane farm of Pastor Pringsheim. The elderly cleric had come forth in his buggy to take a hand in things, having given some thought to the scene in front of the *stavkirche* earlier in the afternoon. He was, by nature, a rigid man. And, as a figure of authority himself, he routinely sided with the powers-that-were, be they secular or ecclesiastical. But upon learning that Eric Starbane was to be evicted, recalling dimly the talk a year ago regarding a September repayment date, he felt vaguely alarmed and somewhat puzzled. These were *his* people after all, he the shepherd, they the flock, and nothing evil was going to happen to his people if he could prevent it.

"God damn it all to Christ," old Adolphus groaned. All priests were idiots; they did not understand how the world worked.

"What is the matter?" inquired Pringsheim, disingenuously.

"There is a misunderstanding about the foreclosures," Eric told him. "I believe them to be fraudulent."

The crowd quieted. The minister stood up in his buggy, as if it were a pulpit. Kristin, in the group of people, re-

Vanessa Royall

membered when a much younger Pringsheim had threatened Eric with a beating, only to learn that a Starbane spoke the truth. Clearly, Pringsheim still thought so.

"The law states," pronounced Pringsheim carefully, "that in the event of contention over a matter of law, the issue must be appealed to the judiciary."

"And what do you know of law?" snapped Gustav, his voice heavy with mockery. "Best remain with devils and brimstone, or—"

Old Adolphus restrained his son with a harsh glance, and Gustav fell silent. Adolphus was determined to have the land and the minerals beneath it, but he wished to do so by using the law to his advantage, not by illegality. He did not consider bribes illegal, however, merely a part of shrewd business.

Kristin, watching from the crowd, was growing more and more uneasy, not to say fearful, for a combination of reasons. First and foremost was her concern for the fate of those she loved best: Eric and her family. Everything for which they had worked, everything for which they lived, now lay in grave jeopardy. From Oslo, the great capital, had come these Rolfsons to threaten devastation in the little village that was her home. Second, there stood Johanson with the notice of foreclosure in his hand and in his mind the memory of what he had seen at Sonnendahl Fjord. With such a secret, he had power over her, over Eric. She did not care for the feeling of being subject to the crude caprice of the subsheriff. Third, and most unsettling, she felt the eyes of Gustav Rolfson upon her, and she knew what his gaze meant. A beautiful girl learns early in life what that particular male gaze means. When the look of raw desire is in the eyes of a man one loves, then it is wonderful. But otherwise . . .

"The nearest justice is Amundsen, in Dovre," Thorsen was explaining. "And since these foreclosures have already been signed by him, there is really no need for an appeal."

Pastor Pringsheim was not to be intimidated. "The law does not prescribe the identity of the judge who hears the appeal, merely that the procedure is the right of anyone desiring it."

The people were silent now, listening, hoping to find in their pastor's words some hope of retaining their lands.

"Why waste our time?" Gustav barked. "You think the judge who signed these papers will reverse himself? You amuse me."

But Eric, once again, saw the opportunity to buy time.

"The law is the law," he said. "If it works for you, then it may also work for us."

"Christ and St. Olaf!" Johanson swore. "Take this paper, Starbane, and get it over with. You can't win."

"No," said Eric. "I want a hearing. And," he added, gesturing to the Rolfsons and Johanson's deputies, "I want you off my doorstep. You have no right to be there."

For a long moment, everyone was stunned, the Rolfsons not least. "Why you disrespectful farmer . . ." Gustav began, making as if to come down from the steps and teach Eric a physical lesson in good manners.

But Eric had had enough. Noting Rolfson's aggressive intention, however attenuated it was, he sprang forward and grabbed the man at his collar, where the knot of the fine silk cravat lay like a scarlet fist against the white silk shirt. Rolfson was startled, and cringed momentarily, waiting for a blow. The two young men stood face to face, so alike in appearance, save for the wolflike quality Gustav possessed due to his bony bridge of nose. They were quite alike in appearance, true, but other than that they were opposites. Eric felt and smelled Rolfson's breath, sensed the very odor of his soul, and at that moment he knew that he caught the stench of something hard and unyielding and evil. And he sensed, rather than understood, that this young man had come into his life not merely for the moment, but for a long, long time. The insight was unbidden and uncanny, but it was there, just as real as the feel of Rolfson's solid neck in his hands.

Kristin saw them there, facing each other. She had been surprised to see Eric, usually so self-contained, rush toward

Vanessa Royall

Gustav Rolfson, and even more surprised to see Eric reach out and grab the other man. True, he was angry because these men had presumed to take away his house, but the immediate threat had been removed, at least until a judge would hear the appeal and render a decision. Without knowing why, she, like Eric, experienced a hint of something ominous and foreboding, as if Gustav Rolfson were a harbinger of grief, and she remembered the feel of his eyes on her body. She shuddered.

"Unhand him, Starbane," Johanson was saying. "Or I'll have to arrest you."

"Yes, let me go, *Gunnarson*," said Gustav in an oozing manner. He realized now that Eric was not going to strike him. The knowledge served to restore his haughty grin.

"Certainly I'll let him go," said Eric, with a smile of his own, and spun Gustav slowly in a half-circle that forced him from the steps onto the ground in front of the house. So easily did Eric move the other man, with no obvious show of force, that it seemed almost as if they were performing one small movement in a dance, the choreography of which was, as yet, incomplete. Then Eric dropped his hand and stood back.

"You'll pay dearly for your impertinence," vowed Gustav, straightening his cravat.

In response Eric just looked back at Rolfson, calm again, his blue eyes clear as a mountain lake in winter.

Thorsen, old Adolphus, and the deputies clomped down from the steps, too. Thorsen was explaining to the elder Rolfson that he would dispatch a rider to summon Judge Amundsen to the village for the hearing.

"It's got to be held *here*?" grumbled the aspirant tycoon, dyspeptic and distressed that his plans for summary acquisition had been thwarted by a farm boy and a preacher. No, not thwarted, he corrected himself. Simply delayed.

The Rolfsons followed Thorsen on horseback, riding to his house, where they would be staying overnight. The deputies stood around Eric's yard for a bit, waiting until most of the people dispersed. They were trying to decide

WILD WIND WESTWARD

if they would have to pay some farmer to sleep in his hayloft.

"Rolfson is paying for everything," Johanson assured them, "just go on down to the inn and tell the innkeeper."

Eric, who was just about to enter his house, along with Kristin and her father, turned to say, "And is Rolfson paying the judge as well, Sheriff?"

"Stick to matters you know something about, Starbane. Planting your fields and herding your cattle and—"

He was about to say "ruining pretty young women in the grass," but he held his tongue. In the first place he did not trust Eric not to stride right over and grab *him* by the collar. It was not a prospect he savored. And, secondly, he recalled seeing the look in Gustav Rolfson's eyes when he first caught sight of Kristin. Since spying upon Eric and Kristin, Johanson had been wondering what best use could be made of what he had seen. Thorsen would pay him for his efforts, naturally, but that was a pittance. Embarrassing the couple might backfire: people would ask what he, Johanson, was doing, voyeur in the hills, when he ought to have been attending to official duties. Jailing Eric and Kristin was too absurd to contemplate. If all the men and women who stole away to the mountains to make love were to be locked up, the country would collapse. There would be too few free people to carry on the business of the day.

He guffawed to himself and swung up into his saddle. His deputies did likewise, to the creak and strain of harness leather, and the skittish prancing of the horses.

"Are you coming with us to the inn?" asked one of the men.

"I'll be there in a little," answered the industrious sub-sheriff. "I just remembered something I have to tell young Rolfson."

III

Arne Vendahl, fairly quivering with impotent fury, sent his son Piet home. "You and the boys see to the cattle," he said, "and have Magda prepare supper for you all. Tell your mother Kristin and I will be home later. We have talking to do."

He said it with a show of optimism, as if by talking about disaster some means might be found to forestall it. But all spirit left him when he sagged into the chair by the fireplace in Eric's kitchen.

Eric drew three huge mugs of ale from an oaken barrel in the corner, while Kristin put several small logs on the fire that always burned beneath the porridge kettle. Two staples of the mountains: ale and porridge. The ale thick, foamy, very strong; the porridge half-soup, half-stew, composed of scraps, leftovers, and occasional fresh additions of vegetables, meats, milks, cheeses, and almost any spice. Even measures of ale were added to the porridge for flavor, and it was eaten from large bowls, steaming hot, and served with goat cheese and huge chunks of black bread.

"What will we do?" moaned Kristin's father, uncheered by several deep swallows of the powerful brew. "If I lose my land, we are lost. I have no other skills. I will not even have my name. Oh, we shall all starve, it is true."

"It may not be that bad," said Eric, more to comfort the older man than to state his real feelings, which now, after the confrontation with Rolfson and its attendant excitement, had become rather gloomy. "It may still be that the judge from Dovre will listen to our story of the strange alteration in the repayment date on the notes."

WILD WIND WESTWARD

Arne said nothing, drinking. Kristin brought to the table three steaming bowls of porridge, placed them there, and sat down with the men.

"Father, it will be all right," she said, quietly, cutting slabs of bread from a loaf and passing them around.

But, in her heart, she did not know if it would be all right at all. She did not know what would happen. To be born a beauty into a rich family is to risk splendor and presumption, languid arrogance and ease. It is to risk being worshiped and patronized, never having to sharpen one's wits, never having to grow. But to be born into a poor family as a beauty, surrounded by other poor, plain people, is to face a harsh world, having constantly to adjust not only to the demands of life but also to the natures of crude, hard people. Kristin had come early to know the darker natures of her playmates and peers—envy and jealousy, mean, bleak rage—and it did not seem a shock to her when she realized that, like children, adults also were driven by savage and apparently inexplicable furies. So she knew that nothing would be all right. If Rolfson had gone so far as to recast by forgery the original loan documents, he would not now shrink from a further sullying of the law. The judge coming from Dovre would not help the citizens of Lesja; he would be coming to aid Rolfson.

Again, her body remembered Gustav's eyes upon her, and there at the table, she trembled.

"Let me get you a shawl," offered Eric anxiously. "The night is becoming chill." He was afraid that she might have taken cold after the long dive in the icy pool.

In spite of her father's presence, Kristin could not help but give Eric a secret smile, letting him know she knew what he was thinking.

"It is the coldness of men that makes me shudder," she said, spooning her porridge.

"All men?" he asked, reassured, smiling.

"Not all."

"What shall we do?" asked Arne, coming back from some dark, distant region of thought.

Kristin had a suggestion. "Father, if need be, I shall

go to Oslo and find work in a grand household. I shall wait upon table, and do laundry, and what money I earn I shall send back to you and the—"

Before Kristin knew what was happening, before Eric could stop him, Arne Vendahl slapped his daughter across the face.

She cried out in surprise and pain, and then began to cry with deeper hurt. Arne would have slapped her again, but Eric grabbed his arm, leaping to his feet, stepping between father and daughter.

"We are not servants! We will *never* be servants!" Arne cried. He meant to be strong, defiant, but in the middle of the declaration his voice went beyond his control, rose into a ragged, pathetic shriek. "I will do *anything* to keep that from happening." But then he realized all the more powerfully the dark degree of his imminent plight—landless, unskilled, seven children and a dying wife—and sank back down into his chair. Father was crying. Daughter, too. Eric stood helplessly over the table, a young man with his own life and new love threatened by the devil Rolfsons, who had suddenly descended, like precursors of doom, like apparitions in a bitter dream.

"I will beat them if it's the last thing I ever do," he vowed to the ancient stone walls of the Starbane house that had stood among these mountains for centuries, shielding within it both the love and the love of freedom in the hearts of his forefathers. *"If they move against me, they will never be able to sleep. Because always I will be outside their door!"*

Kristin was drying her eyes with the hem of her dark-blue skirt, an ugly red blotch forming on her face. Arne was weeping softly, his head down on the table next to his porridge bowl. Eric was just about to sit down, too, when a heavy, peremptory knock sounded on the thick, wooden door.

"Who is it?" called Eric, moving toward, but not grasping, the only weapon in the house, a huge Viking's axe, long-handled, curved-bladed. It was kept in an almost ceremonial position above the hearth, but it was a real axe and could do much damage.

"Gustav Rolfson," came the voice outside the door. "Let me in."

"I have nothing to say to you," answered Eric.

"Nor have I to you. I want to speak to Vendahl."

Eric and Kristin exchanged glances. Arne lifted his head from the table, wiping his puzzled eyes.

"I won't let him in unless you wish it," said Eric. "He has no right here."

Kristin's father turned the matter around in his mind a time or two, then decided that he must see what Rolfson had to say. Eric swung the door open and Gustav pushed into the house as if he owned it. He wore a long black flowing cape. But instead of his contemptuous manner on the steps only an hour earlier, he was now relaxed and smiling. One would have thought he was a friend to Eric, Kristin, and her father; his charm seemed easy and genuine. Kristin was not swayed, however. She surmised that he used charm as a weapon, used it when he needed it, just as he might use cruelty, or wile, sword or notice of foreclosure. She saw that he was as ruthless and unprincipled as his father, and potentially more dangerous, because of his greater gifts as an actor.

"You wanted to see me?" Arne managed.

"A matter of delicacy. Alone, if you please."

Arne Vendahl looked scared. "Does it have to . . . to do with my farm?"

"Tangentially, I believe." Gustav flashed his widest, most ingratiating smile. He nodded toward Eric, then Kristin. "Really, it is a private matter. I assure you that it is in your best interests and those of"—he glanced again at Kristin—"your family."

Looking puzzled and apprehensive, Arne got up from the table. It was clear that Gustav expected Eric and Kristin to leave the house, that he might speak with Arne inside, but Eric made no move to go. Gustav, realizing he could not insist upon the point without losing whatever advantage his display of charm had gained, decided not to press the matter. Arne went out, and Gustav Rolfson followed.

The sun was down now over the blue tops of the mountains, the twilight sky red and gorgeous, purple shadows of the peaks falling upon the Rauma Valley. The air was cool, almost cold. The bark of a shepherd's dog sounded high in the hills, and the thin silver tinkle of bells. From the window of Eric's house Kristin watched her father and Gustav walk over toward the well. Gustav seemed to be preparing for a long speech. He urged Arne to sit down, dropped a bucket down into the well. After he pulled it up, full of water, he filled a dipper and handed it to Arne. The older man drank.

"What do you think it's about?" Kristin asked, staring out the window.

Eric came up behind her, put his arms around her, and hugged her for a long moment. "Whatever it is, it's no good to us. I feel something about Rolfson."

"I, too."

"That this business of the foreclosures is only the beginning of his effect upon our lives."

"How rich do you suppose the Rolfsons are?"

Eric frowned. "Richer already than any man needs to be, nor yet as rich as they desire to be. It is a kind of life I do not understand."

Kristin smiled to herself, turned within his embrace, and they kissed. But the pressure of the day's events weighed upon them. "This house and this land," Kristin sighed, "are all we would ever need."

Eric looked sad. "I fear the judge will not help us at all. A strange form of darkness is falling across Norway now. I do not know what it will bring."

She looked into his eyes. "If they come to take your land, what will you do?"

It was a while before he answered. "My instinct is to fight," he said. "Yet what good is that? Then instead of being simply unlanded and bereft of my name, I will also be a criminal, imprisoned, no good to you or myself. There is but one way I can think of to put these foreclosures aright, and that is to go beyond Judge Amundsen and make an appeal in Oslo."

"How does one do such a thing?"

"Solicitor Thorsen would know. But he is serving the Rolfsons now. I think I will wait until we have the results of the local hearings, and then see a solicitor in another town, perhaps Tynset or Eagernes."

Arne Vendahl came back in just then, to see his daughter in Eric's embrace. His expression had changed; whatever Gustav had said to him had had a profound effect. His attitude was altered, too. He was standing straight and tall.

"Get away from him, girl," he said, gesturing for Kristin to move from Eric's arms.

"What?" Stunned and surprised, the young lovers parted.

"It is bad enough what you have done. Let us hope no one else finds out. Meanwhile, try not to bring further shame upon yourself."

"Father . . ."

"You do not know how fortunate we are. Even your sin will be kept secret." Arne tried, but was unable to meet Eric's eyes. "Come along now," he said to Kristin. "We are going home."

"Sir," asked Eric, "what is happening? Nothing sinful or shameful has occurred, nor will it, save possibly the timorousness of our people in failing to stand up to the Rolfsons. What have you been told by Rolfson? More to the point, why did you believe him? The man is a menace."

"No, no," cried Arne, grabbing Kristin by the arm, as if to drag her from the house. "I was mistaken. Rolfson has our best interests at heart. And he is the only one who can save Kristin's reputation, and the honor of the Vendahl name."

"What?" asked Eric. Kristin pulled herself away from her father's grasp. Clearly Rolfson's effect upon Arne had been sharp and bracing. But it did not seem that his effect had been charitable. Seeing their consternation, Arne shrugged, and explained.

"I understand the Rolfsons now," he said, speaking vigorously but still avoiding Eric's eyes. "Young Gustav was quite direct, and he made a great deal of sense. This is how things are to be. He and his father will not foreclose upon our farm, in spite of the loan. The loan, in fact, will be canceled. I have his word—"

"His *word!*" interrupted Eric scornfully.

"—and our family, alone in this village, will be able to retain its ancestral name. And you, daughter, in spite of your sin—oh, I know all about it; Johanson told Gustav and his father—in spite of your sin, you will not have to face public ridicule. Rolfson guarantees that the subsheriff will hold his tongue."

"Father . . ." Kristin began.

"And why," interjected Eric, "is Rolfson willing to do such fine things for a Vendahl?"

Arne tried to hold his ground, to retain his tone of moral superiority, but he was not quite able to carry it off. "Gustav wishes to marry Kristin," he said. "He has never seen a woman like her. Those were his very words. He will take her to Oslo and she will live splendidly. It is all you could hope for in life," he added, turning to his daughter. "And by marrying him you will save our family and our name."

"Never!" cried Kristin, her eyes wide with horror not only at the thought of Rolfson, but also upon the realization that her father was serious. He truly believed he was doing what was best.

For his part Eric fought to restrain his own tumultuous reactions. He, too, knew that Arne Vendahl was serious. The old farmer thought in terms of Kristin's honor, which he now believed to have been tainted by Eric. He thought in terms of a future for Kristin that he, Arne, truly believed to be splendid. And he thought, naturally, of his land and his name. It all made sense to Arne; to Eric, it all meant disaster. He recalled that moment in front of the farmhouse, when he'd seen Gustav Rolfson's eyes rest on Kristin. Oh, yes, Rolfson had known, had seen what everyone in Lesja had known and seen for all these many years. Kristin Arnesdatter had been born out of place.

Perhaps, Eric admitted to himself, I always knew it, too, but simply refused to believe. Kristin was not meant to be a farmer's wife, milking cows, scrubbing clothes, breeding children, to grow old too soon and to come early to the knowledge that the promise of youth is but a trick, a lure, a trap to catch you until it is too late to flee.

"Rolfson says he has never seen anyone as beautiful as you," Arne was saying. "His father has told him he can do whatever he wants, and he wants to marry you, take you to Oslo, give you education, fine clothes—"

"Never!" Kristin cried again, still unable to grasp the depraved enormity of her father's words.

"Think of your brothers and sisters," he said, pleading. "You alone can save them. Think of your mother. Think even of *me*, girl."

"I am. I always have," she responded, fighting back tears. Eric came over and put his arm around her. Arne didn't seem to notice. He was growing panicky again, fearful that his daughter's willfulness would ruin everything that had seemed so hopeful only minutes earlier.

"What will you do, then?" he asked, attempting, from his jittery perspective, to reason with her. "What will you do when we lose our livelihood? When Eric loses his? As he surely shall?"

"Perhaps not," Eric told him, explaining how he planned to seek a court hearing in Oslo if Judge Amundsen ruled against the citizens of Lesja.

"Fool! They do not listen to poor farmers in Oslo. That is a place run by people like the Rolfsons, who know how to manage high affairs."

Eric could not restrain his contempt, in spite of old Arne's pitiful quest to save himself. "I hardly think what Gustav has offered you could be considered a *high* affair."

"Your brash words will be the ruin of you," accused the older man, pointing a thick, work-blunted finger. "You are still young. What do you think life holds, anyway?"

"Life holds everything. If the worst happens here, Kristin and I will go away."

"To be a man for hire? To be a bought slave? Oh, fine, fine, lad."

"And what will you be, father?"

"I will have my land, my name."

"But not your daughter," countered Eric.

"It is for her own good. She will grow to love Rolfson."

"Oh, father . . ."

"You are young, girl. You know nothing. Nor do you," he said to Eric.

The three of them stood there glaring at one another. Kristin was near tears, Eric white faced and taut, Arne agitated and perspiring.

"Let us leave it until tomorrow," Eric said finally. "Tomorrow is another day."

"Tomorrow may be the last day," the older man shot back. "Kristin, come along. We're leaving."

But she shook her head. "I will follow in a moment, father. But I am not coming with you just now."

Arne seemed to nerve himself for yet another struggle, but then his shoulders sagged, in fatigue if not in resignation. "All right," he said, "all right. But you will do what you must when the time comes, you hear me?"

Then he was gone, beyond the heavy slam of the old wooden door.

Kristin fought back the tears, and succeeded. Matters were too serious for tears. "Let's go away," she said, looking up into his troubled, steady blue eyes.

He gazed down at her darker eyes, which were almost violet, held her with one arm, ran his fingers through her long, lovely hair. "Go away where?"

"There must be a place."

"Where?" asked Eric, not because he did not know the world and what it offered, but because the centuries-old traditions of the family Starbane were inextricably tied to the land, the independence, the very name of his narrow mountain farm. Yet both he and Kristin knew that, during recent years, emigration had begun to burgeon. Eric had always thought sadly of those people forced to flee to

America. What might they find there? What *could* they find that was even half as good as a homeland?

"We could go to Oslo," suggested Kristin, without spirit.

That possibility held small attraction: tens of thousands had recently flocked to Oslo, the streets of which were not paved with gold. There was gold on the tables, and around the fingers, and about the necks, and within the vaults of the rich, true, but outside the high walls of their palaces there was, as in the mountains, only poverty and struggle.

"Without my land, I am no Starbane anymore," said Eric, knowing the irony of what was happening in his country. The Rolfsons themselves were upstarts. Shrewd, vicious, cunning, successful upstarts. But they were neither of old family nor mighty name. Adolphus, son of some forgotten Rolf, set upon making grand his own son's life. Young Gustav could never have hoped to wed a daughter of the actual nobility, be she ugly or beautiful, so instead he had apparently decided to take Kristin, a mountain girl promising and lovely as a legend, and to make her a veritable princess, to outshine whatever women the aristocracy possessed. In terms of origins, history, dignity, the Rolfsons were nothing. But they did have the harsh, modern things that seemed to matter: iron will, money, and an eye for potential. Gustav had seen Kristin's potential, and he wanted it, so that he might enter the greatest ballrooms with the most stunning woman on his arm.

Eric's sadness, and Kristin's too, filled the stone house. Night had fallen. The cold moon rose above the mountain peaks. Pale light hung in the very air above the Rauma; fog drifted from the river, down among the houses of the village. Softly, Kristin left his arms, and moved toward the table, bending over the oil lamp, which she blew out. Moonlight came in through the window, casting the old farmhouse in soft glow and friendly shadow. Eric could not see her for a moment while his eyes adjusted to the new, natural light, but then he saw her approaching, felt her come into his embrace, and exulted to her nakedness within his arms, against his body. He did not even remember taking off his own clothes, and it did not matter if he

Vanessa Royall

remembered it or not. What had taken place between them at Sonnendahl Fjord was nothing compared to the love they now shared in his old bed in the room with the small stone fireplace and the high, wide windows that looked out upon the mountains of ancient Norway, their home, and upon the holy moon beyond. It was as if, without speaking, both sensed something strangely final about being together tonight, and the exquisite pleasure they gave each other could not, in the end, eradicate a gossamer feeling that combined both promise and sadness.

When a great ship leaves the harbor of dreams for a voyage long envisioned, the sea stretches out before the bow, all promise and wonder, but behind lies the land upon which the dream of the voyage has been fashioned. Nothing is yet forgotten, nor is any new thing held within the hand. Time, at a delicate, lambent moment, is held suspended in the sad, bursting heart that is both wellspring and vehicle of human wish.

So it was with their love that night. Neither of them wanting to end the anticipation of pleasure to come, and yet, as they wrapped themselves around and about each other's body, neither wanted to possess the final pleasure that would mean the end of the lovemaking.

He is me now, thought Kristin, *I have drunk him with my body and my mouth, tasted him with my heart, held him and made him mine forever with my arms and all of me.*

Eric moved upon her for a long time with deep gentle strokes, she wrapped all about him, giving her own stroking body to him, until it seemed that nothing would ever end and that everything would end in the next instant. Once, when it seemed almost too much to bear, she cried, "Stop, Eric, stop," and dug her fingers into the soft flesh of his arm, a distraction for him and for her that held the pleasure at bay, and yet somehow increased the ecstasy, too. Ah, pleasure is a strange thing, and love stranger. Night comes, spread by a blanket of wafered moon, but in the darkness, in the small, far places, there is as much love as God has ever dreamed. She felt his kiss upon her breasts, once when he withdrew from her to hold the final pleasure back again. She felt his kiss, and every nerve in her being trembled and exulted, as his lips and tongue found what they were seeking, what she was seeking, what it had all been willed by God for them to seek, even since the beginning of time. That which slow creatures had ferreted in the undersea trees, that gasping apparitions had come out of those seas to seek on the land, that beings had once for the first time stood upright upon African savannahs: Those things had happened only so that upon this sacred night Eric and Kristin could love one another, flesh and blood and being, this once, perfectly, for all time, and enough to last all time.

She reached for him, when he was in her and slowly thrusting again, reached for him, found and held the strange twin throbbing vessels that made him a man, felt their swelling and the swelling throbbing of the great length inside her as delicious as the feeling he sorcered in her, sorcered and ever enhanced in her until she prayed for it to end and never to end. Then, because God also knows time, and time has end to it, the moment came that was the end of this world, a world created in this bed this night by love and their two bodies. Slowly through her fingertips Kristin felt the first throb of him, her body, mind, both leaping to join him in delight. If they were shaken and the earth trembled with them, or if it was the earth that first spun away into abyss, carrying them along with it, who could say? But the moment was coming and finally it was there.

And then it was over, except in memory. So it was never over. All was a mystery. Kristin could not help but puzzle it, even as they kissed long and slowly in the afterglow. New to love, she knew nonetheless that she would never be able to know with clear mind *exactly* what ecstasy felt like. Because while one waited for piercing delight, there was room in the mind neither for imagination nor reflection, there was room only for anticipation and the blood-riven exultation of the flesh. And when delight was done, mind and body were still in shock, and so were incapable of recapitulating the exact feeling when love was at its flaming height. Even the ultimate moment was, in essence, lost, because to possess it was to be lost oneself at the precise moment of possession. So it was a mystery, and one could only, in memory, recapture a shadow of what it had been.

Kristin sighed.

"What's the matter?"

"Is it always this way?"

"Is it always what way?"

She hesitated a moment, as if undecided about speaking.

"Tell me. There is nothing you cannot tell me."

"It is . . . it is as it was at the fjord," she said. "I feel this . . ."

"Yes?" Eric propped himself up on an elbow and looked down at her. She was gold and ivory in the moonlight.

"I feel this terrible *hunger*," she said. "Is it always that way? After?"

He could not help but laugh with relief. "For everyone, it is different after," he said.

Immediately, she sat up beside him, breasts firm and flushed and glowing. "And how would you know?" she demanded, actually jealous, even though, moments before, he had been utterly hers. She knew he had had other girls, women. But never until now had they seemed to threaten her. That was another part of the mystery of love: there is more potential pain attached to something you possess than to something you do not, or have never, or could never, call your own.

"Kristin," he was saying, "Kristin, darling. Do not think of these things. I am yours and will aways be."

"Whatever happens?"

"Whatever happens. Forever."

The word hung there above the bed, powerful but disturbing. Forever was a long, long time.

"You had better eat something," he suggested then. "I do not wish to be the cause of your wasting away."

Kristin got out of bed, cut a slab of bread and a piece of cheese, folding the bread around the cheese. She asked

WILD WIND WESTWARD

if he wanted any, but he said no. She came back to the bed, got in, and snuggled beside him, eating happily.

"What happens afterward, to you?" she asked.

"I become hungry again myself," he admitted.

"Why," she exclaimed, "I just asked if you wanted some bread and cheese! Here, let me get you some."

She made as if to leave the bed again, but felt his powerful arm around her.

"I did not say that my hunger was for food," he said.

IV

Gustav Rolfson had tossed restlessly most of the night, soothed little even by solicitor Thorsen's luxurious feather beds. So when dawn came, he did not so much awaken as simply decide to put an end to the sporadic dozing that had passed for sleep. He tossed the coverlet away, and swung his bare feet over the edge of the bed and onto the bearskin rug. The bedroom, like all the rooms in Thorsen's magnificent house, was large and spacious. Gustav glanced toward the bed on the far side of the room, beneath the French windows he admired so much, but it was empty. As always, his father was up and at work. Gustav stepped into his fine leather slippers, sheepskin lined, and pulled on a robe of magenta-colored silk. One must dress always to be noticed: that was a lesson. Let the poor wear black and brown and gray.

Gustav trudged downstairs, into the dining room. His father and Thorsen were drinking coffee from steaming bowls, and eating fresh-baked white bread with butter and strawberry jam. Two maids scurried from the kitchen to the dining room and back again, bringing in more food: piles of spicy sausages, eggs fried in butter, fragrant sweet rolls, and bowls of fruit. Old Adolphus was eating with relish, and helped himself to half a dozen sausages and three eggs. Gustav heard his stomach rumble with anticipation, and his mouth turned to water. He gave the two men a short greeting, pulled up a chair, and started to load his plate with three or four of everything. A maid poured him a big bowl of coffee.

WILD WIND WESTWARD

Then he noticed Thorsen was just picking at his eggs, shoving a sausage around on his plate.

"You don't eat breakfast?" he asked, his mouth full of egg and bread and jelly.

"The solicitor finds his heart a little faint this morning." Adolphus chuckled. "After handling the foreclosure business for us he knows the people of Lesja will never stomach him again. If, indeed, they do not, some dark night, put an actual dirk in *his* stomach." Adolphus stopped chewing to guffaw at his own wit. "And, on the other hand, our poor host is not yet sure we will be forthcoming with that job he expects in Oslo."

Gustav smiled. The Rolfsons had old Thorsen right where they wanted him. "You've got some yolk on your beard there, solicitor," said Gustav, enjoying the sight of the man rubbing yellow juice into his red whiskers.

"Now, to business," declared Adolphus, still eating. "Son, are you sure you want to persist in this matter with the girl?"

"Yes, father."

"What girl?" asked Thorsen, seemingly alarmed.

"That blond one with the violet eyes. You know, Thorsen, the one you sent a spy after?" Adolphus was enjoying this; he knew Thorsen had wanted Kristin Arnesdatter. "I had expected merely that my boy here might give her a roll in the haymow. In fact, I had seen her on an earlier trip and picked her for just such an eventuality. But now he says he wants to take her to wife."

"Wife?" croaked Thorsen.

"That's right," Gustav spoke up. "She is more lovely than any woman I have ever seen in Oslo. A little training, some clothes, the right setting, and her mere presence beside me will gain us acceptance into the highest circles."

"What does she say to this?"

"And what care I about that? Her father has agreed. She has no choice. If she does not accede to my wishes, her family loses everything."

Thorsen had always realized that, in their operations and schemes, the Rolfsons always strove to place their

Vanessa Royall

victims in a dilemma that was intricately, exquisitely cruel. But not until now did he grasp that, to them, matters of the heart, of emotion, even family, were no more than chips in a game of skill. His own personal feelings were mixed. He divined that Gustav Rolfson would have his way, and that was good because it meant Eric Starbane would not be able to marry Kristin. But it also meant he would never have a chance with her, either. So it became of crucial importance that he please the Rolfsons, that they, indeed, take him with them to Oslo, where Kristin would be.

"The judge is due here quite early this morning," he noted eagerly. "We can hold the hearings, have his decision, and get on with the foreclosures before noon."

"You do not think there is any chance Amundsen will rule against us, do you?" asked Adolphus with a broad wink. He rubbed his thumb and forefinger back and forth, a broad parody of someone counting money for a bribe. The three men laughed loudly.

"There is only one possibility . . ." Thorsen began.

"What is it?" snapped Gustav, immediately alert for danger. His eyes narrowed, slitty and wolflike, over that vulpine nose.

"Judge Amundsen may, nay, *will* find for us. But if the matter goes to the supreme judiciary in Oslo . . ."

Adolphus snorted, and spoke with great emphasis, jamming a finger down onto the tabletop with each word. "Then . . . you . . . see . . . that . . . it . . . doesn't . . . get . . . to . . . Oslo," he commanded.

"And tell your cook to fry some more eggs," suggested Gustav. "I only had five."

Gustav dressed carefully in his swallow-tailed morning coat, striped trousers, white silk shirt, and white cravat affixed with a gold pin. Glossy black boots of kid leather and a top hat in the English mode completed his costume. When he went out of Thorsen's house to admire the day and await the judge, everyone who saw him—children, stablehands, women scurrying about the village on errands

WILD WIND WESTWARD

—just stopped in their tracks and stared and stared.

Exactly as they would stare at a crown prince, thought Gustav, pleased. He called for his horse, having decided to ride over to the Vendahl farm and inspect his woman.

"I want to see Kristin," he demanded, pushing into the poor little house without even a knock.

Arne and his children were huddled around the table, taking a breakfast of bread crusts and boiled pigeon eggs. Good, they were even poorer than Gustav had surmised. He would have no problems with them. But where was Kristin?

Arne got up from the table, but seemed to have difficulty answering the question. "She has . . . gone out," he finally managed to stammer.

Something about the man's eyes ignited Gustav's always-flammable suspicion. Where had he seen Kristin last? At that farmer Gunnarson's house! Was it possible that she had spent the night there?

In an instant he was on his horse again, pounding down the country lane. Then he was in Eric's yard, off the horse, vaulting up the same stone steps Eric had forced him from last evening. He threw himself against the wooden door of the house, felt it give way to his shoulder, and then he fairly flew into the house.

Eric, naked, was half out of bed. Kristin, beside him, was just awakening, the dreamy, content, pleasure-filled look on her face beginning to give way to an expression of shock and violation.

A current, hot and red, flashed through Gustav's already febrile brain. This farmer! He had slept with the girl of Gustav's choice even after Gustav had picked her, had arranged everything with her father. On the *very night* Gustav had sealed the bargain with pathetic old Arne, this benighted son of Gunnar had humiliated a *Rolfson*! As for the woman, he would teach her her place later, but the humiliation must now be expunged. Gustav wished mightily that Norway shared the Russian practice of punishing peasants by tying and beating them. But Eric, who was putting on his trousers, did not look as if he would permit himself to be tied too readily, so—as Kristin sat up in bed, pulled a sheet over her breasts, and cried out to warn Eric—Gustav lifted his mean little braided riding quirt and prepared to bring it down on Eric's flesh.

He never did.

Eric, bending to pull on his boots, heard Kristin's cry, and spun away from the blow. Recovering, he grabbed Gustav's white-cuffed wrist while the other was still off balance, and, using Gustav's momentum for added leverage, sent him sprawling on the soot-covered stone slab in front of the fireplace. Gustav cursed then howled with rage when he discovered the black soot on the palms of his hands, on his cuffs, on his fine striped trousers. His top hat had gone spinning away beneath the bed.

And Eric Starbane stood before him with the riding quirt.

"'You have made a major mistake," Eric was telling him, coldly, clearly, slowly. "You have entered without invitation the home of a freeman."

"Not for long," hissed Gustav, getting to his feet. What would be best? A kick? A rush? A feint and dive? Out of the corner of his eye he saw Kristin pulling on her clothes beneath the bedcovers. Oh, my God, but she was a luscious piece. . . .

"Get out now and you won't be hurt," offered Eric.

Gustav didn't even bother to think it over. He had to punish, he had to destroy, he had to eradicate utterly this big blond country boy. He could do it, too. No fair fights. No frontal assaults. He remembered the snowy day in Oslo, lying in wait for Lars Sondheim, who thought he was so great because his father had once served as minister to the King. Pieces of glass in an ice-crusted snowball. Lars Sondheim would have to go through life with one eye, always suspecting, but never quite knowing for sure, just who had done it to him.

Gustav came out of a crouch, feinted with a rush, twisted sideways, kicking as he did so. He felt the toe of his boot connect solidly and satisfyingly with Eric's belly. Too solid.

WILD WIND WESTWARD

Eric doubled up for a moment, gulping for air, but he recovered! He didn't go down! This farmer must be made of iron! thought Gustav, and way down deep inside his gut he felt a little liquid quiver of fear. Off balance from the kick, he regained his footing and turned to send a blow to Eric's jaw.

Then his face was on fire, a burning hot streak of flame from his left cheekbone, down across his mouth, and ending at his right jawbone. He screamed. He felt as if the pain would make him faint, and it probably would have had he not been so intent upon getting out the door, into the yard, and back onto his horse. The river of fire flowed across his face, a pain such as he had never imagined, and then he tasted his own blood.

Eric stood there in front of him, holding the riding whip. There was blood on it, too.

Gustav was out the door before he realized what had happened to him. That mean little whip, which he used to break horses and discipline dogs, had cut a bloody, ragged trail across his face. He traced his tattered lips with his tongue. His face! His looks!

"Now I shall destroy you utterly, Gunnarson," he muttered bloodily, when he was safely mounted on his horse. "Now you are a walking dead man!"

Eric was standing in the doorway. Kristin stood behind him, one arm upon his shoulder.

Gustav, dabbing at his bloody face with a white silk pocket scarf, wheeled his horse and galloped away in the direction of the village.

"Eric, I'm afraid for you," Kristin said, as they watched the younger Rolfson disappear down the trail. "Let's go away now. Right now."

But Eric shook his head. "I don't run," he said.

From the village, borne upon the pure bright morning air, they heard the sound of the bell in the *stavkirche* steeple, summoning the townsmen.

"That means the judge from Dovre has arrived. We had best get over to the church."

69

Vanessa Royall

* * *

Judge Amundsen wore a long black robe and a crafty, sour look. He sat upon a peerlessly bred Arabian stallion, waited until the citizens of Lesja had gathered in front of the church, and then rode with Thorsen to the village inn, the only place large enough to accommodate the crowd. To hold legal hearings in the church itself would have been unseemly. Amundsen had looked quite striking up on his fine horse, but when he dismounted, Kristin saw that he was very short, almost runty, with ugly twisted legs. Perhaps his lack of stature explained the apparent dour malevolence of his nature.

Thorsen had arranged with the innkeeper that the dining room and the spacious beer garden adjacent to it be used for the hearing. Wide doors gave on to the garden from the dining room, and these, flung wide open, would permit those unable to find a seat inside the inn to hear the proceedings, even if some of them might not be able to see everything. Eric managed to find seats for himself and Kristin near the table at which the judge was to preside.

Arne Vendahl entered, saw them, and came quickly through the crowd. He was red faced with anger, and his eyes were wide with fear.

"Where have you been?" he demanded, grabbing his daughter by the wrist. "You'll ruin everything for us!"

Before either Eric or Kristin could answer, the judge pounded the table.

"I declare these proceedings open," he called, in a grating, rasping voice, which sounded as unpleasant as he looked. "All must be seated. *You*," he shouted, selecting Arne as an example. "Be seated or it's contempt of court, and ten days in the county workhouse!"

Arne, confused, afraid, let Kristin's wrist fall, and scurried to find a seat. She found herself trembling. Although she sympathized with her poor father, she knew for certain that she could not submit to his wishes. Too much had happened. Her life was taking a different track, as if fate were governing her future. But she knew the only worthwhile future could be with Eric.

WILD WIND WESTWARD

For his part, Eric stilled Kristin with a touch, and looked about the inn. Thorsen was there, and so was Subsheriff Johanson, hanging about by the door with his hefty, slow-moving deputies, who resembled slugs if you half-closed your eyes to regard them. But the putative plaintiffs, the Rolfsons, were nowhere to be seen. The people began to murmur, and even Judge Amundsen looked up from some documents he was examining, as if wondering where the two were.

"Perhaps Gustav won't appear, after what you did to him," Kristin hoped.

"I do not think it would alter his father's plans, though. Not after so much time and money have been spent."

Another thought came to Kristin. "Could not Gustav make trouble over the fact that you struck him?"

"Perhaps. But I doubt he would, since I was defending my property against trespass."

"Well," Amundsen was saying, "if I have come all the way from Dovre for nothing . . ."

But he had not. From the village street outside the inn, a great commotion arose, as riders came dashing up the road and reined in.

"They're here, Your Honor, they're here," called Johanson happily, and, sure enough, the crowd parted to allow the Rolfsons entry. Father and son marched through the staring people, not deigning even to look upon them, and certainly not to apologize if they happened to bump or jostle one of the townsmen. The mood in the room, which, moments before, had seemed to cradle the seed of a feeble hope that the Rolfsons would not appear, now plummeted, turned gloomy and quiet.

We have no spirit, Kristin thought, sadly, watching her own father duck his head, lick his lips. *We call ourselves free, but we have no confidence.*

Adolphus Rolfson, thick and splendid in morning coat and a pearl-gray sash, sat down slowly and heavily in a chair near the judge's bench, withdrew his gold watch from a waistcoat pocket, inspected the time, replaced the watch. The mountain farmers watched him, fascinated not only by the great timepiece, the price of which might well have surpassed the worth of a good-sized farm, but captivated also by the man's concern with time itself. The mountaineers rose with the sun, retired with it, their lives drifting easily with the cyclical rhythm of the seasons. There was little need to know which hour it was, much less which minute. What they did not yet understand was that the Rolfsons emerged from, personified, *represented* a hard new world in which minutes were worth money. The law, in such a world, must work with alacrity. And so it could be bought.

Gustav had followed his father into the inn, keeping his back to most of the people, but when the Rolfsons reached the front of the room, several farmers felt they had to stand in order to show respect to such powerful personages. There was a slight crush, a bit of confusion as bodies shuffled about, and in the process Gustav was forced to turn toward the onlookers. A sudden gasp rose from the citizens of Lesja. The slash on Gustav's face stood out scarlet and deep, like a mark of horrible sin.

"What are you looking at?" he screamed at them. "You'll all pay for this!"

Then his eyes found Eric, seated there beside Kristin, and his lips tightened in hatred, as much as the jagged cut would permit. But he did not speak, simply fixed Eric with a long glare, which Kristin's beloved returned, unflinching.

"We will proceed now or not at all!" thundered Judge Amundsen.

Gustav sat down next to his father. The crowd quieted, listening intently.

"This hearing is convened," the judge growled. "At issue: notes of loan signed by individual landowners, in agreement with the Rolfson firm of Oslo. Plaintiffs contend payment is now due. Defendants aver initial payment is not due until September, after the harvest. I have the signed agreements here on the table in front of me. I have examined them thoroughly. In every case, the agreements specify a June repayment date. Consequently, I rule in favor of the Rolfsons. Now, my appearance here has satisfied the requirements of the law, and I declare the proceedings . . ."

Amundsen had intended to say "terminated," and then to get back up on his sleek Arabian mount and get out of Lesja as fast as the beast would carry him, but that was not immediately to be. Long accustomed to the laconic, even phlegmatic ways of the mountain people, and inured to their slow respect for authority and tradition, he had for too long a time been used to his own power. He expected subservience, as in the old days, not realizing that the farmers were far more threatened than he had thought. Threatened enough, possibly, for violence. The roar that rose inside the inn, the answering tumult that broke out in the garden, now impressed upon him the fact that his job was not going to be as easy as he had expected. He made a mental note to demand more bribe money of Rolfson, and began pounding his gavel. Johanson and the deputies began to move among the crowd, calling for order. A hundred people were on their feet, all of them clamoring to speak. Finally a semblance of order was restored. The judge had decided upon the necessity of prolonging the charade. These farmers would eventually be dulled by mere procedure—he thought—and since the outcome of the hearings was immutable no matter who protested, a little more time was not too great a price to pay.

"Who speaks for the plaintiffs?" called the judge, assuming a bored, bureaucratic drone.

"I do, Your Honor," answered solicitor Thorsen, bowing obsequiously.

"And the defendants?"

All eyes turned toward Pastor Pringsheim, whose original knowledge of the law had caused this hearing to be held. "I cannot speak here," he protested. "It is not fitting in the light of my office."

The judge frowned, although not without pleasure. A glint of satisfaction appeared in the eyes of the Rolfsons. No one was prepared to make the case for the landowners; they were untrained in public discourse, afraid to speak on their feet.

All save one. "I shall make the case," Eric declared, standing.

Gustav Rolfson spun around to look at him, his torn lips parting to show a grin of bloody teeth. This upstart might fight well, but how could he have the wit of words?

"Get up here in front, then," Amundsen ordered.

Kristin touched his hand before he left the chair, heard with pride the murmurs of approval and encouragement from her neighbors as Eric strode to the front of the inn.

Thorsen, whose right it was to speak first, was already on his feet. Portentously, with rounded pomposity of phrase, he declared the proceedings to be pointless at best and ludicrous at worst. "It's right here in the papers," he said, thumping the loan agreements. "Everything in order. Everything in black and white. The defendants have simply allied to thwart the just foreclosures of my clients upon lands and properties clearly due them." Then he sat down. Adolphus Rolfson could be seen nodding his approval of the solicitor's sagacity.

"Young man?" prodded the judge, waiting.

Momentarily Eric seemed nervous, but when he began to speak the unease quickly passed. His words were sure and strong.

"I, too, have examined these papers, upon which your signatures or marks appear to be affixed. I have also examined the paper signed by my father, whom you all knew and respected. I was there when he signed his name. And I tell you with all the certainty in my heart"—at this point he picked up his father's loan agreement, the one for which he was now legally responsible, and showed it to the people—"that this paper is *not* the one he signed, and that the signature on this paper is not his."

Thorsen was on his feet. "This is an outrage!" he shouted, agitated, almost blithering. "Why, this nonsense is—"

"Furthermore, I think *all* the papers have been forged," Eric went on, shouting Thorsen down. "And I also feel—"

"Silence! Silence!" yowled Amundsen, excited himself, his short legs, which did not reach the floor, kicking back and forth. "What is your name, son?"

"Starbane. Eric Starbane."

"Listen well, then, Starbane. I tell you that, in order to make this kind of accusation, you must—"

For a moment the judge seemed to lose the thread of his thought. His glance fell upon the Rolfsons. His glance flew guiltily away from them. They all *knew* the papers had been forged, and here before them was a forceful young man not intimidated by the machinery of the court. If Starbane could stand here now and make an accusation of forgery, why, he might very readily take the matter to Oslo! There would be a royal inquiry, at the very least. The judge's dealings in Oppland County were not of a quality that could withstand disciplined scrutiny.

"Son, you must give a good reason, a very good reason, for your accusation." The judge was sure no reason would be sufficiently rational. "Or else I will be forced by law to dismiss you forthwith." This was not true, but what did Starbane know about it?

Eric stood before the people in the dining room. The crowd in the garden listened for Eric's words. The rustle of leaves could be heard, and the ripple of the Rauma River over the stones. It was that quiet.

"I will give you reason," Eric affirmed. "All of these people know that, when my father made the loan agreement, he was a sick man. Is that not so?"

Eric's neighbors to a man, called out their corroboration. Even Arne Vendahl added his voice.

"And," continued Eric, holding the paper up again, "the signature on this note is strong and sure, a hand of which my father, at that time, was incapable!"

Instantly the townsmen were on their feet, clamoring to see their own signatures, shouting angrily, triumphantly, for an end to the proceedings. They underestimated the tenacity of the Rolfsons, the niggling desperation of the judge to accomplish that for which he had been bribed.

"Sheriff! Sheriff!" bellowed the judge, standing on his chair for height, and shouting over the din of the crowd. "I declare these proceedings out of order. Your duty requires action!"

The subsheriff and his men drew weapons, which, since the townsmen had not come to the meeting armed, served to inflame them all the more.

"Hold it!" warned Johanson, leaping to the judge's table, scattering loan papers all over the floor. "I vow my men and I will fire if you people dare to make a move!"

He waved his big pistol to underscore the seriousness of his threat. Meantime the deputies, training their weapons on the townsmen, took up strategic positions at entrances to the garden and the dining room.

"I mean to enforce the law," Johanson bellowed. "What is it, Judge?" he asked, obsequiously.

Amundsen looked around. He saw the farmers tensed in readiness for physical action, but he saw also that they were confounded. Johanson saw it, too. "First one who moves gets it in the head," he roared.

"This hearing is concluded," Amundsen intoned. "Sheriff, you are charged with the duty of presenting notices of foreclosures and carrying out evictions in cases of recalcitrance."

"No!" shouted Eric. "You cannot do this. The hearing has been as fraudulent as the papers now on the floor."

"And what are you going to do about it, Gunnarson?" goaded Gustav, still dabbing at his face with a blood-streaked handkerchief. He leaped to his feet, overturning his chair, and beckoned Kristin with a crude, peremptory gesture.

"Get up here, woman!"

"Not now," old Adolphus could be heard to say. "Not now. First things first."

Kristin looked at Eric, and he at her. The people, as individuals or as a group, had not yet decided what to do. The guns were still upon them. Kristin felt as if now, finally, this overwhelmingly insulting attack upon her people would be met in kind, even by her father. She felt that her neighbors, lifelong freemen, innocent, uneducated, unsophisticated though they were, would seize the moment they had, would respond with brawn and strength they

WILD WIND WESTWARD

so clearly possessed to the courage of words and will Eric had, just as obviously, displayed before them.

Kristin learned a great lesson, then. She saw how the fine smooth gears of the world's machine were oiled and spun; she learned a lesson in deftness and cunning that she would never forget.

Adolphus Rolfson stood, and, by his bulk and bearing, took dominance and command of the gathering.

"We do not wish you harm," he explained sonorously to the taut mountaineers, speaking authoritatively yet soothingly to these enraged but directionless country people. "Do not now engage in an act of violence that might, nay, that *will* jeopardize your very freedom!"

Having said that, he admonished Johanson and his deputies: "Enough of this. Not here. Let us see about the business that has been ordered by the judge."

He waved the subsheriff's gun down, and the deputies followed suit. Within a minute they departed from the gates. Judge Amundsen himself left the inn, and walked toward his horse. The citizens of Lesja began to cheer. Such easy victory, and how sweet.

A great, savage howl cut them off.

"Fools!"

What was this? The cheer died.

"You fools!" shouted Eric Starbane. "Don't you know what has happened?"

The sound of Amundsen's horse's hoofbeats could be heard: a clatter over the stone of the walk, the soft thudding of a canter on the road, the long full pounding of a gallop.

"Where are Johanson and his deputies?" Eric cried. The people looked around, puzzled. They had thought the departure of the lawmen meant an end to all problems.

"They are on their way to serve the notices of foreclosure," Eric explained. "They will meet you upon your own doorsteps, exactly as they met me yesterday afternoon."

"Get the Rolfsons!" someone shouted, but it was too

Vanessa Royall

late. The cunning architects of perfidy had slipped out with the forces of the law.

"Here," Eric called to Kristin.

"Wait!" cried her father. "Who is the fool now? Things have happened just as I said. What good has this hearing done, except to anger the Rolfsons, with whom we will have to live."

Then he smiled, or, more accurately, *smirked* at Eric.

"Fool," he said again. "Daughter, you come with me. I want you ready when Rolfson calls for you."

Kristin shrank from her father as he approached, his hand outstretched to seize her. The townsmen were wondering about what he had said to her. Assured now—he thought—of continued possession of his land in exchange for the offer of his daughter in marriage, Arne could not resist a boast. "Alone among you," he declared, "I had the wit to deal with the Rolfsons. Alone among you—"

"If you stand here, saying who is brilliant and who dull," Eric interrupted, "all is lost. Later we can take this matter to Oslo, but as for now, I fight! Kristin, come!"

He held out his hand and she ran to him. "It will do you no good," Arne howled after them. Hand in hand they raced from the inn, through the village, and up the hill trail toward the Starbane farmstead. Behind them many farmers did likewise: ran to their homes, wanting to protect them without quite knowing how. Those who had already given up slouched hopelessly outside the inn, admiring Arne Vendahl's sagacity. Lord, if only they had a daughter as gorgeous as Kristin, they too would have found a way.

Halfway to the farm Eric saw ahead of him the mounted party of deputies, led by Subsheriff Johanson.

"Just as courageous as I expected," he said. "When the dirty work is being done, the Rolfsons are nowhere to be seen. *I* will never be that way."

But there was no time for talk. On foot Eric and Kristin could never overtake the men on horseback.

"There is a quicker way," he told Kristin, leading her down off the trail, through a grove of ancient birch, up along a stone wall that marked the border of his pasture, and into the yard behind his house. They came around the house and confronted the lawmen just as the latter were riding into the yard.

"Don't resist the inevitable." Johanson scowled, dismounting. He carried the foreclosure paper in his hand.

"I will fight for my land," said Eric, taut but cool. "I give you fair warning."

The deputies drew their black pistols.

"Eric," cried Kristin, in real fear for his life, "give it up. Let's go away."

He shook his head. "I cannot. If evil is not resisted, what is honor worth?"

"You can do it another way. You can go to Oslo." She remembered the lesson she had learned at the inn, observing the casual stealth of the Rolfsons. "You do not have to confront this directly," she cried.

"Yes, I do. Johanson with his vile paper is directly in front of me."

"A wise man," grinned the subsheriff, holding out the paper. "Take it," he told Eric. "The law says I must place it in your hands."

"I will not," Eric answered, retreating backward up the stone steps and into his house, keeping Kristin behind him, and his body between her and the guns. Then they were inside the house. He slammed shut and bolted the heavy door.

"Don't be a lunatic," Johanson shouted from outside.

"Eric, it's all right. Give in," pleaded Kristin. "We can go away."

"Don't you think I want to?" he snapped, turning toward her. It was the first anger he had ever shown toward her. "And don't you know I can't?" he added, not apologetically, yet almost tenderly.

Kristin understood. He was what he was, a strong and honest man, and that was why she loved him. Would she have him if he were but some finer variety of Rolfson, cunning and deadly with charm? She would not. She recalled Pastor Pringsheim's annual sermon about Martin

Vanessa Royall

Luther. *"Ich kann nicht anders,"* Luther had said, when evil men demanded that he forsake his beliefs, *"I cannot do otherwise."*

Oh, but what a hard world to knock one's head upon.

"Eric, let's go," she tried once more.

"No," he said.

Johanson and the deputies were already battering at the door. Eric took up the great Viking's axe.

"Come out or you're a dead man," Johanson was shouting, over the pounding on the door. The deputies were battering away with thick lengths of firewood.

"Come in and you're the same," Eric yelled back, lifting the axe.

Kristin, once again, was about to caution restraint, but it was too late. The bolt, assaulted beyond endurance, shot into splinters. The door flew open and Johanson dived through it, pistol uplifted to fire.

Eric Starbane, past and future poised upon that moment, brought down the great axe, parting Johanson's flaxen hair, his skull, his brain, parting his nose, palate, jaw, parting his neck and shoulders, chest and heart. Johanson's right eye rolled up, his left eye rolled down. He crashed down onto the floor, two bodies almost, divided to his pelvis. And blood was everywhere.

"My God!" exclaimed one of the deputies in horror, as the others gathered in the doorway, observing for one unspeakable moment the fate of their superior. "Oh, my God!"

Eric lifted the axe once more.

V

Kristin's wedding day, and a horn sounded in the mountains. She held her breath, and waited. She did not hear its mournful blast a second time. And so she breathed again.

Because they were hunting for Eric in the mountains. Not only the deputies were hunting, those survivors of hapless Johanson, but also most of the lawmen of Oppland County, and a goodly number of the Lesja men as well. Eric was a criminal now, with a price upon his head.

Kristin could not and would never forget the moments after Eric had struck down Johanson. The deputies, after taking a terrified look at their superior's axed and bloody body, seeing Eric advancing upon them with the same Viking weapon he had used to kill Johanson, now turned and fled to get help. Clearly the young man had gone berserk; vast numbers would be required to subdue him.

"Eric!" Kristin had screamed, shrinking from the split and bloody carcass on the floor.

He watched the deputies flee, and turned to her, throwing the axe into the corner.

"God, what have I done?"

"He had a weapon. He would have killed you. Killed us both."

Eric was thinking furiously. What Kristin said was true. He had no doubt of it. Johanson had been sent by the Rolfsons, sent first to the Starbane house, to serve notice upon the only man in Lesja willing to fight for his rights against the legal machinery arrayed against the town. Eric had fought as a Viking would have, but the Viking way was dead now, and modern times were different. He had no illusions about what he had done, or how he would be regarded: he was a criminal now. To be captured would mean death.

Immediately he began shoving blankets, clothing, foodstuffs into a canvas rucksack.

"What are you doing?"

"Leaving." He put a hunting knife, a second pair of boots, and a woolen scarf into the sack. Kristin had knitted him the scarf as a Christmas present during the preceding winter.

"I will come, too."

He stopped packing and looked at her. "I can do you no good. If they catch me, they will kill me. If you are with me, they will kill you, too."

"I don't care," she vowed, in bitter, outraged defiance. "I don't care, I . . ."

Eric came to her and put his arms on her shoulders. He wanted her to come with all his heart. But it would not work.

"How could you?" he asked. "I can promise you nothing. No one would believe that I acted in self-defense. They will hunt us down in the mountains as they hunt down animals. Perhaps I will get back someday. Our life as we knew it is over now. I can promise you nothing," he said again.

She gave him a long level look. "I never asked for anything, either," she said. "Except to be yours. Remember the water from which we drank each other's image? I go where you go."

He saw that she meant it, and would not be dissuaded.

"All right," was all he said.

Together, they packed another rucksack, tossing into it anything that might conceivably be of use: another blanket, a half-loaf of black bread, a pair of woolen socks, mittens, three apples. Neither looked at the bleeding body on the ancient floor of the Starbane house. That house had seen ages pass, had seen another world rise and fall. When

Columbus set forth on the Atlantic, the Starbane house was already two centuries old. Generations of toddling blond children had played upon it, savoring cool stone in the summer, and in winter basking before the fire. Generations of love had arisen, been made, been spent in warm beds beneath the roofbeams, and, as in all lives, hurt and anguish had found their way within these walls, to be suffered and endured, vanquished or solaced, or both. Perhaps it was merciful that time was so short, that Eric had no moments to consider either the enormity of his leaving, or the long tide of centuries upon which he was now forced to turn his back.

"I will be like them now," he said to Kristin bitterly, as they were about to go out the door. "I will be like the Rolfsons and their kind, and if we survive in the mountains and make our escape, I will look upon the world as they do, and bend it to my will."

In spite of their haste, she stopped him. "Don't ever say that. Don't even think that."

He looked about his ancestral home for one last time.

"I will get even with them if it is the last thing I do," he swore.

"Eric, no. I will be with you. I will help you in all things. But you must stay as you are." Her voice was full of sorrow, but in her tone also there was courage. "I will love you whatever," she went on, as he looked down into her dark, compelling eyes, "but I will never forget what you were when I loved you first, and that is the way I will always love you best."

He took the time to kiss her, but in the new, hard world there was no time for gentle things, and the kiss cost all. Had they run from the house even seconds earlier, they would have avoided the first hunters, pathetic villagers eager for the bounty money Rolfson had instinctively promised upon learning from the deputies what had befallen Johanson. In truth, Rolfson had been pleased at Johanson's death. It meant that, as a killer, Eric would never take the forgery matter to Oslo. It also meant that,

Vanessa Royall

by holding open the offer of bounty money for Eric's capture, Rolfson would have additional leverage over the villagers.

But Eric and Kristin took time to kiss. For such indulgence, great woe.

Three of the most disreputable men in the village, having stolen along the pasture wall, clomped excitedly around the corner of the house and saw the young couple there.

"Get him!" yelled Hønefoss the barrelmaker to his cohorts, barman Larsen and stablehand Teversen. "You fellows get him and I'll subdue the girl."

Under normal conditions Eric would have been more than the three of them could handle, but these were not normal conditions. Surprised by the men, Eric thought first of Kristin, who could run fleetly but not as fast as himself. So he took valuable time to drop Hønefoss with a ramming right to the chin. The barrelmaker's jaw crumpled like an empty paper box beneath a lead weight. Eric had just turned to deal with Larsen and Teversen when Arne Vendahl's voice could be heard in the nearby woods.

"Kristin! Kristin! You obey me now! The fate of our family rests with you!"

Arne and another contingent of men came swarming up out of the woods; the deputies were galloping up the drive, on fast horses. Eric tripped the flabby bartender, Larsen, and sent him sprawling, incapacitated Teversen with an elbow to the gut. "Run!" he yelled to Kristin. He grabbed his rucksack and they dashed toward the back of the house. A stream ran through the yard, with large stones upon which one might step to cross. Eric and Kristin started across, to the rising pine forest beyond. In it, and up into the blue mountains beyond, were places to hide until night fell, and in the night they could move on.

Arne Vendahl, the other men, the deputies, were rounding the corner of the stone house now, yelling jumbled commands to stop, halt, give up.

Kristin slipped on a wet fording stone, fell into the water, and cried out in pain. "My leg!" she screamed, as the

WILD WIND WESTWARD

freezing water of the mountain stream soaked her to the skin. "My leg! It's broken!"

"Here. It can't be. I'll carry you."

"No. Go. You must."

The pursuers were rushing toward them now, closing the gap.

"You must go," said Kristin. "If you stay, we're both lost."

Eric turned and ran, splashing toward the opposite shore. One of the deputies fired, then another. Eric ran zigzag into the pines. The deputy leading the pursuit pounded into the stream, pistol raised. Kristin, unable to rise from the water because of her broken leg, nonetheless had a good arm. Taking a smooth rock from the bed of the creek, she took aim and let fly, sending the man sprawling down into the water with her.

The delay she caused was minimal, but sufficient. First pursuit of Eric faltered in confusion. He made it into the mountains. Kristin was taken back to her father's house, to have her leg set by old Dr. Sarpsborg from Sonndalsøra, to listen to lectures from her father. By the time those twin agonies had been endured, the hunting horns were sounding in the mountains, and Gustav Rolfson was standing by her bedside.

"What do the horns mean?" she asked.

"It is the newly formed search party out after that . . . Gunnarson," said her father. "One blast of the horn reveals a searcher's position in relation to his fellows."

"And two blasts?" she asked.

"Means they have found the killer."

The killer. Eric.

"And what is *he* doing here?" she asked, looking up at Rolfson. His eyes glittered down at her from the sides of his wolflike nose. His lips were puffy. The slash of the riding whip was deep. It would heal but it would never disappear.

"In Oslo, Kristin, you will have everything . . ." Arne began.

"Get out of here," Gustav ordered. "Kristin," he said, when the father had bowed and scraped his way out of this closet of a bedroom, "it has been decided by our fathers that we marry immediately."

"Never."

Rolfson was undeterred. He already knew that he would have his way. "Your father may keep his land. Your family will not be displaced, nor will anyone starve. I will see that your mother is afforded a good doctor."

"Why?" she asked. "*Why?* I find you contemptible. Ugly, too."

Gustav flared, but held his anger in check. "I find you extraordinarily beautiful," he explained. "I admire that for what it is, and also because you will be of use to me. Just as I will be of use to you, and your family."

"It sounds much akin to a business transaction."

"If you like."

"Then what is my measure? Where is my advantage?"

"You will live in comfort and splendor and ease. We will travel to England and America, where my father and I plan ventures. You will bear my children." He said this last as if it were the crowning jewel to which she might aspire.

Never, Kristin thought. In the far mountains the horns were sounding again. Single blasts. Night was falling. If Eric could find shelter for the night, and get away in the morning . . .

"I want one thing more, then."

"What is it?"

"That you and your father call off the hunt for Eric Starbane."

Gustav gave her his glittering grin, but shook his head.

"He is a killer. The law must have him. The matter is out of my hands."

"It was self-defense!" Kristin avowed fervently. "Eric had no choice but to—"

"Hah! And how many people saw him grab me by the throat just yesterday? Not to mention the vicious cut he gave me! Oh, he is violent by nature, and everyone knows

WILD WIND WESTWARD

it. Self-defense, indeed! And how much will your word be worth in a court of law, eh? You, the known consort of the rogue!" Kristin looked back at his cold blue eyes, forcing herself to appear contained, but calculating furiously. No, Gustav was determined. He would not call off the hunt. And, with all those men looking for Eric, at least half the male population of Lesja in their number, men familiar with the mountains and the mountain caves, Eric could never break out of Oppland County and make his way to the sea. Rolfson had her, had Eric, between the horns of another of his cleverly fashioned dilemmas. She saw a way out, not for herself, but for Eric.

"All right," she said, "I agree. I will marry you. But it must be tomorrow. You will get me to the *stavkirche* somehow, on a cart if need be. And, if I am to leave my village for Oslo, I want a traditional wedding, with all of the townspeople there for the ceremony and the celebration afterwards."

Rolfson was so stunned by her easy acceptance—he had estimated a long siege—that he immediately agreed, and gave the necessary instructions, to a shocked Pringsheim and the others. On the morning of Kristin's wedding day one or two lone horns sounded in the hills, random hunters looking for Eric still. The rest of the men had come back down into the village, to enjoy the free food and drink offered by old Adolphus Rolfson to glorify the marriage of the son in whom he was well pleased.

Arne was also pleased with his daughter, and could not understand, as he lugged a mattress out to the haywagon, then carried her out and placed her upon it for the trip to the *stavkirche*, why she was not happy, too.

"You will have everything," he said, over and over. "Wealth, position, power. You will be married to a Rolfson!"

Kristin had a full, lovely mouth, but when she was determined about something, her lips set firmly, and there was no doubt about the strength of her will. Her lips set in just that way now, and she said, "Gustav Rolfson will believe himself married to me, but I was married already

Vanessa Royall

at Sonnendahl Fjord, and my heart will always know it."

Old Arne had no idea what she was talking about. Besides, what did it matter? He climbed up onto the wagon, slapped the broad rump of the horse with the ends of leather reins, and started toward the church.

In the high mountains a hunting horn sounded again, but only once.

From the shadow of the cave in which he had concealed himself, a cave well known to him from years of hunting elk in these high hills, Eric watched the men who were hunting him. The entrance to the cave was deceptive, well hidden, but the searchers were combing the mountains thoroughly, in vast numbers, and Eric knew it was only a matter of time before one or another of them discovered or stumbled upon or even fell into his hiding place. Thus it was, with considerable bewilderment, that he witnessed the apparent withdrawal of his pursuers. Had they given up? He did not think so. A man charged with murder was not so quickly forgotten. Was the withdrawal some form of ruse? That was more likely. He waited in the cave, watching the men—so many of whom he knew, had worked with, had grown up with—as they regrouped on the slope below the place where he lay waiting, and then set off down the steep trail that led to the valley and the village.

What was happening?

He waited until he could no longer hear the men or the blasts of the hunting horn, and cautiously edged out of the cave and into morning sunlight. He looked about. Sunlight glimmered on the snowcapped peaks of distant mountains, and green, sloping pastures, pristine and lovely, swept from the timberline to the shepherds' huts in high regions. The sky was clear and royal blue.

Eric did not know what to think. He heard again the far blast of a horn, and then another sound: the bell in the old *stavkirche*, chiming and chiming again. What were the villagers being summoned for this time? After ascertaining that no pursuers lay in wait for him in the area surrounding the cave, he made his careful way behind trees and shrubs to the crest of the hill overlooking Lesja, from which he could see the church and the village.

There are certain moments in life which, for each person, are indelible. Some of these moments are inherently similar, though they differ from person to person because each person is different: first love, marriage, the death of a dear one. These events occur for almost everyone. Yet there exists, too, another category of special moments, singular and recondite, which mark the souls of those who experience them, which mark their souls with joy or sorrow. When Eric reached the crest of the hill and looked down at the crowd of people entering the little church, he suffered one such ineffable moment, and his heart, his very life, were stricken. Horrified and disbelieving, he saw Kristin, dressed in a bridal gown, being carried into the vestibule. He could not but think that she was being forced into this union, that old Arne's greedy dream was finally being realized.

Kristin's father half-pushed, half-carried her into the church. With her injured leg she could not have fled, however much she wanted to. Rolfsons, father and son, entered the *stavkirche* then, too, but before they disappeared inside, Gustav looked up toward the mountains, almost as if he knew where Eric was hiding. He looked long up toward the mountains, as if he saw Eric, and it was as if he were saying, "Farewell, Gunnarson, you nameless, landless beggar. I may have your scar upon my face, and it may remain forever, but do not be conceited, do not be so proud. Because every time I gaze into a mirror, that scar will remind me that I also possess your woman and your ancestral home."

Then the church doors were closed and, a moment later, resonant chords from the ancient organ rose upon the pure blue mountain air, followed by the swelling voices of Pastor Pringsheim's choir.

What was it that Kristin had said, at the glistening pool

Vanessa Royall

high above Sonnendahl Fjord? *"Take me. Drink me. I am yours. Anywhere and for all time. No matter what happens or how things appear."*

Eric looked down at the church, heard the organ and the choir, and felt as if his heart would break. He could imagine his beautiful Kristin in every way, in every place and pose. He could imagine her in his bed, naked with him, beneath him or upon him, and he could picture her in the mountains, in the forests, at the stream or in the house. But he could not bring himself to shape her image in the place where she now stood: before the altar in a white wedding gown, with scar-faced, wolf-nosed Gustav Rolfson standing triumphantly beside her, waiting for the words that would make her his forever.

Forever.

Was not the terrible finality of *forever* more imposing than Kristin's promise to him, and his to her, on the day they had taken and consumed each other's images from the waters of the pool?

Eric had a momentary impulse to race down the mountain, crash into the church, and steal Kristin away. But he was not too desperate to understand that such an act would be his last, and would do Kristin no good whatsoever. At least now, with all the villagers bent upon the ceremony and the celebration to follow, he could get away. Where? Oslo, first. He could lose himself there for a time. And then what? Get some kind of mean, back-breaking laborer's job? Become a hired arrangement of flesh and muscle for any man who deigned to pay him a wage? No. He rejected such a fate as soon as he thought of it. That kind of life was not for him. But, as a dispossessed landsman, what else might he do? Where might he go? Sweden or Denmark, perhaps, or maybe Germany. But if he did so, he would be an outsider in old societies that were organized for and manipulated by old, established families.

Then he knew. The first fateful glimmer of his destination came to him. He would go westward, across the sea. He would ride with the same wild wind that, centuries earlier, had filled the strange square sails on the ships of his Norse forefathers. He would go to America and from there, somehow, some way, someday recoup his fortunes and fashion a way to regain Kristin and his ancient name! He did not know how he would do these things, but he knew that if he ceased to believe or to hope, he might just as well end his life now, here in the hills of home.

So, twenty years of age, utterly defeated save for a strong blond body and beating heart, Eric Gunnarson threw the pack upon his broad shoulders, turned away forever from the village of his youth, and set off down the road toward Oslo, and destiny.

PART TWO

NEW YORK, OSLO, LONDON 1860–1863

I

"Hey! You! That's right, you, the big Scandihoovian lummox. Where in hell do you think you're going?"

Those coarse, scornful words welcomed Eric Gunnarson to America.

He had climbed up out of the boiler room of the United States merchant ship *Anandale*, to take a look at New York, and, stunned to sheer astonishment by the swell and size of it, had wandered down the gangplank and onto the pier.

"Get your ass back on that boat, Sven or Lars or whatever your name is. Hell, I bet you can't even understand a word I'm saying, can you?"

Eric turned, without real anger, to look down upon a wizened, crafty-looking man in a blue cap and uniform. The man's little pig eyes stared out at Eric from beneath the wool cap pulled low for warmth. It was cold, brutal January in New York, and an icy wind howled down the Hudson River. Eric stared back at the man for a long moment.

"Yes, I understand English," he said slowly, with the lilt and roll of Norway still on his tongue.

"Then do as I say and get the hell back on the *Anandale*," snapped the man, somewhat surprised but undeterred. "Foreigners like you got no business in America."

"Yes, I do," said Eric, before turning and reboarding the ship. "That is why I have come all this way."

He went back down to his bunk in the boiler room, which had been his home for six months of slow peregrination across the oceans of the world. *Yes, I do have business in America,* he repeated to himself, lying down on the bunk. Soon he was lost in thought. He had to think of a way to get off the ship. He had served it well, feeding coal into the boilers to fuel its long voyage. And it had served him well, too. From its unprincipled captain, Hubert Dubin, he had learned more than a speaking knowledge of the English language: he had learned that life in the new land of promise might not be vastly different from that practiced by the Rolfsons.

"I like you," Dubin had said one night. "You're a big blonde *dumbkopf*, and you shovel coal like a machine, but I don't mind saying that I don't find you too pathetic to share a brandy."

The S. S. *Anandale* had been off the Azores that night, and over a month out of Oslo. Her itinerary was, as Captain Dubin put it, "catch-as-catch-can," a phrase that both intrigued and mystified Eric, until Dubin explained it in simpler terms. "You go where the wind blows," he chortled.

Eric had had, at that point, only a month's exposure to the dull, manifestly beaten-down and dim-witted Irish crew, nor did he grasp, in its English form, the not-too-complicated metaphor of "catch" that Dubin had used. But he understood instinctively the significance of "wind."

"A man goes where the gold is," Dubin clarified. "You know, the shekels, the *gelt*, the bucks."

"Bucks?" Eric asked, as Dubin downed a brandy and poured himself another. Eric thought of male elks in the mountains. One month on the sea, and he had only begun to trace the connections of tongue to tongue.

"Yes, bucks. Dollars. America is ruled by them."

Eric thought back upon his homeland, and the Rolfsons. Kristin must be in Oslo now, living in the Rolfson mansion. Money. That he understood. But to learn America operated in the same way was more than a disappointment. It was saddening. Captain Dubin noted his crestfallen expression.

"What's the matter, Sven, hey?"

"I had heard other things of the land to which . . . to which I want go."

"Sure you have. You Europeans don't know nothin' yet.

WILD WIND WESTWARD

But you just wait. Don't be in no hurry, mind you. America's just like any other place, 'cept more complicated. That's why I'm sailin' all over hell an' gone."

Noting, too, that Eric had not understood the idiom, he clarified himself. "I'm just out to make me a buck," he said. "But don't you go worryin' your Viking heart none. I'll get you to the good old US of A just like I said."

Indeed, that was what Captain Dubin had promised.

Eric, having come out of the mountains and down into Oslo, had immediately made his way to the docks. He was tired and hungry, and always watchful. He had killed an officer of the law. The current state of affairs in Norway did not benignly countenance the death of an official at the hands of unpropertied malcontents, a characterization which would be applied to him should his apprehension be effected and his person called before the court. But neither did Eric lightly countenance what had been done to him, nor accept without bitterness the fact that flight was his only safe haven.

If he could achieve it.

Oslo port disconcerted him. There was so much going on, all at the same time. Activity never ceased. Dozens of ships filled the harbor, either tied to the docks or lying at anchor out in the water, waiting to load or unload. He could not understand many of the languages spoken along the quay, and even more was he anguished by the smell of stews and sausages cooking in the shops along the waterfront. He had no food with him, and the few coins in his name had been left behind a chimney brick in the house that now belonged to Gustav Rolfson. All around him sailors and laborers babbled and rushed. He walked onward, trying not to attract undue attention, his belly shrinking and rumbling.

Then, as he passed a ship bearing the letters U.S. S.S. *Anandale,* he heard the sounds of a struggle. He did not understand the words—although he presumed them to be English because he knew *U.S.* meant the United States of America, of which he had read—but he knew the sound of conflict well enough. There was a fight going on up on

Vanessa Royall

the deck of the vessel. He stopped. A couple of Norwegian dockworkers came up beside him, listening, too, to the quarrel. They laughed, seeming to understand.

"What's going on?" he asked them, in his native tongue.

They laughed again.

"Lars Ingersoll has just lost his berth," jeered one of the men. "He hired on as a boilerman, but he's drunk as a skunk all the time. I guess the American captain found him out."

And with that two figures appeared at the top of the *Anandale*'s narrow gangway. One of them, a hulking blond youth, staggering and flushed, braced himself on the gangway rail and started down to the dock.

"And *stay* off my ship, you soused Nordic turd!" yelled the man behind him. "I already got enough whiskey-swilling micks aboard to keep the stillmasters of the world in clover."

He punctuated his cry by giving the unfortunate Ingersoll a solid kick in the rump, which caused the young man to lose his balance and tumble down to the pier. Ingersoll was shaken, but too loose in drunkenness to have been hurt.

On deck the captain was wailing and bellowing in the guttural English tongue.

"What is he saying?" Eric asked the docksmen, who were laughing at Ingersoll's attempts to rise.

"What? He wants a new man for his boiler room, that's what. He plans to sail in an hour."

"And what would such a man have to do?" Eric asked.

The man and his companion regarded Eric as if he were daft.

"Are you some kind of farm lout or ninny?" one of them shouted. "It's like living hell. You live in a room of iron and shovel coal into a furnace of iron. The heat will drive the living God from your soul. But the ship will move."

"Modern times," added his companion. "God goes but the ship moves."

Above them, on the railing of the *Anandale*, the cap-

WILD WIND WESTWARD

tain was still shouting and gesticulating. Ingersoll lurched to his feet and staggered drunkenly toward the nearest dockside tavern.

"What manner of man is he seeking?" Eric asked.

The two dock workers slouched away, laughing. "Somebody even dumber than Ingersoll," one of them called back, over his shoulder.

Eric stood there on the pier, his pack still upon his shoulders, and looked up at the captain, who was pointing at him and shouting. And Eric knew. This opportunity would not come again. He would be gone from Norway, true, but never would he come before the court, and never be lifted to the gallows. Boiler room or no, hell or worse, it would not be more than a man born Starbane could bear. He dropped his backpack and began to make shoveling motions, there on the dock.

The ship's captain ceased to gabble, regarded Eric in wonderment for a moment. Then he laughed. "Ya, ya, Sven," he said, motioning Eric up the gangway. "Ya, ya, you come on up here, Sven. You good strong boy. You shovel coal real good, ya, Sven?"

Eric went on board the *Anandale,* wondering why he was being called Sven when his name was Eric. He did not understand until he met the Irish crew, that everyone from Norway was called Sven. Or worse.

It bothered him, because he was Nordic, and had always thought himself and his people to be lords of the mighty earth.

Captain Dubin showed considerable interest in Eric as the *Anandale* passed down the North Sea, through the English Channel. The cliffs of Dover were white to starboard one evening, and Eric was taking one of his twice-a-day walks on the deck. Above him the stacks were smoking black and full, and the *Anandale* was moving fast. Her itinerary included the Azores, South Africa, across the South Atlantic to Buenos Aires, then north to Rio, Caracas, Havana, and finally New York. Eric, was making progress

Vanessa Royall

at English but was by no means proficient, sought to explain his hopes to the wily captain who had given him a job.

"In America, I work," he said. "And after some time is passing, I have money."

Dubin thought that was terrific. "Hey," he cried, lifting a glass, "that's the spirit that made America great. Only there's one fly in your ointment."

"Fly in my ... what? I understand that not so much."

"Ha ha ha," roared the Captain, "but I don't think you'll do much of anything in America."

Eric looked very perplexed, and Dubin thought that was funny, too. "You see," he said, "I suspect you're running from some kind of big trouble. But you just stay on the boat and work for me, and I won't tell a soul."

Eric knew, even as he heard Dubin chortle and yap, that he would somehow get off the ship. But he grasped, too, the peril of his position. Having so recently been confronted with the legal apparatus of his home country, he suffered dark imaginings as to what might happen to him were he to seek escape from the floating world of the *Anandale*. But he *had* to. He would not win the right to take back his name by spending a life of virtual servitude in the grimy boiler room of a decrepit freighter. Nor could he hope ever to see Kristin again, trapped forever between one shore and another. He would wait. He would see what New York looked like.

In the meantime he did his work, served his watches, shoveled coal into the fiery maws of the engines. His mates were Kuffel, a pale-eyed loutish specimen who said nothing, merely responded to events in his dull life with a phlegmatic, all-purpose grunt, and Flynn Maloney, a wiry, toothless Irishman, who never got the coal dust out of his hair because he never tried. Maloney had the gift of gab, and from him Eric learned many words, if not great wisdom. Kuffel, however, resented not only Eric, but Eric's conversations with the chattering little Irishman. Even the dullest of men do not wish to feel excluded from the camaraderie of their peers.

WILD WIND WESTWARD

"Uhhh," Kuffel grunted one night in the galley, where the crew was eating a watery stew of indeterminate ingredients, "I tink duh Svenska buggers duh mick."

Everybody laughed, the rough, mocking laughs of hard men. Flynn Maloney leaped to his feet, swung at Kuffel, who blocked the punch and returned a shot of his own, slamming the bantam Celt into a steel bulkhead. Maloney cracked his head against it, and dropped unconscious to the deck.

Eric, who had not understood the expression to which Maloney had taken offense, looked around, puzzled. The crew members were laughing at him, now. They looked down on boiler room personnel to begin with, and moreover Eric's strong good looks and strange language threatened them, made them uneasy.

"The Viking buggerer," somebody yelped.

Eric still did not understand. Kuffel was grinning his doltish, gap-toothed grin. Then cook's helper Smythe, recently promoted from cabin boy, told Eric what the expression meant. Kuffel was fully as big as Eric, and at least as strong. He was already on his feet, standing beside Eric, waiting for him to make a move. But Kuffel did not have a chance. Eric spun to his right, catching Kuffel in the solar plexus with a powerfully driven blow. The boilerman snapped forward, a momentum hastened when Eric grabbed him by the back of the neck and slammed his face down into the steel galley table. Kuffel's teeth scattered like ivory chips across the tabletop, and he let out a great bloody bellow of pain, grabbing at his face. Eric then shoved Kuffel forward across the table, sent him flipping like a cartwheel onto the deck. Three crewmen stood in Eric's path as he made for the downed man.

"That's enough," they menaced, fists raised and ready, "that's enough, Sven. Anymore and we'll be feedin' you to your own furnace."

"Some things I do not take," Eric told them and, in further answer, sent one reeling with a crashing right cross to the jaw, slipped his leg behind another and slammed him

Vanessa Royall

to the deck, and made for the third, all in the space of seconds.

"Okay, okay, Sven," the crewman said, dropping his fists and backing away, "that's okay, no harm intended."

Eric seized him anyway, and applied a brutal hammerlock. The crewman winced and cried out. The rest of the crew looked on in awe at the speed and authority of this Nordic savage, whom they had previously thought dull witted due to his unfamiliarity with the language.

"The name is Eric," Eric informed the man he was gripping. "Say it." He wanted to say *Eric Starbane,* but he had no right to that name now. He was not his own man. He was a hired hand.

"Eriiiic!" bleated the man, as the pressure on his arm was tightened.

Then Eric released his grip, and the crewman flopped forward, landing next to the bleary, half-conscious Kuffel. Maloney was coming to, looking around dazedly.

"Hey," he cried, observing the crewmen lying all over the galley deck, "I didn't know I had that much of a punch left."

After that incident the crewmen left Eric alone. Dubin, upon learning of the quick work Eric had made, sent for him. Eric was wary when he entered the captain's cabin.

"Sit down, sit down." From his ubiquitous brandy bottle he poured two healthy mugsful, and handed Eric one of them.

"Drink up. I think maybe I seriously underestimated your potential. How about we strike a deal?"

"Deal?"

"Yep, a business deal. That's what every smart man in America ought to know how to do."

Eric's interest quickened. "If you are speaking, I will be listening," he said. He was still having a bit of trouble with tenses.

"How'd you like to be first mate, on a permanent basis? Pay you twice as much as for shoveling coal."

Eric thought it over. The *Anandale* was steaming northward now, her long voyage almost over. Venezuela lay behind her, and Cuba, then America, awaited.

"Dropkin is first mate," Eric observed. Indeed, there was a considerable amount of tension between the manipulative, rule-bending captain and his punctilious first mate, who was, nonetheless, respected by the crew. Becoming a pawn in a struggle between ship's officers was not Eric's idea of wisdom.

"I plan on cashiering Dropkin in Havana, anyway," Dubin was saying. "You're a natural replacement. Big, strong, smart, and—"

He did not continue. He did not have to. The unspoken words were: "*—If you jump ship, I'll have the authorities check into the trouble in your past.*"

Eric thought quickly. Among the first mate's duties responsibility for managing docking activities ranked high. Dealing with harbor masters, supervising the unloading and loading of cargo, analyzing and not infrequently haggling over the difference between the actual amount of a shipment and the entirely fictional count reflected in bills of lading. In port, at dockside, on ship, this meant that the first mate made the acquaintance of, and was known by, many people at each port of call.

If Eric hoped to leave the ship, to be well known or even recognized in port would be to jeopardize everything.

"I do not think I am ready yet," he told Dubin.

The captain reacted in disgust. *"I do not think I am ready yet,"* he repeated, mockingly. "I guess I overestimated you. You are just another dumb Sven down off the mountain farm. Go back down to the boiler room and don't come up until you're ready to make a deal. You'll never get anywhere until you learn how to make a deal. And you'll never get off this hunk of iron, either, unless I say so," he added for good measure as Eric left his cabin.

But, descending the ladder back to the boiler room, Eric was of another mind. *We shall see,* he said to himself of Dubin's threats, *we shall see.*

* * *

By day, feeding the fierce furnaces of the engines, he wondered what New York would be like, how he might safely—if not legally—go down from the ship and enter into a new life. By night, on his narrow bunk in the overheated boiler room, he thought of Kristin, thought only of Kristin, until he seemed to himself as red and fevered as the mighty fires that ran the ship. He writhed in agony, knowing that now, this very moment, his beloved might be in the embrace of quirt-scarred Rolfson, the rich arrogant scion pounding her with his body, enjoying the vast pleasure for which Kristin's own body had been fashioned since the beginning of time. Red flashes shot behind Eric's eyes when he suffered that vision. *Yet she will always be true to me,* he told himself, *just as I shall always be true to her, no matter what.*

It was a fine, high promise, a holy vow, but it did not help much when he was fiery in his hot bunk in the fierce boiler room, lost from his home country.

Kristin, I will never betray you with anyone, he prayed to the furnaces, the bulkheads, the iron rind of hull. What else had he left to pray to?

Oh, Kristin. He remembered everything. How she looked and how she felt to his hands and lips and body, how she kissed and moved and made him feel. And then he remembered, with a tiny laugh that was almost like a sob, how hungry, how famished she was after lovemaking. *The next time,* he promised himself, *the next time I shall have a feast waiting for you.*

Fine world. Great vow. Black ocean. Gray ship.

Eric slept, waiting for America.

Finally, Havana was behind them. First Mate Dropkin was a new resident of Cuba, and the holds of the *Anandale* were filled with bizarre fruit Eric had never seen in Norway: bananas, mangoes, peaches and pears. The shipment was off limits to all crewmen—fruit meant money, and money was not to be eaten—but Dubin called Eric to his cabin again and offered a huge basket of bananas and peaches and pears. Eric took a pear and bit into it. Softer than an apple, sweeter.

"Sven," he said, "about that first mate business . . ."
"Eric."
"All right, Eric. Eric, let's talk turkey. As first mate you'll do the work for me, but you'll have access to every delight this world offers. Every port. This ship will *be* your world. I'm tired of the responsibility. You do the work and make the money for me, and I swear the sweetness of that pear on your tongue will be surpassed onehundredfold by the taste of the juices of young girls hungry for *you*. My next voyage, after New York, is to the South Pacific. And Asia," he added, for good measure. "You make a deal with me, and—"
"All right," Eric said. "I accept. I'll take the job."
Dubin was startled by this sudden change of mind.
"You agree?"
"Yes. But one thing."
"What's that?"
"I do not wish to take up the duties in New York. It is too large a thing for me. Let me observe you, and how things are to proceed. Then, when we leave for the South Pacific, I shall begin in earnest."
Dubin the dealer thought it over. Was there a trick, a ruse, in Eric's offer? There did not seem to be.
"It is agreed," he said, offering his hand.
Eric shook it, conscious of his falsity. He did not like the feeling; it seemed as if he had compromised, if not abnegated, some ancestral core of strength and purity deep in his soul. Yet Dubin was a master of trickery and deceit, and it seemed not unclean to fight him with his own weapons and on his ground.
Still, Eric felt tainted as the *Anandale* steamed into New York Harbor in gray January, ice forming on her masts, the hard cold wind of America buffeting her steel. Eric came up on deck for a moment to see the land he meant to conquer for himself, and at the moment of first sighting he floundered even in his staunch brave Viking heart. Such

vastness, and such wonder. Compared to this raw, sprawling city, great Oslo was but a fishing village! And when he looked up the mighty river, which Dubin told him was called Hudson, and when he looked off to the western wilderness, called Jersey, and saw the untrammeled expanse of this land, Eric stood on the deck in awe. Here in this harbor, confluence of city and river, ocean and wilderness, spirit and sky, was a force beyond the mere natural. America was not a country. No, it was a creature, a being, a *living thing*. Eric sensed it, felt it, felt drawn toward it and simultaneously judged by it, as if he had suddenly, against all expectation, come faith to faith with an alien god.

So here you are, Eric Starbane, said America to him.

Eric Gunnarson, corrected the new Viking. *My old name is gone.*

Ah, replied America, undisturbed, *what does it matter? In my cities and forests, upon my plains and prairies and hills, up and down my rivers, atop my soaring mountains, all within my borders which are as large as the borders of the earth, I give you the chance to win back your name. So how is that to you?*

That, said Eric to waiting America, *is what I am here for!*

It will not be easy, America said.

No, thought Eric. First I must find a way off the ship. The officious-looking man at the bottom of the gangway, blue cap pulled low on his head, was a discouraging omen, a harbinger of the many difficulties lying in wait for Eric. After being denounced as a foreigner by this miserable creature in uniform, Eric went back to his bunk to plan. Dubin had men watching him; he knew that. The American officials kept a close eye on the comings and goings of ship personnel. A hue and cry had arisen in America in recent years over "foreigners." New York had, it seemed, too many already. And then there was the city itself. Should Eric escape the shop and elude the authorities what would he do? According to standard procedure half the crew had been given liberty by Captain Dubin, to swell the coffers of the more disreputable bars and brothels of lower New York, and the remainder of the men stayed aboard the ship, to await their own pleasure the next evening. Briefly, Eric had considered liberty as a chance to drift away into this vast city. Dubin divested him of this notion.

"I know you want liberty," he soothed, "but no can do, my friend. I plan to keep you under my thumb. What did you do back there in Norway. Kill a man mebbe?"

"We all do what we have to do," Eric said.

Dubin gave him a suspicious look. "What would you be thinkin' of, young man? What you need that city for, anyway? Just get drunk, get in a fight, catch yourself a dose of something to make your peter burn like hell. Look, just you wait, when we get to Tahiti, I'll have some native girls brought up on deck. We can do that sort of stuff out in the Pacific. No one gives a damn, least of all the girls. They'll suck you off in broad daylight, lick their chops, and smile."

"Well, can I have my wages, at least?" Eric asked.

"What for? Don't you trust me? You don't need 'em now, anyway."

The *Anandale*, Dubin had estimated, would require roughly three days of unloading, during which time cranes aboard the ship would dip into the holds, be attached to crates of cargo, these crates to be swung onto the docks for distribution in the city. Three days during which time the boilers would not require stoking. Eric would be, for those three days, superfluous. Lying on his bunk, forming and rejecting plan after plan to escape the ship, he finally fashioned a ploy that might work.

"Captain," he asked, as unloading began the next morning, "since there's no work for me in the boiler room, I might as well help transfer the cargo."

"Hey! Good man," Dubin agreed, distracted somewhat, having to handle more work than usual due to his dismissal of First Mate Dropkin. "Get down in the hold there, and straighten things out. Some of those guys down there are still drunk from last night."

So for an entire morning, Eric worked in the hold, shouting guidance to the crane operator, and himself fastening

Vanessa Royall

the huge hook of the crane onto the cables which bound the cargo crates. Then, after a wolfed lunch of bread, sausage, and pale American beer, when work was beginning again, he assigned another sailor to his task in the hold and rode a cargo crate up onto the deck of the *Anandale*. The blustery clouds of the previous day had blown inland; the weather now was harsh, bright, bitterly cold. But all afternoon, his fingers and toes growing numb, he supervised the crane as it lifted cargo from the ship to horse-drawn wagons along the dock. While he worked, Eric also kept a close watch on Dubin, who remained on board the ship. The captain disappeared more and more frequently into his cabin, there to nip brandy. Late in the afternoon Dubin made another such foray, and Eric had to decide. It was now or never. The winter sun dropped almost visibly toward the frigid, gold-and-rose-blasted horizon of the American wilderness, and the silhouettes of New York's buildings stood stolidly against a cold and darkening sky.

Now, he decided, as the sunlight waned. "Lift!" he yelled to the crane operator, and the machine yanked into the sky yet another crated increment of Caribbean cargo. It was a risky business, running fruit, but cold weather prevented spoilage. On the other hand, a shipper must make certain the goods did not freeze. This particular cargo of bananas, swung now from the *Anandale* to the New York pier, were quite ripe and highly succulent. Eric ate two of them, guiding the cargo to the dock, and jammed another half dozen into his coat pocket. If he ate but one a day, he calculated, he could live at least six days in New York, if he did not freeze first. Or perhaps he could sell one or two. He might have to. He had no money.

The man in the blue cap, whom Eric now knew to be a police officer, was inspecting his watch when Eric rode the cargo down to the dock. He did not see Eric, or, if he did, presumed him to be just another working sailor. The men who took the crates and grunted them onto wagons did not pay attention to Eric either, and, amid the frenetic jumble of activity along the wharves, no one saw or cared about the tall blond sailor who walked hurriedly from the

West Side docks, through the great barns of warehouses, and then into the dark swarm of streets in gray and freezing New York.

But Eric did not feel the cold, just then. The only thing he felt was exhilaration. He decided to eat another banana before *they* froze.

He walked fast for a time, head down, hands thrust deeply into his coat pockets for warmth, studying what he found. The buildings along the pier were obviously not places made to shelter people, but, as he walked north, many apartment houses, close against each other, filled block after block. Eric saw a number of hotels, some of them quite respectable, but he had no money. He saw a church, dark inside, and its doors were locked. He walked onward, found another church. Its doors were open, but inside it was stone cold. He decided against the church, at least for the time being. He could always return if he grew desperate for a place out of the wind. He walked on.

Strangely, he did not feel discouraged, or fearful, or even anxious. He was in America. He was off the ship, his floating prison. No more could fate or desire be circumscribed by any man. Ahead, up the sidewalk, he saw a low building, its narrow windows flooding a glow of warmth upon the dirty snow. He went inside and recognized what it was: a tavern. Men were drinking along a bar, behind which jugs and bottles were arranged. The place was noisy. Half a dozen wooden tables stood near the iron stove, which was positioned in the center of the tavern, and several rough-looking men sat at the tables, eating and drinking. A few of them glanced at Eric when he entered the tavern, and a couple of them stared openly.

Drawn by its warmth, Eric crossed to the stove and held his numb hands over the glow. He was aware of the men watching him, but tried not to pay them attention. He did not want a fight. At this moment warm bread and brandy would surpass the wealth of the world. Then, from a doorway behind the bar, appeared a young woman as beautiful as any Eric had ever seen, Kristin excepted. She had long, glossy red hair, cut in bangs across a fine forehead. Her face was oval in shape, at once strong and delicate, with soft, full lips, and wide, perfect cheekbones. Her eyes were green and brilliant, and her eyes met Eric's as soon as she came out of the door. She was wearing a white apron against which pressed high, full breasts, and he could see the lush curves of her body, even beneath the loose, rude dress she wore. Instantly Eric was aware of himself as a man, the more so when the girl crossed to him. Her smile was warm, yet somehow tentative, as if she were simultaneously revealing and concealing some nameless, incalculable secret.

"What can I bring you?" she asked, with a half-smile that teased and yet did not.

Eric drew his hands away from the stove.

"I have no money," he said.

A young man, who had been drinking, slouched over from the bar. A rangy, mustachioed, ruddy-faced roughneck, he looked solicitously at the girl, then truculently at Eric.

"What's the trouble here?" he demanded.

"I'm sorry. I just wanted to warm my hands. I will be leaving now."

"That's all right," said the girl softly.

"Foreigner, aren'tcha?" pressed the roughneck, his eyes narrowed and threatening.

Eric turned to leave.

"Mick, hush," the girl said. "Mister, it's all right. He didn't mean no harm."

"Dammit, Joan, you are too kindhearted," complained the young man, but the fight had gone out of him. He seemed amenable to the girl's control. He addressed Eric again. "Well, you move along now, anyway."

The girl, Joan, demurred.

"As a brother," she told him, touching his face gently, as if she were soothing him, "you have your strong points. But as a charitable human being, you could use a little improvement."

"Ain't too many people got rich being charitable human

beings," Mick protested dourly, hands thrust deeply into the pockets of coarse, patched trousers.

Eric, sensing that Joan's gentle instincts had, at least for the moment, prevailed over the harsher inclinations of her renegade brother, sought to bargain for food.

"I have no money, as I said. But I am very hungry, and will do work for whatever you are able to give."

"Where the hell did you learn to talk like *that*?" Mick demanded, leaning forward. "I ain't never heard that kind of la-de-da-de-da before. You just get off the boat? What country you from anyway?"

"I think it's kind of cute," said Joan, looking at him closely with her large and lovely eyes.

Mick was still staring, awaiting an answer to his questions. Eric was not sure how to respond. He did not want to mention the *Anandale*, or his manner of jumping ship, since it was not inconceivable that there existed a police procedure for capturing deserters. On the other hand, each moment he delayed in replying to skeptical Mick made Eric's veracity more questionable.

"I am from Norway," he said simply, but truthfully. "I am here in your country to live and work. And I would gladly work now for a meal."

Mick, the roughneck, scowled and grunted.

"You said you could use somebody," Joan said, turning toward him, and putting her arm around his waist in a way that reminded Eric of a clever girl wiling a favor from a boy.

"Yeah, but can we trust 'im?" retorted Mick, in a subdued, guttural grunt.

One of the men who had been eating at a table mopped his face with a napkin, stood up, dropped a large silver coin next to his plate, and strode toward the door. He opened it peremptorily, and was just about to walk outside into the cold. But, suddenly, he froze there in the open doorway, muttered an explanation or curse in which God and damn played a part, slammed the door shut, and ran for the doorway behind the bar.

Vanessa Royall

"Cops!" he cried.

Joan's eyes flashed to her brother, whose ruddy face was growing pale.

"What is it?" asked Eric, puzzled. He had not understood the words "cops."

"Bloody police, that's what it is," Mick yelped in alarm, heading for the door through which the customer had disappeared.

"Don't worry, I'll handle them," said Joan, going toward the door that led to the street.

Eric had little time to make a decision. If Mick was afraid of the police, they might indeed come into the tavern, looking for him. But they might also be looking for Eric himself, having been alerted by Captain Dubin, or the customs officer. It would be logical for them to search barrooms and hotels, especially the former; the sailors of the world were known to frequent taverns now and again. Eric heard hard footsteps crunching the snow on the street outside. He made his decision and rushed into the back room, a flight observed with interest by the beautiful Joan.

The room behind the bar, lighted by kerosene lanterns, was a combination kitchen and storeroom. An iron cooking-stove glowed a dull red from flaming logs in its chamber, and a rickety, soot-ridden pipe led from the stove to an opening in the wall, exhausting the firesmoke. A side of beef, from which cuts had been taken, hung from a hook on the ceiling, jars of preserved foods occupied shelves along the walls, loaves of bread filled a wooden bin, the loaves looking like squat, golden lengths of firewood. There were several kegs of beer in one corner, and a stack of empty barrels stood beside the back door, which was open.

Eric was just about to flee through it, when Mick appeared, frightened and panting. "They're coming around in back," he muttered, looking frantically for a hiding place in the kitchen. "Jesus Christ, what are you doing here?" he demanded of Eric.

Now the footsteps of the advancing police could be

heard in the alley. "Jesus Christ!" Mick moaned again. "You're going to jinx it for me, sure.

"No, you're not," he decided in the next moment. And, shoving a barrel aside, he reached down to the plank floor, jerked a length of flooring aside, said, "Any port in a storm," and dived in.

Before he had a chance to pull the plank back into position, Eric had also made his decision. He dropped down into the opening, too, a cold dark hole that smelled of musk and earth, and of the alcohol on Mick's breath. "Jesus Christ," groaned the mustachioed roughneck, "what the hell?" But he slid the plank into place just before the police tromped into the kitchen.

Eric held his breath, and waited. He felt Mick's presence close beside him, felt beneath his feet round objects that shifted and rolled away. He bent down and picked up one of them, felt its rough yet not unyielding exterior. A potato. They were in a storage space, a root cellar. Above them the police prowled the kitchen, to be joined by more men from the taproom. Then they heard Joan's voice, sweet and calm.

"Certainly, you may search," she was telling them. "And while you're here, would you care for a cup of soup? Or a whiskey?"

"If we get it free like you get it free," returned the gruff voice of one of the police.

"I'm sure I don't know what you mean," Joan said.

There was rough laughter. "We can't prove it yet, but we will, we will. Anyway, I have a warrant here for the arrest of Michael Leeds. You seen him?"

"Who?" asked Joan.

Beside him Eric felt Mick struggle and succeed in stifling a laugh.

"Your brother, that's who! And, long as we're here, we're looking for a man who jumped ship, hour or so ago. Big blond guy. Speaks broken English. His captain reported him missing."

Eric felt the fine hairs on the back of his cold neck stiffen and quiver. But Joan Leeds, after a pause, said no,

Vanessa Royall

no, she hadn't seen anyone fitting that description, but she would certainly let them know if she did.

"You must have been sayin' your prayers," hissed Mick. "But don't you go gettin' any big ideas about her, hey?"

Then the police shuffled out, and slammed the door. Mick waited for five minutes, ten. Eric used the time to jam several potatoes into his coat pockets. Bananas and potatoes. A meager diet, but better than none. If the police were already looking for him, New York would be an even harsher world than he had anticipated.

Finally, a tap on the wood above them. "They're gone," Joan said, "you can come out now."

Mick climbed out of the root cellar first, and embraced his sister warmly. They both watched Eric as he, too, struggled out of the hole.

"Look, the bastard stole some potatoes," Mick denounced. "A ship-jumping thief."

"I'll pay you for them when I can."

"Sure you will. Just get out of here. You're probably the reason they came in here anyway. I knew you were trouble first time I laid eyes on you."

Eric and Mick faced each other, tension palpable between them. Yet, in some way Eric could not decipher, it was a strange, unusual tension, touched and colored by a force perverse and unfamiliar.

The pressure was broken by Joan, who said: "Mick, it is just as mother always says. You are far too hasty and you don't use your head. Mister," she added, turning to Eric, "go out and sit down at a table by the fire. I'll bring you some hot food and—"

"You'll do no such thing . . ." Mick began.

"Be quiet," she snapped back. "Sometimes I think Liz is right when she says you wouldn't recognize a gift horse if it kicked you in the teeth."

Liz? Gift horse? Eric went out to a table in the now deserted barroom and sat down by the stove. He did not yet know what to think. The police were after Mick Leeds, and that was not good. He ought to get out of here. And yet Joan was about to bring him a hot meal. Who knew

WILD WIND WESTWARD

when he might get another? And perhaps she might tell him where he could find work, and how to go about looking for a job. She seemed friendly, and intelligent, not to mention being beautiful. She had handled the police splendidly. Perhaps it was all a mistake.

Mick sauntered out of the kitchen after a few moments, flushed, smiling a slight, private smile of satisfaction. Joan seemed to have calmed him down. He drew himself a mug of ale, then, almost as an afterthought, drew another, and carried them over to the table at which Eric sat.

"Mind if I join you?" he asked, sliding one of the mugs across the table to Eric, sitting down without invitation. He took a long swallow of the ale. So did Eric.

"So you're off a ship, eh? Didn't like it?"

"The captain would not pay me my wages."

"Is that the truth? Norwegian ship?"

"American."

"It figures. Why did you leave your country?"

Too many questions. Eric felt alarm. Perhaps, while Mick pumped him for information, kept him occupied, Joan had stolen out into the night to call the police back.

"There was no . . . no chance for me in my country to make a success."

Mick gulped some more ale, snickered. "And you think this is the place to do that, eh? The new world and everything?"

"I must try."

"You got a lot of surprises in store for you, if you think we live in a land of milk and honey over here." Mick laughed at his own wit. "I don't know what it's like where you come from. Hell, I don't even know where Norway is. But I can tell you this: It's tough times here, tough times. I only know of one sure way you can make money. Maybe."

"What's that?"

"There's going to be a war, I think. Everybody's yammering about it."

Eric was confused. A war? How did one contrive to make money in a war?

"North and South are fixing to fight," Mick was ex-

115

plaining. "Over the nigger issue. That new president, who's going to be sworn in come March, Lincoln's his name, he's a fanatic about the nigger issue. If there's a war and men are called up to fight, you can go to the army as a substitute."

"A substitute?"

"Sure, see. Some rich guy gets drafted and he doesn't want to go get a cannonball through his private parts. So he gives you some money and you go in his place, hoping to avoid that cannonball."

"That is unfair."

Mick laughed. "I said you got a lot of surprises coming. All you foreigners get off the boat thinking this is some ideal kind of place. Fair. Unfair. Either you want the money or you don't. Fair don't have nothing to do with it. It's all just as anonymous as the cannonball. But Joan, she was thinking . . ."

Mick let his voice trail off, as if he did not altogether agree with whatever his sister had been thinking.

"Yes?" Eric prompted.

Then Joan came in from the kitchen, carrying a large plate heaped with steaming boiled potatoes, and a thick, juicy chunk of broiled beef. She set it in front of Eric.

"Eat up," she said, sitting down next to her brother. "Have you mentioned it to him yet?" she asked Mick.

"Just broaching the subject," he grinned. "I'm not sure he'll be interested."

"Let's let him be the judge of that, shall we?" she interrupted, patting his shoulder lovingly.

Mick fell silent, as Joan explained what they had been discussing in the kitchen.

"It's up to Liz, of course," she began, "but I think she'll approve of a man like you. We need someone who's strong"—she eyed him appreciatively—"honest, and, above all, discreet."

"I am those things," Eric admitted, "but who is Liz?"

"That's our mother," Mick answered. "She owns this tavern, and the boardinghouse on the next block."

"That's where we live," said Joan.

WILD WIND WESTWARD

"Assuming that your mother agrees to let me work for her," Eric wondered, "exactly what would I be doing?"

"You know how to drive a team of horses? You know how to lift heavy objects?" Mick demanded.

Eric nodded. This job, whatever it was, did not seem especially promising. But he had to start somewhere.

"You'll be hauling cargo, essentially," Joan said. "Here in New York and farther out on Long Island. It's a bad time of year, but . . ." She seemed on the verge of saying something, then changed her mind. "Mick, let's close up and take this foreigner to meet Liz. What is your name?"

"Gunnarson. Eric Gunnarson."

"I like that," she said, smiling at him in a way that was promissory and insinuating, yet totally innocent. "Eric. I like that very much."

"Well, let's not moon on about it now," snapped Mick, his temper flaring.

"Oh, come," Joan soothed him, patting his cheek gently. She kissed him quickly, as one would an angry child, and, again, he quieted under her influence. Buttoning his coat in preparation for the foray out into the cold, Eric reflected that it would be wonderful to have a family as warm and affectionate as that reflected by the behavior of Mick and Joan Leeds. Truly, Liz, their mother, had a sound influence upon them. It was fortuitous that he should, so quickly, have made this connection, which might in turn lead to a job. He did not know too much about it yet, but he would be a fool not to explore the possibility further. Perhaps he might work out an arrangement allowing him to stay the night in their house. Surely he could cut firewood, or perform some other task, to make recompense.

Collars pulled up against the cold, heads bent into the icy wind, the three rushed up the street toward Liz Leed's boardinghouse. On the way Joan told Eric a little about their family.

"Father was a businessman," she said. "He owned four ships. Sailing ships. He imported sugar and molasses from the West Indies. But one year, when Mick and I were real little, he borrowed a lot of money to buy two of the new steamships, because the sailing vessels were getting old. He had bad luck, though. One of the new ships blew up, right here in New York Harbor, and the other sank in a typhoon."

"In the same year," Mick said. "And he didn't have insurance. He figured, what could happen to a steel ship?"

"He couldn't bear the thought of failure," Joan went on, a touch of pride in her voice, her father's demise notwithstanding, "and he took to beating Liz."

"He also took to drink," Mick said. "It's a tendency we in the family have to watch out for."

"He died of drink," said Liz. "They found him on a streetcorner one February, almost frozen. Took him to the hospital. But it was too late."

She seemed to shudder, affected more by the memory than the icy night.

"Luckily, Liz carried on. She's a very strong lady."

And, indeed, Liz Leeds did seem quite formidable. She sat knitting before the fireplace, a broad-shouldered, big-bosomed woman, with streaks of gray in thick dark hair. Eric noted that Mick resembled her more than did Joan. Liz seemed as steady and secure as the house, which, in the firelit darkness, Eric had judged to be a dusky yellow. Inside, the rooms were not large, but neatly arranged.

"What is this?" she asked her children, looking at Eric as she did so.

Quickly, Joan explained how Eric had come into the tavern, what had transpired with the police, and how they had discussed the possibility of a job.

Liz nodded, thinking it over. She bade them take off their coats, went out into the kitchen, and returned with four cups and a pot of tea. "Tell me about yourself?" she asked Eric, in the too casual tone that reveals suspicion.

Guardedly, Eric complied. He did not mention the man he had killed in Norway, but, since Mick and Joan already knew he'd jumped ship, he had to tell that part.

Oddly, Liz Leeds seemed not overly disturbed by this fact. In the weeks to come Eric would learn why this was so. Liz Leeds knew an advantage when she saw one. "You can start work tomorrow morning?" she asked abruptly, after Eric had finished speaking.

"I would be very eager to do just that."

Liz thought it over for a few minutes, as Mick, Joan and Eric waited.

"It would be a good idea, really," Joan implored her mother quietly. "Mr. Gunnarson has everything we've been looking for."

This seemed to convince the older woman. She looked Eric in the eye. "Yes, I think he does at that," she said slowly, with what private thoughts Eric could not guess.

They finished the tea, and Liz told Joan to give Eric bedding and show him to one of the upstairs rooms. "It's empty at the moment. We had a boarder who skipped out on us. Couldn't pay the rent." She shrugged. "It happens. But if it's all right with you, board and room will be part of your wages."

The arrangement, at the moment, seemed a necessity to Eric, who had no money. He agreed. If he did not like the situation, he reasoned, a different procedure could be determined after he had some coins in his pocket.

Joan led him up the stairs, holding a whale-oil lamp that lighted a flickering way down a gloomy upstairs corridor. There were at least six doors, behind which unknown, transient people slept. Joan handed Eric the lamp, opened a closet door, and withdrew blankets, sheets, and a rumpled pillow. Smiling, she motioned him toward one of the doors. Behind it was a small, rude room, but there was a bed, one chair, and a washstand.

"We'll get you water in the morning," she said, expertly putting the sheets on the bed. "It would freeze here overnight."

"Thank you," said Eric, when Joan had finished making the bed.

She came to him, as if to take the lamp, which he had been holding. Her beautiful green eyes shone brilliantly in the light, and Eric saw on her mouth that soft, vexing, indecipherable smile.

"It's nothing," she said. "I like to please." And, saying this, she slipped close to him, moved her body once, twice, three times against his, moved her body in the way a woman moves for a man. Then, with one hand, she took the lamp from him, and with the other touched softly but lingeringly the staff of his manhood which she had stirred into throbbing life.

Then she was gone from the room, which was dark. But Eric was on fire in the night.

II

Kristin found Oslo both exciting and depressing. The great port city, jewel of Norway, teemed with life and bustle unknown to her mountain youth, and she enjoyed the constant movement of people, horses, drays and carriages. She exulted, as with a sense of adventure, to the sight of mighty ships in the harbor, along the quay. The tutors Gustav Rolfson had engaged to give her a knowledge of English and French offered refined, intellectual companionship. Madame Lonnerdahl, who taught her dance, was a source of constant encouragement, with her praise of Kristin's natural grace and ability. And Herr Borcher, who was to teach her the ways of society, echoed Gustav himself: "Your husband was right, if I may say so, madame. Properly trained in the rituals of society, and in the arts of genteel discourse, you will be able to charm serpents down from the trees. If that is, indeed, where they reside."

I know one such serpent very well, thought Kristin, smiling the while, *and he resides in my bed.*

It was her personal life with Gustav, her family life with the Rolfsons, that left her irritated and depressed. Even on the road from Lesja to Oslo, after her wedding to Gustav, Kristin had been planning some trick, some ruse, some feint which would allow her to escape. She would wait until her leg had healed, find Eric somehow, and the two of them would run away. But Rolfson senior had scotched such a wild notion. He spoke to her bluntly, in private, several days after they had arrived at the tall, walled, luxurious Rolfson manor.

"My son is quite smitten with you, young lady," he

barked, "but I can tell you do not fully reciprocate his ardor. Have no ideas of leaving, however. If you do, remember that we can do terrible things to your family in Lesja. We can also leave them in peace and a relative prosperity. The choice is entirely yours."

So, even now, perhaps forever, the Rolfsons would hold over her the specter of her family, homeless and starving. And, if they were, it would have been her own fault. These Rolfsons were vicious; they always plotted things so that in the end they held a devious, wicked advantage, a black ace, a glittering sword suspended by a hair.

Kristin thought long and hard, trying to find some way by which her family might writhe free of the Rolfson yoke, and by which she herself might approach independence. In the end, when Gustav decided she had learned enough to manage the household and servants, Kristin began each week to withhold and secrete a small part of the household allowance, and send it by post to her family. She placed neither her name nor address on the envelope, lest the money fall into the wrong hands. Her family might guess— but would never know for certain—the identity of their benefactor. She would have liked to do more for them, but, for the time being, further aid was impossible. And she had other matters with which to deal.

"Now that you are fully in charge of my house," Gustav said to her one morning while he was dressing for the day, "I want you to arrange a formal dinner."

He adjusted his tie with a flourish, pulled on his morning coat, and stood arrogantly before the full-length bedroom mirror that showed all too clearly the deep, liver-colored scar across his face. His eyes narrowed dangerously, and he turned to Kristin, who lay abed. She was thinking of Eric. She always thought of Eric when she saw her husband inspect that scar. She was certain that he knew her thoughts, but she didn't care.

"Did you hear me?" he asked, with just a trace of harshness in his voice. He came over and sat down next to her on the bed. "I said I want you to organize a formal dinner. Saturday evening, a fortnight hence. The minerals and mountains of Lesja have given us massive collateral, which father and I intend to use in the attainment of major capital loans. Lord Anthony Soames, the British banker, will be here in Oslo, and if we show him a great time, let him see what we are worth, perhaps he will authorize the loan."

"Yes, husband," Kristin replied, without expression. This was the method she had adopted in all her dealings with him. She showed no emotion whatever. She showed no passion, or resentment, or even disapproval. She showed neither delight in the gifts he gave—rings, gowns, furs, necklaces—nor disappointment when, suddenly vexed at her lack of response to him, he withdrew some favor he had promised. Her coolness, which yet was always totally proper and sedate, drove him wild. Gustav could do nothing, it seemed, to stir his wife to life, much less to passion. When he took her at night in their marriage bed, he had at first done so with intensity, feeling, hot desire, his whole body shuddering in anticipation as he poised to enter her. She had let him take her, opened herself to him, but never had she returned his embrace, or moved her body for him in the way of a woman making love. They had been married now for half a year, and already he took her less and less, angered and puzzled and, yes, even though he was a hard man, *hurt* at what he had come to call her "incapacity." It would, he felt, cure itself in time, perhaps with a child. He very much wanted a child and was sure he had good seed. Perhaps if his wife warmed somewhat toward him, her body would in its turn grow receptive to his seed.

Now he sat down beside her at the edge of the bed and placed his large hand over her warm, glowing breast, caressing it. The delicate nipple stirred, and Gustav felt exultant.

Perhaps now . . . ? He would have to undress, after such long and careful preparation. But it would be worth it. Kristin was looking at him coolly, levelly, as if totally unaware of his hand on her, of her own nakedness beneath the bedsheets, of anything in the world but the prospect of a dinner party, which she also regarded with exquisite neutrality.

Gustav decided to be tender. "What are your thoughts, my darling?" he asked, still petting her breast, bending to whisper closely in her ear.

"I was wondering about Lord Anthony Soames. I never heard you mention his name."

Gustav was disappointed. He had hoped she would respond to the overture he was making. "Soames is unimportant just now. Let us make love as we did last night."

"If you wish," said Kristin, without inflection, without eagerness or reluctance.

Disappointed at her casual air, yet thoroughly excited once again by her naked beauty, Gustav pressed on. "Kristin, darling, answer me something."

"Yes, husband."

"Why are you not with child? We have made love at every time, and I have worn no device. The Rolfson name must be carried on. And, I feel, a child will draw us even more closely together."

Kristin had to make a considerable effort not to show aversion to his words. A child would bind her closely to Rolfson, too closely, forever. She had to avoid having his child at all costs, and had, thus far, relied secretly and with success on an old Greek method known but unused by her pious God-fearing mother. Each night, before bed, she would insert a piece of cheesecloth treated with olive oil, oil of cedar, frankincense, and hope. The procedure had not failed yet, except that the lack of pregnancy was beginning to disquiet Gustav. Kristin knew from bitter experience that a Rolfson unable immediately to have what he wanted would bend himself even more forcefully to get whatever the desired object was.

"I am quite sure I will conceive someday," she told him, quite beyond desire, "or you may rid yourself of me."

He leaned back, and drew his hand away.

"Oh, so that is it, eh? You think I will no longer wish to have your beauty simply because you are not yet with child? You have much still to learn."

WILD WIND WESTWARD

Kristin watched resignedly as Gustav stood, divesting himself almost frantically of his elegant morning clothes. During a normal business day he often dressed four times—morning coat for the office; riding attire prior to the noon meal; a casual suit for the afternoon appearance at his club; and formal clothes for the evening meal. The Rolfsons dressed always like the nobility because they were not yet secure enough to flout by jot or tittle any part of the societal code, written or unwritten.

But now, having ripped off his expensive outfit, he ripped away also the sheets by which Kristin was covered. He was hard and throbbing above her, and then he was upon her, and then he was in her. Gustav had a certain vague contempt for his weakness, his overwhelming desire to have her, when Kristin herself so obviously did not seem to care if she had him, now or ever. And yet it was her soulless and dispassionate yielding that goaded him, time and again, to try to ignite her, inflame her, sorcer her to writhing, thrusting, unfettered passion.

He had never succeeded, and as he felt the moment of his pleasure approaching, felt it down along the base of his spine, and deep within himself, and all along the rending rod of lust and ecstasy, he knew that he was failing again.

"It's the mountain farmer, isn't it?" he said, thrusting, thrusting, battering into her. "It's that—" But then he could say no more, think no more, possessed by the gorgeous sweetness of the flesh, the pulsing rushes of luminous enchantment. And then he was there, and then gone down from it, shaking along the spent, gray landscape of aftermath, doomed and sorrowful.

"It's that farmer, isn't it? You can't get him out of your mind."

"Is that it? What are you talking about, husband?" Gustav would have groaned with disappointment, but he would not give her the satisfaction. What was wrong? In the world of affairs, in business, everything was progressing so well. Soon, after they charmed Lord Soames, gained liquidity from his vast bank, Gustav and his father would move on to exploit the riches of the New World. Nothing would stand in their way. They would gain everything, everything: power, fame, money beyond belief. Gustav was sure he would have those things, and yet he could not truly, completely, have the spirit or soul of this beautiful young woman in his bed. It was unfair. Any other mountain girl would have given her eye teeth, an arm, a leg, to enjoy what Kristin Arnesdatter had now at her beck and call.

"Are you finished with me, husband?" she was asking him. "I must wash, dress, and begin preparations for the banquet you wish."

Conscious that he was still lying, spent and limp, upon her, Gustav withdrew from her, and a hollow, popping sound marked his leaving, empty and sad. He slid off and lay there beside her, panting. Everything was turned around. He was married to a beauty, and yet she was remote and unknown to him. Other men envied him, and yet had wives and lovers, or both, to give them happy pleasure. He had pleasure that seemed to melt beneath him, seemed to turn into futility and loneliness and chagrin even as he possessed it, even at the precise moment of his spending within the lovely body he had chosen, both as the receptacle of his pleasure and the wellspring of the generation of titans he dreamed to create.

"For how many guests shall I plan?" Kristin was asking, as she crossed the thickly carpeted bedroom and began brushing her hair at her dressing table.

"What?" Gustav asked, in a daze. He collected his clothing and began, again, to dress. He would be late to the Rolfson offices now, and, depending upon his mood, old Adolphus would either rage or snicker. "What? Oh, yes, the dinner. I would expect about forty or fifty. There are many who will thank us merely for giving them a moment of Lord Soames's time."

"I am sure that is true, husband."

Then Gustav could not take it, could not take one more moment, just then, of Kristin's infernal remoteness, her studied calm. It mocked him, goaded him, maddened him, though he was captive of it, servant to it.

"You'll be sorry one day!" he raged at her, before departing the bedroom amid the stomping of boots and the slamming of doors. "You'll be sorry!"

Kristin went on brushing her hair until he was gone. She heard him clomping down the great circular staircase of the mansion, built with other people's tears, with other people's blood and toil.

"I'm already sorry," she said to her reflection in the mirror.

Eric was ever on Kristin's mind, and she sought him whenever she could. At first, in her early days in Oslo, looking for him had been an impossibility. She was too closely watched at the mansion, and she had too many lessons to attend. But gradually, as time went on, she enjoyed more and more free time, and suffered less suspicion. True, she did not trust any of the servants—they had been long and loyally in the Rolfsons' employ, and one of them, quick, nervy Giselda, who was head of housekeeping, seemed to resent Kristin in some particular way the girl from Lesja did not understand. But then, she did not know Gustav Rolfson had often petted and bedded Giselda prior to his unexpected marriage, a marriage especially unexpected by Giselda, who had been given vague promises of permanent union, during passionate moments of sexual union, by Gustav himself.

Kristin breakfasted on bread and butter, coffee and cream, in the morning room. Her tray was silver, her cup and saucer of delicate china. Her butter plate and knife were of gold. None of it meant anything to Kristin. She would much rather have been in a rude stone house with Eric, eating dried apples and drinking mountain-flower tea. Having eaten, she summoned the head of housekeeping.

"Yes, madame?" Giselda inquired. She had dark, straight hair, striking, gelid-blue eyes, and a slender, full-breasted body. There was about her an air of barely controlled recklessness. Kristin admired her spirit and competence, but, try as she might, could not seem to enlist the young woman's trust.

"Giselda," she said, "we will be having an English banker to dinner, Saturday fortnight. Forty guests, perhaps more. We shall dine in the great hall. Have the table prepared, the gold plate polished, as usual. The English are said to prefer beef or lamb. Let us give Lord Soames roast beef as the main meat course. Also caviar, salmon, turtle soup, herring in cream, potato soufflé, mince pie, and the usual fruits and cheeses. I myself shall see to the orchestra."

"Oh, madame?" asked Giselda, as if convinced Kristin would not properly handle such an arrangement.

"Yes, Giselda. Now, set about this business, and there'll be something extra in your pay if all goes well."

"Why, thank you *so* much, madame!"

"And tell Ellison I wish to see him. I must go out and I'll want my carriage."

"Go out again, madame?"

Kristin looked at the other woman. Giselda was getting suspicious. She ought not to have mentioned going out, even casually. She had gone out often of late, explaining her absences in terms of shopping for dresses, or furniture, or antiques in the quaint shops along the harbor. And, indeed, she did visit such shops, and she did buy items that pleased her, but her purpose was quite different.

"Yes, Giselda," she told the servant. "Now, go about your duties."

The head housekeeper went out, her fine body moving gracefully, slyly, like a cat's. Presently, Ellison, the butler, came in. Kristin ordered her carriage. His eyebrows lifted but he bowed and went out. Half an hour later Kristin was in the coach, riding out the gate of the Rolfson manor. She was mistress of that manor, and it meant less to her than a crystal of sugar dissolving in sweet tea.

"Down to the waterfront," she told Fensterwald, the dribbly, fawning driver.

He looked at her oddly, as if wondering: *The waterfront again?*

Kristin realized she would have to be more careful. Yet

where else but on the waterfront did she have even half a chance to learn of Eric's whereabouts? A man on the run, with a murder charge against him and almost no hope in the courts, would almost certainly seek to get out of the country. In many a shop along the quay, she had made purchases, made herself known, and finally asked her question:

"It would have been last June, possibly early July? A blond man, tall and strong? He would have had a pack on his back?"

"Sorry, madam. Norway is filled these days with tall, strong blonds, with but one pack to take them to the ends of the world."

"He was a man of extraordinary comeliness."

"Aren't they all, madam? Aren't they all? You know him well?" The shopkeepers studied the huge diamond, the ruby-encrusted wedding band on her finger.

"My brother," she lied.

But, shop after shop, no news of Eric. She grew desperate. She grew reckless. Sooner or later, she was certain, she *must* get a lead, win a clue. Eric could not simply have disappeared into the whirl and abyss of life.

Once she had thought of going to detectives, but had eschewed the idea. She could not trust them. They might go to Gustav with news of her clandestine activities. She did not want that. Gustav himself might get the idea to have Eric traced.

The day was bright and cold, with white scudding clouds, and the waters of the winter harbor were thick with floes of ice. Fensterwald eased the horses to a walk. Horses and carriage, driver and rider, moved slowly along the waterfront. Kristin had a premonition that something was going to happen today. She was sure it was going to be something good. "Tell me when you wish to stop?" blubbered Fensterwald, the drool freezing on his chin.

Kristin unwrapped the rich bearskins in which she was esconced, and climbed down from the buggy. "Right here is just fine," she said.

Vanessa Royall

"Here?" blithered Fensterwald, shocked in spite of his hazy dim-wittedness. "Here?"

Before them, alongside the narrow waterfront street, was a grogshop of decrepit and sinister appearance. It had one window, now grease-blackened and totally opaque, and it had once possessed a door, too, but that had long ago been torn off in some trackless, incalculable brawl. Now a heavy blanket hung in the doorway, keeping out what cold it could, and holding in more cheap tobacco smoke than any man would have believed possible.

"You oughtn't to go in there, madam," Fensterwald bleated, even as he helped her down to the street. "Somebody might be seeing you and telling tales."

"If you don't, and I don't, who will?" She smiled at him.

Fensterwald licked and enjoyed some dribble, and looked pained. He threw up his hands, said nothing.

Kristin went into the bar. It was small, dark, and narrow, not a table, not a chair, not even stools for its itinerants and habitués, but just a rude counter all along one side behind which a slutty barmaid sloshed liquor into dirty glasses and collected soiled coins in payment. The place smelled of urine, vomit, and cheap liquor. Four sailors stood along the bar as Kristin entered, drinking over their fates, lost opportunities, and lost loves. Their backs were toward the door, but when they saw the look of surprise in the barmaid's eyes, they turned, ready either to fight or flee.

"Don't think you ought to be in a place like this here, honey," warned the barmaid.

"Ursula, shut your mouth," contradicted one of the sailors. "She had a date to meet me here."

Everybody laughed, even Ursula the barmaid.

Kristin knew she would have to take control quickly, or leave before her mission was accomplished.

"I'm seeking information," she said, "about a man."

Everybody laughed and hooted.

"I'm willing to pay for the information."

There was attentive silence now.

"Ursula, here, knows a lot about men," snickered one of the sailors, which evoked a few raspy chuckles.

"Go ahead," demanded the most physically imposing of the sailors, a deep-chested, dirty-blond brawler with the bright red nose of a hard drinker. "We're waiting."

"I'm looking for my . . . brother."

A few wicked laughs.

"He may have been here sometime last June. I have reason to believe he might have shipped out from this harbor. Eric," she said risking his name. "He was known as Eric Starbane, or Gunnarson. Tall and very blond. He would have been wearing mountaineer's clothing. If any of you remember him, I—"

"Hey!" cried the big sailor. "I think I recall something like that!"

Kristin was on guard. They would want the money, would invent information in order to get it.

"And who might you be?"

"Ingersoll. Lars Ingersoll. Seagoing boilerman. *Former* seagoing boilerman. The captain of an American ship threw me off her just before she was to sail, and I recollect a man fitting your description getting called on board."

Kristin's heart quickened. This Ingersoll might be lying, but he seemed too deeply in his cups to fabricate a story very readily.

"How's your coin?" Ingersoll demanded, taking a step toward her.

"It is reliable. But tell me, what ship was it?"

"American. The *Anandale*. A tub. Captain name of Dubin. Like to kill the bastard, he ever sails back into this port again. Now, *give*." He stood before her, reeking of whiskey, and held out his hand.

Keeping her part of the bargain since she now had at least some information to pursue further, Kristin opened her purse and reached inside to select a couple of half-krone pieces. But, like a flash, Ingersoll's big hand grabbed her wrist, twisted, trying to tear the purse away from her.

"Lars!" cried the barmaid, alarmed. "I don't want no trouble!"

"Help!" cried Kristin, trying to wrench away from him and make it to the blanket-shrouded doorway. She would gladly have relinquished the purse, but Ingersoll's half-drunken exertions had succeeded in wrapping its leather shoulder straps around her wrists and forearms. "Help!" she cried again.

"If you'll just let go of the goddam thing . . ." grunted the sailor, still struggling with her.

"Lars! For God sakes, stop it. Do you want the King's police down here after us?" yelled one of the sailors, coming forward not so much to rescue Kristin as to extricate Ingersoll from the mess he had created.

Then the blanket across the doorway was thrown aside, and everyone in the bar turned to see who was about to come in. Kristin, for an instant before she grasped what was happening, wished for the police. But it was not. There, standing in the doorway against the bright cold winter light, was Giselda, the head housekeeper, and behind her, equally aghast though not as diabolically pleased as Giselda, was Fensterwald the driver, dribbling onto his chin.

"I'm gettin' out of here," growled Ingersoll, and, followed hastily by his mates, they all but pushed Giselda aside as they raced from the dive.

Giselda did not mind. "So, madam, you have been out shopping, have you?" She glanced around the pitiful barroom. "Shopping for the men who like this place?"

Kristin was humiliated, and furious, too. Giselda had actually followed her down here, had perhaps arranged it with Fensterwald. The circumstances were terrible. No lady of wealth and breeding would be caught dead down here by the docks in a filthy grogshop like this one.

"Why don't you all leave?" muttered Ursula the barmaid. "You've scared away my customers and caused enough trouble."

It seemed more than a good idea. Gathering what dignity she could muster, Kristin squared her shoulders, marched past her tormentor, and walked outside. The carriage was there alongside the dock. She walked toward it. So did Giselda.

"Do you not have some explanation for me?" the other woman goaded.

Kristin decided that, however compromising her situation appeared, Giselda, as a servant, was in no position to cause real trouble. After all, Kristin was Rolfson's wife, however little the fact pleased her.

"I do not have to explain anything to you."

Giselda's lovely lips twisted into a sneer of knowing malevolence.

"We shall see," she retorted. "I know as well as you how to account for the household funds."

Kristin started. True, she left most of the details of running the household to Giselda. Could it be that the wily servant had noticed the small weekly discrepancies, the money Kristin was sending to her family in Lesja? If so, the situation was more dangerous than Kristin had surmised. The only way to deal with it was to be as truthful as possible, and to act as a member of the class into which Rolfson had brought her.

"You are quite right, Giselda," she said. "I am pleased by your perspicacity, as well as by your diligence. Yes, of course a portion of the household fund is being withheld. It is for a special gift"—this was true—"and it is none of your affair whatever. As to my travels about the city, I owe you no explanation. But since you have gone to such trouble to follow me, I shall tell you this. I am seeking information about the man who marked my husband so horribly upon his visage. If you had been thinking of telling tales"—and, saying this, she looked at both Giselda and old Fensterwald—"do you think you would very much elevate my husband's estimate of you by passing on such information?"

Fensterwald was having some trouble following the conversation, but Giselda saw the point all too clearly, and began to form an apology.

"It is all right, Giselda. In a way, I am touched by your concern. And I am sure we do not need to discuss the inevitable consequence to a servant who involves herself in matters not within her jurisdiction."

Giselda blanched. She did not wish to be dismissed. And it was with new respect, even a measure of fear, that the housekeeper accepted Kristin's invitation to climb into the carriage and drive home warm within the lush sleek furs.

On the drive, watching the fine houses of the moneyed class come into view, Kristin suppressed a sigh. She had narrowly avoided a great deal of trouble. It was still possible, although unlikely, that Giselda would mention this trip down to the docks. Then Kristin brightened. At long last, she had at least one small sliver of information. The American ship *Anandale*. If Eric had sailed on her...

Her brain worked rapidly; currents and connections flickered and flashed. The Rolfsons were heavily involved in shipping, and somewhere in their offices must be a list of the vessels serving Oslo. If the itinerary of the *Anandale* could be traced, she might learn where Eric had gone. But how could she inspect such listings without making Gustav suspicious?

It was something to think about.

Upon returning to the mansion Kristin gave instructions for the evening meal—roast goose with a dressing of herbs and truffles, flounder basted in white wine, carrots baked in sweet molasses, baby onions stewed in gravy, and cheese toast—and then retired to her room. She ordered her bath drawn, undressed, bathed long and splendidly in hot, fragrant water, then consciously selected an evening gown sure to have its effect upon Gustav. His awe of her was a weapon, her weapon, and his awe of her made him faintly contemptible in her eyes. Eric had been a man who accepted her beauty as a natural gift, but who loved her *beyond* mere beauty. But Gustav thought the loveliness was all there was to her, and so he was a victim of Kristin's comely face and lissome body. Standing before the mirror, she admired the glistening white satin gown. It was a French design, and, in fact, had been a gift of old Adolphus, who admired the way it revealed her breasts almost to the nipple, and how it hugged her narrow waist and showed the curve of her hips. Perhaps Gustav's father would permit her into the offices one day, if she could fashion a sufficiently compelling reason.

Summoning a maid, she asked for tea and sherry, and

sat down at her writing table to think. Alternately sipping the hot tea and the sweet, heavy wine, she began to prepare a list of the pieces the orchestra might perform on the night of the Soames dinner. The occasion was a crucial one for the Rolfsons. Their plans for an international business empire depended heavily on the ability to secure capital. Kristin felt a sudden anger that was close to hatred. The poor people of Lesja, her people, those who shared her own honest origins, were financing with their lands and mountains the underpinning of the Rolfsons' vast schemes. How would she feel if the Rolfsons failed?

She had never really considered the question before because, initially overwhelmed by their position in Oslo and by the wealth surrounding them, she had not entertained even the possibility of a Rolfson debacle. But she did now, at first with a certain bitter pleasure. Soon, however, her intelligence superseded her emotions, what she had learned of wealth and power took precedence over hurt and passion, and she began to understand that Rolfson's standing was also hers, if she could but find a way to use it to her ends. Of what good would she be to herself, to her family, should Gustav's fortunes flounder? And, cast off and impoverished, she would never find Eric, would never see his sweet strong face again, nor be held and thrilled by him. Penniless women did not emigrate; penniless women did not ship away on steamships as deckhands or boilertenders.

No, it was true, she had a stake in the Rolfsons and their enterprises. She resolved to find out as much about business as she could. *That* was it! She would convince Gustav to permit her into the offices of the company, professing a desire to learn more about mercantile affairs! That her desire was real in no way diminished her resolve; in fact, just the opposite was true.

When dinner was announced, she went downstairs eagerly, looking radiant, and prepared to work her wiles.

But she came upon a scene of dark, gloomy pessimism. Gustav and his father, already seated, were hunched over their wineglasses at one end of the huge table, muttering to each other, lower lips thrust out in quirky and not entirely convincing defiance.

"Why, gentlemen, what is the matter?" she asked, as Ellison, the butler, pulled out her chair. She sat down, signaled for wine. Old Adolphus was studying her neckline and breasts, but dully, without spirit. A bad sign. Truly, the day must have gone bleakly for these rapacious and brassy connivers.

"We have had something of a setback," Gustav grumbled, turning to her. His eyes widened when he saw the gown, and her inside it.

"Not a setback," grumbled the old man, in hoary admonition, "more like a disappointment. But it would have been better to have him here, on our own grounds. Then he would have been able to *see* our wealth. Otherwise . . . oh, I know what they think in London. I know how they think. They feel that we here in Norway are mere pikers, useless for knowing and fruitless to consider."

"And not worth a loan of money, either," added his son, "especially the amount of money we so desperately need if we are to expand our business."

"Would you please tell me what you are talking about?" Kristin asked. "What is the cause of such dismay?"

Gustav shrugged and told her. "We have had a message from Lord Soames. He has canceled his plans to come to Norway. Instead, he has invited father or myself to London."

"Why, and what is wrong with that? You yourself are very much a champion of things English, and I should love to go to London."

"You?" Her husband laughed, in a condescending way that angered Kristin. "You go? This is business, my dear, and not a promenade."

"Wait a minute," grumbled Rolfson senior. "I believe I have thought of a new angle for us to exploit." He was still staring at Kristin's breasts, but with much more alertness now. His mood was improving. "Yes, I believe I have a new angle indeed. We had intended to impress Lord Soames with our houses, or lands, wealth he could see, which he cannot witness from London. But we have something else he can see and appreciate, which will give him evidence of our exquisite style and taste."

He raised his glance from Kristin's breasts and met her eyes. His own eyes were glittering fiendishly. "You see, I know a little about Lord Soames. He has certain tastes all his own."

"What do you mean, father?" asked Gustav in a tone that seemed not disingenuous to Kristin.

"When I was in England last September, attempting overtures to financing after we had acquired the Lesja property, I learned that Lord Soames is . . . how would one say it? A connoisseur of beautiful women? And surely Kristin is that."

Kristin watched her husband's face. For a brief—a very brief—moment, he seemed shocked to grasp that his own wife might play a part, based merely on her sex and beauty, in the fortunes of the Rolfson future. But that brief moment passed, and it was all too clear to Kristin that, whatever personal or passionate needs Gustav had for her, when it came to business she was but another item, another element, another pawn in the game. But then, why would she ever have thought otherwise?

She surprised both of them with her agreeability. "If the Englishman in question means so much to you, then he must mean a great deal to me as well, because our fortunes are joined." She thought again how she would learn as much as she could, how she would use these two unprincipled moneygrubbers exactly as they were using her. She felt a quick pang of conscience. *"Don't become like them,"* she had pleaded with Eric. *"Don't ever become like them."*

I'm not, she reassured herself, *I shall simply be the dutiful, compliant spouse.*

"Whatever you wish of me, husband," she said, dropping her eyes.

There was a long silence as the waiters began to serve the meal.

"Ah . . . what precisely did you mean by Lord Soames's

Vanessa Royall

tastes?" Gustav asked his father, when the fish course was being cleared. The flounder had been splendid.

The older man looked up. "He appreciates beautiful women, that's all," Adolphus answered, with a wink. "Nothing wrong with that, is there? So do I!"

He reached over and pawed Kristin around the shoulders a little, let his hand trail down her back, around her ribcage.

"Oh, *father*!" she cried, with a counterfeit but convincing giggle, as Gustav's face reddened. "If I'd only known earlier how much you cared. . . ."

"That's enough of this!" Gustav cried, angry and embarrassed at the same time. "This is enough."

The old man chortled but withdrew his eager, exploratory hand.

Then the goose was served.

"How could you have let him do that to you?" Gustav raged later in their bedroom. He was dressed in a silk robe, almost as scarlet as the mark across his face.

Kristin, sitting at her writing desk, looked up without interest. She had begun to wonder why Eric had not tried to write her or send her a message. Surely he knew where she was living, in Oslo with the Rolfsons. Perhaps some tragedy had befallen him.

"Let who do what to me?" she asked.

"You know what I am speaking about!"

"Husband, I assure you, I do not."

"My name is Gustav. *Gustav*."

"Yes, husband."

With difficulty he forced himself to keep control. "My father," he said, between gritted teeth. "Pawing you at dinner."

"He was only showing affection, in his way," Kristin replied, in a voice absolutely without inflection. "You do the same," she added.

His face darkened the more, becoming almost as colorful as scar and dressing gown.

WILD WIND WESTWARD

"He is simply using you, for the cheap, vicarious delight of an old man."

"Using me? Is not Lord Soames to use me, too?"

"That . . . that is ridiculous! That is preposterous. You will merely accompany me to London. If he appreciates beauty, he will find favorable his visual experience of your charms."

Kristin gave him a level look. "Is that all? But, even so, then who is using whom?"

Gustav turned, and paced away, irritated.

"When do you sail for England?" she asked.

He turned back to her. "What? Oh. It is now January. The North Sea is treacherous. And there are many papers and preparations I must see to. I doubt that we will sail until the summer."

The summer. By then a year would have elapsed since she had seen Eric, since that last fleeting moment, when, leg broken and lying in the stream, she had last seen him race away up the mountain. But had she not promised him, *We shall always belong to each other, no matter what?* Yes, she had. And that was still true, it would always be true.

"I wish," she said, "to learn more about your business. So that when we reach England, I am conversant on the subject. Do you think it would be seemly for me to spend some time in your offices? To gather a feeling for what it is you do at work? A feeling for how your enterprises are managed?"

Gustav misread her request. To the extent that he could be demonstrative, his face showed softness, even tenderness.

"My darling, of course," he said, coming to her, taking her into his arms. "How foolish of me not to have suggested it before." He thought it was the beginning of an entirely new closeness for them.

Overcome by desire, he stripped her rudely and carried her to the bed, only to be confounded again by her limp, maddening acquiescence to his physical assault, her entire responselessness. But that, he assured himself once more as he had so often before, was only the temporary "incapacity" of a young mountain girl brought suddenly into the house and surroundings of a great family.

What else could it be?

Later that night, after Gustav had drifted off into a sex-satiated sleep, Kristin removed from herself the protective wad of cheesecloth, red with the remnants of wine, red with hopeful blood, white with the seed that had not taken.

Not this time, nor ever, she thought.

Due to business preparations and various delays Kristin and Gustav were unable to sail for England until the autumn of 1861. At the Rolfson offices Kristin had been able to determine only the ports at which the S.S. *Anandale* had long since visited and departed. Eric might well be in the Azores, or Africa, or South America, or New York. He might even be rolling white and lost beneath the wild waves and dark cold waters of Cape Horn, where the *Anandale* had gone to the bottom in a typhoon some months after leaving New York on a voyage that had been planned for Tahiti, the Dutch East Indies, China, and Japan.

No, she thought, upon learning of the tragedy through the notices of various mercantile shipping lines, *no, I will not let myself believe in disaster.*

So she and Gustav left for London, aboard the *Viking Serpent,* an oceangoing yacht Adolphus had acquired by cheating a drunken young nobleman in a card game. Adolphus was sure the yacht would impress Lord Soames. Its master cabin was walled with mirrors; there was a mirror on the ceiling, too.

Kristin saw herself looking up at the mirror every night on the voyage from Oslo to England, saw herself, arms and legs limp and outstretched, motionless beneath the wildly thrusting Gustav, who was determined now more than ever to have a scion, a son, a Rolfson heir. Kristin watched him bucking and battering at her, but somehow she could not feel him. It was as if another man entirely was making love to some woman she had never known. The woman she *did* remember had felt desperately hungry, famished, absolutely starved after love.

Four days after they had left Oslo a letter addressed to Mrs. Gustav Rolfson arrived at the mansion. A mail coach brought it from the U.S.S. *Ticonderoga*, where it was received, along with other dispatches, by Ellison, the butler.

He wondered what was in it, of course, but he had always felt kindly toward the young Viking beauty who had come down from the mountains and had adapted so naturally to the rich life of Oslo. A Giselda might have opened it, read it, and destroyed it later, knowing its importance. It was the first letter from America ever received in the Rolfson household. "It is unfortunate she missed it," Ellison said to himself, as he slipped it into the pouch of business dispatches that would be sent to Gustav on the next ship bound for England.

III

A week before Eric posted his circumspect letter to Kristin, in the summer of 1861, things had seemed to be going well for him. He had a little money saved, and was thinking of moving out of the Leeds house, buying a horse and wagon and going into business for himself. He was not certain how Liz and Mick would react to his departure, but it was something he had to do. Eric had become very suspicious of Mick's "business," and he did not want to become involved in it any further. But, more crucially, he felt a need to move to a place of his own because of Joan.

Over half a year had passed since the first night in that cold, darkened upstairs bedroom. Eric, who had known women early, who had known rowdy mountain girls in cool summer glades below the timberline with the sun dappling the leaves, the grass, and the burning bodies of lovers, and who had known rough, eager older women in a room behind the store in Dovre, downriver from Lesja, thought he knew immediately what Joan Leeds was offering when she pressed her body momentarily against his own, when she reached down to touch him with a tender, exploratory hand.

But now, half a year later, he had to admit that his initial estimate did not begin to explain the mystery of Joan Leeds.

In a sense Eric was relieved. He was intensely attracted to Joan, to her mystery, allure, and enigmatic smile. However, not only could he not embark upon a dalliance with her right in her own household, but his memory of and need for Kristin was with him constantly, like a companion, as if Kristin's spirit and palpable physical presence stood beside him by day and lay down with him at night, when his labors were done.

Joan, he decided, was simply a lusty, affectionate girl. Her touching him on the first night, he decided, was instinctive, brought on by the excitement of the evening and what he, she, and Mick had been through together. He could accept that without judging anyone, neither himself nor her. She had never touched him in that intimate manner since, though often in tossing dreams he formed her image and felt her fingers. She was naturally expressive, he concluded, outgoing with hugs and kisses for her mother and brother, and never failing to give Eric himself one of her full, lovely smiles when she saw him in the evenings.

In truth, once Eric entered upon his work routine with Mick, he saw Joan quite seldom. She kept the tavern, Liz the boardinghouse, and Mick, with Eric's help, saw to the transport business. The only time Mick had spoken to Eric with regard to his sister was during one of their first drives from the boardinghouse to the isolated East River ferry slip that Mick favored.

"Don't you go gettin' no ideas about Joanie," he advised. He spoke, habitually, in a manner not exactly rude and not precisely arrogant either. One might make of it what one wished. Mick did not bother Eric, so he made nothing of it.

"I have a girl in my homeland," he told Leeds.

"Oh, yeah, is that right? Is she good looking like Joanie?"

"She is very attractive," replied Eric, diplomatically, "as is your sister."

"Yeah, ain't she a sweetheart, though? I don't know what me and Liz would do without her. How come you left your woman back in . . . where was it again? France?"

"Norway. I had no money. When I get some, I hope to send for her."

"Hey. Is that right? Well, you just stick by me an' do what I say an' before long you might just be writing that sweetheart of yours a little letter that says, 'Come on across, lover, I've got the bed all warm.' "

He laughed his rude laugh, which was as indeterminate as his speech, neither good humored nor mean spirited. It was beginning to impress Eric that, somehow, the Leeds existed in a certain middle world of their own, ventured into the life of the community when they had to, but afterward retreated to a secret, special haven of their own, that Eric had sensed though not observed.

The matter was not of importance to Eric anyway. He wanted money; he had work to do. Mick provided the work, Liz the bed and board, and Joan—sometimes—touched him and smiled at him in a tantalizing dream.

Very soon after Eric began to help Mick in his shipping business, the young immigrant could not but observe that the roughneck's methods were eccentric, if not erratic. Yet he was a hard worker, and he made money. So at first Eric kept his own counsel and held back his questions. After all this was America, not Norway, and Eric was just beginning to learn its peculiar ways.

New York had grown first along the harbor at Manhattan's southern end, and spread inexorably northward until, at the time of Eric's arrival in America, the city stretched, teeming and sprawling, to the middle of that slender rocky island and beyond, a symbolic, haphazard organism of wealth and elegance, ugliness and poverty and greed. Great mansions shadowed pathetic hovels; perfumed tycoons strode the streets beside feckless beggars and hapless urchins; thoroughbred horses cantered past the stray, rooting pigs of the poor. America, Eric observed, seemed very much like Europe, except it was harsher in its contrasts and it held, always, always, the promise of quick money, sudden power.

Eric pondered the contradictions, riding on the wagon beside Mick, as Leeds drove his team of big brown Belgian draft horses up the island, past the mansions and hovels, to the ferry slip. The tides of American life seemed founded on money; money was the only nobility. The fat, wealthy man being helped into his carriage in front of his new, raw Park Avenue palace might by some turn of fate become the ragged, scrawny beggar lurching along Canal Street. And the reverse was likewise true.

Eric resolved to have the mansion and the carriage and the gold. If to get it he had to put up with Mick Leeds, he was willing to accept the hand that destiny had dealt.

"Why do you use this ferry? It's so far out of the way," Eric had said, on one of their first trips.

"Don't ask no questions!" Mick snapped, then seemed to think the better of his harshness. "Two reasons," he explained. "First, not too many people cross here. It ain't crowded an' we don't have to wait. Second, it's a shorter route to where I buy supplies, out on Long Island."

That made sense to Eric, although he had come to wonder why, so often, Mick preferred to leave Manhattan at night and also, inevitably, return at night as well. But at first he didn't ask, and in time he knew.

At first, in fact, Mick did not even require Eric to make the entire trip out to Long Island. Eric would load empty barrels onto the wagon at the Leeds's own tavern, and at several other taverns and restaurants in the city. Then they would drive to the ferry slip, cross the East River, and drive out onto Long Island until they reached a grimy inn at which waited a number of other wagons, teams, and drivers. Mick seemed to know the other drivers, although they were not a communicative lot. Eric was left behind, to shoe horses and repair harnesses at the livery next to the inn, while Mick went farther out on Long Island with the other teams. When he returned, the barrels were full, and, touching with his fingertips and tasting on his tongue some slight seepage between the barrel staves, Eric knew: Mick was shipping whiskey.

What was the American law? He did not know. But, while travel by night may indeed have been an honest preference on Mick's part, certainly it also carried disconcerting connotations.

Eric decided to ask someone about it. But whom? If he acted rashly, what might befall him? If these shipments were illegal, he was already a participant in that illegality.

Vanessa Royall

And the Leeds family knew he had jumped ship. He was, quite soundly, in a trap. If, indeed, something was amiss.

He said nothing to Mick about his misgivings, said nothing to anyone for several weeks, although he worried about the matter.

Joan, perceptive as she was lovely, noticed his preoccupation late one night, when Eric and Mick made a liquor delivery at the tavern. Eric had been working for about a month, and a sudden February thaw, turning the roadways to muddy ruts, had made the trip more arduous than usual. The tavern was empty. She poured him a glass of whiskey, then checked to make sure her brother was not within earshot. Smoothing her thick, silky red hair, she asked Eric what was troubling him.

"I know you have a beloved in Norway," she said. "Mick told me. Is she heavily upon your mind?"

"No," he said, "it's not that." He did not think it was wise to confide in one of the Leeds. They were too close. They told each other everything. But Joan seemed so kind, so worried about him, it was late and he was very tired.

"The liquor we bring in from the country," he said, "and the manner in which we do it. Is that not . . . ?"

He didn't finish. He didn't have to. Joan interrupted his worrying with an easy, gentle laugh. "You mean is it against the law?" she asked. "Of course not."

"But those police who were here the night I left the ship? The ones looking for Mick?"

"Oh, that was just a personal thing between Mick and a cop," she answered, dismissing the incident. "No, it's all very simple. I'll explain it to you. See, there are powerful men who want to force all tavern owners to buy liquor only from them. At very high prices," she added, nodding her head. "So we buy ours out on Long Island from farmers who distill privately, and thus save money. Mick must work by night, because these powerful men have been known to intercept and destroy shipments, and even to burn down the taverns of people who do not cooperate with them."

Eric was incensed. All the old unfairness of the powerful

in his own country, all of his contempt for the chicanery and high-handedness of the hated Rolfsons, came flooding back to him. Joan leaned forward, her face close to his, her eyes locked on his.

"I like you, Eric, very much. We *all* like you. And we would *never* involve you in something bad. We would never do *anything* bad ourselves."

Mick never mentioned this conversation, if Joan did tell him about it, and by springtime Eric no longer had to remain behind at the inn, tending horses, but was invited to accompany Mick out to the still, there to unload the empty barrels, load the full. He was not permitted to observe the still itself, nor to meet its operator, who, Mick told him, "is a sort of recluse. You know, like an artist. It takes time. One day, when he's in a good mood, I'll take you up and introduce you. You know, naturally, I'm thinking of letting you make some of these runs on your own. I could use a rest, now and again."

Eric nodded, feeling almost flattered.

"Naturally, too, there'll be more money in it for you."

Money. Eric skipped meals to save it, sewed his own clothes to save it, mended his own boots to save it. And, by July of 1861, he had three hundred American dollars, which he kept hidden in his room, just as, once, the Starbanes concealed coin in a hollow place behind the chimney brick. Here in his bedroom, however, he had pried loose a floorboard plank beneath his bed, wrapped the bills in oilcloth as protection from chance moisture, and returned the board to its place, putting one leg of the bed directly over it, in a precise position at the corner, so he might tell at a glance if his cache had been suspected or disturbed. Not that he worried. All was going well. And storing his money in this secret place seemed safer than a bank. The freemen of Norway were suspicious of banks. Banks were run by unprincipled deviants for the benefit of the rich. Banks failed. Indeed, American banks were failing all the time. Moreover, if he put money in an American bank, would they not ask questions? Who are you? Where are

Vanessa Royall

you from? When did you come to America? How? Are you a citizen?

That was something he would have to explore: becoming a citizen. But he was a man of property now. Three hundred dollars. He would write Kristin and tell her, somehow phrasing his letter safely, should other eyes read his words. Could she escape Rolfson? One hundred dollars would buy her passage. With one hundred fifty he could get a wagon and a team of horses, and go into business. With the rest he could acquire an address of his own. It was true: three hundred dollars was more actual money than he had ever possessed. He did not regard as money his house and land in Norway. Those were part of his soul, pure and simple, and of a value incalculable. So was the name he had not yet won back.

Eric's life was progressing with extraordinary felicity that summer, and it mattered to him not at all when Confederate gunboats fired upon Fort Sumter, and when the new president Lincoln took the North into war against the South. Everyone spoke of war, ranted of war, reveled in the prospect of war all along the way out to the Long Island still for another shipment of liquor, but Eric barely heard. He was working out, in his mind, the phrases of the letter he would send to Kristin. He was loading the last of the barrels onto the wagon when Mick Leeds emerged from the woods that shielded the still.

"It's your day of honor, Eric," Mick proclaimed. "Old Krich says to come on up and have a drink on him. You're about to be accepted by the man himself."

Eric had never heard Mick, or anyone else, refer to the stillmaster by his name. He did not want a drink, nor even to delay, now that the wagon was loaded, but curiosity won out. They walked through the woods along the north shore of Long Island, down a trail overhung with leafy branches, and came upon a small clearing. High, ancient oaks and maples surrounded the clearing, protecting it from all but the most resolute—or accidental—visitor. Tree stumps of various heights stood in the ground, like tombstones in an old cemetery, and the wood from felled trees, now split into lengths of firewood, was stacked next to a weatherbeaten shack. Smoke rose wispily from a pipe on the roof of the shack. Mick motioned Eric inside, where a small wiry man was busy putting more firewood beneath a huge metal tub. Thin coils of pipe rose from the tub, circles and circles of a pipe that emptied into a big barrel just like the barrels Eric had just loaded onto the wagon. The man turned from the fire when Mick and Eric entered the shack, and permitted his thin mouth to twitch into a cagey grin.

"So you're the new man, eh?" he rasped, pulling a pewter jug down from a shelf on the wall. "How about a sample of the product?"

He pulled the cork from the jug and handed the container to Eric, who raised it and took a tentative gulp.

"Na, na, not that way," complained the stillmaster, grabbing the jug. Deftly he swung it over his shoulder, turned his head, clamped his mouth over the neck of the jug, and took five or six gurgling swallows. "Ahhhh," he said, handing the jug to Mick.

Eric, trying not to cough in reaction to the fiery liquor that had burned his mouth and throat, and which was now etching the walls of his stomach, took the stillmaster's outstretched hand, and shook it.

"This here's Krich," said Mick, corking the jug.

"So you're the new man," Krich observed, studying Eric with a wary eye. "Figure it's time I met you. Does he know the ropes?" he asked Mick.

"He sure does. And can keep his mouth shut, too."

Krich nodded sagely. "Let's hope so, an' let's hope he can do it if the cops catch his ass and start beatin' his brains in to find out where we distill the juice."

Eric was simultaneously startled and angry, startled because he knew now, for certain, that Mick's shipping operation was illegal, angry because Joan, in her sweet voice, had lied to him. Eric was also angry at himself: deep down, had he not known, all along, exactly what was going on? Had he not taken advantage of a dangerous situation simply because he was making substantial money from it?

"Eric's all right," Mick was saying. "We been watching him for quite a while now. Besides, he's a ship jumper. Knows he'd be in a mess of trouble if anybody ever found it out."

Old Krich gave Eric a measuring look. "He-he-he," he cackled, slapping Eric's shoulder, "looks like them Leeds got you by the short hairs, son."

Eric forced himself to smile. "They take care of me and I take care of them," he said easily, hating himself for the hypocrisy as well as the need for it. He was already thinking how to go about breaking away from Mick and Joan and Liz, once and for all.

"Eric, here, will be making trips on his own, starting next month," Mick was telling the stillmaster. "See you don't shortship the barrels on him."

"Hell, have I ever done that to you?"

"Damn right you have an' you know it," Mick retorted.

Old Krich just chortled and cackled some more. Then the two young men walked back to the wagon and started for New York. It was already late afternoon, and Mick had no doubt that they would make a safe crossing of the river, unmolested by the forces of the law. Eric, whose trip out to Long Island had been brightened by his intended letter to Kristin, now found himself dwelling upon dark matters.

"What did Krich mean," he asked Mick, feigning innocence, "about the cops beating my brains?"

"Aw, that's nothing. He just talks that way. Tries to scare new men a little. Don't worry about it."

Eric caught Mick giving him a suspicious, sidelong glance.

"I won't," he said. "I'm looking forward to making some more trips. How much extra will I get?"

"Well, Liz'll have to figure that out. Should be at least five bucks a trip more, though."

Ah, the temptation of money. Two trips per week, and

ten more dollars than Eric was already making. That would be an extra *forty* dollars a month, a fortune! But he could not have it. Another thought came to him: What if the Leedses were setting him up in some way? What if they would send him on a trip, inform the police, allow him to get caught, thus throwing suspicion off themselves, should the police be getting ready to strike?

All the more reason to break away now, take the three hundred dollars he had already saved, and try to make a living on his own.

But Kristin! Eric's mind worked furiously. If he left the Leedses, would they make trouble for him? True, he knew about their whiskey running. He might make trouble for them. No, he couldn't. He was compromised. Besides which, what if Kristin could not get away from Norway, could not come here? His heart plummeted, and all his plans spun away, frail wraiths fashioned in happier times by a too sanguine heart. But he would write Kristin. He did have some money now; he could offer her something, at least.

"Looks like you're thinkin' mighty hard," observed Mick, as he urged the big horses down toward the darkened ferry slip.

"Just tired," Eric said, "just tired."

Eric mulled his situation for several days after the trip to Long Island, the trip on which the stillmaster, Krich, had unwittingly revealed to Eric the depth of his involvement in crime. He was tense and tried not to show it; he knew he had to get out, but did not yet know when or how. Mocked by his own lofty ambitions of independence, mocked as well by his paltry three hundred dollars, he hovered on the edge of action, decision. Were he a rich man, or even a sworn citizen, his bonds would be as nothing, nor would he have considered for even a moment the possible reactions of the Leeds family to his departure. But he was neither rich nor a citizen.

Around the boardinghouse, too, he noticed tension. Uncharacteristically, Liz snapped at her children, and they at her. Several boarders quarreled, and moved out. No new occupants appeared to take their places.

"I don't trust this bunch a tinker's damn," one of the departing boarders muttered to Eric, as he left. "It's a strange and devil-blasted lot. You give them the finger, they take the whole hand."

Eric said nothing, but he agreed. The Leedses were corrupt. And yet. And yet the beautiful Joan seemed, somehow, immune even to Eric's conscious attempts to place the Leedses all together in his mind. She had a hold on him; she was a lambent, shimmering presence all the time.

A spell of hot weather fell upon the city, and life slowed, slowed, until everything came almost to a stop. In the evening people sat on their doorsteps, or on porches if they had them, trying to find the hint of a breeze. One such evening Eric returned to the house and found himself apparently alone. Enjoying relief from the nameless tension of past days, he tore off his sweat-stained work clothes, washed thoroughly, and put on a clean pair of trousers and a new shirt of blue cotton, light and cool. Then he decided to write Kristin, finally, and trust to luck and fate. Weeks earlier, he had purchased paper and envelopes, and these he took downstairs to the table at which the boarders usually dined. It was not yet twilight, and he needed no lamp. He uncapped a small container of black ink, dipped his pen, and began, telling her that he was safe in New York, describing his voyage briefly, explaining that he now had the wherewithal to support himself and "whoever else might choose to be with me." He lingered over that phrase for many a long minute. "I cannot say more about it now, but for strong and sufficient reasons, I must immediately depart my current situation. . . ."

"What are you writing, Eric?"

It was Joan, coming down the stairs. She had been in the house all the while. She was barefoot, and her rich red hair fell upon a white robe, wrapped loosely about her. She looked cool and lovelier than ever. She walked over to the table and, without embarrassment, scanned what he had written.

"What strange letters!"

"Norwegian."

"You are writing your beloved?"

"Yes." Eric was glad she could not read his language.

This did not hinder Joan's desire to know. "What are you saying?"

"That I am well. That I hope she is."

Joan seemed to think something over a moment, then: "Eric, you are suspicious of us, again, aren't you?"

"No," he lied.

If she believed him, he could not say, and had no time to consider. Because there at the table, right next to him, she let her robe fall open, to reveal her breasts, full and firm and perfect. Eric's eyes were drawn to them, and he felt the sweet rush of his masculinity, instinctive and ungovernable, responding to her. She was bending toward him, bringing her mouth down to him, lips parted, soft and red as lust, glistening like the dew-laden petals of a flower.

"You must never think to leave us," she was saying, as he felt her tender hand on the back of his neck. "You must never leave us and I will give you a reason not to...."

And he was already getting to his feet, his arms going out, embracing her. The rest of her robe opened, and she came into his embrace, kissed him hard, her mouth open and her tongue probing, snaking around his own. Her body pressed savagely against his, and she ground her hips and moaned. There on the table lay a letter of love to Kristin, who was far away across the cold Atlantic, but in Eric's arms was flesh as hot as the night, and ten times more yielding. Eric had not loved a woman since Kristin, in June, more than a year ago. However desirous of fidelity his mind might be, his body knew its needs. Already he was burning with lust, the force building, ready to blast from his body, and that was what Joan seemed to want. Her hands were everywhere on him, unbuttoning and plunging.

"Upstairs," she gasped, "upstairs, in my room."

Eric tried to fight his own desire, but it was useless. Joan held him, led him up the steps, he in her tender, ever-stroking grip, and they fell, gasping and clutching, upon the bed in her little room. Joan was just about to pull him into herself, to wrap herself about him, close upon him, when the door downstairs opened, then banged shut.

"Joanie!"

"It's Mick!" Joan cried, in a stifled gasp, and in her eyes, by twilight, Eric saw again that bizarre, half-buried aspect of concealed meaning once again, of a portent teasing yet sinister, veiled but profound.

Boots coming up the stairs. *"Joanie!"* A cry of urgency. Something must have happened.

"Quick," Joan told Eric. "Get in the closet. Get in the—"

He did not have to be told twice. Grabbing shirt and trousers from the floor—he would dress inside—Eric slipped in among her perfumed dresses, and pulled the door closed. He heard Mick enter the room.

"Joanie?"

"I was trying to get a little rest."

But there was something in her voice.

Eric expected Mick to say something, to tell whatever it was that had caused him to burst into the house and mount the stairs with such urgency. Instead he heard Joan say, "Not now," in a voice quivery and irresolute, as though she had not the strength to hold away whatever it was. The closet was a drugged chamber of perfume. Eric felt weak and wavering, assaulted by the hot fragrance. Outside, over the city, twilight had settled, and in Joan's bedroom the very air was dusty-rose and drowsy; sweet, almost palpable air, that caressed and softened the golden-bare skin of riding lovers, lovers seen by Eric through a crack in the wooden closet door.

Yes, he saw it, but he did not grasp what he was seeing. Horrified, he pulled on his clothes, and leaped from the hiding place to do battle for Joan's honor, fearing that she was too ashamed to cry out for his help. So, with murder in his heart for the unspeakable Mick, Eric plunged from the closet. A guttural, maddened, challenging cry was already on his lips, could not be retrieved, when he saw Joan's face, and recognized the truth. It was there in her glazed, heavily-lidded green eyes; in the dazed, unsmiling slackness of her soft red mouth; in the animallike flare of her fine nostrils. The truth was there, too, in the wrap of her legs high around Mick, and in the clutch and pull of her strong haunches as she milked him.

Eric's cry filled the room, absorbing and blotting out the lesser cries of pleasure.

"Eric!" cried Joan. "I told you—"

Mick, his face twisted and slack, looked up and saw Eric standing there, his fists upraised. Then he looked down at his sister. "He was *here*?" he accused her, with hurtful incredulity. "You let him in *here*? With *you*?"

Still reeling at what he had witnessed and heard, Eric was stunned all the more by Mick's rueful cry of lover's jealousy. Now he understood fully the dark attraction, privately savored but imperfectly veiled, between Joan and her renegade brother.

With a muted snarl, like a sob, Mick sprang naked from his sister's body, from the bed, and hurled himself at Eric, who, however confused, was nonetheless braced and ready. Eric dealt a blow whose force traveled back up his arm, through his shoulder, all down along his spine. Mick hurtled backward twice as fast as he had been rushing forward toward Eric, flipped over the bed, and came to rest, unconscious, against the wall.

"You've hurt him!" cried Joan, sliding down the bed to inspect and caress her brother, her lover. "Oh, you've hurt him."

Apparently Mick was still alive. He breathed. He stirred.

"I didn't know . . ." Eric began.

Joan, still naked, sweaty from love, her matted red hair trailing tendrils of passion, slid up onto the bed again.

"It doesn't matter whether you knew or not," she said, "but you'll have to leave now. He'll kill you. He'll come after you and kill you."

On the floor, against the wall, Mick groaned.

Joan was very composed now. "Don't judge," she said. "Love is hard to find. It's simply the way things are. Can you understand that?"

She was looking at him with her muted half-smile, that held still the hint of some forgotten meaning, a knowledge of love more perverse and indomitable than death.

Eric retreated toward the door.

"What will you do now?" Joan asked him. "Don't stay in New York. He'll kill you if you stay in New York."

Eric left her there, and did not answer. He went to his room, pulled on his boots, threw clothing into his pack, and pushed the bed away from the loose plank. It was almost dark now, but his fingers closed around the oilcloth. He felt the paper bills inside, and thrust the packet into his shirt, stuffed it down into his belt. Racing downstairs, he seized his half-finished letter from the table, and jammed it into his pack, along with the bottle of ink and the pen. Then he was outside and walking down the street, jostled by people standing on corners, trying to avoid the full weight of the summer heat.

"Hey, what's the big hurry?" complained someone Eric bumped into. "Where do you think you're going, anyway?"

A good question.

Eric walked at least a mile before he realized that, however shocking his departure from the house of the Leedses, he was, at least, quit of them. The knowledge made him feel better, and so did the thickness of the money-filled oilcloth at his waistband. He had money. He would go to a hotel, get some sleep, and plot his future course.

It was not until he was in the lobby of the Stuyvesant House, unfolding the oilcloth for a bill to pay his lodging, that he found he had been robbed.

"Those shreds of newspaper won't buy you a bed here, mister," the desk clerk was saying.

Fighting a sense of devastation, Eric went back out into the heat and the night.

The letter he mailed to Kristin, some days later, was not at all the one he had intended to send, in happier times now gone.

IV

The Rolfson yacht, *Viking Serpent,* sailed south on the rolling North Sea, and entered the English Channel. Each day, as England drew nearer, Kristin felt more and more exhilarated. The green coast of Britain glided by to starboard, and, leagues behind, Norway fell away. *Now I am out in the world, just like Eric,* Kristin thought, *and surely we will meet somewhere.* It was more than a hope; she believed in it with all the passionate conviction of her young heart.

"You certainly seem to be enjoying yourself, my dear," remarked Gustav gloomily.

Kristin was standing at the yacht's railing, luxuriating in the sun on her face, the wind in her hair. Her husband had come up on deck after another long stint working on his business papers in the stateroom. Each day, in contrast to Kristin, Gustav grew tenser and more irritable. Kristin thought she knew why. Hitherto, in all business dealings, Gustav had been able to rely upon the native cunning, not to mention the physical proximity, of old Adolphus. Now, however, he was alone to face Britain's leading banker, alone to manage perhaps the most important business deal upon which the Rolfsons had yet embarked. Lord Anthony Soames was no Lesja farmer, to be deuced by forgeries and a bought judge. And Soames, once crossed, was capable of waiting for years to get even. Gustav was suffering from a bad case of nerves.

Kristin admitted that, yes, she was savoring the voyage. He gave her a speculative glance. "And you have no sense of trepidation about meeting the English?"

"Should I have, husband?" she asked, thinking that he was referring to the role she might have to play with Lord Soames.

Gustav had been thinking of that, indeed, but it was a matter far outweighed by his own tension. "We *must* make a fine impression," he muttered. "Everything depends on it. And you, particularly, must do everything Lord Soames wishes."

"Everything, husband?"

"Well, perhaps it will not be necessary. But . . ." He stared morosely out upon the tumbling waves, running his hand over the pristine polished mahogany railing of the vessel, but not even this vast gorgeous toy of a ship gave him pleasure today.

"Husband," Kristin told him, "I have told you I shall do what I can, and you should know that I am one who keeps her promises."

Including the promise made at Sonnendahl Fjord, she thought, smiling inwardly.

"If your business goes well in England," she asked carefully, "how soon will it be before you embark upon your American adventures?"

"And why do you want to know?"

"I thought you knew. I am your wife."

He accepted her curiosity, and explanation, without much thought. "Oh, sometime next year, I expect." He sighed. "*If* all goes well with Soames." Then he returned dourly below decks to his work.

Next year. Kristin was worried. Even if, somehow, she managed to find Eric, two years would have elapsed. Two years. And he was a young and handsome man. His body was sure to grow hungry, demanding that its needs be met.

No, she would not think of that, she would not think of it.

According to plans made by letter during previous months, Gustav was to dock at Southend-on-Sea at the mouth of the Thames, and send a messenger to Lord Soames's house in London, announcing his arrival. Soames would arrange to have the yacht escorted up the Thames to a berth along the river, from which Gustav and Kristin would disembark before proceeding to the Lord's home. Consequently Gustav's anxious discomfiture was very great when, docking at Southend, he found Soames's man waiting with a message of his own. Gustav had been enjoying a fine mood for a change, noticing how splendidly the *Viking Serpent* compared to so many of the vessels sailing in and out of the Thames. The flag of Norway rippled and snapped atop the mast, blue St. Olaf's cross on a bright field of red, and beneath it the personal crest of the Rolfsons (recently designed) stood out just as proudly in the brisk offshore wind. The crest, gold on a field of white, displayed two Viking battle-axes, crossed, and in the V formed thereby was the plumed and visored helmet of a medieval knight. The crest was imposing but, Kristin felt, presumptuous. It was a crest for Eric, she thought, for in it was the spirit of the old Vikings from whom he was descended. From whom Gustav was not.

Lord Soames's man barely noticed the flags, however, as he came on board inquiring after Rolfson.

"I am he," Gustav said, striding across the deck.

The messenger tried very hard but could not keep from staring at the lurid scar on Gustav's face. "What is your business, man?" Gustav demanded, both angry and unsettled.

The man handed over an envelope, which Gustav ripped open and read. His face darkened. "Thank you," was all he said.

When the messenger had departed, Gustav ordered the yacht back out to sea. "Soames is not in London," he declared irritably. "He has gone to Cowes, on the south coast. Queen Victoria is summering there, and Soames has been called to offer his counsel upon some matter." He thought it over, not without a touch of fearful despondency. Gustav Rolfson had never advised the King of Norway about anything. "It is probably just a British trick," he decided. "He is undoubtedly trying to throw me off balance, and then he will demand more than the usual rate of interest."

"Yes, husband," Kristin agreed dutifully.

Under pressure as he was, her quiet reply, with its hint of counterfeit obsequiousness, served to goad him, and he lifted a hand to slap her across the face. But her cool, level stare held back the blow.

"Go ahead," she said, "if it will please you."

"You," he rasped, "oh, but you will learn, you will learn."

I hope so, Kristin thought.

Cowes, on the Isle of Wight, off the south coast of England, was the summer retreat of nobility. Warships of the British navy patrolled the waters of the English channel, in attendance upon the royal yacht of Queen Victoria, and the lesser vessels of lesser nobles. Gustav's captain made the proper hailings, received appropriate authorization, and soon the *Viking Serpent* glided along Spithead channel to the port of Cowes itself, where Lord Soames had said his yacht would be. Kristin was amused, watching her husband wringing his hands, lest this beautiful ship his father had unjustly won be outshone by the craft of his intended benefactor. Gustav turned almost as white as the great gleaming yacht that bore down on them from the west, and recovered slowly and slightly when it proved to be the royal yacht itself, out for an afternoon cruise. "I'll have one like that someday," Gustav promised himself, in a low menacing growl.

He was considerably cheered to see that Soame's yacht, *Dare*, which they soon hailed, was somewhat smaller, though no less elegant, than the *Viking Serpent*.

"He can't help but be impressed," Gustav gloated as the two crafts moved together on the water.

But, once again, Gustav was rendered rueful and crestfallen. Lord Soames regretted, in another missive, that he had been compelled to return to one of his country houses in Kent, southeast of London, but he would be there for several days, and the Rolfsons might make haste to join him, if they pleased.

"The *bastard*," Gustav roared that night, pacing up and down in the mirrored master cabin, "he is making sport of me, and trying to unnerve me. He shall see, though. He shall see!"

But Gustav was more than a little fearful now that everything would go awry, that he would return to Oslo a failure. The fear unmanned him, temporarily, and he was unable to bed Kristin.

"It is all right, husband," she told him. "I do not mind."

By the time Gustav and Kristin drove into the vast, sweeping green grounds of Daredále, Lord Soames's Kent estate, Gustav was as jittery as a victim of the St. Vitus's dance. "I hate to admit it," he admitted, "but this Soames fellow knows how to soften a man, the better to gain advantage. It is something I shall remember in my own business dealings in years to come."

Gustav had hired the most elegant carriage in Dover, where the *Viking Serpent* had docked, but it was clear that Daredale had seen far more splendid vehicles. Every hedge, every tree, every flower that grew upon the hundreds of green acres was in precisely the right spot. Gardens were laid out with mathematical precision, and even the rippling streams had been channeled perfectly to delight the aesthetic eye. The great house itself, with gables and chimneys, reflected solidity and power, a quiet splendor that was almost indolent, like the home of a careless god. By comparison the Rolfson mansion in Oslo was but a gardener's cottage, residence of nervous usurpers.

Although her husband was decidedly tense, Kristin, by contrast, felt a quiet, anticipatory excitement. So many things were happening, and she was learning much. In addition her husband's anxiety had given her an opportunity to put the Rolfsons in proper perspective. They were not so rough and indomitable as they had seemed! It was not folly to think that someday she might wriggle out of their grasp.

Inside, Daredale was a sumptuous museum of paintings, tapestries, statuary. The Rolfsons were admitted by a butler of cold bearing, shown into a long, dark room that seemed part library, part conservatory, given tea, and informed that Lord Soames would be with them shortly. But the tea remaining in the pot had long since grown cold when the butler returned to say that, through some mistake, Lord Soames had been out riding. Gustav and Kristin were to be shown upstairs, given rooms. They would dine at Daredale, and stay the night.

"I believe this is a good sign," Gustav whispered, as they followed several servants and a baggage-bearing footman up the grand staircase. Gustav seemed only mildly surprised, and Kristin was quite relieved, when they were shown to separate bedrooms, at opposite ends of the third story. And, once inside her room, Kristin was delighted.

The room was fully twice as large as the house in which she had grown up in Lesja, with her brothers and sisters scrapping and fighting for space. The bed was wide as a cornfield, canopied in yellow silk, with tassels hanging down; a fireplace stretched across one wall. Deep, lush couches waited beneath windows that looked out upon the blue-green glitter of Daredale in summer, a luxuriant piece of paradise, an island, a safe haven of soft mossy murmurs, verdurous gloom, and easy sunlight drowsy on peaceful leaves. Enchanted, she drank in the beauty for a while, then moved to find what the closets contained, what further wonders lay behind the three evenly spaced doors on the wall opposite the fireplace.

She tried the first one, but it did not open.

Nor did the second.

Well, doubtless, the closets contained wonderful gowns, the finest in satin, silk, and fur. Why should they not be locked?

But she tried the third door anyway, turned the knob easily, swung the door open.

Half-smiling, arms crossed, leaning indolently against a row of plush dark capes that hung from hooks in the closet like the drooping wings of dead bats, the man met Kristin's eyes. It was not as if he had been waiting there; it was as if he had suddenly *appeared* there. She was too startled even to cry out, although, an instant later, she raced for the bedroom door.

It, too, was locked.

When she turned to face him again, she found that he had not moved, but the smile had been replaced by a bright bold grin.

"Kristin," he said, still not moving, "how do you do? I am Anthony Soames. Welcome to my house."

He came out of the closet, closed the door behind him. No taller than Kristin herself, he was markedly slender, but with square shoulders of respectable width. He wore black riding boots, tan breeches, and a red hunting coat. "So it is true," he said quietly, in a voice deeper than one might have expected from a man so slight, a voice oddly soft as well, "so it is true, you are as lovely as I had been told to expect."

"What?" she asked, as he came toward her. "By whom?"

"Why," he replied, smiling that suggestive smile again, "by your husband, of course."

Mention of Gustav nerved her to regain self-control, a self-control somewhat shattered by Soames's bizarre entrance. Now she thought she knew what Gustav had been hinting about all this time: Soames was going to use her for delight. Giving that delight was her part in gaining the loan for the Rolfsons.

"Your husband and I, naturally, have been corresponding for some time," Soames was saying, as his eyes moved up and down her body. She was grateful for the neck-to-ankle travelling cloak, but, at the same time, conscious of how her body pressed against its fabric. "And, naturally, too, reports of your beauty reached me from Cowes and Southend-on-Sea, and—"

"Unlock this door," she told him.

"What?" he asked, quite surprised. He was unused to being told to do anything.

"I said, unlock this door and let me out of here. What on earth is in your mind, anyway?"

Like a spoiled child, he flared and whined: "Do you know what you're saying, and to whom you're saying it?"

"Yes. Somebody named Anthony Soames, from whom my husband wishes to borrow a great deal of money."

Vanessa Royall

Soames came closer. He was directly in front of her now. She could feel his breath, and even the heat of his body. But she could not read his expression. His moods shifted quickly. He was no longer angry, but what he was she could not gauge. His lean body was probably quite strong, she thought, but if he tried any kind of assault upon her, she was perfectly capable of putting up a struggle.

He seemed to guess her thoughts. "So you think I want you," he said, laughing easily.

Unsure how to reply—to say yes would be presumptuous, to say no would be, faintly, debasing—she shifted her ground: "What does one expect from a man who lurks in closets?"

Again, his anger flared. "I'll not loan your precious husband a ha'penny!"

"Then don't."

Soames could not believe what she had said. "You don't care?"

"I have lived through many things without money. And I can live without yours."

Now he was truly studying her, face to face for the first time in his wealthy, luxurious life with a spirit whose independence and fire he could not fathom.

"I think you are lying," he said, at length, still watching her. "I have had many wives and mistresses in this room. It is my test, so to speak, my litmus cloth of the human animal. The husband or lover, driven almost to idiocy by my delays and ruses, is resting blissfully in his room at the far end of the corridor. His mistress or wife, greed riddled as he, finds me in this room. I make my promise, and then I receive whatever I demand."

Kristin was appalled at his arrogance. "There is nothing you can promise me, nothing that I want from you."

The dim smile reappeared. "Divest yourself of that cloak," he said, "go to bed. I shall join you and you will pleasure me in every way, hands and mouth, body and lips, and your husband will receive his loan."

"No, I won't."

WILD WIND WESTWARD

"You had better, or I will mark your face exactly as your husband's is marked."

Kristin felt fear for a second. Lord Soames did not seem the kind of man who made idle threats. But anger overrode fear. "If you try that," she said, "we shall see what part of you is scarred as well."

Once more he was amused. "Hah!" he cried. "A Nordic spitfire. By the by, how did your husband receive such a terrible cut?"

"Another man gave it to him. In a fight."

Soames considered this. "Was the fight over you?"

Kristin admitted that it had been.

"So, this Rolfson is more a man than I had expected. And he won you, too, did he?"

"So it appears," Kristin said.

Suddenly, unnervingly, young Lord Soames began to laugh. At first it was a deep, clackety rattle, down in his throat, but it rose in volume until he was fairly gasping with glee.

"You are . . . you are wondering at my mirth?" he managed, collecting himself after a time.

"Such curiosity does not seem unreasonable."

"No, no, I suppose it does not. Who was the other man?"

"What?"

"The man who marked your husband's face."

"A mountaineer, whose land was taken from him."

"By whom?"

Kristin looked him in the eye and did not lie.

"Rolfson, eh? Did you love this other man?"

"I did. I do."

Soames seemed to think about it. "Where is he now?"

"I don't know. In America, I hope."

"Ahhh! In America. Your husband wants loans so that he can build a business in America, and you know your lover is there—or think he may be there—and yet you would not go to bed with me, even if my money bought you passage, so to speak?"

"That is correct," she told him. "There are some things I will not do."

He reached for her, grabbed her upper arm. His grip was surprisingly strong, brutal, and she cried out.

"I could force you to do my will," he said. "I could have my servants hold you down. I am perfectly capable of having you degraded and debased and whipped until you should come crawling across the floor."

"That may be true, but, free and of my own will, you shall not have me, no."

Soames released her arm, and a playful light danced behind his eyes. "So," he said, almost to himself, "you have been tested. Now it is your husband's turn. We shall see, we shall see."

Kristin and Gustav dined that night at Daredale, dined alone on succulent fish chowder, asparagus, roast pork with barley, candied potatoes, and Stilton cheese. Lord Soames did not appear.

"What happened? What happened?" Gustav demanded. "I became restless, and walked about upstairs. I saw a man leaving your chamber."

"That was he. Soames."

Gustav was fairly beside himself with excitement. "What did he say? What did he want?"

"He said very little. Something about testing me. He wanted to take me to bed."

Gustav was not especially startled. "Thank God. You did as he expected, I hope?"

"No, I refused him."

"What? Refused him? Oh, good Christ! I hinted to you that he was said to have strange ways. What are you? A peasant ninny? A mountaineer's fool daughter?"

"Neither," she replied, fighting to maintain her customary neutrality in his presence. "But do not worry, husband. All is not lost."

"It isn't?"

"No, he said he had tested me, and that now he will test you."

Gustav sagged with relief. "Oh, thank God." He sighed. "You can be sure I won't fail him as you did."

WILD WIND WESTWARD

* * *

Gustav's spirits, raised briefly upon learning that he would be given some chance to prove himself, soon fell again. Three days passed, four, five. He and Kristin rode, played tennis and croquet, read, walked, dined. But it was as if they were phantom guests in a mystery house, long since abandoned by its master. Soames was nowhere to be seen. Finally, after they'd been a week at Daredale, nine men, officers at Soames's London bank, came down from the city to hear Gustav's formal presentation. Kristin was invited to the meeting, at the specific request of Lord Soames, who was, again, absent. She saw the way the bankers looked at her; she felt their eyes even when she was looking elsewhere, lost in thought, or when she followed Gustav's speech.

And he spoke well. Whatever his personal qualms and uncertainties, he knew the worth of Rolfson collateral, the vast mineral deposits along the Rauma valley, beneath the Lesja mountains. He had the reports of surveyors, he had titles, deeds, timetables, plan after plan. The bankers were clearly impressed, and so was Kristin, who drank in every bit of information.

"And, in America," droned a stodgy, goutish old factotum in a pearl waistcoat, "what is your proposed area of investment?"

Gustav unrolled a huge map, and spread it out upon the table. He bade the bankers leave their chairs for a look.

"Oil," he said, pointing to a map of Pennsylvania, in the United States. "I am going to invest in oil, recently discovered right *here*!" He pointed to a little town called Titusville, close to Lake Erie. "I intend to get there first, fastest, strongest. In years to come oil will run the world's machines, and new machines of which, right now, we cannot even dream."

A few of the older bankers snickered, but not many of them.

"It's a great risk," one commented.

"*Dare*," said Gustav, not without wit.

The bankers smiled. They knew their master was not

without a hunger for the speculative edge. Indeed, he thrived on risk, especially if the collateral covered any possible losses. And Gustav had collateral.

"How much do you think you would need?" the old factotum asked.

"Five million pounds sterling," snapped Gustav.

The bankers let out a collective gasp, followed by an awed hush. Five million pounds exceeded the combined annual budget of the British army and navy.

At length the bankers rose and departed Daredale for their return trip to London.

"Lord Soames will give you his answer in due course," they told Gustav.

That night Gustav acted like a triumphant king, like a wild, victorious knight. He took Kristin once, then took her again. Not long before dawn she awakened to find him enjoying her once more, but lay still beneath his furious, closed-eyed, intensely private assault. He dreamed of gold and glory, she of Viking axes, age and love and time. When he had done with her, she was hungry for nothing but more sleep.

London thrilled Kristin to the soles of her feet, the marrow of her bones. Surpassing even the excitement of her ride from Dover aboard the new "iron horse" was the panorama of London itself, sprawling along the Thames, populated by every manner and type of human being conceived in the mind of God or man. And then there were the buildings, the churches—Westminster, Whitehall, St. Paul's, Buckingham Palace—of which she vaguely recalled seeing pictures in her little mountain school.

"Is it not grand?" she asked Gustav, as Soames's carriage brought them to his sedate, expensive city home in St. John's Wood.

"What? Ah, yes, yes it is," Gustav agreed distractedly.

He was worried about the "test" Lord Soames had mentioned to Kristin; he did not intend to fail.

Neither Gustav nor Kristin was surprised, however, to learn that Soames was not in residence. They had become

WILD WIND WESTWARD

inured to his enigmatic appearances and departures. The house, small but more opulent than Daredale, was fully staffed, that their every whim might be met, and several attractive young men, friends of the lord, were stopping there as well. The young men, one French, one Greek, one English, were bright and witty, and were charmed by Kristin's beauty. Dinner conversations were quick and amusing, which fact irritated the stolid Gustav, but he found no true reason for complaint, as the young men treated Kristin with utmost respect, even deference. Obviously Lord Soames had informed them she was not to be bothered.

During the days, Gustav brooded and worked, while one or two of the men ordered up the carriage and took Kristin lunching or shopping in London. The French youth, Pierre LaValle, took her one afternoon to a stage play, a musical called *Her Majesty's Holiday*, and afterward to tea. They were drinking tea, and chatting about the play, which had been occasionally hilarious and sometimes faintly risqué, when LaValle let fall that Lord Soames would be at the house upon their return. He seemed excited by the prospect.

"I owe him everything," he told her. "He is a strange man, often petulant, but if he loves you, he will do everything for you."

Kristin was a little startled at the passion with which he spoke. Did Pierre mean Soames had fallen in love with *her*?

As if guessing her thoughts, or perhaps reading her expression, Pierre laughed soothingly. "No, no," he said, "I did not mean that. He loves me. He also loves Vitas and Rob"—these were the Greek and English lads—"but he loves me best. You understand?" he asked, with an air at once defiant and pensive.

Yes, Kristin understood. She had heard of such things.

"Did your husband truly receive that terrible scar from a man you love?" Pierre demanded suddenly.

Kristin had the strange feeling that Soames might have

put Pierre up to asking this question, as if he might be trying to catch her in a lie or a contradiction.

"Yes," she said, "it is true."

Pierre seemed impressed by the fact, or possibly by the violence implicit in the scar, but the afternoon was ebbing.

"We must return now to the house," he said. "The lord has entertainment planned for tonight."

When they reached St. John's Wood, Kristin entered the house and went up to her room to bathe and dress for dinner. As at Daredale she and Gustav had been quartered separately, so she was surprised to see him in her own room, slouched in an easy chair. He leaped to his feet as soon as she entered, and waved a piece of paper in her face. He was furious. She had never seen him so angry, and anger was an emotion with which he was not unfamiliar.

"I demand an explanation!" he raged. "Close the door. Let us have it out."

"Have what out, husband?" she asked, sweetly. She thought, somehow, he might be angry because she had spent so much time with Pierre.

But it was not that. She took the paper from him, and read. The actual words were bland, obviously meant to be, but between the lines was much.

> July 26, 1861
> New York
>
> My Dear Kristin,
> It is not my wish to intrude upon your life, should this not be your desire, but to let you know that I am well and safe. The life is hard, but not without prospect, and you might well think to see these shores one day, should the chance come to you. The Norwegian consulate is most cooperative to visitors, in every respect. I think often of home, and the beauty of Sonnendahl Fjord.
>
> Most sincerely,
> E. Gunnarson

WILD WIND WESTWARD

* * *

By the time she finished reading, Kristin's heart was pounding with hope and joy. Eric had told her that he still loved her, wished she were with him. He had told her that he wanted her in America, and where in New York to get in touch with him: the consulate. And he had mentioned Sonnendahl Fjord, where they had consumed each other, and the image of one another, in a mystical ceremony, the magic of which would endure forever. Kristin decided to take the offensive.

"What is this?" she demanded of him. "Opening my private correspondence?"

"It arrived in the pouch of business mail," he explained. Then, realizing he had sounded slightly defensive, changed tack.

"Private correspondence!" he raged. "With a murdering pauper. It is the duty of a husband to make certain his wife does not court foolishness!"

"How responsible and considerate of you."

"You will not return his message!"

There was no point in discussing it. "As you wish, my husband," she agreed softly.

He ripped the note to shreds. "The gall of the man. The boldness. He has sought aid, or some such, at our own consulate in New York. Why did not our diplomatic personnel note his name? They ought to have. He is a criminal in Norway. A criminal, a *murderer*!"

"Yes," Kristin could not help saying, with considerable pleasure at the irony, "but he is a criminal under his true name, Starbane."

Gustav got the point. Eric had gone to the consulate, had given Kristin a place through which he might be located should she ever reach New York, by using the common name, Gunnarson, that Gustav had been so eager to pin on him!

But Gustav was not without malevolent resourcefulness. Going to the mirror, he ran his fingertip along the scar Eric had etched. "Well, he will get the surprise of his life," Gustav vowed. "I shall immediately send a message to our people in New York, informing them of Gunnarson's ruse, demanding his arrest and extradition. *That* ought to end this matter quickly enough."

Now Kristin feared for Eric. Gustav would not shrink from carrying out his evil promise. "I promised to ruin him utterly," he was ranting, "and I shall. Just you wait and see. And do not think of warning him, much less of flying to him, or you yourself shall see what befalls a poor family named Vendahl, in Lesja."

"Yes, husband," she said, with counterfeit meekness and fear. Just two days earlier she had sent her family a portion of the money Gustav had given her to buy fine gowns.

Gustav and Kristin were just about to dress for dinner, in their formal evening clothes, when one of the maids knocked at the door, opened it shyly, and laid two sets of clothing on the bed.

"What is this?" wondered Gustav, appalled.

"There must be some mistake," said Kristin.

One set of clothing was that of a common seaman: canvas breeches, rope-soled shoes, striped shirt, bandana, and a shapeless cloth hat. The other was a dress of bright hue and minimal fabric, such as Kristin had glimpsed on women walking the alleys and streets off Piccadilly.

"No mistake," answered the maid apologetically, retreating toward the door. "The master requests that yuh wear these t'dinner and t'night."

"Pierre told me Soames had entertainment planned," Kristin remembered. "Perhaps a costume party?"

Gustav was of another mind. "My *test*," he cried. "It must have something to do with my test!"

And, excitedly, he gathered up the sailor's uniform and raced to his room to dress.

After a rather hurried dinner of beefsteak and kidney pie, during which Lord Soames saw fit to ply his guests with all manner of wines and spirits, several carriages were brought round, and everyone climbed in. Vitas, Pierre, and Rob, dressed like Gustav as sailors, went in one vehicle,

WILD WIND WESTWARD

while Soames, whose baggy sacklike costume suggested a beggar or pickpocket, rode with the Rolfsons.

"Where are we going?" Kristin asked.

"To hell," replied Soames, laughing. And, indeed, passage from the refined West End of London to the pitiless and unremitting squalor of the East End was like a descent into nether regions. It was night, and scattered streetlamps failed to penetrate, much less to dispel, the fog drifting in off the Channel, up the Thames, and into the city. Curses of the destitute followed the rich carriages, curses against privilege and fate and luck, and frequently a beggar would pound on the door of a passing carriage, whining and begging for bread. Soames gave no alms, but always tried to look out, to see the face of the beggar.

"I wonder what it's like," he kept repeating, "I wonder what it's really like."

"Is this not . . . ah . . . dangerous?" Gustav asked tentatively, apprehensive about the area into which they were driving, yet not wanting to seem actually afraid, lest a display of fear should render him a failure in whatever strange test Soames contemplated.

"No, no," replied the lord, dismissing Gustav's provincial squeamishness with a wave of his hand. "My coachmen are strong and well-armed. Moreover, we have been to the Skull and Raven many times."

The Skull and Raven proved to be a smoky tavern and dance hall, more disreputable by far than the bar in Oslo at which Seaman Ingersoll had sought to steal Kristin's purse. An ambience of dangerous, edgy futility suffused the entire bar, a mean-spirited atmosphere of gin, opium smoke, and quick, raw, bitter sex. Kristin was revolted by the air and odor of the place, and Gustav was clearly doubtful, but Lord Soames yelped with glee as he led them in. Vitas, Pierre, and Rob, too, strutted expectantly into the crowd and din. The men and women there, Kristin noted, were dressed much like Soames's party, but such clothing, for the denizens of the Skull and Raven, did not constitute a costume.

Soames passed money to a huge woman, with missing teeth and one eye askew, who showed them to a corner table and then, once they were seated, drew a beaded curtain on a wire from one wall to another giving them a measure of privacy. They could readily see what was going on in the Skull and Raven, but were set apart from it. Soames ordered wine and gin, ale, and called for an opium pipe. The ugly woman went to fetch these. Meanwhile the three young men had grown suddenly animated, happy and excited, as if wondrously released from the formality of decorous social routine.

"Oh!" exclaimed Pierre, brightly. "There's Dirk, over at the bar. He's *so* strong! Perhaps he'll see me!" He waved. "Yo, Dirk, Dirk!"

Vitas was laughing bitchily. "He already saw you come in, silly. And he looked the other way. He doesn't want to see you, that's very clear."

"That's not true!"

"Is so."

"Is *not*."

"It's true. I distinctly saw him turn away from you."

Pierre's mouth was twisted, as if he were going to cry.

"Oh, hush up," Rob told his quarreling mates. "I'm *très* bored with your infernal fussing. *I'm* going over to talk to Dirk myself."

"You *won't!*" cried Vitas and Pierre, in unison.

"Watch me," said Rob. And, smoothing his hair, he left the table, walked to the crowded bar, and very soon, arm in arm, was engaged in earnest conversation with a broad-shouldered, narrow-hipped young ruffian who wore a golden earring.

"Now see what you've done," Vitas accused Pierre. "You had to go bragging and carrying on, so now Rob gets him."

Pierre, overcome, began to weep, got up, and left the table, rattling the curtain of beads as he departed.

The big woman brought them drink and the opium pipe.

"What do you think of it?" Soames asked the Rolfsons. "This place?"

"It's a little . . . frightening," Kristin confessed.

WILD WIND WESTWARD

Gustav shot her a disapproving look. "Doesn't bother me any," he told Soames.

"Like it, do you?"

"One must adapt," answered Gustav, sudden cavalier and bon vivant. He had decided that Soames would lend money only to businessmen with sangfroid and savoir faire.

Kristin declined the opium, but sipped red wine. Gustav, following his host's example, drew deeply on the pipe. He was used to strong cigars, and did not mind the raw smoke, but never had he tried opium before, and the effect was soon evident.

"I have been considering your loan," Soames said abruptly, lighting a second pipeful of the drug.

Mention of business, juxtaposed so suddenly against the perverse desuetude of the Skull and Raven, startled Kristin, and caused Gustav to struggle back upward toward mental acuity. "Yes?" he said, with eager wariness. Where was the test? When came his time of trial?

"Exactly how much would you be able to do in order to insure the loan?"

"What do you mean, how much?"

"I want you to meet some friends of mine," Soames said, standing. "Come with me. Vitas, you stay with Mrs. Rolfson."

"Oh, Anthony, I see somebody over there I want to—"

"Do as I say. You'll get your turn."

He left the table, passed through the beaded curtain followed by Gustav. Soon they were lost in the crowd.

"Where is Lord Soames taking my husband?"

"What do you care?" said Vitas petulantly. "I hear you have a lover in America?"

No use to deny it. Anthony Soames and his three resident pederasts obviously spent much time in the dissection of those with whom they came in contact, those who needed Soames's limitless wealth.

"Someone I know and care about is in America," she answered, cautiously. She meant to add: "I know and care about many," but Vitas, short, burly, tousle-haired, and blunt, cut her off.

"What is it like?" he asked. "How does it feel to a woman?"

"I don't— What do you mean?"

"The pleasure part," he said bluntly. "Do you think it's better for the woman or the man?"

"It's only good if you really love somebody," she told him. "Whether you're a man or a woman doesn't make much difference."

He took a long pull of the opium pipe, smiled lazily, leaned away, and studied her. "You know, I would be very pleased if you would be my first woman. I have always wanted to know what a woman felt like." He reached out and put his hand over hers. She nodded toward the crowded tavern. Men were dancing drunkenly with savage-looking women. Men were dancing with other men. Women were embracing women and pretending to dance.

"You may take your pick of anyone out there," she said, "man, woman, or combination thereof. I'm sure your benefactor's money will buy whatever prize you desire."

He grinned. "And it will buy you, too."

"You are very wrong," she said.

He laughed. His mood shifted, and he no longer wished to pursue possession of her.

Lord Soames returned to the table. He looked self-satisfied, secretly pleased, like a sleek, lazy cat. "All right, Vitas," he said.

"Oh, dear me, at last." And, with that, Vitas was gone among the swirl and swarm of Skull and Raven.

"Where is he going?"

"I promised him something special."

Kristin was disgusted. Soames, with his good looks, youth, and fabulous money, might have bent his efforts to improving the world, or at least his part of it. Instead he chose to be a corruptor, to dally with persons like Rob, Pierre, and Vitas, who were empty husks, given to frivolity and pursuit of pleasure, narcissism and night.

"You disapprove of me, don't you?" Soames smiled.

"I think you are a corruptor. You play with people."

He laughed. "No," he disagreed. "I am merely a diligent

WILD WIND WESTWARD

student of human nature. There is always something new to learn."

Kristin was just about to ask what had become of Gustav, when the fat, toothless hag who seemed to be in charge of the Skull and Raven came pushing through the throng. She threw the beaded curtain aside, looking alarmed.

"What is it, Maloney?" Soames demanded.

"Two of those fools with you are fighting in the back room," she growled accusingly. "I don't want no trouble. You got to do something about it. If you please," she added grudgingly, in deference to his rank.

Soames just laughed. "All right, I'll take care of it. We'd best leave anyway. I got what I came for." He threw a handful of ten-pound notes down on the table. "Rob and Vitas," he told Kristin. "Probably fighting over Dirk. They do it all the time."

He left the table again, leaving Kristin alone. She sipped wine and tried not to took at the reprobates who were staring at her through the beads. Presently Soames, followed by his three friends, returned. Soames looked merely irritated, Pierre amused, but Vitas and Rob seemed furious with each other. Gustav accompanied them. He had been drinking, appeared disheveled and slightly distracted, but on his face, along with the scar, was the hard, almost bitter expression she recognized: it meant he had won something, gained an advantage, closed the deal.

In the carriage returning to Soames's house, Gustav and Kristin were alone, the lord having elected to ride with his friends. Gustav was very quiet, and now and then would drop into a doze.

"So you secured the loan?" Kristin asked him, trying to ascertain the actual nature of the situation.

"Hmmmm? Yes."

"Was it difficult?"

A pause. "No."

"What sort of test did he give you?"

"It's none of your concern," he snapped. "It was a matter for men."

177

Not wishing to seem prying, lest his suspicions become aroused, nonetheless she had to know one more thing: "Will you be taking me with you to America?"

He gave her an odd glance, which she could not decipher in the fog-dimmed light of the streetlamp they were passing.

"Yes." He sighed. "I would have anyway, but now it is part of the bargain to which I agreed."

She wanted to know what he meant, but Gustav would say no more. He fell asleep, riding, and when they reached Lord Soames's home in St. John's Wood, he managed to come only half awake.

"Poor soul," Soames commented, and directed Vitas, Pierre, and Rob to help Gustav to his rooms. They did so, chuckling. This Norwegian might look fierce enough, indeed, but, as a carouser, he lacked stamina. No wonder Britain ruled the world, or most of it.

Kristin was about to go upstairs to her own room, when Anthony Soames laid a hand on her arm, delaying her ascent. Momentarily she thought he meant to make her another proposition, or perhaps to take her summarily. The servants had retired for the night, and the great house was dark and quiet. London lay sleeping all about, both the prim see-no-evil London of Queen Victoria, and the dark netherworld into which, this night, Kristin had been plunged.

"Let us talk."

"Please, Lord Soames. I fear I am very tired."

"Anthony. Call me Anthony, my dear."

"Please . . ."

But he brooked no refusal. "Your husband is a good investment," he said, leading her into the library and bidding her be seated. "As a businessman very little can stop him, save possibly his capacity to do anything he thinks necessary."

If he expected Kristin to comment, she disappointed him.

"But what may be necessary might not be wise," he went on. "As a human being, I think less of him."

WILD WIND WESTWARD

"Less of him than what?"

"Than *you*."

"But you are going to provide him capital?"

He laughed. "I would be a fool not to. Your husband is willing to sign over to us a mountain range of wealth in return for some of my petty cash."

"Five million *pounds* is petty cash?"

For the first time since she had met him, Soames dropped his casual, supercilious demeanor. "Kristin," he said, addressing her directly, "there are two kinds of noblemen in the world. The first kind is, like me, hereditary. One of my forefathers had the wit to realize that William the Conqueror was going to take Britain. And so, instead of being branded a traitor, he was given lands in quantity sufficient to make a god exult. Those lands are now mine. Another of my ancestors decided that it would be wise to back Henry VIII against the Pope. He did not suffer, nor do I. We have guessed right, and we have won. That is the kind of 'nobility' I am. Ha!"

He walked across the library to a sideboard, and poured himself a glass of whiskey.

"What is the second kind of nobleman?" Kristin prodded.

Soames took a swig, another, then shrugged. "Nature's men," he said, "gentle warriors. They may lose, but they are the best in the end, because they will not do *anything* to achieve their goals."

"Anything?"

Soames made a sound, somewhere between a laugh and a sigh. "Tonight I gave your husband my test," he said. "The human animal is more predictable than generally supposed, but always interesting nonetheless. I told him, 'Rolfson, you may have that loan if you do one thing to please me.' 'What is it?' he asked, eagerly. 'Three friends of mine wish to make love to you,' I told him."

Now Kristin knew, and knew she had known all along, what had happened in the back room of the Skull and Raven. The monstrousness of it was underscored, in her mind, by Anthony's blasé demeanor now.

He noted her revulsion.

"It is true," he said. "It happened. I do not lie. And it is why I am giving money to your husband. He will do *anything*, and so my investment is in good hands. He is the perfect modern businessman"—here Anthony's voice grew bitter—"and he will allow anything to be done to him, even degradation against his nature and being, should such an assault make him more money. But you . . ." His eyes turned tender.

"What about me?"

"But you," he continued, coming across the room and sitting down beside her, "deserve a better thing. My own life has been determined long ago, by money and biology. However, I am, as I said, a student of human nature, and not without gifts of appraisal and appreciation. You love another, he is in America, and it was my condition, which your husband had to accept, that you go to America with him. Whether you find there the kind of nobleman I described, the one you claim to love, is your concern, and not mine. My gift to you is that I have given you the chance."

Kristin looked at him, holding back words, holding back a tide of commingled emotions, which included hope, anger, pride, revulsion, fear, and yes, a knowledge that Anthony Soames was like her husband, only far more dangerous, far more corrupt. And yet . . . And yet good and evil are brothers more than they are enemies.

"Gustav gave in to my demands," he said. "And I love that. You did not. But I love that the more."

He stood, a bit unsteadily, and motioned her to leave the library, climb the stairs.

"When the times comes," he said, "bon voyage."

PART THREE

NEW YORK, PENNSYLVANIA 1863–1865

I

The heatless room in the rat-trap tenement had only one occupant on that raw March morning of 1863. He was Eric Gunnarson, over two years now in New York, and he was ill. He coughed, cursed, waited for the uncontrollable burst of gasping and hacking that had been plaguing him for months. It did not come. A good sign. Sam Lapin, the dockmaster, had told Eric he could return to work as a stevedore when his health improved, if the job was still available. *If* the job was still available. Eric knew he was weak, but he was down to his last half-dollar. He forced himself from the bunk, one bunk in a room he shared with fourteen other men and fourteen other triple-tiered bunks. The men were out now, a few of them working, and the rest looking for work. The bunks rented for a nickel a night, which was more than some of the men earned in a day, sometimes a week.

Outside the door, coming up the cold, hollow stairwell, Eric heard the sound of footsteps. At first he thought Jake Goldstein was on his way up, to make sure no transient had purloined one of his fifteen bedbug-ridden mattresses, but the footsteps were lighter than Jake's and more hurried. Eric pulled on boots and cap; he had been sleeping in his coat. Presently there was a tentative knock on the door.

"Come in."

A young man entered, good looking, but soft in an apple-cheeked sort of way. He was about twenty years old, and Eric recognized him: Bobby Lapin, son of Sam Lapin, the dockmaster for whom Eric had worked before

Vanessa Royall

coming down with pneumonia just prior to Christmas.

The youth looked with real horror at the stained, grimy room, then at Eric. "You're Gunnarson?" he asked.

Eric nodded. Yes, his luck *was* changing! Sam had sent his son to fetch Eric back to the docks. Upon fleeing the Leedses and finding himself robbed of all his savings, Eric had fought back against fate with the forced optimism that is probably the last refuge of the undeservedly unfortunate. It had not been easy. Hubert Dubin, unprincipled captain of the S.S. *Anandale,* had once told Eric: "Son, in America you got to know how to make a deal." To this rude maxim Eric had added a corollary: "But first you have to survive."

And he had done that, so far, barely.

Staff members at the Norwegian consulate in New York were helpful, and for a time Eric had had several acquaintances there, bright career men who condescended only slightly to him because they wanted to hear their own tongue amid the barbaric babble of many-tongued New York. They were unable to get him a job, but they suggested that he gain American citizenship if he wished decent employment. Eric agreed, and, he reasoned, the consulate might serve as a meeting place should Kristin come to America, and he wrote her to that effect. Months later, after Eric had found temporary work removing offal from the streets of New York, one of the young foreign service officers brought him a letter. It was from Kristin. Unable to wait, Eric tore it open in the man's presence. His face must have registered immense shock, because the other asked sharply, "Why, what's wrong? What's the matter?"

"An old friend died in the homeland," Eric fabricated, trying to keep his wits. But he never returned to the embassy after that, or saw the consulate personnel again, because Kristin had written:

WILD WIND WESTWARD

June 10, 1862
London

My Darling,

This is written in haste and in the hope that it reaches you in time. G. intends to inform New York of the Subsheriff Johanson matter that caused you to leave Lesja. He may have already done so. I fear for your safety, although I was overjoyed to have received your letter, and to know there is hope for us. There will always be. We shall come to America next year when winter departs to open the Atlantic lanes, but I do not know if we sail from here or from Oslo. Be safe and well. Where you are, there I am, and where I am, so are you, too.

All my love,
Kristin

So, thereafter, Eric frequented the consulate no more, nor did he send Kristin another letter, because that would have given Rolfson further cause to anger, and further need to see that Eric was hunted down. Nor could Kristin write again. To have sent mail in care of the consulate would have been as pointless as it would have been foolhardy of Eric to send her his address, lest Gustav learn it. Gradually, as the year dragged on, Eric's life wound down, reduced itself to bleak need and high, private hope. On the one hand he had to stay alive. On the other, somehow, he had to meet Kristin's ship.

The former need was met when Eric applied for a job as stevedore. Dockmaster Sam Lapin liked his looks, appraised his strength, and hired him. Working on the harbor likewise rendered less unlikely Eric's expectation of meeting Kristin: harbor news carried word of all ships, their arrivals, departures, points of origin, and destinations. While lying abed with pneumonia, Eric had grown somewhat anxious. What if, already, Kristin were in New York? What if Gustav had already dragged her off to some other part of the country? The world? But she had written:

"... when winter departs to open the Atlantic lanes ..." And that undoubtedly meant Kristin would be on one of the first ships arriving in spring. Yes, she would be on it, but so would Gustav.

Lying sick in a dirty bunk, Eric imagined Gustav Rolfson in America, moneyed and powerful, courted by American businessmen, politicians, perhaps even people of society. Oh, he had observed it many a time, sometimes with amusement, sometimes bitterly. The penniless foreigner, just off a freighter, or up out of the steerage section in a passenger vessel, the person as ridden with lice as the ship was laden with barnacles: that person would be cursed, reviled, shunted aside, laughed at. He would have to fight for a crust of bread, not to mention a job. But the rich foreigner, one who came grandly to the New World's shores, no, he would be treated as a celebrity, a prince, and courted as a wonder of wit and civility by Americans who had not yet gotten over the idea that European rich were more intelligent, more refined, indeed, better in every way, than anything America had yet invented or conceived.

Gustav Rolfson! And Kristin on his arm!

But young Bobby Lapin had no idea what thoughts possessed Eric Gunnarson, or what passions stirred and guided his life.

"Pa told me you'd been laid up with the pneumony," he was saying. "How you feeling?"

Eric felt a coughing fit coming on, but held it back. "Fine," he said. "All ready to go."

Lapin looked doubtful. "I got a proposition for you," he said.

"So the dock job is still open," answered Eric, pleased. "What?"

"The job I had. Working for your father ..."

Young Bobby waved away the matter, a thing of no consequence.

"You must be kidding," he said. "The war has ruined business. Shipping is less than half what it was just last year. It's all the fault of that damnable ape-man, Lincoln.

WILD WIND WESTWARD

Freed slaves have come north to work for almost nothing. The Irish, who previously held jobs taken by the Negroes, are up in arms. The city is a vicious place, just now. And, to make it worse, Lincoln has imposed a draft. The immigrants don't see why they should be called into the army, and they are on the verge of becoming violent. In fact, that's why I'm here to see you."

So there was no job, Eric thought, sitting down on his bunk. He motioned Lapin to do the same, but the youth, after another brief disgusted glance at the mattresses, declined.

"I've just been drafted myself," Lapin said. "I'm supposed to report in early May."

"I wish you well."

"But don't you see? That's why I'm here. Pa has a soft spot for you. This is your big opportunity."

Eric was astonished; Lapin made no sense. "What do you mean?" he asked.

"You can be my substitute!" Lapin explained happily. "It's all legal, and everything. I'll pay you the required three hundred dollars, and—"

"I'll go off to war and be killed," Eric finished.

"No, no, *that* won't happen. The war will probably be over before you finish training. It might even be over by the time I'm . . . *you're* due to report for service."

Of that estimate Eric was very skeptical. He had made it a point to learn as much about America as he could, its society, its economy, and its politics. The war was tearing the country apart, and it seemed to be far from over. Newspapers, from 1861 on, had reported disaster after disaster for Lincoln and the North. General McClellan, commander of the much vaunted but seldom active Army of the Potomac, claimed always to be on the verge of taking Richmond, the Confederate capital, but this was difficult without giving the order to attack, which McClellan hesitated to do. Ulysses S. Grant was more pugnacious, but the North's victory at Shiloh cost the Union thirteen thousand dead. The South lost eleven thousand men. No sweetness in such victory, and Robert E. Lee held on, hoping, fighting, retreating to fight again. Lee's were the tactics of Washington in the Revolutionary War: maintain an army, in hiding, in the fields, in the trenches. Just keep the army together, and you are not defeated. Keep the army together and *wait* until the time is right to strike. That time had not yet come. Bull Run, Antietam, Fredericksburg: these were the names of places that, forever, would be marked also by blood, and the memory of blood. More battles waited to be fought. Many more. Eric knew this. Besides, he could not leave New York. Even now Kristin might be aboard a ship on her way.

"I can't do it. I must stay here, work . . ."

"There are no jobs," said Lapin emphatically. "I just told you that."

Eric did not wish to discuss the matter further. He felt bad enough already, without having to consider himself a piece of cannon fodder, capable of being bought and used to keep this chubby son of a wealthy man out of the army. A life for a life: one loses, one wins. Eric saw that he would not be the winner in such a human equation.

"I can't be in your army anyway," he said bleakly. "You see I'm not a . . . that is, I haven't finished my citizenship process yet."

"That doesn't matter!" Lapin declared. "They'll take care of that for you in the army."

"They will?"

"Certainly. It's being done left and right, all the time. What is it, anyway? Just a piece of paper. You've been here now . . . how long?"

"Two years."

"Two years! That's a whole generation these days. Lincoln is drafting micks and paddies just in off the boat, still stinking of cabbage from their last meal on the auld sod."

"Micks and paddies?"

"The Irish. On account of they're all named Michael or Padraic or some such. Watch out for them. They're vicious and they're dumb."

Eric dismissed this outburst. As an immigrant, he, too,

had been called these things, and much worse. Young Lapin simply did not understand.

But do I understand anything either? Eric asked himself, disconsolately. Dubin's words returned to him, kept resounding within his mind: "You got to be willing to make a deal, you got to be willing to make a deal."

What other prospects do I have? Eric asked himself. *None,* he answered, *and little hope of finding any.*

"How soon would you have to know my decision," he asked Lapin, "should I decide to go into the army as your substitute?"

Lapin relaxed a little, and congratulated himself on being a clever persuader. He did not even have the insight to know that a hungry and desperate man is less difficult to manipulate than a secure, healthy one with money in his pocket, food in his belly. And now he was happy, too, thinking he had worked his way out of the army, out of the prospect of dirt, orders, obedience, training, and— quite possibly—maiming or death. In this war the dead were lucky. The wounded lingered in awful agony, and died slowly, by the tens of thousands: there were almost no medical supplies, and even fewer doctors.

"I would have to know definitely by the first of May," he said. "Before that if possible. Pa told me to give you first chance. I'll be speaking to others, of course, should you make the wrong decision and not take this fine opportunity."

Lapin went on talking for a little while longer, using the verbal touchstones Eric had come to know in America: "opportunity" and "freedom" and "progress" and "individual worth." He had heard these words, and believed in them, but they were used sonorously, emptily, and all too often by people like Bobby Lapin, who would never be compelled to struggle for possession of the reality behind the meaning.

"All right," Eric agreed, gambling with himself and with time. If Kristin were on her way, she might well be in New York by May first, and then he would make with her whatever plans they could. With Lapin, Eric decided to deal as he had with Captain Dubin. He would not lie, nor give his word of honor, only to renege upon it, but if this young man presumed so readily to use Eric, a portion of the favor might, with no lack of justification, be returned.

"I expect I shall have a good word ready for you by the first of May," he informed the happy young man.

After Lapin had gone, Eric walked downstairs and out onto the cold street. A fine, icy drizzle was falling; the entire city looked grainy and gray. Eric invested a nickel in a huge mug of cream-filled coffee, and a roll of hard bread with a thick spear of yellow cheese stuffed inside. He had forty-five cents left now, but he felt better, even though he knew jobs were tight. He wasn't coughing either; he actually felt quite fit, if a little weak. He decided to go down to the harbor and check the names of inbound ships. Then, too, there was also the possibility that Bobby Lapin had been wrong about the scarcity of jobs: people who do not need to work always say, accusingly, that *anybody* can get a job, or, with secret gloating, false pity, that *nobody* can get a job.

The trek to the harbor was a little over a mile, and Eric had not walked that far in several months. Normally he would have gone additional blocks out of his way to avoid the Leeds house, but he felt his energy waning, and took a chance. If anyone happened to be home at this time of the morning, it would be only Liz. And she would be inside. Eric approached the dusty-yellow house, walking fast, on the opposite side of the street. But as he drew nearer, he saw a cluster of people standing on the walkway in front of the house. Nearer still, he saw that they were police officers, along with a half-dozen neighbor women who had come to gape not only at the police but at the Leedses' furniture, which was scattered along the street. Eric recognized the dining-room table at which he had begun his happy letter to Kristin, a letter never sent.

He also recognized the frame of his old bed, and the leg he had used to press down the plank over his money. Anger rose in him, along with curiosity. Had the Leedses been fire victims? He stopped but did not cross the street, not desiring to come into contact either with the police or the Leedses. No, the house did not look as if there had been a fire, although the front door was wide open. Just then two more police officers emerged, carrying a couch.

"That's the last of it," one of them yelled to his mates.

And in the open doorway appeared the beautiful redhaired Joan. She stood there and watched with her strange detachment as the police began loading the household furnishings into horse-drawn wagons. In spite of himself Eric could neither walk on toward the harbor nor take his eyes away from her. Even at this distance she emanated an aura: she gave off the spirit, the air, the very *scent* of the soft and lovely girl-child in need of protection, the shield of a man's love and strength and being. Eric sensed this aura, as he had from the beginning, but sensed it with his body alone. His mind refreshed him with reality: Joan, no matter how gorgeous, no matter how apparently helpless, was to the hard rock bottom of her soul a schemer and conniver, a manipulator and user of others, not even perverse, because the admission of perversity implied an awareness of good and evil, and Joan was beyond both.

"Eric!" she cried, with fervent, ruthless, penetrating and triumphant helplessness.

He turned away.

"Eric! Eric! Everything's fallen apart!"

He began to walk.

The police wagon, piled high with her mother's household goods, pulled away from the curb.

"Oh, Eric! Please!"

Lot's wife is in everyone, and the vestige of Lot's wife in Eric looked back. Joan started down from the steps, then faltered, seemed to stumble, and fell. She rolled down the steps and came to a rest on the wet walk, motionless.

He watched for a moment. She lay there motionless.

Damn her, he thought. But no one else went to aid her, and he could not let a human being lie injured upon cold earth.

It would seem to him later that fate had preordained that it should be he who crossed the street to her, not she who pursued him, begging for help. But he did not have an opportunity, just then, to consider the distinction. He went to her and helped her up. Sudden tears came to Joan's lovely green eyes, her arms were open, and Eric found himself in her embrace. She *seemed* desperate, and yet the futility was oddly superficial. Again, the people and events she experienced seemed somehow not to touch her nor to affect her as much as she affected them. Her body was warm against Eric's, but he fought the wile and spell of her, remembering his lost three hundred dollars, the mean way in which the Leedses had used him, and Joan's lies, too. He reached behind his neck, caught her wrists, and extricated himself from her embrace.

Joan looked startled for a moment. Perhaps few men had ever done such a thing; certainly Mick had not.

"Oh, Eric! I'm so glad you've come."

"I was passing by, that's all. What's the matter here?"

Tears trembling, she told a terrible tale there on the cold March street. Liz, her mother, had caught the flu earlier in the year. It had turned into pneumonia, and she had died. Joan and Mick had been sad, of course, but they knew Liz had owned tavern and house. They would survive, even prosper. But, very soon, strange, hard men began to appear, either at the house or the tavern, demanding money, showing unpaid notes signed by Liz Leeds.

Eric's interest quickened. Well did he know the cruel power and leverage of forged notes!

Joan's tale, however, had a different twist. The men were legitimate creditors, in quest of proper reimbursement. Liz had put up as collateral tavern, house, and household furnishings in order to make purchase of a business enterprise down near the harbor. "She could have paid cash for at least half of it," Joan said. "She had a lot of money. I'd seen her count it on the dining table."

WILD WIND WESTWARD

"Then why didn't she?"

"Liz didn't like to part with cash. So she took out the loan."

"What kind of business was she buying?" Eric probed. These Leedses, crooked to the core, could think of acquiring more wealth, while he had to struggle to stay alive!

Joan looked away, but did not blush. "It was a house having to do with women and sailors."

Eric's expression of disgust must have been very clear, because she immediately added: "I'm sure Liz just wanted the property. I'm sure she didn't mean to—"

"Of course. But whatever became of the money Liz had?"

New tears pearled on the ends of Joan's long lashes. "We don't know. Liz kept it hidden and we can't find it."

Eric could barely keep a smile off his face. How fitting. The Leedses had been caught in their own shivery web.

"Where's Mick?" he asked.

"He's been drafted into the army, and sent south to Maryland for training."

"Perhaps it will do him some good. You must be lonesome."

"Oh, Eric!" she cried, remembering what he'd seen. "That night . . . you don't think . . . oh, Eric, no! That was just one time. He was frightfully drunk. There was nothing I could do."

Her eyes showed such purity and innocence that Eric, against his will, wanted to believe her.

"Have you been ill?" she asked, either to show concern for him or to change the subject.

"I'm getting better."

"Where are you staying now? Do you have a job?"

He told her of Goldstein's rat trap, and his former job on the docks. "I'm going to see about that now."

"May I come with you?"

"Why would you want to do that?"

"Eric. Oh, Eric. There's nothing left here for me. The new owner will arrive presently to take over the house, and I'll . . . I'll be alone. Please let me come along with you. Just for a little while. I promise I won't be a bother."

Vanessa Royall

What harm could come of it? Eric thought. Joan read his expression before he told her she could walk along with him if she wanted. "I must go back inside the house and fetch my cloak," she said.

In a moment she was with him again, holding on to his arm as they walked down along the cobblestone streets of lower Manhattan. When they reached the wharves, the shuddering sight of a vast, swirling mob greeted them, the great hue and cry of angry men.

Joan clung more tightly to Eric's arm, but not from fright. An unusual, recondite gleam came into her eyes: her response to, and acceptance of, danger and violence.

The mob was blocking entry to Lapin's warehouses and offices. Eric approached a man at the outskirts of the crowd and asked what was happening.

"What d'ye think?" the other returned, his tone as coarse, bitter, and full of futility as the expression on his unshaven face. "We caught us another one of them niggers, an' we're burning him."

"Ohhh!" exclaimed Joan.

"Where are the police?"

"Safe and out of here. They took 'em a beatin' at the draft riot just this mornin'. They won't be wantin' 'em another beatin' over one dumb darkie slave." He scowled suspiciously at Eric. "Hey, you wouldn't be one of these here abul-eesh-unists, would you? That support the darkie against decent white men like me, looking for work?"

Before Eric could answer, Joan pulled him away from the man. To his surprise she drew him into the crowd, pushing her way with a strength born of strange, fierce desire.

"I have to see it," she kept saying, "I have to see it."

A great, bloodthirsty howl arose from the mob then, and the smell of firesmoke drifted over the crowd. It was followed by a shrieking, hopeless plea for mercy, then by a savage, unearthly howl, as fire found flesh. Joan pulled Eric into the very heart of the crowd, right to the inner circle where hard men stood watching a black man tied to one of the great wooden pillars upon which this section of the wharf was founded. All around the pillar were bundles of kindling and shafts of firewood, already aflame. Tongues of fire lanced upward, swirling around the Negro, flashing and shifting in the harbor wind. The man was screaming at the top of his lungs, calling upon gods unknown to men of the West. His rude garments were aflame. Still he might be saved if . . .

Eric sprang forward, and began to kick away the burning pieces of wood. He managed to dislodge several of them from the burning pile, kicking them from the pier. He heard them hiss in the water below. He felt the blow on the back of his head, but that was all.

"When you going to wise up, hey? This is America, dammit. You're no knight in shining armor. You almost got yourself killed, you know that?"

Faces wavered in and out of Eric's field of vision; his head pulsed and pounded with currents of pain, woefully enhanced by the thundering sounds of the words being spoken to him. He squinted and focused: Dockmaster Sam Lapin was looking down at him. Behind Sam, spinning into view, came Joan's face, and then the faces of other men. Joan appeared concerned, but the concern was tinged with lingering, subdued excitement, such as might be present following some strenuous contest, or exciting activity, or lovemaking. In contrast the faces of the men showed little but disgust.

"You dumb bastard," Lapin was saying, mopping Eric's face with a cold, wet rag. "What the hell did you think you were doing out there?"

Memory drifted back as Eric's head cleared. The pain receded a little. The image of the burning black man came to him, and he recalled kicking at the flaming logs.

"Lucky that Irishman thought he killed you with one blow of cordwood," Sam said. "Even luckier this girl here" —he jerked his thumb in Joan's direction—"dragged you into the office."

Eric sat up and shook his head.

"What a goddamn dumb thing to do," Sam pronounced yet again.

"But they were burning that man."

Sam's dockworkers drifted off to their tasks, convinced now that, while the big dumb foreigner might live, he would never develop even half a brain.

Sam Lapin was shaking his head, wringing out the rag above a bucket of water. "Look, I'm going to give you some advice you should have had when you first got off the boat. This is, as I've said, America. Fight your *own* damn battles here. Not everybody else's. What the hell did you think you were going to prove out there? By saving that nigger? Hell, them Irishmen burned two yesterday, three the day before, and likely they'll burn some more tomorrow. Every freed nigger that Lincoln and the damned abolitionists send north takes the food out of a white man's mouth. Why, you're lucky they didn't decide to burn you. Probably would have if they hadn't figured you were already dead."

He stood up, lending a hand to help Eric to his feet.

"How are you feeling?" Joan asked, as Eric stood there, swaying unsteadily.

"Awful. I just came down here to see about . . ."

"The job?" Sam finished. "Forget it. Did Bobby find you? About the draft?"

Eric nodded, winced. "Yes."

"You going to do it? Take his place as a substitute? Jesus, I hope they don't reject you now, because of health reasons."

"You just told me not to fight anyone's battles but my own."

Lapin threw up his hands in exasperation, and looked at Joan. "Are you his girl friend? Can't you teach him something?" Then, again to Eric: "What I meant was, do things to *your* advantage. It's to your advantage to take my boy's place in the ranks of the Union army. It's to your advantage because there are no jobs for you here, and you'll starve to death if you don't somehow first contrive

WILD WIND WESTWARD

to get the brains kicked plumb out of your head. You got that? You see what I mean?"

Eric didn't speak. A wave of uneasy self-realization came down upon him, like the assault of a dark, accusatory conscience. The events of the past years flashed along the gray, furrowed curves of his brain. Everything—almost everything—that he had done since the glorious day with Kristin at Sonnendahl Fjord had been misguided, or disastrous. He had been true to himself, yes, but how worthy, how applicable, were the old ways, the ways of a country freeman in the old world, to the harsh, complicated requirements of this new land? How applicable were those ancient values, in fact, to the assurance of his own survival? Kristin had asked him not to change, had asked him to remain strong in the ways he had been strong, and to retain the virtues she had admired. He wanted to do this, because he *was* those virtues, they were his. His attempt to save the burning Negro proved that. And yet what had his persistent devotion to the cause of truth gained him? He was as penniless today as he had been upon fleeing the *Anandale*. Moreover, his health was threatened. Could he offer Kristin naught but poverty and illness?

"I'll be all right," he told Lapin, with as much certitude as he could muster. "You'll hear from me regarding substitution for the draft."

Leaving Lapin's office, he tried not to stagger. Joan helped him, and he leaned on her, grateful for the support, but wondering about her motives.

"It was wonderful!" she said. "You were splendid. I love action. Bravery. I love to watch it. Somehow I didn't think you had it in you."

He stopped walking and looked at her. "Why didn't you think so?" he demanded.

"Because you were always so . . . *gentlemanly. Too* . . . gentlemanly."

Eric remembered what a willing dupe he had been to the Leedses, running whiskey for them, believing Joan's lies.

"But now I can see you're going to change," she said,

appraising him. "Let's find a place to stay, and we'll plan some things."

Ah, this time Eric would not let himself be gulled. She meant to use him for something; he knew it. She meant, again, to manipulate him for her own ends. Find a place to stay? The two of them?

"I have forty-five cents," he said. "That's all."

"It doesn't matter. My brother Mick went into the army as a substitute. He got three hundred dollars, and he left it with me. He said I had to have it because of what happened to Liz."

Eric could not help thinking that Joan had probably stolen her own brother's money. Mick would have arrived at the training camp in Maryland, would have slipped the cachet out of his waistband or legging or pack or boot only to find . . . strips of newspaper. But he held his tongue. He would be one mite wiser than he'd been upon awakening this morning.

"Just one more thing," he told her. "I must check the registry of vessels."

"Why?" she asked suspiciously.

"Maybe I can get a job on one or another of them," he lied.

"But I have plans for you," she said, her eyes narrowing slightly.

He did not reply, but instead led her down the wharf to the building in which records of incoming and outgoing vessels were listed. A Mercator map of the world stretched across one wall in the main room of the office building, with all sea lanes mapped and charted. Joan was interested in spite of herself; her horizons, previously, had been limited to mother, brother, house, tavern, and the contours and parallels of the dollar sign.

"Where did you come from?"

He showed her Europe and Norway on the great map.

"That long thin country way up there? Where are we now? Maps always confuse me."

He pointed to New York, the United States, America.

WILD WIND WESTWARD

"I can see why you left," she said. "This is much bigger. And so where's Mick?"

Eric found Maryland on the map, and indicated its location.

"Why, that's not far at all," she said, with a measure of delight that, Eric deduced, was somehow counterfeit. Perhaps she had really taken her brother's money, in which case, given his personality and inclinations, he would certainly think of getting it back. Not to mention getting even.

Eric's head was fairly clear now, but he still had to make an effort to focus on the printing of the registry. Joan stood beside him as he went down the long list of vessels bound for New York.

"How do you know from that list which ship might have a job for you?" she asked warily.

"I speak Norwegian and English, so it seems intelligent to seek employment on—"

"Back to the bottom again, is that it?" Joan was asking, while she watched Eric study the registry. "Didn't you hear what Mr. Lapin was telling you? Can't you make big plans? If you go back to some silly job, you'll never get anywhere. Why, I've thought of something for the two of us . . ."

She didn't finish. She saw the look on Eric's face, and knew that it meant much more than he had let on.

And she was right. Because he had found the listing he sought.

H.M.S. *Valkyrie* (Passenger Vessel)
Departed Oslo: March 2
Docked Southampton, England, March 12–14
Estimated arrival, New York, April 18–22

Kristin was on her way! Eric was so delighted, there was no way he could have held back his joy. Joan, quick and shrewd, wondered what could have made him so happy. In her experience, destitute people were not made happy except by an escape from their destitution. She followed his eyes to the registry listing.

"That's a passenger ship," she said. "The likes of you, at least the way you look now, won't get a job on a passenger ship."

Then her mind cast back over what she knew about him, and what he had told her.

"So," she exclaimed, with a smile of slow cunning, "don't think I didn't see the light in your eyes. Your beloved, the one you used to tell me about, is on that ship, isn't she?"

Eric looked at her. Joan seemed excited, even challenged, by the possibility. She was standing straight, breasts forward, displaying her womanhood. He was witnessing yet another facet of her complicated, unpredictable nature.

Joan studied the register more closely. "April eighteenth to twenty-second, eh? Unless there's a storm at sea, or something."

"I have no idea who will be on that ship," Eric said.

"Don't lie to me. You can't lie anyway. I swear, you'll never make anything of yourself. Without proper training, of course," she smiled, taking his arm.

Eric thought of leaving her, and going off by himself. Surely he could make his way back to Goldstein's tenement on his own, and by the time the *Valkyrie* docked, his health would be completely restored. Just *thinking* about Kristin had a recuperative quality. But, outside the building again, the cold hit him like a punch, his head throbbed, and he sagged. Joan was there, and he braced against her. He was vaguely aware that she was hailing a hack, and then he was inside it, she still there, and his head pounding with every rut and jounce of the carriage.

". . . time someone made proper use of you . . ." he thought he heard her say.

Eric took fever again that night, and although he was not conscious of the passage of individual days and nights for some time thereafter, he did perceive, as through a dark glass, certain wavering, incandescent episodes: He was being helped into some hotel or hospital; an intelligent-looking man was bending over him, examining him; he was being fed; Joan was there next to the bed upon which he lay, alternately looking down upon him and talking to someone else who was outside Eric's field of vision. Whether he was asleep and dreaming, or awake and hallucinating in the delirium of fever, Eric could not have said. High rock walls of the brilliant blue fjords swayed against the blood-red membranes of his affliction. Viking swords and axes marched across a landscape of sere and battered weeds. The port of Oslo sank into the sea as he left his homeland, and somewhere Captain Dubin was giving him advice. The face of Gustav Rolfson appeared in his trance, a livid scar upon it like the mark of original sin, and before Eric's very eyes, Subsheriff Johanson's skull parted like an apple halved by a paring knife, to reveal, within its gray and pulsing depths, the head of Gustav Rolfson once again, laughing. Trapped within the spell of his own delirium, Eric nonetheless fought against it, tried to swim upward out of its insidious depths, to attain clarity again. Then he was moving upward, dreamlike and borne upon water. It was as it had been in the icy blue pool at Sonnendahl Fjord, when he and Kristin had pledged themselves eternally to each other. He shot upward, upward, and all about him hung brilliant curtains of shadow and ice, but above, above, it was light, like the light of the Solstice suspended there evermore, and he swept upward toward it, toward Kristin, who was waiting for him there. . . .

"I think he's finally shaken the fever," Joan Leeds was saying to someone in the room with her. "My goodness, Eric, my dear, you do look a fright. I shall send out for a barber."

Eric tried to speak, but his mouth and tongue were sawdust and sand. He was lying in a bed in a large room, a well-appointed room of high windows, long draperies, and two low couches. A man in a dark suit rose from one of the couches now, and walked over to the bed. By his very manner, Eric judged him to be a doctor, which the man proceeded to corroborate by giving Eric a brisk, professional examination. Joan stood by, watching. She smiled at Eric encouragingly, but, as always, there was on her face an expression he could not read.

The doctor lifted Eric's head, and let him sip a glass of

water. He seemed satisfied that his patient was out of immediate danger. "Stay on the water," he instructed Joan, "and try some broth later in the day. It's very important that he get all the liquids he can take, and he must absolutely remain on his back. I'll drop by tomorrow, midmorning."

Joan saw the physician to the door. Eric noted that she was dressed in a fine, floor-length gown of azure velvet, against which gleamed her shining red hair. He also noted, looking out the windows, that the room was high up in some building. He could see several rooftops and the steeples of a few churches. He must be in a hotel, and a good one at that. Joan certainly had not been shy about spending Mick's draft-substitute money. Then he thought of something far more important.

"What day is it?" he croaked anxiously.

Joan came back to the bed and sat down beside him, smiling her dazzling, enigmatic smile.

"Don't you worry about time. Everything's taken care of."

"But I must know if . . ."

Joan's face darkened as she guessed what he was thinking about: his beloved and the arrival of the *Valkyrie*.

"I should think you might wish to thank someone before making inquiries regarding the news of the world."

"Oh, yes, Joan. I didn't mean to . . . There is no way I can repay you—"

"Perhaps I can think of something."

"—but how long was I—"

"In fever? Let's see. This is Thursday, so that makes"—she tallied on her long, fine fingers: aristocratic fingers, they were—"about nine days. You were lucid some of the time, but not often." She gave him a searching look, even as Eric reckoned the passage of time and calculated that Kristin was still at least a month out of New York.

"Tell me, did you kill a man named Johanson?" she asked abruptly.

My God! thought Eric. What dangerous secrets had he babbled from the caverns of delirium?

WILD WIND WESTWARD

"Kristin is the name of the woman," Joan was saying. "I know that beyond doubt. Even in fever, you spoke the name in a special way. But what of this Rolfson? What is he to you? When you spoke his name you"—and here Joan shuddered, in a way that was almost sexual—"you seemed to hate him enough to kill."

Her body quivered again, as if the thought of such violence thrilled her more deeply than sex could or love might.

Exhausted by the fever, and still terribly weak, Eric tried to fashion a response. If Joan already knew these secrets, she must also have guessed . . .

"You're no simple ship-jumping immigrant, are you? You're an escaped murderer."

The idea seemed to please her, pleased her in itself, above and beyond the fact that the knowledge extended her power over him. She looked at him a long while, then said: "Rest now. Forget about your past. All of it and everyone in it. I'm the best thing that has ever happened to you, and we'll do splendidly together. Rest now, because I have plans for you."

During the next weeks, as Eric slowly but steadily recovered his health and strength, he knew there must be a madness in Joan's method, but he could not deduce what it was, or of what elements it might be composed. She had him examined regularly by the doctor, saw to his food, brought in a barber to groom him and a tailor to prepare him new clothes, fashionable in cut and expensive of cloth. Where had she gotten the money for these things?

"Liz's creditors missed some things," she explained. "For example, Mick's horses were stabled on Long Island at the time of mother's . . . death. . . ."

She had difficulty with the word *death*. Eric reasoned that such hesitancy was natural, in the light of all that had happened to Joan recently. It was amazing that she was holding up so well.

"Anyway, I sold the horses and . . . certain other things.

Vanessa Royall

We have enough to live on until you recover fully, which, judging by your eyes and appetite, ought to be soon."

He watched her, wondering. She was standing at one of the high windows, her back to him, looking out over the grit and sprawl of the city. Or was she studying his reflection in the window glass? He had not mentioned the *Valkyrie* or Kristin again, not only because he had to be genuinely grateful to Joan for what she had done for him and thus did not want to offend her, but also because he sensed that Joan, in her particular feminine way, regarded Kristin—whom she had never seen and of whom Eric had never spoken save with the greatest circumspection—as a challenge or threat. It was now mid-April, and within days the *Valkyrie* was due in New York Harbor. Eric had to decide how to proceed. He was bound, by gratitude as well as honor, to repay Joan in some way, or at least promise to repay her, and to bring to an end—hopefully an amicable end—his strange relationship with her. He considered his situation: his health was almost back to normal, and although he had no money of his own, two fine suits Joan had bought for him hung in the closet next to his old dockworker's tatters, vestiges of a past life.

Eric was just about to speak, to try and discuss things with Joan, but she turned away from the window and came to him. Dressed in a warm robe, he reclined against piled pillows on the bed. Her lips were soft with a smile; her eyes gleamed with a woman's sudden hunger. Eric's body read the gleam before his mind did, and the hot blood of arousal coursed within him before she did what he knew she was about to do: pull down from her shoulders and full perfect breasts another of her elegant gowns, this gown soft and rose-pink as the concavity of musk and flesh by which she meant to hold and pleasure him.

"I know we have much to discuss," she whispered huskily, letting the gown fall about her ankles, the gown beneath which she was solid and splendid and lovely and altogether bare, "but that is for later. For now, I have another need. And so do you."

With that she knelt upon the bed, leaned forward, and

with utter naturalness, reached beneath his robe and touched him, smiling with pleasure and knowledge to find he was already in her spell. Eric groaned, both in pleasure and woe. The image of Kristin flashed through his mind, but there was no time, because, expertly, Joan had thrown open the robe, swung upon him as if mounting a horse, and slid down upon him, taking him into herself. She rocked easily upon him for a moment, leaning forward also to kiss him—a kiss he could not help but return—and then suddenly she was up and away from him, smiling wickedly, and he felt cool air tingling where he had been enclosed and voluptuously warm. He gasped in surprise and despair.

Joan knelt above him, grinning wickedly. "Whoever is the one you remember," she said, "I shall now make you forget."

And Joan tried. She made Eric's brain dance, his body burn, stripping him for herself, for the pleasure of her eyes and body. Cooing sofly in anticipation of her own eventual glory and release, she prolonged everything, every glance, touch, kiss, every caress of finger or body or tongue. She sensed, from the beginning, that Eric, because of his love for the girl of his homeland, would try to hold something back, would try to keep from her some private part of himself, even though she might milk him, and milk him again and again, of every drop of his essence. Oh, yes, she wanted his essence, but she wanted his spirit more, and she advanced to have it, trailing kisses all along his body, and coming down again and again to stroke and kiss the utter length of him, only to leave him free and open and begging.

Beneath her, Eric lay quiet at first, entranced and dazzled by the sensations she gave, feeling his mind and all control flow away from him, like sweet water into the quiet earth, like sweet raindrops feeding the seed. That seed was pure passion, and soon it sprang forth. There was neither place nor time, only pleasure and need and need of pleasure. Breath left him as he felt flick and swirl of tongue, soft fingertips teasing the rise of his juice. *No more, no more, no more,* but then she would take away her kiss, and in the silence of his mind, Eric would cry: *No, more, more!*

Then for a long, long time Joan spoke only with her tongue. Finally she came up to him and stretched out long beside him, telling him to roll upon her, telling him not with words but only with that smile he would never read, would never be able to read. At that moment her power over him was virtually limitless, a witch's brew of hunger, dark knowledge, and sex. He thought of her in bed with her brother, but that meant nothing now. She might have been to bed with God. Who cared? Now it was his turn and he took it, knowing all the while that, in the strange heart of her enigma, Joan was taking her turn with him, putting her hold upon his soul.

It was a contradiction which did not escape him: if this were a joust, he rose and she fell, but only because she chose to fall. And he knew, even as he gave up his body to itself, to shoot and shoot and shoot again, shoot deep within the belly of her pleasure and desire, that, for trackless reasons of her own, she had decided neither to give him up nor let him be.

"Did that make you forget?" she asked, much later. Eric struggled up out of a drowsy, lascivious miasma that was at least as gripping as delirium, but a trance he was loath to relinquish.

"Joan . . ." he began.

"Shhhhhh. Let me talk. You rest quietly. I've taken a lot out of you, and I don't want you to go getting sick on me again. We've got a lot of work to do."

"We have?"

There in the bed she explained it to him. Pulling the covers up to their chins, snuggling next to him like the most tender of fleshly conspirators, stroking him easily now and again where he alternately waxed and waned in the subdued brilliances of ecstatic torpor and remembered delight, she told Eric what she meant to do, and how she wanted him to help her do it.

"War is a sad time for so many people," she began, "both for poor guys like my brother Mick, in the army,

WILD WIND WESTWARD

and also for everybody at home. So many people are lonely, and even more of them can't find work. Well, you know about that. But you haven't been out on the streets in weeks. It's even worse out there now. It is. More darkies come north every day. More immigrants arrive by ship. Having a boardinghouse was all right—"

Eric remembered the money stolen from him there.

"—and having a tavern was also good business—"

Eric recalled how gullible he had been.

"—but now I want to do something bigger, something that will make *real* money."

"Is that right?" he asked. He did not doubt her sincerity. He simply felt that her ideas of "big" money were founded on a lust for quick money, and were therefore insubstantial. "Real money in America comes from industry and commerce."

She laughed. "The poor boy speaks. And how would you know?"

"I have nothing. But that doesn't mean I haven't observed how this country works. The great fortunes are founded in shipping, or coal, or steel, like Andrew Carnegie's fortune. And next there is oil."

"Oil?"

"Yes, I've read of it. It will be the fuel of the future. To run engines. Provide light, heat. Oil has recently been discovered in Pennsylvania, too."

"Pennsylvania?" Joan echoed, with considerable interest. "Why, that's not so far away."

"What did *you* have in mind to make *real* money?" he asked her.

"Well," Joan answered, "before you said that about all the money in oil, I was thinking of doing something that would help people."

"Help people?" That hardly sounded like an idea coming from the Joan Leeds Eric knew. He looked at her closely. She seemed to mean it. Was it possible that he had misjudged her all along? After all, she had paid his expenses all this while, had cared for him when not another soul in all New York would have given him the time of day.

Vanessa Royall

"I want to help poor young girls like myself," Joan was saying. "That's what I want to do."

Eric lifted himself up upon one elbow. "That's fine, but how?"

Beneath the covers, she squeezed him tenderly, erotically. She kissed him. "By giving them a home," she said.

Eric knew before she told it. He knew her well enough now; he had been through varied and sufficient forms of travail and deceit, trickery and grief. Trust has its place, but wariness ought always to be sent first through the door. Joan in her fine gowns and Eric in his new suits were to meet ships in the harbor, scour the streets of New York, walk the blocks of tenements and hovels. Looking for poor young girls to "help."

"And New York is a bad place for them, too," Joan was saying. "We might send some of them south, to places like Maryland and . . . what is it? Virginia? Where they could meet some nice army boys, and—"

"Where are you going to get the money to do this?" he asked, feigning innocence. "Living in a hotel like this one, not to mention food and clothing, must have pretty well exhausted Mick's draft money and the proceeds from the sale of the horses."

"You are not so innocent as you contrive to appear," she rejoined. "The girls will trust you. You bring them to me and I'll take care of the rest."

Eric recalled Joan telling him once of the "house" Liz had intended to buy, a house for sailors and girls.

"We'll live with money, and in style. You weren't meant to be a poor but honest backbreaker. I saw that from the beginning. In addition to which," she continued, squeezing him gently where the processes of nature were filling him again, "I will give you what I gave you before, only longer and better, whenever you have need of it. Or even for no reason at all."

Joan moved to come down on him again, but this time he held her off. He was still weak, and she was a strong girl, but she held back, wondering.

"I owe you so much—"

"I'm glad you realize that."

"—and I will repay it someday."

"You don't have to. Just join me, work with me, be mine."

"But I simply cannot do what you are suggesting."

Eric could see that Joan was growing angry, but she held it in check. "Then what will you do? I swear I've seldom—if ever—met a man who could accomplish as much as you, if you'd just *use* your good looks and your brains. But you don't!"

Eric was stung by this, even from Joan, who had blithely offered him a position as a procurer of girls for whoredom.

"Your mind is still probably on that ship that's due, isn't it?" she went on. "Yes, your *darling* from the other side is coming, to whom you have been oh, so true . . . or is fidelity a part of being the fool you are?" Then she had another idea. "Could it be," she demanded, wrapping a length of his hair in one hand and putting her face down next to his, "could it be that your lover is rich? Wealthy? Could it be that you are waiting for her to save you, so to speak?"

"It doesn't matter if she is or not," Eric blurted.

Joan laughed, genuinely amused. "What a quaint idea! What a truly quaint and noble notion. Tell me, is she beautiful?"

"Yes."

Joan showed her breasts, posed. Lifted her chin. "As beautiful as I?"

"Look, you have been wonderful to me, taking care of me as you have, and—"

She flared again. "I don't care how wonderful I am! Can't you see it doesn't matter? *You* look. I want you, and I always get what I want."

"It's not as you think. Kristin and I have promised one another that—"

"I don't care what you've promised this Kristin, whether to buy her the Hudson Valley, or the Union army, or to do her ten times a night, I—"

Then, seeming to realize that her tone was all wrong, her manner doomed to antagonize Eric, Joan changed course.

"But enough of this," she said soothingly, and kissed him on the cheek, as if the kiss were a signal to end a small lover's spat. "I am sure you will come to your senses."

Eric tried, once more, to tell her his truth. From her manner, he had no doubts that she possessed a strong vengeful nature, which she might exercise with delight if he crossed her. And she had heard God only knows what revelations while he'd babbled in fever.

"Kristin and I planned long ago to join and go away together."

"Where?" The question was quick and cold.

"West, most likely. There are homestead lands available—"

"Farm?"

"It is what I did in the old country. Kristin was also from that life, until—"

"Until what?" Joan asked. Eric could see her eyes, see how they darkened as she concentrated, putting things together. She had a whip-and-trap mind; it missed little. "Rolfson!" Joan exclaimed. "The one you talked about with such hatred. She—Kristin—is with him, is she not?"

Eric admitted it.

Joan laughed, this time sympathetically. "What a poor fool you are. Poor *and* a fool, for all your big talk of oil and money! I ought to have figured it out sooner. It is unlikely a marriageable beauty would go untaken, and she has not. In fact it is my surmise that this Rolfson has money. Perhaps a great deal of money."

"Money beats in your blood," said Eric, not without bitterness.

"Why not?" Joan shrugged. "I shall have it, but I doubt you ever will." And then she said something that bothered Eric very deeply, not so much at first, but more and more as the minutes crept by.

"A couple of years have gone by since you last saw this legendary sweetheart of yours. Things happen. People change. Except you. That is true; face it. You are the same as you were. A murderer on the run, without citizenship, or money, or a job, or the prospect of one. So tell me: What will your darling see, what will she think, when she comes down the gangway and sees *you*?"

"This is only temporary," retorted Eric. "It will not matter to her. We plan to—"

"Temporary!" she cried. "Temporary for two years. I would hate to hear your definition of permanent."

Eric had begun to feel quite badly, under her accusatory and irrefutable words. His current plight would not matter to Kristin. He was sure of that. But it mattered to *him*! He began to feel a pale giddiness where his heart should have been.

"Oh, my words have finally begun to sink in, have they?" purred Joan, kissing him on the lips. He did not respond. "You just tell me now, my fine strong Viking, that you will do as I say, and be mine. As friend, I'll give you a start toward riches and power. But as enemy, I'll leave you to flounder in the dirt, and don't think I'll forget, either, that you turned me down."

But she did not give him a chance to answer. Instead, she roused him again to hard throbbing length—he, powerless to resist—and kissed him down his broad chest and flat stomach, took him into her wileful, smiling kiss. He lay there, immobilized in body by the agony of the pleasure she gave, immobilized in spirit by the plight to which his life had led him. *This should not be!* his spirit cried, for Joan was the profane one, utterly and beyond redemption. But his spirit was weak, and Kristin, however pure, was far away. The kissing and stroking of Joan was all the world, and Eric gave himself up to her, could not help himself, and when, triumphantly, she brought him to the heights, it felt as if she had drawn all of him into herself: blood and marrow, bone and gristle, skull and brain and beating heart.

If Kristin had drunk his image from the waters of Sonnendahl Fjord, he realized suddenly, with a quickening sense of imminence, then just now, this very moment, profane Joan had drunk and swallowed his own body!

Now she slithered upward, serpentlike, and made him taste her tongue. "Did you feel that well and good?" she wanted to know.

"Yes."

"That is for you, and always for you."

Eric said nothing. Joan ordered them up a fine dinner of roast chicken, gravy and dumplings, baked apples, strong red wine.

"Tomorrow we'll begin planning in earnest," she whispered, settling down next to him for sleep.

"No, Joan, I can't."

"Don't be silly. Oil. You told me yourself. We'll go out together to Pennsylvania and get rich. You've given me the idea of doing big things. No small-time business for me anymore. Or for you either."

"Joan, I can't go."

There was a long silence. Then, very calmly, so quietly her words did not distress him nor jolt him from the path toward sleep, Joan said: "You must learn the hard way that I am right about how life is. So, that is your choice."

II

Eric awoke to a pounding on the door of the hotel room. Still half-asleep, he struggled to open his eyes. The light of midmorning slanted in through the windows, formed long golden rectangles on the wine-colored carpet. Where was Joan? Neither in bed with him, nor in the room.

The pounding on the door, which had ceased momentarily, now began again. "Mr. Gunnarson? Mr. Gunnarson!"

Eric sat up. He was naked, as he had been upon going to sleep. Where was his robe? He could not see it, nor was it beneath the covers.

"Come in," he called.

The door opened slightly and one of the room clerks peered in. "Mornin', Mr. Gunnarson. Sorry for the noise, but you was asleep." He seemed expectant, as if waiting for something.

"Yes? What is it? What do you want?"

The clerk looked confused. "Hope there wasn't no mistake, sir," he said. "But Miz Gunnarson said you was ready to check out of the hotel."

That news brought Eric fully awake. *Miz* Gunnarson? Joan had claimed to be his wife, here at the hotel? Well, he had to admit, how else could she have gotten them registered? The Madison Hotel was one of the finest in the city, and guarded its reputation assiduously. But why would Joan have left the business of checking out to him? In fact, why had she gone? *Where* had she gone?

Eric experienced the sick flicker of premonition. Joan, angry at his refusal to accommodate her venal strategies, had maneuvered him into a situation that could do him little good: with no money to pay the hotel for this long stay, he would be thrown in debtor's prison for certain!

"I'll be ready in a few minutes," he told the waiting clerk. "Sorry for the inconvenience."

"That's all right, Mr. Gunnarson. I'll be expecting you at the front desk then?"

"Yes."

The clerk shut the door, and Eric got out of bed, went to the closet, and reached for one of the fine suits Joan had bought him to pimp with.

One suit hung in the closet. His old worker's rags. His new suits, all her gowns, were gone. Now he knew, too, where his dressing gown had gone: She had taken everything. She had taken everything, left him with the bill, and probably jail as well. He had certainly been right about her possession of a vengeful nature.

There was no hope in going down to the front desk and explaining the situation. Eric might have done such a thing once, a long time ago, in Norway, where the word of a freeholder was his bond, and better than money. He would have done it, too, in his early days in New York, not knowing any better. But he knew better now, or, if not "better," in the sense of *good,* then in the sense of wisdom, however coarse. Desperation does not ennoble.

His old clothes itched when he donned them, and he could not help but recall with regret the soft sleekness of the suits and dressing gown Joan had given, then taken. But to his surprise he found in the pocket of his old jacket the forty-five cents he had had on that March morning he'd met Joan, gone to the docks, tried to save the Negro. All that seemed a world away, now, but yet he was in the same clothes, no further ahead than he had been. *Except,* he told himself, *you have your health back.*

He left the room, walked down the thickly carpeted stairway—Joan had really chosen an expensive hotel—down three flights of wide, carpeted stairs. Descending toward the lobby, he saw a vast marble floor, lights, chandeliers, men and women dressed in stunning clothes.

WILD WIND WESTWARD

The aroma of good cigars drifted in the air, and the animated chatter of rich, satisfied people tinkled and echoed in the vaulting chamber. And there was Eric, a penniless, ragged workman on some errand among these people. He embarrassed them. They turned away from him, and went on with their conversations, conversations about plays, parties, travel, people they knew.

The clerks at the front desk, and even the bellboys, turned away from Eric. They, who were not far removed from his own financial plight, nevertheless saw his rags and decided they, too, were a part of the rich world discussed and enjoyed by guests in the hotel lobby.

Then Eric was on the street. Free, anyway. He went first to the harbor. The *Valkyrie* was due any day. He paid ten cents for a loaf of bread and a chunk of Thuringer, drank water from a public fountain, waited, paid a nickel for a bunk in a waterfront hostel. From its window, at twilight, he watched a group of recruits form up and march aboard a ship. Future members of the Union army. They were young and scared and thin and poor. Most of all poor. Their bodies had been bought. He thought of Sam Lapin and his son, who wanted to buy his body. No deal. Kristin would come, and would go with him. They would go west, and find land. In only a day, two days more . . .

What would Gustav Rolfson do?

It did not matter. Nothing mattered but Kristin, and soon she would be here.

But then Eric remembered Joan's taunt: What *would* Kristin see when she left the *Valkyrie* and came down the gangway, onto American earth?

"Well, sir," said Captain Sonntag, wiping his mouth fastidiously, putting down his napkin, and lighting an afterbreakfast cheroot, "we'll reach New York by midafternoon. Pleased about that, eh, Mr. Rolfson? And I know your wife will be. I've seen her watching at the rail for days now."

Sonntag blew fat donuts of smoke, through which he grinned at the Rolfsons, his *premier* passengers, who always

Vanessa Royall

sat with him at the captain's table. All Scandinavia knew of the vast capital loan Gustav had gotten from that Englishman, Soames. A great number of Norwegians, led by patriarchal Adolphus, awaited further news of Gustav's splendid forthcoming triumphs in America. Gustav's complexion tended to be pale in the morning, setting the scar in stark relief, like a newly gouged canyon on the surface of the moon. Moreover, he had not spent much time on deck during the voyage, and had not the color of sun and wind that most of the passengers had acquired. He had spent the crossing mainly in the stateroom he shared with Kristin. Whatever one might say of Gustav, he could not be accused of failing to apply himself diligently to his mercantile enterprises. If anything, he was too steeped in them, to the exclusion of other enjoyments, save his continued, obsessive enjoyment of Kristin herself.

"I daresay my wife looks forward to making the acquaintance of the New York couturiers," Gustav told Captain Sonntag, a remark that, for him, was almost witty.

Kristin forced a smile. Fashion was the last thing on her mind. Difficulties and decisions faced her, no matter what the new world held in store. Would Eric be there, waiting for her? If he was, how might she meet with him, what would his reaction be? How could she get away from Gustav? These things weighed on her mind. Indeed, *could* she get away from Gustav at all? She had sent her family a considerable amount of money during her married years, but by no means enough to insure their independence if, back in Sweden, old Adolphus seized their land and livelihood. And then what if Eric were *not* to be found? What if something had happened to him? It had been so long since she'd written him.

"Your thoughts this morning seem uncommonly grave for a beautiful woman," Captain Sonntag oozed.

"Yes," agreed Gustav, studying his wife. "Be that as it may, Captain, we must retire now and prepare for the landing."

They rose from the captain's table, Sonntag standing, too, as well as five other guests, three lesser businessmen

WILD WIND WESTWARD

and the wives of two of them, all of them somewhat in awe of both the captain and of Gustav Rolfson, rising titan of Norwegian capitalism. The wives were frankly envious of Kristin, being themselves more sturdy than lithe of carriage, but veiled their true sentiments with comments such as: "Isn't she a darling?" "She might show a bit more affection for her husband, though." "Yes, but do you think the American women will resent her?" "Oh, my goodness, I hope not."

In the stateroom Gustav turned to her. "I must ask a favor of you," he said, "as a woman and a wife."

"Yes, husband."

His face colored slightly with residual anger. He had ceased begging her to use his given name, but her refusal to do so continued to rankle. "When I begin to set up appointments with the important American bankers and businessmen, I would like you to keep your days free so that you might accompany me."

"In other words you wish me to play the part as I did with Lord Soames, charming bait for your trap. They should be looking at me, while you pick their minds for information and their pockets for—"

It was more than he could take. She vexed him, as always, and he bore the vexation because, in his own hard way, he was in love with her. But a woman had her place, and decorum must receive its due. So instinctively that Gustav was only slightly more aware of it than Kristin, he brought up his hand powerfully, in a wide hard swinging arc, and slapped her across the face with such force that her head snapped sideways. She spun across the stateroom, and fell upon the bed, too shocked to cry out. Kristin glared at him, her hand on her wounded cheek. Never had she hated him so much! Never had *he* been this angry.

"You are my wife," he told her, gritting his teeth, "and so you shall remain. I asked you, with all courtesy, to aid me in New York. I have neither the time nor patience to put up with any more of your cute or evasive rejoinders. You are going to play your part as a Rolfson, willingly and

Vanessa Royall

gracefully, or you are going to learn the hard way that my tolerance wears distinctly thin."

"If I no longer please you, husband," Kristin returned, gauging him, "put me aside. Divorce me."

He smiled, a hideous grimace. "That is what you think you would like, is it? Oh, no. Oh, no. Don't you worry. You will come to love me and the wealth I shall acquire. You will savor it dearly, believe me. You will, and when you do, then I will know your heart is finally mine."

Judiciously she held her tongue. Gustav advanced, put his hands on her shoulders, forced her backward upon the great stateroom bed, straddled her, and glared down into her eyes. "And don't have any romantic dreams about your long-lost mountaineer lover. My friends in the consulate tell me he's dropped utterly out of sight. He's probably dead by now."

Kristin understood. Eric was, at base, at least partially the cause of Gustav's anger this morning. She did not believe what he was telling her, of course. Eric would be vibrantly alive, would he not? And prosperous. Prosperous enough for the two of them to go off together. Anyway, what did it matter? Certainly prosperity mattered not at all to her. She had loved him when he had but a stone house and a few stray coins stashed behind a loose chimney brick.

Now she sensed that Gustav was about to rip off her clothes and take her, to show her again that she belonged to him, that he would do what he wished with her. But she could not bear him inside her, on top of her, just now. Besides which, her protection against pregnancy was not in place. She must never have his child, never ever. His hold over her, already powerful, would be virtually indissoluble with a child involved.

"Please, husband," she said imploringly. "I am sorry. Take me now and pleasure me. I need it now to make me feel whole again."

Gustav heard that, and grinned meanly. "So," he said. "At last you beg. Well, get this straight. I shall have you when and where I want, but not now. Your punishment

218

for impertinence to me is that you must suffer your need unfulfilled."

He got off her, off the bed, and stood looking down at her. His expression was one of victory, almost as if he had taken her and, finally, worked moans of passion from her throat.

"Oh, husband, please! Please!"

But Gustav was adamant, and he refused to yield.

New York stunned Kristin, first by its size, then by its quality of rough, vibrant, almost savage intensity. Everywhere was movement: on the ships, the docks, up and down the streets. Everywhere was shouting and yelling and apparent chaos. Yet the *Valkyrie* glided swiftly and smoothly to the pier, and Kristin stood at the railing. The April day was warm with sunlight, clean with wind. New York, the new world, America itself, lay waiting at her feet. Her heart quickened, in wonderment and expectation, as she studied the scene along the harbor, tried to pick out faces of individuals. *Eric has been here,* she knew. *Perhaps he is here even now.*

While Kristin stood on the *Valkyrie*'s glossy oaken deck, waiting for the gangway to be lowered, Eric raced toward the harbor. Three days had gone by since his ignominious departure from the hotel, and he had turned the three days to good use. Knowing there was no chance of getting a workingman's job, he had instead decided to use a skill many others did not possess: he'd called on boardinghouses, visited tenements, met incoming ships. "Letters," he'd cried. "I can write letters in English and Norwegian. Letters to relatives, employers, government officials. Letters. I'll write letters for you."

There had been some customers, and as Eric rushed down to the pier to meet the *Valkyrie*, his old clothes were cleaned and pressed, patched, too. In one jacket pocket he had fourteen dollars and thirty-five cents, enough for train fare for two out of New York and into the vicinity of

Vanessa Royall

Harrisburg, Pennsylvania. He had never been there, but many had told him that the land was rich in Pennsylvania. In the other pocket of his jacket Eric carried several sheets of rude tablet paper, upon which he had copied—from information garnered at the New York Public Library—what one had to do in order to acquire a homestead. The day was bright; he felt fine, save for a subliminal quaver of nervousness. He could not forget Joan's words: *"Tell me, what will your beloved think when she comes down the gangway and sees* you?"

He passed down along the docks, and saw the *Valkyrie* shimmering there, riding the blue-green water like a lazy lover on the mount, moving gently up and down as dock workers tied her to the pier. He could imagine the gleam and power of her engines, the gloss of her appointments, the comfort of her staterooms. Kristin had crossed the Atlantic in *that*—Eric had by now discounted any thought that his darling would not be aboard the vessel—and he himself had come over, laden with coal dust and grime, in the bowels of the *Anandale*.

Then he saw her at the railing, Kristin, his own. She was wearing a dress of pale blue, with ruffles of gleaming white at collar and cuffs. The dress showed her figure, and the color enhanced the golden tone of her skin, the glossy darker gold of her hair as it shifted in the easy wind. She was looking down at the docks. Trying to find him? Eric did not know why, just then, but he stepped behind a wharf piling. He felt strange. Then he knew why. He felt ashamed. He cursed himself for it. In the old country, he had, in terms of actual possessions, been poor. But that had never bothered him, because it had not mattered. What had one needed there but land and one's name? *Eric Starbane, what has happened to you?* he asked himself. He felt powerless; he felt unmanned; he felt poor.

And there on the *Valkyrie* was Kristin, born to be a princess, and finally in her state. How could he presume to take her away from such heights, he who knew so well how cold the world could be?

At that moment a man came up to Kristin and stood

beside her. Casually he put his arm around her waist, and spoke to her. She nodded, but did not look at him. The man wore a coat that, even at this distance, spoke of money. When he lifted his head to look out across New York Eric observed, faintly but readily distinguishable, the diagonal manner in which his features were marred. Rolfson. Then, as casually as he had draped his arm about Kristin's waist, as possessively as he had let his hand rest upon the swell of her hip, Rolfson now withdrew, and walked away to see about his business.

Eric's chest flooded with pain, and his mind fought assaults of uncertainty. He had to believe Kristin wanted *him*, and at some deep point in his soul he knew that she did. But he was deeply anguished with the knowledge that Kristin would never suffer want or need or hunger if she remained with Rolfson. All of Eric's bright hopes fell away from him, dropped down like a glass vase, and shattered on the ground. Except that the pieces flying away were not glass but dream. The fourteen dollars and thirty-five cents laughed in his pocket, mocking him. The homestead information within his other patched pocket, once so bright, seemed now but a shard of disaster, reminder of something valuable, wrecked through stupidity, and discarded.

"I've had a man order us up a carriage, the finest in New York," Kristin heard Gustav tell her. "I've arranged with Sonntag that we should disembark first. The other passengers will be held back for a time. There are newspaper reporters waiting. I shall bestow upon them a few words, and invite them to a reception at our hotel on the morrow. We'll be staying at a place called the Madison. I am told it is quite excellent, and much frequented by people of good standing."

"Yes, husband."

It was with relief that Kristin felt his arm leave her waist, and sensed his withdrawal. Then she was free again, alone with her thoughts. Oh, yes, it was passing fair to wear fine clothes and ride great ships. But in the end, what was it? It was nothing. It was nothing because she was not happy, and could never be happy, with Gustav Rolfson. All of it was hollowness and ashes. All she wanted was Eric, and a simple life of work and love, children, happiness, and growing old together. That was all she needed. The greatness, the wealth, and all of the accoutrements of power, seemed to her to be sham and illusion and façade, from the manner in which the commoner Rolfsons sought to portray themselves as princes of a new economic order, to the blatant perversions in the life of much-respected Soames, and even to the pecking order apparent in the line of vehicles on the dock below.

First in line was a big, glittering high-wheeled affair—Gustav's, no doubt—drawn by four fine thoroughbreds. Half a dozen other carriages stood behind it, reasonably decent in appearance, and hitched to healthy horses. Then came the rest: poor, dirty hacks with tattered canvas awnings, wheels on which spokes had broken and been tied or wired back together. Plug horses pulled these, or swaybacked nags displaying ribcages and festering sores where raw harnesses had worn through hide. As Kristin watched, another fine carriage drew up onto the pier, and stopped some distance away from the other vehicles. Kristin could see the shining blond hair of a woman inside, a woman alone. Perhaps she is here to meet some elegant man on the *Valkyrie*, Kristin thought. If so, that passenger had certainly kept his identity secret from Kristin during the voyage. The only man on board who was at all interesting had been Captain Sonntag, and that owed less to character than to the experience of his many voyages. All of which, due to innumerable times at table, Kristin knew by heart.

Then, just as the gangway was being lowered, she saw Eric!

Almost at the same moment, even while her heart prepared to pound in joy and triumph, she realized that something, some nameless, sinister, unexpected thing, was terribly awry.

Why did he appear to be concealing himself? No, he *was* concealing himself!

Her skin grew instantly cold, and fine hairs quivered at

the back of her neck. She stood for the first time face to face with something terrible in this new world, and she did not know what it was. But she knew it was there, all right, out there in that mighty city, or over there, beyond, in the green rolling fields of America. It had to be there, that terrible something, because what else, other than an horrific trackless entity, would cause Eric Starbane to conceal himself behind a wharf piling?

"We're going ashore now," Gustav said, coming up behind her and taking her elbow. He guided her toward the gangway. "All you have to do is smile, and if you show a little ankle while getting into our carriage, that wouldn't hurt."

Kristin lost sight of Eric. And she wondered that Gustav seemed not to sense the terror swarming in this new land.

Or perhaps he already knew it.

Or perhaps he was its brother.

Whatever happened between them, or afterward, Eric knew he must speak to Kristin. But, at first, he despaired of doing so. There were too many people around, and when Gustav and Kristin left the ship first and moved toward the carriage, Eric almost gave up. All he would be able to do was hail a hack, spend a portion of his fourteen dollar fortune, and follow them to their destination. But then Kristin climbed into the carriage, while Gustav remained on the dock to talk to a number of men who flocked around him. Eric saw the sheets of paper and the scribbling pencils. Reporters. Gustav and the reporters stood between the *Valkyrie* and the carriage.

Eric advanced up the pier, toward the opposite side of Kristin's carriage. He did not notice, yet, an equally expensive vehicle drawn up parallel to the first, so that the two carriages were no more than five yards apart.

After climbing inside, Kristin's first thought was to sit next to the door, and try to see if she could locate Eric again. She thought she could see the piling at which he'd been earlier, but now she was not sure. All the pilings looked alike; they all *were* alike.

Vanessa Royall

"Sir, I don't mean to be rude," she heard one reporter asking Gustav, "but how did you come by that scar?"

"Not rude at all," boomed Gustav, in a hearty, open-handed manner he seemed to have devised for dealing with Americans. "I acquired it during a duel, in my university days."

The reporters scribbled furiously; duels were very European, hence fashionable, even noble.

"If you think this is awesome, you ought to see my opponent's scars!" exclaimed Gustav, with relish. The reporters laughed. This Norwegian tycoon would make good copy.

"God rest my late opponent's soul," Gustav added.

The reporters laughed some more. Foreign nobility were always so *distinguished*. The newspapermen, who spent considerable time and creative power mocking Abraham Lincoln for his homespun manner and physical ungainliness, looked at Gustav Rolfson and saw not the red cunning acquisitive eyes above that broad wolf's nose, but rather an intelligent and charming mercantile ambassador, whose acquaintance would be useful to cultivate.

Because the day was warm and clement, the isinglass shade on the door of the Rolfson carriage had been rolled up, so that when Kristin looked out to try and find Eric, she had a clear view of the waterfront. She let her eyes move from piling to piling, looking.

But there he was, approaching her, no more than a few yards away! She had not expected him to appear so suddenly. She had not expected to see him in the clothes he was wearing, which had been unnoticeable at a distance. But she did not care about that. It was Eric! He was here! But he looked so wan and pale.

Eric saw her face, framed in the carriage window. He saw love there, love as great as his own for her. And he saw something else as well, which was actually surprise, but which, in his depressed condition, he misread as pity.

There would be but a few moments to exchange words, Kristin realized, perhaps the most important words of her life. Gustav was regaling his court with prognostications

WILD WIND WESTWARD

of his future in America; he would be the first—hence greatest—oil baron in the whole wide world.

Then Eric stood by the carriage.

They spent one moment looking at each other. Kristin wanted to leap from the carriage into Eric's arms; Eric wanted to erase from the world all but the two of them.

"Kristin, my darling—"

"I love you."

"I don't know—"

"We will be at the Madison Hotel." She did not know why Eric winced. "Come there tomorrow morning."

Did she not see how he was dressed? Did she not know he couldn't enter a place like that?

"I am prepared to leave him," she was saying.

"But I have *nothing!*" Eric hissed urgently, hoping to make her see, understand.

Kristin spent a moment turning that over in her mind. She seemed confused to the depths of her being. "What does that *matter?*" she asked, genuinely puzzled.

"That will be all," Gustav boomed to the sycophantic reporters, on the other side of the carriage. The horses pranced, eager to be off. The driver, attired elegantly, as befit the owner of a first-class rig, clucked to soothe them a moment more.

"Thank you, sir," the scribes said, in unison. "I wish you every success America has to offer," added one of them fervently. It was Horace Greeley, noted New York journalist and dyed-in-the-wool abolitionist. "Remember, go west. The place to go is west. That's where the future is."

"I shall give that advice considerable thought," responded Gustav, heavily judicious.

"The Madison Hotel," Kristin said again. She was worried now. Eric did not seem in good spirits, and he looked worn down. All the more reason for her to be with him. Tomorrow he would come to her, and somehow everything would work out.

Eric had time to say, "I love you," before Gustav opened the opposite door and jumped into the carriage. He was too delighted with his fine reception and tremendous interview to catch more than a fleeting flash of some man's head as it disappeared from the open window on the other side of the vehicle.

"Who was that?" he asked, without interest. "Some American tramp looking for a handout? You must be careful here, my dear, not to mix with the peasants. These Americans regard us as nobility, you know, and we must set a proper example."

"Yes, husband," Kristin said. *Nobility!* she thought.

The driver cracked his whip and the carriage wheeled smoothly away from the ship.

III

Eric waited in the shadow of a dock warehouse until the carriage was out of sight, then trudged disconsolately uptown. He had no plans. He would have to find a place for the night. He needed money. He ought to have decent clothes if he went to see Kristin in the morning. *If* he went to see her. He *had* to see her. But he remembered that strange look on her face, that he had interpreted as pity. Something in him froze. A ball of ice formed deep inside him, a cold implacable entity he had never known before. Eric had already changed, but he did not know it yet.

He cut crosstown, then walked north on Madison Avenue for a time, reflecting upon Gustav Rolfson's interview with the fawning newspapermen. He did not even notice the elegant shops and great mansions, so deep was his bitter concentration. The same Gustav Rolfson upon whose countenance he had etched what ought to have been a scar of shame for all the world to see was being feted and celebrated on his first day in America. Whereas Eric, who had worked and struggled here for years, slouched aimlessly uptown, his once warm heart turning hard and cold.

Passing a series of expensive shops, he collided with a silk-hatted gentleman emerging from the establishment of Saul Leffert, tailor. The man was crossing from Leffert's doorway to his buggy, waiting at curbside, his head turned away to bid the tailor good-bye. He did not see Eric approach, nor was Eric attentive. The impact was sudden and sharp. Eric staggered, the gentleman was knocked off balance, and his stylish hat fell to the walk, rolling into a pile of horse manure in the gutter. He let out a cry of anguish.

Eric prepared to apologize—there was nothing else he could do—but Leffert, the tailor, made a bad situation worse. A small, lean, flinty man, he stepped onto the sidewalk and began brushing the gentleman's coat energetically.

"Mr. Baines," he bleated, "Mr. Baines, I'm so sorry. It is the fault of this ignorant dolt. You," he ordered Eric, "fetch that hat and clean it at once."

Eric, who might just yesterday have done exactly that, refused. Surprising even himself for a moment, he stood his ground, glared down at the diminutive tailor, and said, "I am no ignorant dolt."

"It was an accident . . ." Baines began, sensing trouble he had not yet consciously identified.

"Pick up that hat, you ignorant dolt," Leffert ordered, shouting now, "or I'll have the police here to drag you in that gutter before I'm through!"

"Come now," managed Mr. Baines.

Eric grabbed Leffert by the collar, lifted him, and slammed him against the wall of his shop. The tailor's eyes popped open in fear.

"You call me *sir*!" he told the tailor.

"Please . . ." Baines said.

Leffert gulped, his face coloring deeply.

"*Sir!*" said Eric, not in a loud voice, not loud at all. But there was something in it. . . .

"Police?" Baines bleated tentatively.

"Say it or I'll ram your skull right though these bricks," Eric advised the tailor calmly.

"Sir," Leffert gasped.

"Sir, what?"

"Please pick up the hat, sir?"

"Police!" called Baines, more determinedly now, backing away from Eric. Passersby were gathering now, asking one another what was happening.

"Please pick up the hat, *sir*," repeated Eric. And, with that, he carried Leffert across the walk, set him down on his feet next to the soiled hat. "Pick it up," he ordered.

Shakily, the tailor did so.

"Now put it on."

"Sir," pleaded Baines, "that is enough. The man meant no harm. You have gone too far."

Poor unfortunate Leffert did not know it, but at that moment he was the forger, Thorvaldsen; he was the crooked judge, Amundsen; he was Rolfson, father and son; he was Kuffel and Dubin of the *Anandale*, Mick and Joan Leeds. He was everyone who had conspired to harry and belittle and ill-use Eric Gunnarson, born Starbane.

"Put on the hat," Eric said again, in that utterly calm, unsettling tone.

Leffert hesitated, but Eric was through waiting. He had changed. He had turned a corner in life, a corner he had not foreseen, and of which, even now, he was only partially aware. He took the manure-spattered hat from Leffert's trembling hands, grabbed it by the wide brim, and pulled it down over the little tailor's eyes and ears.

The gathering crowd gasped, some in outrage, others in frank amazement.

"That will teach you to call someone an ignorant dolt," he said.

"Police!" yelled Baines, at the top of his lungs. He feared Eric would come for him next.

But Eric simply pushed through the crowd, and went his way, astonished at himself at first, then astonished at how he felt. He felt *good*.

In that frame of mind, he felt a measure of optimism return, and he began to make plans. First, food. The April afternoon was fair and clear. He had little money, and did not want to spend it just yet, so he walked over to Turtle Bay, on the east side of Manhattan Island. He found a discarded fishing line, tied it to a sapling, borrowed a hook from an old man fishing along the bank.

"They's bitin' pretty good," the codger reckoned, showing Eric a dozen good-sized perch laid out on the grass beside him. "You want some bait? Here, I got some caterpillars. Been doin' right good with caterpillars."

Eric baited his hook, cast the line, and sat down on the bank. There are some things I'm going to have to take, he reflected, not thinking at all of fish, but I'll only take what I must. Only what I need to survive.

Two hours of patience yielded ten perch. He gutted and cleaned them, built a small fire, and cooked them on a sheet of boilerplate abandoned along the river. He invited the old man to use the fire, and the other accepted.

"What's your trade?" the man asked Eric, with laconic curiosity.

"I don't know yet. So far I've farmed, worked on a ship, and driven a team of delivery horses. I was on the docks lately, but hard times have come."

The other snorted, chewing fish. "There's always hard times," he allowed. "You just got to survive 'em."

"So I intend," agreed Eric. "So I intend."

After eating he rested by the river until the sun began to fall, the air to grow chill. Then he walked back to Madison Avenue and down Madison until he reached Leffert's tailor shop, closed and locked now, the drama of the day long over. The front door was securely bolted. In the window, on a clothier's dummy, was one of Leffert's wares: a morning coat of the latest style, narrow lapels buttoned high, framing a starkly white shirt with uppointed collar, and a rich red silk cravat.

That will do, Eric thought.

He went on down to the end of the block, turned the corner, entered an alley, and followed it to the rear of the tailor shop. The door there was bolted, too, but no one was about. Finding a chunk of paving stone next to the building, he lifted it, took aim, and delivered a powerful smash on one of the door's two hinges. Another blow, and the hinge gave way. Leffert, the ignorant dolt! His door was hinged with nails, not screws. Two more blows dislodged the second hinge, and Eric stepped inside the shop. It smelled dry and dusty, and it was very dark. Waning light from the partially open doorway showed a lamp and several candles standing on a work table. Eric lit the

WILD WIND WESTWARD

lamp. Then, using the paving stone, he made haste to pound the nails back into the blasted hinges. In daylight the damage would be obvious, but he planned to be gone by daylight.

With the door shut and secure, he was alone in the shop. There were two rooms, workroom in the rear, showroom in front, off the street entrance. Dozens of coats and trousers in various stages of completion littered the workroom, but on racks in the showroom were garments of elegant cut, of all sizes and styles, waiting to be claimed by the rich of New York. Eric removed the morning coat from the clothier's dummy in the window and tried it on. A bit tight in the shoulders, but otherwise excellent. He took the shirt and cravat too, replacing these items with others from the racks. Further perusal yielded cape, trousers, and hat. He retreated to the back room, closing the curtain between the two parts of the shop, making sure that no lamplight shone out into the front of the store, where a passing policeman might see it through the window. Then he tried on the clothes in front of a big workroom mirror. Splendid. He had never looked so good. His ragged boots were the only items that would give away his current impoverished state in life, but these new fashionable long trousers almost obcured that fact. Satisfied, he took off the outfit, donned his regular clothes, and dropped into contented sleep on a pile of woolens and flannels, thinking of Kristin.

On the street in the morning, with his fine clothes and fourteen dollars and thirty-five cents in his pocket, Eric felt like a millionaire. He had to spend a dollar and fifteen cents on breakfast in a hotel, however, because patronizing a vendor or a café would have appeared unseemly for a man of his obvious high station in life. He tipped the waiter a dime, and found the Lexington Livery. There he inquired about the rental of a horse, closed carriage, and driver for the morning.

"I will wish to drive about the city," he said, "and

show a visitor the sights. After that, I will want to be taken to Pennsylvania Station. I must catch a train to Pennsylvania."

"That will be four dollars for the morning, sir, payable in advance."

"Certainly," said Eric grandly, peeling off greenbacks even as his heart sank. Now he had less than train fare for himself and Kristin. Possibly Kristin would have money of her own. She would have to. If not . . . if not, he would think of something. The thought of seeing Kristin, of holding her in his arms again, rendered absurd petty considerations of dollars and cents.

He chose a high, rust-colored carriage, with polished spokes on its wheels, and rolled curtains to draw down over the windows. Horses were hitched to the vehicle, and a driver, young and yawning, climbed down from the loft where he had been sleeping.

"Hotel Madison, if you please," ordered Eric.

The driver bounded up into his seat behind the horses, and guided them out into the bustle of morning traffic.

Now Eric considered his next move. It would be unwise to enter the hotel himself, after yesterday's humiliating flight. He might send the driver to the desk with a message for Kristin, but what if Gustav was with her when the message was delivered? He had still not decided upon a course of action when the carriage pulled up in front of the hotel. Then he did not have to decide, because God was with him.

In front of the hotel, ready to enter a carriage of his own, was Gustav Rolfson, off to make calls on bankers and businessmen, launching his adventure in America.

"Go to the desk," Eric ordered the driver, "and have Mrs. Rolfson summoned, please."

"Yessir. And who shall I say—?"

"Mr. Sonnendahl. Ford Sonnendahl."

"Yessir, Mr. Sonnendahl."

The driver went on his errand. Eric waited in the carriage. And time grinned, working its vexing magic. He waited a minute, two. Hours passed in his heart, days. The driver did not return. What had happened? Eric hesitated to leave the carriage, lest he be recognized by hotel personnel, ruining everything. Still Kristin did not come. It seemed Eric had waited for a longer time than it had taken to cross the Atlantic in the wallowing *Anandale*.

The young driver came out of the hotel, sauntered toward his rig.

"I give 'em the message at the desk, sir."

"It took this long?"

"Sorry, they was pretty busy."

And then Kristin appeared in the hotel doorway, lovely as a vision. She wore a long blue dress, trimmed with white piping, and a small cape, also blue and white, clasped at her throat with a golden chain. She looked about, and in her expression he saw a tentative hope that dared not quite believe.

He gestured from the carriage window, and his wave caught her eye. She crossed the distance in the space of a heartbeat, and as she came to him, he knew she brought with her the past and future, both.

"Darling."

"Oh, it is you!"

"I can't—"

"No, wait. Driver, be off. Go up the river to Spuyten Duyvil, and don't stop until you get there."

"Yessir."

The carriage began to move. Eric untied the knots by which the rolled-up window curtains were fastened, and they curled down softly, shutting out the street, the rush, the light. The cab was shut away from earth, a world unto itself, cushions deep and soft, the light itself conspiratorial, tender and gloomy and dusky red.

"Darling . . ." Kristin began again.

"No, don't say a word. Not yet."

He took her and held her to him for a long, long time, not even kissing her yet, just holding her, as if to convince the both of them that they were together at last. Time turned another face now, smiling benignly, and years fell away like floss, like thistledown in wind. Kristin was as she had been the first time they'd made love on the grass above Sonnendahl Fjord, and Eric's suffering and hardship melted away in this mystical embrace.

Finally, they drew apart.

"Yesterday, when I saw you on the docks," Kristin said, "you seemed so——"

"That was yesterday. Something has changed me. Your arrival," he said. "Now I feel as once I was."

Then, again, they held each other, hungrily, ecstatically. There in the jouncing carriage, moving slowly northward along the river road to Manhattan's tip, Eric peeled from her the fine furbelowed gown Gustav had bought, and beheld after so long a time her golden body which so bewitched and haunted him. His fine clothes, too, he removed, and then wrapped the great cape around them both. "Here," he sighed, breathlessly, "face me, like this, and, yes, come down upon me . . . so. . . ."

And together they gasped in ecstasy and delight, as they were joined in body after so long a time. She felt him all the way inside, every nerve alive and throbbing; to him, her body had the soft, wet embrace of a primordial memory, offering, by a passage of infinite delight, the gorgeous rush of creation itself. But not yet. But not yet. All they had to do was cling to each other, hold onto each other, kiss. The jouncing and rolling of the carriage moved them, moved them with a conspiracy of its own, a pact of pleasure, and there was nothing and no one to put an end to it.

"Oh, this is too sweet, too slow," cried Kristin, writhing upon him. "I cannot wait, I must——"

"No, no." He calmed her, holding her tightly so she could not wriggle or move. "There is no rush, none at all. For after this time, there will be another, and after that another still."

Kristin felt him inside her, growing and growing, as if he would burst, or she would. And she felt within her too the spark of old magic, that she had never known or even sought with Gustav, but which she had known with Eric in lost Lesja. The immense fire of pleasure began to burn for her, consuming her rational mind, living tongues of fire flicking over her body, until most of her body was lost to her, too, all of her body save where love was, and from there the fire came burning, fierce and hard. His eyes closed, Eric saw behind his lids the shifting colors of passion, dancing patterns of light, amber and red and blue and gorgeous violet, soft and hot. From a place so deep within himself it must be trackless, sourceless, he felt rising the very splendor of his strength and need, and cried out that it was to be. Kristin's very mind had flown to a far place now, and she did not care. The cells of her body told her now now *now* was the time, and she twisted and rose in his embrace, upon him, twisted and fell, tossing about as if in the grip of an awful wonder. Their communion of pleasure began and throbbed again and again, sweet and divine. Never had they felt such glorious, enchanting surges, and far back in Eric's mind was a dark flash of sadness that he had ever accepted the profane favors of Joan Leeds. Was this delight with Kristin not worth waiting for, no matter if it took all time to have and hold again? Yes, it was, and never would he weaken in the future.

Then he was gasping, and Kristin, still upon him, sobbed with joy in the aftermath of pleasure. So ardent had they been, so stricken with the needs of their bodies, that now they were wet with sweet perspiration, and he wrapped the cape more closely about them still.

"If I had to wait all those months for this pleasure," Kristin said, "then maybe it was worth it after all."

"We are together now. And we shall be from now on. I have a plan. Here in America, one might buy good land for very little. This very afternoon, we shall take a train west, to Pennsylvania, and I will hire out there until I have enough to buy a farm . . . if that is all right with you?"

"Darling, anything is all right, so long as we are together."

"But there is only one problem right now. I don't have quite enough for the train fare. I did, but I had to hire this rig, and—"

Vanessa Royall

"Do not think about it for another moment. Save the time to love me again. We shall stop at the hotel before taking the train. I will take money. We have much with us, some in the suite, and some locked in the hotel safe. You will not have to work in Pennsylvania either, not for money to buy the land. I will take enough to buy the land."

"Is that not dangerous?"

"No, it is my money as well as Gustav's. I have certainly earned it."

And so, with their future stretching before them like a golden meadow, the lovers partook of each other again.

At length, the coach halted, and the driver called down, "Spuyden Duyvil, sir, just as you wished. Care to step out and have a look."

"No," Gustav answered. "Just turn around and drive back to the city. The view is fine from where we are."

Baffled, the young driver clucked to the horses and slapped their rumps with the reins. Mr. Ford Sonnendahl was certainly a man of changeable mind.

The carriage drew to a halt in front of the Madison Hotel in the roaring bustle of a New York noon. The late-April day was warm and perfect, and the streets were jammed with a happy throng, moving hither and thither. The dark cloaks of winter had been put aside, and bright-colored dresses and coats made a gay scene. Even a newshawk in front of the hotel added his positive note to the day: "General Grant and the Union army advance in Mississippi," he cried. "Read all about it. Union army floats downriver past the Vicksburg fortress in the dark of night."

"Oh, darling," said Kristin, just as she was to alight from the coach and enter the hotel to fetch the money, "will this terrible war affect us?"

"Not at all," Eric assured her lovingly. "Mississippi is far to the south. There will never be any battles as far north as Pennsylvania."

"It is high time things began to go our way."

"And they have."

Kristin walked across the short distance from curbside

to hotel, waved briefly to Eric, and entered. He climbed down from the coach, and stood on the street, enjoying the warm feel of the sun.

"Just a jaunt over to Pennsylvania Station," he told the driver, "and then—"

He meant to say, ". . . and then you can take the carriage back to the livery . . ." but he didn't, because at that moment another glittering coach drew up, and Gustav Rolfson leaped exuberantly out of it. The two men were no more than fifteen feet apart.

Gustav had had a good morning at the Morgan Bank, had already made plans to go west to see the new oil fields. He was feeling prosperous and indomitable. Spying the expensive rust-colored carriage, he assumed at once that its owner must be of high class, both socially and in the mercantile sense. He doffed his hat in comradeship and respect, smiling. There was no way Eric could refuse to return the salute without giving offense, and, quite possibly, causing trouble. But if he did lift his hat, and remove from his face the shadow made by the hatbrim, there was little doubt that Rolfson would recognize him. Further, Kristin would be coming out of the hotel at any moment.

Eric thought fast. He doffed his hat, simultaneously bowing slightly, satisfying protocol for the moment, but showing Rolfson not his face but his head. When he recovered from the bow, he was safe again within the shadow of the hatbrim.

Rolfson turned toward the hotel entrance.

Kristin came flying out of the hotel, gloriously happy. "Eric!" she cried, her eyes on him alone, "Eric, I have it. Now let's—"

"You have *what*?" Rolfson demanded, grabbing her arm and yanking her to a halt.

She turned to him, speechless with surprise.

"Eric?" Rolfson wondered, aloud. He turned from his startled wife to the man near the rust-colored carriage.

"Take your hands off her," threatened Eric, stepping forward.

Rolfson could not see the face clearly, but he recognized

the voice and stride immediately. He felt, not with his ruined face but with his vengeful soul beneath, the cut of the riding whip, dropped Kristin's arm, and leaped forward to do battle again with this lowly, despicable upstart.

Eric's mind was pure and cold and clear. It did not matter that this was a busy street in a great city. He was ready for the moment. He would have been ready for this moment had it taken place in the mountains of Norway, in a back-alley bar, on the trackless prairies of North America. When the time comes to demand recompense, you demand. When the time comes to pay, you pay.

Gustav Rolfson was about to pay.

He forgot that arrogance alone is not sufficient armor, and came toward Eric before his fists were raised.

"Eric!" Kristin cried.

Out of the hotel strode the clerk who, on the previous day, had come to the room to present Eric with the bill.

Down the street, trying to walk off a burden of raw anger due to a break-in at his shop, came tailor Leffert.

Gustav, unready, took a wild, high swing, and knocked off Eric's hat.

"Gunnarson!" cried the clerk.

"You!" howled Leffert, recognizing not only his handcrafted suit of clothes but the man in them as well.

"Swine!" grunted Rolfson.

Eric did not spend his energy in words. Braced and balanced, he shot a straight right fist to the middle of Rolfson's face, smashing and widening further that vulpine nose. Rolfson, thrown backward by the force of the blow, was unconscious even before he came to rest against the hotel's foundation.

"Kristin, let's go," said Eric, stretching his hand out toward her.

She came to him, and he swung her into the carriage.

"Pennsylvania Station!" he ordered the driver, getting into the coach himself.

"That man's a thief!" Leffert shouted.

"Eric, what—?" asked Kristin, disbelieving and bewildered. In her eyes Eric saw a glimmer of heartbreak.

WILD WIND WESTWARD

Somehow, because of things she did not understand—because of rash things *he* had done—their dream was not going to be.

Traffic was heavy, and the driver was having difficulty getting his team away from the curb.

"That man in the red buggy! He stole my clothes!" Leffert shrieked, even as he dashed toward the horses. The hotel clerk had the same idea. He, too, ran forward, and grabbed the horses by their bridles. The perplexed driver could only shout at them, wondering what was going on.

"Police!" someone shouted.

Gustav Rolfson came woozily to life, and propped himself on an arm.

"That blond man," he moaned, "get that blond man. He's a murderer."

"Oh, my God . . ." Kristin said, near tears.

"God damn," said Eric.

"What shall we do?"

"I've got to get out of here." He remembered how he had had to flee once before, leaving Kristin in the stream bed, her leg broken, and men closing in. Now, here on the other side of the world, much the same thing was happening. "I've got to get out of here. I can't explain now, but if I'm captured, it's the end of everything. I'll send for you, all right?"

"Police. A murderer!"

"That man in the buggy stole my clothes!"

"Mr. Sonnendahl, what should I do?" the poor young driver wanted to know.

"I'm going to a city called Harrisburg. It's in Pennsylvania," Eric told his beloved. "I'll send for you from there." He kissed her, no more than a touch on the lips. There was no more time.

"Kristin, get out of there," muttered Gustav, staggering toward the coach.

Eric opened the door on the street side of the coach, and leaped into the roadway. He startled a team of horses drawing a supply wagon. The horses reared. Their driver cursed. Another team, coming from the opposite direction,

Vanessa Royall

veered to the side, frightened and confused by the man in the cape who dashed across the street in front of them. For a moment the whole area in front of the Madison Hotel was in a state of chaos, a condition exacerbated when Gustav opened the carriage door and pulled Kristin out onto the sidewalk, lifting his hand as if to strike her. But the young driver, beside himself now with anger and confusion, jumped down from his seat, onto Rolfson's wide back, and drove him to the ground.

Two policemen rushed up, their clubs ready for action. Out of the subsequent babble they were able to deduce that a dangerous man had fled the scene. But by the time they realized it, there was no chance to give pursuit.

"He said he was going to the railroad station," the driver said, helpfully.

Now I can't leave New York by rail, Eric thought. A block from the hotel he had slowed to a walk. People paid him no notice, rushing past to see what the fuss at the Madison was all about. Knowing that the railroad station would be watched by the police, aware that all his plans had once again gone awry, he felt disgusted and ill. Was it more painful never to have experienced heaven at all? Or to have held it and lost it? He was thinking of Kristin. The answer was easy. It was more painful to have held her and lost her. The pain was brutal, almost incapacitating.

But he would not give way to it. He would not become weak again, awaiting the blow of whosoever chose to deliver it. His plight had become critical. He had to get out of New York. But if the police were looking for him—and he would be a fool to assume they were not—getting out of the city would be difficult indeed.

Yet there was one way.

He made his way down to the docks, sought out Sam Lapin's office, and announced his decision.

"Well, Eric my boy. I knew you'd find the wit to make the right decision. Bobby will be so pleased. And the Union army will have one hell of a soldier in you. I can see that."

Sam Lapin pulled a thick wallet from his hip pocket

WILD WIND WESTWARD

and counted out three crisp one-hundred-dollar bills. "Now, don't you be late in reporting," he advised.

"Could I have some twenties," Eric asked, "and an envelope?" He was thinking of tailor Leffert. "I have to pay a small debt before I leave, and I won't have time to do it in person."

"Why, certainly," said Lapin, making the adjustment. "Now, when you report, be on the lookout. Your commander is a fellow named Randolph. Colonel Scott Randolph. Hard but fair. He's from a very old New England banking family, fine as they come." Sam Lapin stopped talking and looked at Eric in a fatherly way. "Maybe *he* can teach you a few things, at long last," he added dolefully.

Eric took the money, pocketed it, and turned toward the door.

"Oh, by the way," called Sam. "I'm sure Bobby would want me to tell you good luck from him. But he's away at a party now with some of his friends."

Eric stepped through the open office door.

"Duck if you see a cannonball coming!" called Sam Lapin encouragingly.

Eric closed the door behind him.

IV

Kristin, who had seen Gustav Rolfson angry many times, had never seen him this furious. She was lying on the big double bed in their Madison suite when he entered, having returned from the ministrations of the doctor and consultations with the police. A wide white bandage crossed the bridge of his battered nose, anchored by tape to his cheekbones. His eyes were small and mean and red above the bandage, and gave him an aspect, indeed, of a wolf peering over a snowbank, seeking prey. He looked at Kristin. She was his prey.

"You were with Gunnarson," he said, slowly unbuckling his heavy belt. "I learned it from the driver. You know," he went on, drawing the belt from the loops on the waistband of his trousers, "Father always told me that if a woman gets a good beating early on in marriage, you don't have to waste your time watching her too closely afterwards."

Warily Kristin slid to the end of the bed, and prepared to get up.

"I didn't pay attention to my father," Gustav went on, speaking very slowly, and doubling the belt, "and so I learned my lesson the hard way. Exactly as you must now learn yours."

He advanced toward her, raising and swinging the belt.

"I'll scream," she told him, in a level voice.

He grinned. "I've already given money to the hotel personnel who service this floor."

"But there are people in the adjacent suites."

"Not now. They are downstairs in the dining room,

preparing to dine on a feast I have arranged. After you have been sufficiently chastised, you and I shall also descend, and there you will be as perfect and irreproachable as today with Gunnarson you were perfidious and unclean."

"You don't dare to strike me," she cried, lifting her chin.

"You shall see what I dare to do. Now you get the beating you ought to have had as soon as we left Lesja. And hereafter I shall have you watched at all times."

"No," she said, her heart sinking. She was not thinking of his belt. She was thinking of Eric. How could she ever flee to him if Gustav had her watched all the time?

"Lie down on the bed," he said, "on your stomach."

Kristin looked at the bed, looked at him. Then she decided. If he wanted to beat her, let him fight to do it.

She leaped from the bed and sprang at him, fingers curled and nails ready. He swung the belt with one hand, fended her off with the other. A streak of fire burned across her right hip, but she felt the flesh of his hot neck in her fingers. His thick forearm blocked her assault partially, but he gave a little startled yelp when her fingernails went deep for blood. This would not do. Already his face was scarred, and he was wearing a most unsightly bandage. Downstairs his guests were gathering. He could not meet them with yet further wounds. But this wife of his, whose beauty so entranced him; whose detachment so maddened him, she *needed* punishment! Why, if those great people of New York now circling around his table in the dining room, if they but *knew* Kristin had been out driving about in a carriage with an outcast commoner of their homeland, what would they think?

Kristin had grabbed hold of the belt now, and was trying to pull it away from him. He jerked it hard, and she spun, off balance, onto the floor. He brought the belt down hard across her lovely shoulders, and she shivered but did not cry out. He hit her again, and she sneered at him.

"Go ahead," she taunted. "But remember, this is not Norway and you are not great here. You will see."

Vanessa Royall

Gustav, the belt lifted to strike again, hesitated.

"What do you know about it?" he asked. "Greatness is where greatness goes."

She laughed at him, in spite of his strength and her pain.

To Gustav, parvenu that he was, scornful laughter was the ultimate weapon. He could not bear it, especially from Kristin, whose beauty was ever a weapon in itself. Suddenly he was on the floor beside her, trying to take her into an embrace.

"I shall not strike you again, ever," he promised.

"That is the truth," she vowed quietly.

"It was just that I was so agitated to see that murdering coward here in the city, and you having traffic with him. Moreover, the driver told me you and he went for a long drive. Thank God he could not ravish you in a carriage!"

He tried to hold her again, but she pushed him away.

"Kristin!" He was hurt now, but growing angry again. Oh, how powerless he was emotionally when he had to deal with her, think about her.

"What did you mean?" he asked coldly. "What did you mean, coming out of the hotel, saying, 'Eric, I have it!'"

"Nothing," she said.

"I don't believe you."

"Then don't."

"Gunnarson will be captured, you know, sent back to Norway, and hanged."

"That *I* don't believe."

"How did he know where you were staying? How did he know . . . ?"

"He is a very intelligent man," she told him, looking straight into his eyes. Gustav's basic uncertainty about Eric was a weapon for her.

Gustav could not bear such praise for his enemy. He had already been wondering where and by what means a lowly Gunnarson had come to have such a great coach, such fine clothes. Was it possible that Gunnarson had risen in America? Had come to great station and power? No, he could not countenance such an idea. That was not the way the world worked!

WILD WIND WESTWARD

"Come now, my darling," he said, getting up, offering his hand to help her to her feet. "We have had a falling out, as sometimes happens between the best of husbands and wives."

"You have struck me, and I shan't forget it."

"Yes, you shall. This is a new, grand adventure for us. We will be rich and more powerful than even I have dreamed. We will have children."

Kristin, getting to her feet without his aid, now realized that, in making love with Eric this morning, she had not used her formula of frankincense, olive oil, and oil of cedar. She had not thought to use it, and had not thought about it afterward either. Everything had seemed natural, perfect, preordained.

"I shall have no child of yours," she vowed. "No matter what. How often you have tried! But it must be something in my body, or my spirit, inimical to your seed."

"Do not say that."

"I have already said it."

Gustav stood there, powerful but powerless, angry but hurt, a conqueror yet all undone. Someday he would manage to interpret and explain this woman. Someday he would make her totally his, tame her, blot out from her mind even a fleeting trace of the memory of her plowboy lover. But now time was running, and guests waited.

"You need not come down to dinner with me," he said. "Affairs of business will be discussed, and you would not find them interesting."

"No, husband," Kristin replied. She believed it was important to know as much about Gustav's affairs as she could. The knowledge might be valuable someday. But she did not wish to tell him this. "I shall go mad if I must dine in this hotel room. Anything is preferable."

Even your company, she thought.

Kristin was not without respect regarding her husband's instinct for and talent in self-promotion. Prior to his leaving Norway, his many letters had put him into contact with a great number of New York's most powerful men.

Vanessa Royall

Gustav was bringing to America the financial backing of Lord Soames, and that was excellent backing indeed. It made Gustav far more than just a legitimate entrepreneur; it made him a prospective mercantile prince. And, if he succeeded, could he not help others on the way up?

This evening, for the entertainment of his guests and potential allies, Gustav had hired the grand ballroom in the Madison Hotel. The dance floor shone like glass, reflecting the thousand lights on three great chandeliers that hung on huge silver chains from the ornate ceiling, forty feet above. Tables circled the ballroom floor, covered with sparkling white linen, glimmering crystal, and the finest gold plate. Gustav had spared no expense. Nor would his guests find wanting the crabmeat canapés, the lobster, the new asparagus, or the tenderloin of beef. Cases of French Champagne had been acquired to lend spirit to the evening, to titillate palates and stimulate wits.

Gustav held Kristin's hand tightly as he moved from guest to guest before the dinner commenced, giving the appearance that he and his sweet wife were also the closest of lovers, but actually—Kristin thought—to assure that she would not somehow find a way to escape, duck out of his life forever, and be gone. She found herself introduced to the Astors, the Lands, Sydney Vanderbilt, the Wainwrights, the Westmorelands, a funny-looking little man named Carnegie, a handsome couple named Van Santen, and another odd duck, unaccompanied, whose name was Percy Phipps.

"He is an artist of some sort," Gustav whispered. "Did you see how he stared at you?"

Kristin *had* noticed. Percy Phipps's stare had been almost reverent.

"Well, don't worry." Gustav snickered. "Mr. Phipps is not interested in women in any *direct* sense."

"Rather like Lord Soames's friends, Rob and Pierre and Vitas? Is that what you mean, husband?"

Gustav colored deeply, stammering, "It . . . it was something I . . . I had to do. . . ."

By the time dinner was served, Kristin was actually

enjoying herself. The handsome people in their fine suits and gowns, the splendid ballroom, and a few glasses of champagne had put out of her mind the sordid struggle with Gustav, had enhanced the wondrous union with Eric in the morning. Then, too, the American men were being very gallant and solicitous, and little Percy Phipps hovered adoringly, although he had as yet been too shy to speak to her.

When they were seated, the Rolfsons shared a table with Mr. Phipps, the Van Santens—Hector and Isabel—and beaming, bandy-legged little Carnegie, who looked so benign and inconsequential in this assemblage that Kristin wondered what he was doing there at all. Hector Van Santen seemed thoroughly upright and sober, but Isabel was bright and effervescent. She was also ravishing: a tall girl with deep breasts, long legs, and the most luscious red hair Kristin had ever seen.

"How was your crossing, darling?" she asked Kristin.

"Uneventful. But the weather was excellent."

"The North Atlantic can be difficult at the best of times."

"Do you sail often?"

"Far less than I would like. We were in Paris last year, and London two years ago. But lately the war has hampered travel, and besides, Horace has been so much involved in business."

The men, except for Percy Phipps, were already discussing tariffs earnestly.

"What business is your husband in?"

"He supplies coal and iron ore for Mr. Carnegie."

Kristin shot a glance in the direction of the beaming little man. To her surprise, watching him talk about commerce, she found his eye hard and shrewd.

Her own surprise must have been evident, for Isabel laughed delightedly. "Many mistake what he is," she whispered, "which is probably the richest and quite likely the most ruthless businessman in America."

Isabel gave Kristin a long look, then a glance of scrutiny and examination, as if trying to decide something.

"Not that many people yet understand how important oil

will be," Hector Van Santen was saying. "I have a feeling that he who controls oil will control the future of business in America for the next fifty years."

"No, it's steel," Carnegie maintained, championing the enterprise in which he had risen to wealth and prominence. "Steel is king, and shall always be."

"I have done much study on oil," said Gustav, making an attempt to appear modest and thoughtful, "and I would say there is a future in it. Has either of you gentlemen"— he ignored Phipps entirely—"visited the region around Titusville, Pennsylvania, where the first oil wells are being worked?"

Hector Van Santen shook his head. "My men have," Carnegie said. "It is primitive. Production is minimal, and no one has as yet determined how best to refine the crude, or, more importantly, how to bring it here to the eastern markets."

"Anyone specializing in that problem as yet?" inquired Gustav, seeming only mildly interested.

"The business is too new," said Van Santen. "No one knows where it will go."

"There is a man in Cleveland who visits the oil fields regularly," Carnegie added. "A young man. Rockefeller by name. But he has little money, and cannot hope to do much. He is, at present, clerk in a produce house in Cleveland."

"Clerk in a produce house!" Van Santen guffawed.

"But my men tell me he is very determined about oil," Carnegie said.

Gustav stored the name Rockefeller in his memory, remembered his manners, and turned toward Mr. Phipps.

"I am told that you are a very fine artist," he remarked in an oily manner which implied that art of any kind was suspect at best and worthless at worst.

"If that is what you have heard, I am pleased," said Phipps shyly.

Isabel Van Santen came to his defense. "Percy is the greatest portrait artist America has yet produced," she

WILD WIND WESTWARD

maintained. "It is only a matter of time until his talent is recognized by all the world."

"I should settle for recognition here in my own country," said Phipps, his eyes on Kristin again. "But it is more than a matter of time. It is also a question of the perfect subject."

"And you have found such a subject?" Isabel prompted, her eyes going from Phipps to Kristin and back again.

"I think I have," the painter murmured shyly.

Gustav caught the drift of the conversation. "You want to do Kristin?" He was pleased. "Why, by all means!"

He was thinking that sitting for the portrait would give Kristin something to do. He was thinking that a portrait by a competent artist—he did not imagine that Phipps could be very good; the man was simply not strong enough to be good—would add luster to the Rolfson reputation.

"Would that be all right with you, Madame Rolfson?" Phipps asked.

Gustav interrupted. "I make her decisions," he announced, not harshly, but with a kind of amused arrogance that made his comment all the more blatantly offensive. He did not notice this, however. "Yes, you may do the portrait. It will afford her some entertainment, I am sure. We men must look out to keep our women amused, is that not so?" he demanded of Hector and Carnegie, who murmured and smiled neutrally.

They went back to discussions of business as the dinner progressed, course after succulent course. An orchestra began to play quietly at one end of the ballroom; there would be dancing later. Phipps studied Kristin even more closely now. "I shall do a wonderful likeness of you," he promised shyly. "But I fear my studio does not have the light required for the effect I wish to create."

"And what effect is that, Mr. Phipps?" Isabel asked.

Phipps smiled for the first time that evening. On any other person it would have been a smile of holy exuberance. He was too restrained to show his excitement, but it was there.

Vanessa Royall

"She is a goddess!" he cried. "You see the beauty! Everyone can see the beauty! But *beneath*, oh, beneath, there is steel of such strength even Mr. Carnegie has not dreamed. Yes, she is a blond Viking goddess."

He gestured indeterminately, unable to describe in words what he meant to do with paint and brush and canvas.

"I have a suggestion," Isabel offered. "Why don't you use my home for the sittings? You know, Percy? The sitting room next to the garden? I'm sure it would be . . ."

"Splendid," agreed the little artist.

"How long will you be stopping here at the Madison?" Isabel asked.

"I do not know," answered Kristin, with a slight edge to her voice. "My husband makes all such decisions."

Isabel smiled. She understood. "I think we should have a long talk very soon," she said. "A private talk. I believe I might be able to help you . . . in certain things."

Kristin smiled gratefully.

Later, when they were dancing, Gustav could not contain his excitement. "I'm going to get in on the ground floor of the oil business," he boasted. "Even Carnegie has no idea of the millions to be made. I shall take these American businessmen and stand them on their heads!"

"But what about this man they mentioned? Rockingfellow? It seems to me that he is laying some groundwork of his own."

"Rockefeller? A clerk in a produce company? Don't be absurd. It is a pity that a man of my standing must do business with such low-caliber people. But Hector and Andrew"—how quickly Gustav had assumed familiarity—"have convinced me that the man knows more, theoretically, about oil than anyone in this wild country. So I . . . we shall journey by rail to this city of Cleveland. I shall take Rockefeller's measure, and use him for as long as I need. He requires money, they say. I have money. Yes, my darling, it will all be easy now."

"Just as you say, husband."

He ignored her detachment this time, and drew her close

to him. She could feel his excitement, and suppressed a shudder.

"Soon the dance will be over. I will take you into bed, and give you delight that will make you forget the mischance that befell us earlier today."

Danger. The musk of Eric was still on her body, within her body.

"I am regretful, husband. But it is the wrong time."

Gustav looked disappointed, but only briefly. "Let me make a vow," he said, holding her to him more tightly still. "Let me vow that this is the last such time you shall have for many months. Nine, at least. If it does not . . . proceed, I think it will be time that a doctor examined you. I want my son now, so that he may grow as my American empire grows."

"Yes, husband," Kristin said.

Even though she was traveling with Gustav, Kristin was having a marvelous time.

They left New York by locomotive on May 3, 1863, striking northwest toward a city called Buffalo that, Gustav told her, was almost five hundred wilderness miles away. There they would change to a steamship, and go farther west on Lake Erie, until they reached Cleveland. New York had been thrilling to Kristin, but that excitement was surpassed once the train left the city behind and headed out over the vast, green countryside. Born and bred in the mountains of Norway, Kristin at first could not believe that the earth was this rich, this vast. What a country! Did it ever end? For a long while the train rocked along the broad Hudson, then cut westward across the Appalachians, so green and dark they evoked for her memories of stories about past centuries, the forest-heavy darkness, with brigands in the trees, sojourners far from home, adventure behind every trunk, every bush, or leaf. Then, beyond the mountains, rolling westward, ever westward, were vast fields at which farmers worked, planting their crops.

She wished that Eric were with her, seeing this! What a

paradise! Was Pennsylvania, too, like this? Perhaps it was better still.

At each stop, when the train halted to take on water and wood, by which the engine was fueled, Kristin, in her fine European traveling clothes, climbed down out of the coach—always under Gustav's watchful eye—and eagerly sought conversation with the people. They looked askance at first, those country people seeing for the first time a beauty like Kristin, descending like a dream from private car to country backwater, but they saw in a moment that she was extraordinarily delighted to be there, to be talking to them.

"Now you be keerful, ma'am," grinned a local character in Poughkeepsie, hoping to frighten her, "they's Injuns all along this route that'd love a golden scalp like yours."

"And wouldn't you, too?" she shot back, laughing, the sharpie's companions laughing with her, the man finally laughing, too, at how she had bested him.

"What are you, anyway? A queen or something?" asked a bold little boy in Binghamton, after studying her for a long time.

"No, I am a little country girl, and when I was growing up, I milked the cows just like you do."

"G'wan," he said, charmed, believing and disbelieving simultaneously.

And, when she found a group of dark-skirted farm women regarding her enviously, suspiciously, on the platform in Syracuse, Kristin walked over to them and bought what they were there to sell, milk and eggs and bread, telling them how she herself had baked the bread of Norway. "I am going with my husband to Cleveland," she said. "What is it like there?"

"A bad town," they answered, liking her, not wishing that she be harmed, "a bad town, so have a care."

"What do you want all this garbage for?" Gustav asked disgruntledly, looking at the things she had bought.

"If we don't use them ourselves, we can give them away. I just wanted to see what the people of America are like."

"And you have found out?"

"These were good people. As good as in Lesja."

"I bested the people of Lesja." Gustav smirked. "It was but an afternoon's work."

"I do not think you shall have such an easy time with Americans," she told him. "They seem unawed, if not downright defiant."

"There is an American saying that goes, 'You wait and see.' You wait and see."

"I am waiting."

She did not say for what.

"Don't go off the train again. I don't wish you to mingle with the commoners."

"But I must have some decent companionship."

"Were it not for this train, on which I have paid your fare, you would never dare to come this far back into the hinterlands. You would have to walk, or go by wagon, day after day."

"I could do that," Kristin said. "I have lived without the finer things longer than I have had them, and—"

"Silence. I do not wish to discuss it anymore."

Gustav was jumpy, preoccupied, worried. Kristin did not mind. When he was in such moods, he let her alone. The pursuit of money was a serious thing, and Gustav had no energy to embark upon pleasures of the flesh. For several nights Kristin prepared her contraceptive, just in case. But when she saw that she would not need it, she ceased to take the trouble.

The train finally arrived in Buffalo. They spent several nervous nights at a bad hotel, bad for Gustav at any rate. The clerks and waiters did not treat him in a fawning European manner. Instead of being threatened by him, he was threatened by them! He fired off telegrams to J. D. Rockefeller in Cleveland, confirming an appointment made in New York. Rockefeller did not respond at first. Then he inquired as to the nature of Mr. Rolfson's business.

"He *knows* my business!" cried Gustav, outraged, pacing the floor in the dingy hotel room he had been forced to accept, there being none grand enough for him. "I sent him three telegrams from New York, explaining exactly what I mean to do: buy his expertise in oil, and take him on as a hired hand."

When a final cable arrived, saying:

FREE FOR FIFTEEN MINUTES MAY 12.
ROCKEFELLER

Kristin thought she knew what was going on.

"He is playing with you, husband. He is a far stronger man than you have supposed."

"He is nothing, the little cowherd," Rolfson replied in a rage. "He is a nobody, a produce clerk. I can buy him and sell him. Why, do you know that his father peddled patent medicines on horseback? Do you know that his father was once suspected of horse thievery?"

"I recall your father telling me that, in his youth, he had to sleep with animals simply for their warmth."

"But he did not *steal* animals," Gustav shot back.

"No," Kristin agreed, in that tone Gustav could not bear, "no, he did not steal *animals*."

"You wait and see," he shot back, practicing the idiom.

Cleveland was enjoying a riot of political and martial emotions when Kristin and Gustav disembarked from the Lake Erie steamer. General Grant was poised for a major attack on the crucial, Confederate-held fortress of Vicksburg, key to the Mississippi River. President Lincoln had called for more soldiers. Men with money were seeking substitutes, and men without money were making three hundred dollars in return—quite possibly—for their lives.

"That is disgusting," Kristin pronounced, after a prosperous but desperate young man had approached Gustav hoping to buy him as a substitute in the Union army. "A real man fights his own battles."

Rolfson just laughed. "That may be true, but a smart man gets others to fight for him."

You ought to know, Kristin thought. Gustav's scar was as obnoxious as ever, and his nose flat and broad now at base as well as bridge.

WILD WIND WESTWARD

A decrepit horse-drawn cab took them from the waterfront to the address Rockefeller had given in early correspondence. It turned out to be an unprepossessing warehouse of unpainted clapboard. Union army wagons were being loaded with crates of vegetables at a dozen docks, and there was an air of vitality and enterprise in spite of the appearance of the place.

Gustav told the driver to wait, helped Kristin down from the cab, and they entered the warehouse. On a high stool, working over a bench, hunched a thin, pale young man. He was carefully entering figures into a thick ledger, painstakingly blotting after every entry.

"Make haste, lad, and fetch me Mr. Rockefeller," Gustav ordered. "I am Rolfson, and I have an appointment with him."

"For fifteen minutes," said the young man.

Gustav frowned, irritated and impatient.

The young man put down his quill, but did not move from the stool. Gustav ignored him. Kristin watched him, though. He was colorless, and did not look at all vital. He seemed a pale body with a pale soul inside, quiet and timid and obsequious. His eyes were wary, but opaque. She could not see behind their shining surfaces.

"Well?" prodded Gustav. "Are you a dunce, or what? I want to talk to Mr. Rockefeller. Time is money."

"I know that," said the clerk, "and you have already wasted a minute. I am John D. Rockefeller."

Kristin was taken aback, and Gustav the more so.

"Well, why did you not say so?" Gustav boomed heartily. He was displeased at Rockefeller's apparent subterfuge, but he thought he could use him, and wanted no trouble.

"I just wondered how you would treat a simple clerk," Rockefeller said, holding out a limp hand. There was very little in it to shake. Gustav made the best of it. Kristin was reminded of a snake with a steel wire inside it.

"Young fellow like you, how come you're not in the army?" asked Gustav, trying to make small talk.

"I bought a substitute," Rockefeller explained, without inflection or emotion.

255

Vanessa Royall

Kristin recalled her husband's words: *A smart man gets others to fight for him.*

"But God has seen fit to send me my duty," the clerk continued. "I have a contract to provide produce to the Union army. That is how I serve."

"And make money too, eh?" Gustav laughed, as if Rockefeller had told a good joke.

"If I receive money, it comes from God," the young clerk replied, soberly, again without inflection.

Sweet Jesus! Gustav was thinking, *a Godster!* He would bargain the very trousers off this naive, pious young fellow. Not that he wanted the trousers: they were colorless, threadbare, and patched at the knees.

"Three minutes gone," Rockefeller said, drawing a cheap watch from his vest pocket and examining it.

The man was not jesting! All right, Gustav could be tough, too. "I have a lot of money to invest in the oil business," he said. "I have it on good authority that you have been studying possibilities—commercial possibilities —with regard to oil, and I think we can help each other."

"How?" asked Rockefeller, as if Gustav had just asserted that he had it in his power to fly to the moon.

"Tell me about the situation around the oil wells at Titusville. How do you interpret events and prospects there?"

"Why should I?" Rockefeller asked.

"What? See here, young fellow. I have come all the way from—"

"I am not especially concerned how far you have come, nor from where. I am a businessman, sir. Yes, I have been to Titusville, and have some knowledge of how I think the oil business ought to progress in America. That is my capital, so to speak. I would advise you to go down to the oil fields on your own, learn what you can, and then perhaps I will think of borrowing money from you. It is true, as you may have heard, that I already know more about oil than anyone in America. It is also true that I will need vast sums to develop the business along suitable lines."

"What do you consider suitable?"

WILD WIND WESTWARD

"That is also a part of my capital."

"And you will not discuss it?"

"Not now."

"Then what am I doing here?"

"You wished to see me, and to invest in my business. I am a busy man, sir. The fifteen minutes are drawing to a close."

"Why you . . ." began Gustav, in a state of raspy indignation, "why . . . from what I can gather you do not yet have an oil business, and yet you are sitting here and making terms, setting conditions. Why, this is intolerable!"

"As you say."

"I shall go to Titusville myself."

"I think that would be wise of you," said Rockefeller. "Good day, sir."

"Good day! And I doubt that we shall meet again."

"I must differ with you on that, as well."

Again he offered his oddly strong, oddly limp hand to Gustav, who shrank a bit, but shook it anyway. Rockefeller gave Kristin a small bow, barely civil, and regarded her with those cold, bright, opaque eyes. Something had bothered her about him from the moment of first sight, and now she knew what it was: He did not see her as a woman at all. Kristin had seen, in the eyes of almost every man she had never known, a special, instinctive recognition of her presence, her womanhood, her beauty. John D. Rockefeller did not manifest such a response; to him, she felt, she was simply another human being, to be labeled, categorized, and entered on some vast, impersonal ledger in his mind. To him there was only profit and loss; any given person could aid him, and thus be entered in the profit column, or harm him, in which case an entry would be made under "loss." A colder human being she had never met, nor one as potentially dangerous. Compared to Rockefeller, bold, irascible Gustav was but a troll beneath a child's story bridge.

"God be with you," called the young clerk piously, as Kristin and Gustav left the warehouse.

"If that wasn't the strangest man I ever met, I'll eat my

Vanessa Royall

hat," Gustav said, climbing back into the hired coach. Lately he had taken to using American slang, and although Kristin was mystified as to why anyone would wish to ingest a headpiece, she had to admit it was a colorful expression.

"What will you do now, husband?"

"I shall go down to Titusville. It is only a hundred-odd miles east of here. Young Rockefeller may know a lot about oil, but I am a fast learner. Also, I am the one with money to be lent. He needs me; I don't need him. When I finish, he will not know what hit him."

"I am not so sure about that, husband," said Kristin, who had seen, beneath the faceless clerk's impersonal manner and bizarre piety, a deeper reality that was like a serpent fashioned from spring steel, implacable ambition, and ice.

Titusville, a little farm town in the rough country of northwestern Pennsylvania, was rude and unprepossessing. One road led into it, rutted and bleak, and also a rickety new spur of the Pennsylvania Railroad. The importance of transportation was not lost on Gustav; oil was of little use to anyone if it remained in Titusville. It had to be moved out in order to reach the big markets in the cities, and before it reached market, it had to be refined. Refining the crude required manpower, and he knew that the surrounding agricultural communities did not have enough available men to service the kind of enterprise he hoped to establish.

There were other problems, too. After he and Kristin checked into the town's one inn, nothing more than a big, warm country house with a sign in the window that said "Free Mashed Potatoes with Every Meal," Gustav explained the obstacles to his wife. Normally he would have burdened his coterie of sycophants with such complexities, but he had not taken them with him because he did not want them to learn too much about oil. It was harmless, he felt, for Kristin to hear of such matters. He liked to hear himself talk, but she was only a woman, and any concrete information would bead and roll off her brain like water on oilcloth.

"First," he said, "there is the matter of leasing rights to the oil. The farmers on whose land the substance has been found are, doubtless, unsophisticated and doltish, similar to those in your hometown of Lesja. I shall get leases from them as easily as father and I acquired the minerals in the Rauma Range. It would not be efficacious to refine the oil here, so it must be shipped to the nearest large city where a work force exists. That would be Cleveland. Hauling oil overland by wagon would be chancy; the roads wash out in the rain, and are all but impassable from November to March. Thus I must make arrangements for shipping the crude with the Pennsylvania Railroad. Finally I must build a refinery in Cleveland, right on the Lake Erie waterfront. From there the refined marketable products, kerosene, gasoline, and lubricants, can be shipped to cities east and west, either by boats on the Great Lakes, or by rail. Arrangements will have to be made with shipping agents. I do not think the refinery will take too long to build. On the way into Cleveland harbor I noted a fine, empty plot of land, right by the docks, that would be perfect for such a factory."

Kristin listened. She well knew that, in spite of his twisted personality, Gustav was a man of brutal directness. His intelligence, narrow but undeniable and tending toward bold action, was not to be underestimated. And he had access to the Soames millions, whereas Rockefeller, the clerk, could not hope, on his own, to fashion the series of arrangements necessary to market oil nationally, much less overseas.

But something was not right. *Something doesn't fit here*, Kristin thought.

That evening they dined with other boarders at the inn: a young man clerking in the general store and reading law by night, an old couple retired from their farm, the local schoolteacher, a shy young woman who looked at no one, and the innkeeper, Mrs. Prendegast, who assumed an easy familiarity which unnerved Gustav.

"Here on business?" she demanded, passing the mashed potatoes.

"Perhaps," he said.

Mrs. Prendegast glanced at Kristin, calculating. *Rich man. Lovely young woman. What gives?* She glanced at Kristin's hand. Kristin had always worn Gustav's diamond readily enough, though it was at present locked in a New York safe. But she had always refused to wear a gold wedding band. In her heart she was married to Eric Starbane, and she did not need a ring to remind her of that.

"You a prizefighter, or something?" the innkeeper prodded Gustav. "I mean, look at your nose and face and all."

Rolfson frowned. "No," he pronounced slowly, "I am here about the oil. I am a businessman, as you guessed."

"Ah, I knew it!" the woman cried, delighted with her acuity.

"It's about this oil discovery. That's why I'm here."

"Ach! The oil again!" muttered the old farmer. "It will ruin everything. A man should be left alone to farm peacefully."

His wife nodded vigorously, gumming a length of pork chop.

"I disagree," said the store clerk and prospective lawyer. "Oil is progress. That man Rockefeller from Cleveland. He knows. He knows where the future lies."

"Rockefeller?" asked Gustav, alert and suspicious.

"Yes. A wise man, in spite of his years. He has bought up all the oil leases in the county."

"What?" cried Gustav, getting to his feet. "All the oil leases?"

It could not be true.

It was.

The next morning, when Gustav drove out to the oil wells, little more than grimy pumps in grubby shacks, surrounded by great stacks of barrels and blasted earth from which native trees had been uprooted, he learned, to his chagrin, that the clerk had been right.

"Nope, can't deal with ya," shrugged Ebenezer Tilton,

WILD WIND WESTWARD

farmer. "I done signed on with Mistah Rockefeller in Cleveland."

Herman Bellows averred that, yep, he reckoned he had signed the same deal as had Ebenezer.

Virgil Watts was another who had seen his star with the produce clerk from Cleveland.

"What are you doing with the oil you're producing?" Gustav demanded.

"Oh, we ship out a little to build up demand," Virgil said. "Mr. Rockefeller, he said to do that. But we barrel the crude and keep it right here."

Gustav saw his chance. "Well, let me make you an offer. I'll buy up everything you've produced, and everything you can produce, and ship it out of here on the railroad."

"No can do. We've signed leases to Mr. Rockefeller. If we renege, according to the agreement, he gets everything, land included."

"Land included? Why did you ever agree to anything like that?"

"Because we're making money, mister. For the first time in our lives. And we like the feeling."

"But . . . but . . ." Gustav sputtered. "Rockefeller can't be doing that well. He isn't even shipping any of the oil out. I can get the Pennsy Road in here, and . . ."

"Beggin' yer pardon, but no you can't."

"What?"

"Rockefeller's gone and signed an agreement with Pennsy Road. He agrees to ship only with them, when he's ready to ship, and they give him a freight rebate for the business."

Gustav slapped his forehead with the heel of his hand. The Pennsy was the only road into this backwater, and this was where the oil was. That young son of a horse thief had the deal all locked up, nailed down, shut tight, and he wasn't even *in* business yet. He must have used what meager funds he had in bargaining for the leases and the railroad agreement. Well, there was one end of the enterprise he could not have had the cash to secure.

Vanessa Royall

"What is the rush?" Kristin asked, when Gustav came dashing into the inn.

"We're going back to Cleveland right away," he told her. "I'm going to buy that piece of land along the dock for my refinery, cash on the barrelhead, as they say in these regions. If I control the refinery, I control the oil business. Simple as that."

The train clattered back into Cleveland, and a buggy bounced them over to a waterfront shanty, on which a sign read:

CLEM A. TUGWELL
LOTS, HOMES, AND HOMESTEADS

Clem, a massive man liberally spattered with tobacco juice and gravy stains, was very helpful. He judged Kristin and saw class; he measured Gustav and saw money. Fast, easy money. He also saw that Gustav was in a hurry. Best kind of person to sell to.

"That big stretch of land by the docks, eh? What you want it for?"

"I'm going to put up an oil refinery," declared Gustav proudly.

"Is that right? Is that right? Can't put 'er there, though."

"I can't? Why not? Is there some kind of zoning restriction? Perhaps we could get it changed, or work our way around it. That place is absolutely perfect for a refinery. We could load the product and ship it right out . . ."

"Yeah, I know," agreed Clem, "but I can't let you have it. Not for five years, anyway."

"Five years!" wailed Gustav. "In five years the oil business will have advanced to a point we cannot even dream! But why can't I . . . ?"

"Because just last month I sold an option to buy that land. It's tied up until then, unless you can persuade the man to relinquish his option."

"That's it," brightened Gustav. "That's what I'll do! Where can I find him?"

"In the produce warehouse, no more'n half a mile from

here. Young guy, but sharp. Rockefeller's his name. John D."

"Turn your head slightly more to the right, Mrs. Rolfson," said Percy Phipps, sighting with his brush. "There. The light strikes just so. . . . Now, lift your chin a little, no, that's too much, no, yes, yes!"

Delighted, he bent to his canvas again.

"How did you find the western regions?" asked Isabel Van Santen.

Kristin had come to sit for Phipps in the Van Santen mansion on Fifth Avenue. It was a solid, blocky palace of white marble, with massive portico, a turret, and a row of bleak dormers upthrusting from the slate roof. But while the façade was forbidding, the large rooms within were cheered by bright rugs, large, comfortable furniture, and sunlight pouring through the tall windows and skylights.

"It is a raw country, but very vibrant. I have never seen anything like it. You would think a race with a country like this would have too much work to do to fight."

"Oh, that awful war. I dread to hear it mentioned, even obliquely," said Isabel, stirring sugar into her cup of tea. It was mid-June now. Vicksburg had fallen to General Grant, but the Confederacy still held Richmond, and the papers were full of news that General Robert E. Lee was on the move into the Shenandoah Valley. And that was the road to Pennsylvania!

Where Eric said he would be!

Kristin did not want to think of the war. Too many other things were on her mind. Since their return to New York from Cleveland, Gustav had hired men to be with her at all times. They drove her carriage; they waited outside the stores in which she shopped; one of them waited now outside the Van Santen house. It was maddening.

"Hector," said Isabel brightly, introducing a new subject, "is very curious to know how your husband fared in his dealings with Rockefeller."

Kristin could not hold back a short, derisory laugh.

"Please now, Mrs. Rolfson, lift the chin. That's it. How

Vanessa Royall

can I make you famous if you do not keep your chin up?"

"Famous? I do not wish to be famous."

The painter merely smiled.

"Percy has plans for you, my dear," Isabel said. "Now, why the laugh a moment ago?"

By now the two women were friends and had talked several times, at length, about their respective situations. Isabel was deeply devoted to her husband, Hector, an affection he reciprocated. As a woman in love she could tell that Kristin was not happy with Gustav, but she did not yet know the entire story. She knew there was another man somewhere, far more important to Kristin than Gustav would ever be. And she knew that Kristin was exceedingly watchful and astute. Lately, too, she had grown quite pale of complexion, in spite of the approaching summer, and Isabel thought something might have occurred during the western trip to account for her new friend's malaise.

"My husband is very anxious just now. I believe he has met a nemesis in Cleveland. He struck a deal there, he says. In my own appraisal I think it is more accurate to say that he was struck by a deal."

She herself had read the letters of agreement drawn up and signed by Gustav and young Rockefeller.

"You seem to know quite a lot about business," Isabel commented. "Me, I am such a goose in those things."

"I had a hard early lesson in Norway," Kristin replied. "There my husband and his father maneuvered the citizens of my village out of their rightful title to lands that might have made them rich."

"And in Cleveland?" Isabel prompted.

"In Cleveland there is a petard. And who shall be hoist upon it in the end, Rockefeller or Gustav, is yet a question."

"But I sense beneath your words a feeling that it is your husband who shall be hoist one day."

Kristin nodded, but said no more. That cold icy snake of a produce clerk in Cleveland possessed mind and jaw like steel traps, and his appetite was insatiable. Perhaps, had Gustav not been so angered at Rockefeller's skill, the business prescience that had led Rockefeller to acquire the basic step-by-step elements to an enterprise before he had the enterprise itself, perhaps if Gustav had not been so outflanked, he would not have signed the letters of agreement.

Those letters were dangerous.

For Gustav had agreed to loan Rockefeller millions—the millions loaned to Gustav by Lord Anthony Soames, the collateral for which was Lesja, and the minerals of the Rauma Range in Norway. In her mind Kristin imagined a house of gigantic cards, and Gustav within that house. If a wind should shiver it, if a storm should come, if the very earth should quiver and quake, ah, then . . .

Who knew the future?

Gustav thought he did. "I have the limp-handed little Godster now," Gustav had told her, studying drafts of the agreements in their Cleveland hotel. "The land on which the refinery stands will be his, but I shall build the refinery and it will be mine. I have learned from my experience with your unhappy neighbors in Norway that it is not the land itself that matters, but the valuables in it or on it. According to this agreement, if he is unable to repay my loan in its entirety by 1868, I give him a two-year extension, but automatically the land is mine. If he is able to repay prior to 1868, and that's only five years away, title to the refinery goes to him."

"Do you think you ought to agree to something as indefinite as that?" Kristin had asked.

"What do you know about it? There is no way in the world that oil, in five years time, will afford that much profit. Ten years, yes. Fifteen years, certainly. But, no, the weak-spined—albeit arrogant—little clerk must leaven greed with a hard knowledge of how the world works."

Kristin said no more, that night. In her judgment John D. Rockefeller needed no instruction in how the world worked.

The refinery was to be Gustav's beachhead in the oil industry, the sine qua non of the entire process, from which he would expand and by which he would eventually control everything done with oil and its by-products. After

Vanessa Royall

this Cleveland refinery—which would be built with Soames's money—there would be more, and more. In due course. One step at a time, as the Americans said.

But, upon their return to New York—at which time they moved into an apartment in the luxurious, modern Federal Hotel—Gustav took time to skim over business news that had emerged during his western trip. The headlines moved him to acute mental anguish.

SHIPOWNERS SEE MOVE TO OIL:
FUEL OF FUTURE ALREADY
HERE FOR USE

The news story accompanying the headline was long and enthusiastic, mentioning that, in only a few years, whale oil as lamp fuel had dropped eighty-eight percent in sales, and other areas in which animal fats had served as fuel likewise had registered sharp declines. Oil, "black gold," was the lodestone of a future undreamed.

"I am greatly fatigued," he told Kristin. "You may retire without me. I shall see you in the morning."

"As you wish, husband," Kristin had replied. Something had happened to her, and she did not think she would be able to bear his touch, ever again.

Now, seated in Isabel Van Santen's house, posing for Percy Phipps, she wondered how to proceed.

"You seem unusually pensive today," Isabel was saying.

Percy Phipps had noticed the same thing: a mood of introspection in his subject more pronounced than he had sensed during previous sittings. Her color was also weak. This was not the day to proceed further.

"I think we shall call it quits for now," he suggested gently, putting down his palette.

Kristin did not protest.

When the little painter had departed, Isabel poured tea for her friend, and bade her rest on the sitting room couch.

"Is something troubling you? That I can help with?"

Kristin did not say anything for many minutes, just

sipped her sweet tea and looked out at the garden in back of the Van Santen house.

"I am pregnant," she said quietly.

Isabel did not say anything for a moment, trying to read Kristin's mood, expression. It seemed that Kristin was not unhappy with her condition, nor did she appear to be entirely content with it. Perhaps this eventuality had not been desired, or planned.

"This sort of thing does happen," she said, brightly, "and I trust you are both pleased."

"Gustav doesn't know about it yet."

Isabel pursed her lips, thinking. Yes, there was something amiss here. She guessed, but waited for Kristin to tell her.

"The baby isn't Gustav's."

Isabel made a further surmise. "The man you were telling me about?"

Convinced of Isabel's sympathy and discretion, Kristin let her story pour out. The agony of parting with Eric in Norway. The empty years intervening. The passionate reunion here in New York. And now—

"And now," Isabel finished, "you're carrying his child, and Gustav doesn't know it. What does Eric think?"

"Eric doesn't know it, either."

She told about that, too: the awful scene in front of the Madison Hotel, and Eric having to flee. "He has not been able to come back, or even send a message. I hope he is all right. In any case, I don't know where he is."

Isabel got up from her chair, came over, and sat down next to Kristin, patting her hand. "Come, now, this isn't as complicated as it might seem," she said soothingly, thinking that it was certainly complicated enough. "First, tell me, is there any chance Gustav will think the child is his own?"

"By the time the baby is born, I hope to be far from Gustav."

"But let us say that things do not develop as you wish. Such is sometimes the way things go in life."

Kristin smiled. Isabel had spoken the truth. "It is possible my husband will not guess, unless he remembers and counts days. Lately he has been extremely preoccupied with business. I only wish . . ."

"Wish what?"

"That there were some way I could get in touch with Eric."

"Have no fear," cried Isabel, warming to the challenge. "You just leave it to me."

"Why? What will you do?"

"On my own, I shall engage the Pinkerton detective agency. I shall tell them I wish to trace a man for reasons of my own. The Pinkertons are the best in the business, and if I manage the affair, there is no need for Gustav ever to know."

"What about Hector?"

"If Hector discovers what I am about, I shall tell him the truth. Or part of it. I shall say you must find someone from your homeland, as you have a message for him. I am helping you do it, since, being pregnant, you have neither the time nor the energy."

She smiled, delighted with her inventiveness. Her lovely red hair caught the sun, showing russet and gold. She was a beautiful woman, and also a good one.

"I am lucky to have found you, Isabel."

"Luck had nothing to do with it. Put your faith in the stars. Now, you must tell me everything about Eric: his appearance, his habits, his proclivities. Everything. So I can pass that information along to the Pinkertons."

Summer came, and dragged along. Percy Phipps worked on Kristin's portrait, and completed it early in July. Kristin told Gustav she was expecting a baby—she did not say *his* baby—and he was ecstatic. "A future prince," he raved, "someone to train for ascendancy, exactly as my father trained me!" *Good Lord,* Kristin thought. And the war, like the summer, dragged on as well.

In early July the newspapers were filled with accounts of a great battle that had taken place at a small Pennsylvania town called Gettysburg. Studying the maps printed in the papers, Kristin noted how near Gettysburg was to Harrisburg, the city Eric had intended to go to, and she felt a hot ball of fear form deep within her, curling where the baby grew. The battle, by all reports, had been horror, and mayhem, and death triumphant. The South had lost the battle, but Lee's army, although badly savaged, had managed to escape intact.

And that meant the war would go on.

One hot afternoon in late July, Isabel called upon Kristin at the Rolfson apartment.

"Gustav is not in?"

"No, he has gone down to Philadelphia for a few days, to discuss some dreadful banking affair. He has left me with the usual watchdogs, however. What is it?"

Isabel appeared very intense. "I have come with a man I think you should meet," she said. "He is outside in the coach. Shall I call him up?"

Eric! thought Kristin, her heart pounding with joy.

But the man who entered the room was not Eric. Isabel introduced him as one Padraic O'Keefe, Pinkerton agent. A short, powerfully built man with reddish hair and a broad reddish face, he came right to the point.

"You the one wanted a report on a Gunnarson, Eric?"

Kristin nodded, not trusting her voice.

"Well, here goes. Subject left New York on April twenty-eighth of this year, after enlisting in the twenty-seventh regiment of the New York Regulars. He signed on as a substitute for a Mr. Robert Lapin, which indicates that Gunnarson either likes to fight a lot, or that he needed money badly. And which, in my opinion, indicates that young Lapin prefers others to fight battles for him. But that's beside the point. Gunnarson departed from New York and, with the detachment of trainees, took his military instruction at Fort Belvoir, in Maryland. He was under the command of Colonel Scott Randolph, of Boston. Gunnarson did extraordinarily well in training, by the way. He was designated an officer, second lieutenant, and was also able to win citizenship, under a rule whereby officers, upon appointment, must also pass citizenship hearings. Were you aware that Gunnarson had not been a citizen of the United States?"

Kristin shook her head briefly, as if the matter were of no import. But inwardly she thrilled. The killing of Subsheriff Johanson in Lesja had always stood in the way of Eric's chances for legitimacy in America. Now that obstacle was cleared. The future looked brighter by the minute, even if Eric had to spend time in the Union army.

"Gunnarson spent six weeks in Maryland," Paddy O'Keefe went on, studying his notes, "and was then assigned as a company commander with the Army of the Potomac, which was, at the time of the big battle, under the command of General Meade. . . ."

"What big battle?" Isabel asked.

"I'm getting to that. Randolph, and with him Gunnarson, moved west with the Army of the Potomac, shadowing the movement of General Robert E. Lee, who shifted northward into Pennsylvania during the latter weeks of June. . . ."

The child stirred within Kristin's belly, and she felt momentarily nauseous. It passed.

". . . No one knew at first how large an army Lee commanded, but by June twenty-seventh the Union knew it was in for a big showdown. Jeb Stuart was there, and Ewell, and Jubal Early, too. It was not a foray; it was going to be a wingding, and everybody knew it by then. . . ."

"Gettysburg," said Isabel, in a hollow voice.

"Gettysburg," corroborated O'Keefe, with a frown and a nod, "and that got around to starting up on July first." He glanced at both of the women. The red-haired one who had hired him did not seem as intensely concerned about Gunnarson as did the blonde. The blonde was obviously with child, early on, true, but showing. Could Gunnarson be her husband? Hardly seemed likely. Somebody who had to hire on as a draft substitute would not live in a place like this. Well, they were paying him to tell them what he had learned, and so he would.

"On the evening of July second," he said, "the forces

WILD WIND WESTWARD

of Confederate General Early broke the Union line at Cemetery Ridge. The battle went on for a long time. Early almost won, but his reinforcements didn't appear—"

"Not to be impertinent, Mr. O'Keefe," Kristin said, "but what does this have to do with—"

"With Eric Gunnarson? Everything. I will now read you the notes of my interview with Colonel Scott Randolph, who told me what he knows when I interviewed him in the federal hospital in Harrisburg, Pennsylvania. He was Gunnarson's commander, as you know."

O'Keefe paused, shuffled a few sheets of paper.

"Ah, here it is. This is Colonel Randolph speaking.

> "Early hit us an hour before twilight, and it was horrible. Eric and I had been riding along the line, inspecting fortifications, as we expected an attack the next morning. We were not under cover, and had no chance to take cover. The Confederate cannoneers opened fire, and their cavalry began the onslaught against Cemetery Ridge. I don't recall any of it. I remember falling from my horse, and looking up to see my boot still in the stirrup. My horse was falling toward me, and beyond my horse I saw Lieutenant Gunnarson. He was no longer on his horse, and he was not on the ground, either. He seemed to be suspended in midair, spinning in a blaze of blood. . . ."

"Oh, my God!" Kristin cried, hugging her stomach.

"Mr. O'Keefe," said Isabel, very calmly, with a nervous glance at her friend, "perhaps we had better—"

"No," said Kristin, gathering herself, "I want to hear it all."

"That's about it," said O'Keefe, shrugging. "Colonel Randolph is recuperating in the hospital at Harrisburg, and learning to get around on one leg. As to Gunnarson, the official report is 'missing and presumed dead.'"

"Missing!" cried Kristin, hopefully.

O'Keefe looked pained.

Vanessa Royall

"But they would have found his body!" Isabel interjected. "Wouldn't they have?"

O'Keefe shook his head. "Either of you women ever seen a battlefield after the action's over?"

Isabel and Kristin had not.

"Well, there are plenty of bodies, and there are many, many *pieces* of bodies that never get matched up, and there are some bodies that vanish all together, just get blasted into atoms."

... spinning in a blaze of blood ...

O'Keefe waited, hoping he would not have to state the obvious. But the women were looking at him, waiting for his words, wanting him to confirm some horrible thing he himself didn't even want to think about. Oh, life itself endures, one way or another. But the individual life was so fragile, like a tiny spark in the hurricane, and it might be expunged in an instant, with no one to see or to mourn.

"The Rebs," he said, "they were using chained balls at Gettysburg."

"Chained balls?"

"Two heavy cannonballs, chained together, and fired at the same time. They come through the air whirling all around. Colonel Randolph is of the opinion that a pair of these hit Gunnarson. And that there's nothing left of him. So 'missing and presumed dead' means—"

"Dead," said Kristin. "No, I don't believe it." She started to get up from her chair. "No, it can't be."

"There, there," said Isabel, going to her.

"Perhaps I'd better leave now," offered O'Keefe.

"It can't be. I won't believe it!" Kristin said.

"That's right, that's right," Isabel responded soothingly. Kristin, Isabel knew, was protecting herself, protecting herself by denying what had happened. The grief would come soon. Denial gave a person one more moment, one more hour, one more day to get ready for the dead empty blackness of bereavement.

Isabel took O'Keefe to the door. "Thank you," she said. "We needed to know."

"At a time like this, I don't like to talk about money, but . . ."

"It's all right. I understand. You've done well. We had to know. Just have the bill sent over."

O'Keefe departed, and Isabel sat down beside Kristin.

"It is not true," Kristin was saying, holding her stomach.

Odd, thought Isabel, *she does not look bereaved, she is not stricken in that way.*

"It is *not* true," Kristin repeated, "it is not *true!*"

"Come, dear. Let's rest now."

"I don't want to rest! Missing and presumed dead. *Presumed* is a big word."

"Big enough," replied Isabel. "Big enough."

For hope.

V

The commanding officer's tent sat, cool and serene, on a hill overlooking the training field. For two weeks now the Union army trainees had marched and run and crawled upon the dust of that field, cursing and sweating in the humid Maryland summer. Beginning as a ragtag assortment of disgruntled and sometimes angry individuals, they had begun to work as a team. Their marching was not yet precise, but marksmanship was improving daily, bayonet drills were effected with brutal efficiency, and teamwork in loading and firing the cannon was so creditable that even the sergeants withheld criticism. Criticism withheld meant praise.

But, eating hard tack and beef jerky around their campfires at night, the recruits wondered.

"Here we are, getting ready to die for our country," complained Wayne Cleavis, a farm boy from Binghamton, "and we ain't even seen our commanding officer. I want to have at least a look at the CO before I go out on the battlefield with 'im."

"Maybe we don't even have no CO," pondered Willis Krantz, a mean-looking renegade from the hills of Ohio, who bragged that he had been given a choice between the Army or the gallows. "All's I see up there is a big tent with a couple of sentries in front of it. You know something? Maybe there ain't a Colonel Scott Randolph at all."

"Sure, an' maybe there ain't any Abe Lincoln, either," shot Tim Finnegan, a tough little Irishman straight from Cork County by way of Boston and New York, "an' maybe there ain't a war, an' we've already died an' gone to the Blessed Mither."

"Shut your mouth, you stupid grinning paddy. I'll teach a furriner like you when to open your yap."

"Easy," Eric Gunnarson cautioned. "We're not here to fight among ourselves."

The men around the campfire quieted. By virtue of skill, discipline, and strength, Eric had been appointed their squad leader. "Sven," Sergeant Rollins had said, "you look like you could whip any of this bunch, so you be the squad leader."

So far Eric had not had to prove the truth of Rollins's estimate.

"An' what the hell business is it of yours?" grunted Krantz. "I'll say what I goddam well—"

"It's a free country," Eric retorted, "say what you please. I just don't care to hear you, that's all."

Krantz glared at him. "Well, I ain't moving from this campfire."

"Then you'd better shut up."

Krantz thought it over. He had killed a man, and he knew he was tough. But the man he had killed was unarmed, and Eric had a bayonet, a knife, and a rifle. So did Krantz, but by his lights even Steven was bad odds.

"You don't know if there's a CO either," he whined. "Ain't that so? All's we see up there on the hill is a nice cool tent. Man goin' into combat got a right to know the warp and woof of his CO. Now ain't that right?"

A subdued mutter of agreement rose from the squad members.

Eric, in fact, had been wondering about Colonel Scott Randolph himself. Sam Lapin had said he was "hard but fair," that he might teach Eric a thing or two. Was that so? Hard to tell, without having met the man and judged him face to face. In the mountains of Norway there was no other way to judge.

Eric stood up.

"Where you going?" asked Cleavis, the farm boy.

"Up to the tent to see Randolph."

Vanessa Royall

"Like hell you are," Krantz guffawed. "You ain't got the balls for that. Ain't any of us got the balls for that. To see him at all, you got to go through the lieutenant, and then the captain, and then the major."

"I don't see any of them around, do you?"

And so, leaving his men gaping over their mess kits, Eric shouldered his rifle and started up the hill toward the commanding officer's tent. The flag of the United States flew in front of it, along with the regimental colors. Seeing Eric approach, a sentry in front of the tent stiffened, lifting his weapon, bringing it across his body.

"State your business, soldier."

"I wish to speak to the commanding officer."

"By whose authorization?"

"Personal request."

"Request denied. Get out of here. He's having dinner."

"It's very important."

The sentry hesitated. It was highly unusual for a trainee to want to see the CO. Most—if not all—trainees wanted to avoid contact with the CO, as well as with other superiors. Superiors almost always meant trouble, or extra work. "Stay away from headquarters," was a common watchword among the troops.

"What is it then, if it's so important?"

"A personal matter."

"You're a soldier now. You don't have any personal matters."

"Let the colonel be the judge of that."

The sentry took another minute, thinking it over. So Eric put to use a morsel of intelligence he *had* acquired. Subordinates were generally fearful of doing the wrong thing, and they so often did not seem to know what was right and what might later be considered wrong.

"You may be in big trouble if I cannot see the CO now," he said. "But if that's what you say . . ."

He turned, as if to retreat back down the hill.

"Wait! I'll announce you. But if this goes bad, it's on your head, not mine."

The sentry entered the tent, and came out. He was

grinning. "Go on in. He's in a bad mood. I want to see how long you last."

Eric pushed aside the tent flap, and went in. The command tent was large and square. A kerosene lantern burned brightly on a table, and seated at the table, knife and fork raised, gleaming white napkin tucked into his shirt collar, was a tall, lean man with closely cropped black hair, and a meticulously trimmed vandyke. In spite of the fact that this tent was on a remote army training post, Eric noted the wine bottle in a silver bucket, the heavy china, and the blood-red rib of roast that the Colonel was eating.

"What is it, soldier?"

Eric saluted, held the salute. Colonel Randolph lifted a fork to his temple. Eric dropped the salute.

"I just came to see if you were here, sir?"

"What in heaven's name . . . ?"

"My men were wondering if you were here. We haven't seen you, and—"

"Silence," said Randolph, emphatically but not loudly. "Stand at attention. Who are you?"

"Private Gunnarson, sir. Squad leader of the—"

"Silence, Gunnarson. Stay at attention. I am going to teach you a lesson."

Eric tensed. He had done the wrong thing. The sentry had been right. So he stood there, waiting, his muscles straining at attention after a fatiguing day on the field. But the colonel paid him no attention. As if Eric were not there at all, he returned to his dinner, eating slowly, sipping the wine. From time to time a steward, whom Eric had not at first seen, advanced from the shadows of the tent, to fill the colonel's glass, and then retreat once more to his position.

"That will be all," said the colonel, at length, and the steward removed the serving dishes, and cleared the table.

"Well now," said the colonel to Eric, after the steward had departed, "you may be at ease. What have you learned here?"

Randolph was smiling. He expected little from a foot

soldier, a raw recruit, save perhaps a request to be dismissed.

"I learned a great deal about command."

"Oh? Is that so?"

"And I learned why you remain aloof from the men."

"Interesting. You learned this by watching me gnaw on beefsteak?"

"Yes, sir. However much the men grumble about him, they want a leader who is special. Few men are special. So the man who wishes to command must consciously set himself apart, by gesture, behavior, even affectation."

"And I have chosen to do this by remaining remote, in my tent?"

"I think so. Yes, sir."

Colonel Randolph pursed his lips, and nodded, studying Eric. "How afraid are you to die, Private?"

"I don't want to die. Sir."

"But are you afraid to die?"

"More at some times than at other times."

"Do you think you would ever turn tail and run in battle?"

This was a question discussed and debated constantly by the men in the training detachment. Everyone denied they would actually do it, but some let on that they were afraid they might, in a moment of panic.

"I don't know, sir. I've never been in combat."

"Surely you must have had the usual number of fights, though, growing up, women, things like that?"

Dangerous ground, thought Eric. Would the bloody corpse of Subsheriff Johanson never decompose, never disappear into the atoms of history?

But Randolph did not seem to know about Johanson. He had something else on his mind. "You haven't your citizenship papers, have you, Gunnarson?"

"No, sir."

"Why not?"

"I meant to apply for them, but many things happened, I was ill—"

"I don't tolerate excuses."

"Sir, I am not giving excuses," replied Eric, stung.

Randolph nodded.

"What are you going to tell your squad members when you go back down to the campfire?"

"I shall tell them that the colonel is an intelligent man, whom I would follow into battle."

Surprisingly Randolph laughed. It was a deep laugh, full of humor and enjoyment, so much at variance with his restrained, severe demeanor. "You have no choice but to follow me into battle, Private."

"Sir, some follow willingly, and others are merely made to march."

The smile disappeared. "Gunnarson," the colonel asked intently, "do you think you could lead men?"

"Yes," said Eric, without pause.

"All right. Gunnarson, I am impressed by what you have done. Not one in a thousand troopers would come up here just to see what I looked like. But, also, in spite of my distance from day-to-day training, I have kept careful watch on the training reports. You have been evaluated in the upper categories. The very highest categories, as a matter of fact. Now, I cannot disclose general plans, but action in battle may not be far off. The conscription has brought manpower back up to standard, but our officer ranks were severely depleted at Chancellorsville. *If* you continue to do well for the rest of this month of training, and *if* I continue to need officers, would you accept a commission?"

"Yes, sir," said Eric, again without hesitation. He was well aware of the dangers. The person most likely to die first on the field of battle was a lieutenant, out there on the line, directing his troops. Even mere privates were but second on death's list. Eric was aware of this, but he had not forgotten something the colonel had said, and that Sam Lapin had mentioned in New York: an officer received citizenship.

"Yes, sir," Eric repeated.

"That is all, Gunnarson. I shall be keeping an eye on you. Dismissed."

"What's he like?" asked Krantz and Cleavis and the others, when Eric came down the hill.

"He said we might be in battle soon."

"But what is he like as a person?"

"I don't know."

"Don't know? Look, we saw yus go into the tent. You mean he's not there? Well, is he or isn't he?"

"He's there. I mean, he did not allow me to see what he is like as a person. But, judging him as an officer, I am very impressed."

The men muttered about this a bit, then gradually drifted off to ready their bedrolls for the night. Eric did likewise, thinking. To be an officer. It was dangerous, but an honor. It was a step upward. A step upward. Upward to exactly what, he did not yet know.

In his tent Colonel Randolph summoned a staff officer.

"Get me all the papers on Private Gunnarson," he ordered. He wanted to know as much about Eric as he could. The young man was clearly out of his element in the enlisted ranks, like a nobleman fallen upon hard times.

Gettysburg, Pennsylvania, was a quiet little farm village, where nothing much ever happened.

"I have just returned from General Meade's headquarters," Colonel Randolph informed his staff. Meade was in command of the Army of the Potomac, of which Randolph's New York regiment was a part. "It is the feeling of the General Staff that there will be no battle here. Lee has entrenched his army near Cashtown, as if awaiting attack, and Meade is not prepared to move. According to him Lincoln feels Lee is here in Pennsylvania not to fight but to symbolize Southern strength."

The senior officers present at this briefing glanced knowingly at one another. Politics. They were convinced to a man that, were the business of politics not allowed to define and decide where and when to give battle, this war would have ended in Union victory long ago.

"Confederate Vice President Stephens," Colonel Randolph went on, "is on his way to see Lincoln, under a flag

...en into formation," the colonel told him, ...to Pipe Creek."

...the following day, June thirtieth, Eric's ...well entrenched along Pipe Creek, and he ...them. But by midafternoon they were ...trenches and fortifications forged with so ...Because by midafternoon everything had

..."ell is going on?" grumbled the men, when ...red to pack up and prepare to march again. ...ug in here, the battle hasn't even begun, and ...ving out already?"
...ric informed them. "The battle is already on, ...to be a lot worse than anyone thought."
..., as Colonel Randolph had feared, because ...new exactly where its adversary was located, ...ded, heavily foliated hills of Pennsylvania. ...te cavalry of General A. P. Hill, out on a ...on, decided to stop in the little town of ...me of the men needed new boots, and ...wn would have a bootery. They did not, ...uch of a chance to shop, because in the ...e Northern troops, riding with the cavalry ...eral Buford.

...ed his defensive plans, and went on the ...ttle took place not at Cashtown, where he ...but in and around Gettysburg. Colonel ...rdered west from Pipe Creek to Cemetery ...ig in and defend. A forced march across ...brought Eric and his men to Cemetery ...nestone outcropping shaped like a fish- ...afederate forces to the west and north. ...e beaten and bedraggled remnants of the ...s, driven from the village of Gettysburg ...rst day of battle. Units of General A. P. ...Ewell had slashed the First Corps to ...retreat to Cemetery Ridge was less a of truce, to discuss negotiations for a peace settlement. There is no hope of such a settlement, as the South will not yield its demand for independence, nor will the North ever accede to such a demand. That is why we are fighting."

"Or not fighting," grumbled Major Stonehead, of the Indiana Regulars, to a chorus of guffaws.

"I repeat," Randolph said, "Lee is entrenched. Meade believes he is not in Pennsylvania to fight, but to give a show of force while Stephens makes his plea for peace to Lincoln."

"Well, let's surprise the old gent," offered Major Stonehead, "and kick his head in."

This suggestion was greeted with considerable enthusiasm, and Colonel Randolph raised his hands for silence. "I was coming to that part," he called. "I said it is Meade's feeling that Lee does not want to fight, and that there will be no battle here *unless we make it ourselves!*"

An outburst of cheering seemed to lift and billow the canvas of the command tent. Second Lieutenant Eric Gunnarson, his gold emblems of rank still bright and new, was surprised to feel a thrill of imminence, and he felt his blood rush faster through his veins. This would be his first battle. If there was a battle.

"General Meade has given me the following orders, which I now pass along to you," Randolph said. "We are going to move to Pipe Creek, and entrench ourselves there. Meade wants Lee to attack *us*. Our reconnaisance parties are scouting the entire Gettysburg area, and so are the Rebel units of Jeb Stuart and A.P. Hill."

"Begging your pardon, sir," asked Major Stonehead, "but we've been up against Hill and Stuart before. If they're along with Lee, I'd say Meade is wrong. Jeb Stuart doesn't come along for a meander in the countryside. I think Lee is getting set to put the fire to our feet once and for all."

"I can only tell you what I have been told," Randolph said, to a mutter of dissent, "but, frankly, Stonehead, I share your view entirely."

The mood of the meeting changed instantly. *Action*

loomed, the hopeful prideful expectation of blood and thunder, cannon and conflict, life and death, for which hardened soldiers live and breathe.

"We march in four hours, so ready your men," the colonel ordered. "Tomorrow, June thirtieth, we ought to be in position along Pipe Creek, covering Meade's right flank. Lee is to our north. So if he can be baited to the attack, we'll see action for certain."

A final burst of cheering ended the staff meeting. Many of these officers, Stonehead of Indiana, Cleveland of Ohio, "Mad Dog" Spaeth of the Minnesota Territorial Irregulars, had served long and bitterly under the timid McClellan. At least Meade would fight, not run, if he got drawn into a battle, although he was still too hesitant for some of the staff.

"The only way to do this," Lieutenant Colonel Spaeth was telling his fellow officers as they left the tent, "is to grab Lee by the throat and kick him in the hind end. That's the way to settle with the fellow. I never liked him anyway."

"Lieutenant Gunnarson," Colonel Randolph called, as Eric waited for the senior officers to exit before he did, "join me for a moment."

Eric was more than happy to do so. Since he'd taken his commission, and been given charge of a company of troops, Colonel Randolph's attention and advice had served him in good stead on many occasions.

Randolph had a steward bring coffee, and the two men sat down at the command table. A large, detailed topographical map was spread upon it, features of the hilly terrain clearly delineated, and the apparent positions of both armies marked by blue and gray flags.

"This is bad," Randolph said, in a voice different from that he had used only moments before to address his staff. "We don't know exactly where their reconnaisance and support units are, nor whether they are quite certain of the location of ours. The whole thing could come to flashpoint by accidental encounter before either side is prepared. And when that happens..."

calculated move than a rout. They sank down exhausted, shell shocked, while Colonel Randolph's men set up the defensive guns.

Eric's men, boisterous and bright with bravado on the march toward the Ridge, now gazed with veiled fear at the wounded and the dead. Cries of anguish rose from the encampment as twilight descended that day, from the wounded men who lay suffering, dying. Campfires were not permitted, so as not to give away the exact Union positions, and every sound from under bush or behind tree was interpreted to have been caused by a Rebel scout. Watchful and jittery, Eric inspected his company's cannon and talked to the men.

"They got hit real bad, didn't they, sir?" asked Krantz, the tough Ohioan. It was the first time he'd ever called Eric "sir."

"It's true, but we can't think about that now. Colonel Randolph has it from headquarters that Jubal Early's men will attack us tomorrow morning."

Krantz and his fellows gave low whistles. Jubal Early. The great names of the war were known to nearly all of them, and, like all great names, they carried an aura. The history of the war was written in the names of men and places, so that men and places had become more than they were, had acquired by repetition and significance and, yes, by death, too, a power mightier than daily reality. The Wilderness and Sharpsburg, Vicksburg and Ulysses S. Grant. Andersonville and Manassas and the golden Shenandoah, and Robert E. Lee. Fighting Joe Hooker was one of the great names, and Jeb Stuart. And Jubal Early, too.

The men listened to the mutter of the night, heard the million trackless noises beneath the trees, and shivered, eating sourdough bread, drinking water from canteens, wondering if one night hence they would eat and drink again.

"Well, it's only Early," said Private Cleavis, trying to cheer himself. "It could be Jeb Stuart himself. That'd be worse."

"Shut up. Early is bad enough," Krantz shot back.

A long, low moan sounded down the line, and Eric walked toward it. Darkness had almost fallen, and he picked his way carefully among the rows of wounded men. Several officers and a doctor bent over a filthy, bloody bedroll, on which a soldier lay dying. The man was still conscious, but suffering acutely. He had lost an arm, and his right leg from just above the knee. He was dying, and he knew it, and he did not like it.

"Kill me now," he groaned, "goddam you bastards. You got me into this, and I'm a goner. Have a heart and put a bullet in my head."

Something was familiar about the voice. Eric bent down. By the last light of day he saw Mick Leeds, by whom he had been so ill used in his early days in New York. Mick's once ruddy complexion was pale now, pale as death, and his thick, rowdy mustache was limp and wet with the sweat of final exhaustion.

"Leeds!" said Eric, in recognition.

The officers turned; the doctor looked up. He seemed relieved that someone else had come along. "You know this man?"

Eric went down on one knee next to the wounded man. "Yes. Mick. Mick. You remember me?"

The big roughneck squinted against twilight and pain. A glimmer of knowledge came into his eyes. "Hey. It's the foreigner. Hey, man, sorry about back in New York. You hate me? You got a right. Look, get even now, and put a bullet in me . . . oh, God!" he wailed, as new spasms of pain shook him, left him breathless. "Hey . . ." he gasped, "come . . . on. Shoot me . . . ah . . . bitch . . ."

"I can't do that. You want to talk? Take your mind off some of the pain? Your sister. What happened to your sister, Joan?"

Mick Leeds struggled up through layers of agony, and a hard glint came into his eyes.

"She . . . she done me," he said. "She got me to go in the army, and then she stole my draft money."

"She stole your. . . ?"

"An' you know what I think?" With his remaining arm

WILD WIND WESTWARD

he reached out and grabbed Eric's sleeve, holding on as if, when he died, he meant to take Eric across with him. "You know, I think she did Liz in. Killed our own ma. I think she did. To get the money. That was all she ever wanted. She didn't love me. . . ."

This seemed to sadden him.

"Where is she now? Joan?"

Mick was gasping irregularly now, and it was clear he would not last much longer.

"You want a priest or a minister?" the doctor interjected.

Mick Leeds shook his head. "No, God damn it . . . no . . . unless you get one who'll shoot me, put me out of . . . Joan's in . . . Pittsburgh now. She's . . . she's got a . . . rich man. Horace . . . is his name. But don't . . . don't mess with her. She's trouble . . . she's death. . . ."

His voice stopped. He gulped, coughed. Blood rose in his throat, and ran down the corners of his slack mouth.

"Remember," he cried, still holding onto Eric's sleeve, his eyes bright and big, "remember those . . . rides out to the Island? Getting the liquor? Those . . . those were good . . . times, they were . . ."

His body shook once, twice. Blood pooled in his open mouth, but no longer spilled over. His blood had stopped running. His heart had quit.

The doctor pulled a blanket up over Mick's head. "So," he said to Eric, "ran a little rum in your younger days, did you?"

But he was only making nervous conversation, separating himself, separating the rest of the living, from the husk of death in the blanket at their feet.

"What was that name he mentioned? The one in Pittsburgh?"

"Horace," said Eric.

"I wonder if that could be Benjamin Horace? The one who's interested in oil? He's the meanest son of a bitch in western Pennsylvania."

"I wouldn't know," Eric said. But it sounded like the

type of man Joan would want. He made a mental note to stay far from Pittsburgh.

Early attacked Cemetery Ridge in the morning. Eric's first battle, his first taste of combat. It was something that just happened, as if outside of time. There was no chance to experience it, study it, certainly not to reflect upon it, as the battle was going on. Men moved by instinct and fear, loaded and fired rifle or cannon so frantically they were seldom aware of the discrete elements of their physical action. But their training had been good. They worked. If a man fell, and many fell, that was as it was. There was no time, in the melee of shouting and blasting and blood, to think, only to act.

Early's men came up Cemetery Ridge, and kept on coming. Eric, with his men next to their cannon, saw the charge begin, far down the slope, and thought, *they will never get past the row of hedges,* and bent to work, passing balls for the cannon, calling out to his men, "Fire! Reload! Fire! Reload! Fire! Reload!" as if he were no longer a man, but rather a piece of some vast killing machine, which he was supposed to be directing but which was actually directing him. But they did get past the row of hedges, the Confederates, and came on. *They will never get beyond the ditch at the bottom of the ridge,* Eric thought, sweat-soaked now, three of his men dead, four, five, another fallen, another. But they did get beyond the ditch and kept on coming, up the ridge now. *They cannot ever get halfway up,* thought Eric then, *our fire is too withering.* And the Union fire was indeed monstrous, a rolling field of thunder beneath heaven. It seemed as if all Pennsylvania were rocking upon the cradle of mother earth, as if the earth herself were shuddering in its depth. And Early's men kept on coming. "They shall never reach the top of the hill," cried Eric to his men, but then, as if in slow motion, removed from the minute-by-minute record of man's sad history on the face of his patient planet, Eric saw his cannoneer turn away from the blazing-hot weapon, and run for cover. A moment passed. He saw the flicker of a tri-

WILD WIND WESTWARD

umphant smile cross the face of an oncoming Confederate cavalryman, saw two more of his men melt away. He *felt* the hoofbeats of the horses coming at him, sensed the bitter pall of fear in the air. All along Cemetery Ridge men were turning, running, a ragged wave of blue abandoning positions and rolling toward the wooded cover on the opposite side of the ridge. Colonel Randolph pounded up on his chestnut stallion, pointing, exhorting. Eric leaped toward his own horse, the beast terrified now, ready to bolt. He was in the air. He saw the Confederates about to crash through what had been, until this instant, the Union line. He heard the blast and the thunder, and felt whirling through the air some device or engine of incomparable power. He saw Colonel Randolph lifted from his saddle, lifted from his horse. How odd, he had forgotten to remove his leg. And then Eric felt himself lifted, too, and struck, and spinning far above the bloody fields of ancient earth. Then everything was soft and lovely, soft and sweet, and he was with Kristin in a blaze of light, far up in the mountains above Sonnendahl Fjord. He was loving her, and she him, bathed in gorgeous light. He drank her image, and she his, and nothing bad had ever happened to them, and never would.

VI

Faces.

Faces came and went, appeared suddenly, dimmed, flickered out like pale fires.

Faces. Worried. Curious. Dispassionate. Coming down out of a cloud to look at him, and then receding, like gods come to study small life on a bizarre and distant world.

One face came more often than the other.

Soft. Comforting. Soft white, surrounded by lovely blackness, shards of blue light, jewels within the face.

"Elaine."

Elaine, Eric thought. *Elaine.*

Faces, and a word. Other words. *Oslo. Anandale.* A slip of memory there, an image: water harbor city cold. More then: thunder . . .

"Elaine?"

Face soft white with blue jewel eyes. Smile.

Thunder. Images in water. Kris . . . Thunder. Boot in a stirrup . . .

"Has he opened his eyes again, Elaine?"

The face moved above him, red lips, white teeth. Music. Music, from those lips.

"I think he's awake now, praise God."

God. Thunder battle and earth, thin blue line of men running for trees.

Himself in the trees, lying down, the earth sweet and soft upon him. *This is my grave. . . .*

He heard other words, felt them come out of himself, as if from a point in his soul so remote that speech had only been invented yesterday, was only now being tested.

WILD WIND WESTWARD

"This . . . is not my . . . grave. . . ."

"I hope not," came the music from the mouth of the face above him, jewel eyes smiling, and teeth smiling, too. "Father, come!"

And then another face, angular, with gray at the top and long gray coming down. Beard.

"You rest easy there, son."

Son! That is who I am. Someone called son. Rest easy there, son. No, I am not son. I am . . . something, something son, I am

"Gunnarson," he heard a voice say.

"Gunnarson," he heard another voice repeat. The melody voice. "Is that his name, father?"

"I reckon."

"Do you think he's all right?"

"Dunno yet. Can't tell."

"Dear God, let him be all right."

"I'm . . . all right," Eric heard someone say. *I said that.* "I'm all right," he said again. *All right. Alive. I'm . . . what of the soft earth in the forest, hiding, the grave . . .* "Where am I?" he asked.

The face of black and white, jewel-blue eyes, came down and close to him. A girl. A woman. Pretty, very. And worried, but with a touch of hope in her expression. "You're in bed. In a farmhouse in Pennsylvania."

Pennsylvania. Familiar. *I have been there. Starbane? No. Gettys . . . something.*

Battle. The battle. Running. He tried to rise. Barely moved. The bearded man touched him on the chest. "Easy now, you ain't goin' nowhere yet."

"But I've got to . . . my men . . . what day is it? Must drive General Early back. . . ."

Then the man laughed. "Son, that's been done long ago. This is August the tenth, year of our Lord eighteen hundred and sixty-three."

August tenth? Could not be. It was . . . it was July the second, and . . .

Hard. To think. The faces wavered, and gradually disappeared into the cloud out of which they had emerged.

But Eric remembered them as he sank away into sleep. He knew they would be there again.

Father and daughter looked at each other after Eric had dozed off. "Well, reckon we know his name now, at least," said Wilbur Nesterling. "Can't tell for sure, yet, but he did ask what day it was. Seems a good sign."

"Oh, I hope so," said his daughter, Elaine. "But oughtn't we to have contacted his unit? Shouldn't we do so now?"

"You know how I feel about that, child. War is evil. All war, both sides. This here's a good man an' he's done all anybody could expect him to do. We're doing the Lord's work now."

"As you say, Father. That he survived at all shows the hand of God in his destiny."

"Ah, my child, and your hand, too. You were the one to find him."

The Nesterlings themselves were almost as lucky as Eric. Their farm, just west of Gettysburg, had felt the ebb and flow of armies while the great battle took place. For three days, July first, second, and third, Confederate and Union forces surged back and forth across the soil, battering down the wheat, the corn. Until, when the tide of battle turned, and the North drove Lee and his men out of Pennsylvania, not a sprout of wheat, not a stalk of corn, remained standing. Yet, incredibly, the farmhouse had not been touched, the barn was still intact. Even the livestock had not been appropriated for food.

"They were too busy fighting, and I reckon they didn't have time to wreck our buildings or kill our cattle," Wilbur Nesterling reasoned. "And God's will, of course."

Wilbur Nesterling put his faith in God, not men, and he had taught his daughter, his only child, to do the same. She was his reason for living, now that his wife had died, but he feared for her, and never had he feared for her more than during the great battle. Soldiers were animals, and Elaine was— Did she know it yet? Was she aware of her power—a great beauty? But for once the armies swept in, fought, and left. They did not remain week after week to despoil the countryside and deflower its women. Wilbur gave thanks to his God when the soldiers left Gettysburg, and it was with considerable consternation that he saw his daughter race across the fields the day after General Meade's departure, calling something he could not quite decipher. She was greatly agitated, and her clothing dirty and in disarray. God forbid if . . .

"Father, Father! I was out seeking berries, and I came upon a soldier!"

Wilbur, fearing the worst, had turned immediately toward his house, to get his shotgun and do what must be done.

But Elaine Nesterling was not without awareness of her dear father's gentle obsessions.

"Oh, it's not *that*! Is that all you can think about? I found a man, and he's alive. Badly wounded, but alive. His men must not have found him, before they left. And we must do something."

The dead—thousands of them—had been buried, and the wounded carted away for treatment. The battlefield had been scoured for survivors. So at first Wilbur did not see how a whole living man could have been missed. Perhaps he was attempting to desert. But when Elaine led him back across the ruined field and into the trees behind Cemetery Ridge, when she showed him the place beneath the fallen tree where the soft earth had been dug for a shelter, he understood. The man was nearer dead than alive, his uniform blasted away by some unimaginable explosion, lacerations covering his body, a limb or two broken, and his breath coming in long, horrible hisses. Such a sound had caught Elaine's attention.

The surprising thing was that the man had found shelter at all. God's will.

Even more surprising, that he was still alive.

God's will as well.

Father and daughter fashioned a makeshift stretcher of saplings and vines, and trundled the wounded man back to the farmhouse. A doctor was summoned. He shook his head, but, because the Nesterlings insisted, he set the broken legs, the shattered arm, bandaged tightly the skull he believed fatally fractured, shook his head again, and left.

"There's no hope," he told them. "This man ought to have died three times already. Once from shock, once from the blow to his head, and once from exposure. Call me if you need me, but there's nothing more I can do."

If God wanted the man to live, Wilbur reasoned, then he would live. But Elaine was less placid, less accepting. Night and day she stayed near the man, whose fairness moved something deep inside her that had never been moved before, but which, mysteriously, was nevertheless very familiar to her, even thrilling. Hourly she bathed him with a damp cloth, holding his fever down. Tenderly she replaced the dressings over his lacerations, and watched them heal. With fearful interest at first, later with a kind of gentle amusement, she quieted him in delirium, listened to him babble in a soft tongue, strange to her, but not unsettling.

The only bad times for her occurred when he would try to start up against the bonds which held him to the bed, when he would cry out, "Kristin! Kristin, darling!" in a voice filled with love and desperation.

Elaine Nesterling was a loving girl, but she hated it when he called that name. And, although she did not believe her own creations, Elaine spun tragic fantasies that a terrible, heartless woman named Kristin had once wronged this splendid man lying near death on a bed in her father's house.

Ah, but she would make him forget that name when he recovered. And she never doubted that he would recover.

When first he opened his eyes, near the end of July, she was there. Every time thereafter, if he stirred or made a sound, she was there. Finally, when he was conscious enough to speak, to seem to see her and her father, she quieted him, saw him back into sleep, and, on the calendar hanging on the pantry wall, made a big star on the date, August tenth. Over a month had been lost to this man Gunnarson, but for herself—she was sure—boon beyond measure had been won.

WILD WIND WESTWARD

By the latter part of August Eric was well enough to sit up for an hour each day. He began to take solid foods, vegetables, a boiled potato, small pieces of beef or pork. The small quantities of broth Elaine had managed to spoon into him before had sustained him, but now, on substantial fare, he began to grow slowly stronger. He was unable to concentrate very well, and his remarks wandered, now about the army, now about things that had happened in New York, which he could not explain in sufficient detail for her to understand. But she read to him, and he liked that. She read him long passages from the Bible, and he nodded in vague pleasure at the majestic poetry of the Old Testament. *Uncle Tom's Cabin* agitated him, though, so Elaine discontinued that, and instead took up the tales of Fenimore Cooper. Wilbur Nesterling had been brought up in staid New England, and had been to school before removing himself to the wilds of prewar Pennsylvania, but he had brought his books along with him. One day in early September, when Elaine was reading Eric *Romeo and Juliet*, the suffering of the doomed lovers moved her to tears, and she had to pause.

Eric was still very weak, and had never really conversed with her, but her weeping struck him deeply, and he was no longer just a convalescent but a man.

"It's all right," he told her. "You don't have to go on. I know it's very sad."

"That's not it, that's not it," she said, wiping her eyes on the corner of her apron, "it's just that it's so beautiful."

"Being apart from someone you love is never beautiful," he said, staring into a middle distance.

Kristin! thought Elaine, suddenly worried, and she put aside the book.

For a long time Eric was not at all sure he would survive. His eyes focused not much better than his mind, and if there was a part of his body that did not throb with pain, he had not yet found it. All he knew for certain, for a long time, was that somehow he had come from the grave of earth beneath the tree to this warm farmhouse, and friends. A man and a woman. Gradually he knew them as a father and a daughter, good people, both, and then, during September when he began to sense a quiver of strength returning, he distinguished them further: he was in the home of a canny old farmer and his beautiful daughter.

Elaine was truly lovely, in spirit as well as form, comely of face, soft of hand, high of breast. He looked forward to seeing her from the moment of waking, and all day he enjoyed her moving about the house, taking care of it, taking care of him. He remembered everything about Kristin now, although he did not speak of her, and sometimes it gave him pain to feel toward Elaine the emotions he had learned with Kristin, from whom he was parted. Where was she now? What had become of her? What had become of the war and the world?

"I must have paper," he said one October morning. The chill of approaching winter already moved through the valleys, and in the fireplace logs burned high.

Elaine finished washing the breakfast bowls, and came over to his bed. There was a look in her eyes he could not read.

"Why?" she asked, quietly.

Eric read her look, her tone. One part of him felt tenderness, even joy, because he knew he was loved. But, because she did love him, loved him so obviously and with such devotion, the chances of hurting her were increased. He did not wish to hurt her at all; the mere thought of it caused tumult in his own heart. But he had to write.

"I must try and contact my army division, and tell them of my whereabouts and circumstances. It is my responsibility. I should also write to New York. I know people there, and they will worry if they don't hear from me."

Elaine said nothing, and dutifully brought him writing paper, ink, and a pen. Eric wrote. He had no idea where, at this point, Colonel Randolph's division might be, and it was quite likely that Randolph himself was dead. Eric wrote to the commanding general of the Army of the Potomac, describing his wounds, his present situation, and promising to rejoin his unit as soon as he was able to travel. He slipped the message into an envelope, sealed it, and then began his letter to Kristin. She must know he was safe, and, if not well, at least recovering. There was no other way but to send the letter directly to her, in care of the Madison Hotel. Surely she and Gustav would have moved from there by now, but perhaps the letter might be forwarded. Perhaps it would reach her somehow. He could only hope. It was a very short message, but it said all that needed to be told:

> Dear Kristin:
> I was wounded in battle last summer, but am on the way to complete recovery. I do so hope that you are well and happy. To me, the future shall be what it seemed when last we met. All waiting eventually ends.

Momentarily he had the impulse to sign it "Starbane," his ancestral name, so that, if Gustav should happen to read it, the wretch should know the man he had bested was indomitable. But Eric had no land, and without land it was not right to use the name. Instead he initialed the page "EG," and, hoping for the best, sealed the envelope.

"New York must be a very fine place," said Elaine, glancing at the envelope. The name *Kristin* stared up at her, and burned into her mind.

"It is not so fine as all that. Great, true, but also cold and hard. I was born in the country, and the countryside will always be first in my heart."

Elaine was pleased. "I shall walk down to the main road," she offered, "and give these to the postman when he rides by."

Eric thanked her, lay down, and dozed off. The effort of the letters had taxed him considerably. It was one thing to write cheerfully that he was on the road to "complete recovery," and quite another actually to be recovered.

Elaine saw that he was covered warmly with the heavy quilt she had made especially for him, then slipped on her coat and left the house. The Nesterling farmstead was about half a mile from the main road, which wandered through the countryside, from Gettysburg to Harrisburg. Usually Elaine delighted in the walk to meet the postman when he made his once-a-week round. And today was splendid, the air clear and sharp, just a kiss of clean wind, the whole world filled with the scent of oak leaves, straw, and crisp dry cornhusks. In a distant field she saw her father cutting and binding stalks of corn, setting them into shucks to dry. They looked like small golden teepees on the reddish-brown earth of autumn. Usually Elaine would have savored this stroll down to the main road. But not today. Eric's two letters burned in her hand. They were his connection to the outside world. Since July she had had him to herself, and the outside world did not matter. The outside world did not even *exist*. But now . . .

When she studied her heart, which was a prayer phrase her father sometimes used, Elaine knew she loved Eric. She knew also that love forced is love rejected. She must wait, and let Eric find her, find her truly, although she had been there before his eyes the entire time since summer. She thought, of late, that he seemed to look at her differently, more intensely, and so one fine day might he not study his own heart, and discover what was already inside?

He might. He *would*!

But not, perhaps, if the outside world intruded, if letters came back, if . . .

Elaine Nesterling had never done a great sin.

Once she had lied to her teacher, Mrs. Dobbs, saying that her primer had fallen into the creek, when, in truth, Elaine had left it carelessly on the porch, and a goat had eaten it.

Several times she had complained to her mother—when her mother was alive—and thus avoided chores she knew she ought to have done.

Several times she had kissed boys in the graveyard in back of the church, and once she had let Vance Trumbull, of Hagerstown, touch her breasts, but that might just have been an accident, and although it hadn't been, not really,

WILD WIND WESTWARD

it would have had to happen sometime anyway, wouldn't it? Vance Trumbull was a nice boy.

That was the problem. Vance Trumbull and the others had been—were—still boys. There was a man now in Elaine's house, and in her heart.

She reached the main road, and looked toward the north, from which direction the postman rode. Far off on the horizon she saw him coming, his horse trotting easily over the golden hills. God, such beauty in this earth, such possibility for beauty and love within her breast. Yet all of it might be ruined by these two letters in her hand. Elaine Nesterling had never done a great sin, and at this moment, she was sufficiently afflicted by imminent loss to convince herself that what she chose to do was no sin either.

The postman rode up to her and reined in his horse, greeted her, and reached into a leather saddlebag.

"Naught but the Harrisburg newspaper, Miz Nesterling," he said, not noticing the pleased expression on her face as he gave this news, not noticing either the two crumpled envelopes beneath her apron. "Gen'l Thomas sure gave them Rebs a licking at Chickamauga. Can't see how the South can last much longer. Anything for me to post?"

"No," she answered, sweetly, her heart resolved and at peace. She took the newspaper with her, bade the postman good-bye, and walked across the fields toward her father. She managed, on this short trek, to shred Eric's two letters into tiny pieces, scattering them as she walked, letting them blow out over the hills with the wind, like flecks of forlorn snow.

"What's the news?" called Wilbur Nesterling, as he saw her approaching. He took the paper and sat down next to a corn shuck, wiping his forehead. He was not getting any younger, and he knew it. Farming was no work for a man getting on in years, but he couldn't afford a hired man, and he didn't have a son.

"Father," Elaine said tentatively, as Wilbur read the war news and shook his head in perplexity at human folly, "what do you think will happen if—when—Eric gets better?"

Wilbur looked up. He had, many times, seen her looking at the young man. He knew the look. It was natural, God's will. Wilbur didn't mind. Long as looking was as far as it went. Right now.

"I don't know," he allowed. "Why don't you ask him?"

"Oh, I couldn't."

"Why not?"

"He'd think . . . he'd think I was too interested."

Wilbur smiled, tenderly but shrewdly. "Why, honey, I thought that's just what you were."

"Oh, Papa."

"Now, now. I understand. He's a fine-looking man, and he seems a smart one, too. But he doesn't talk much. What of his friends? His kin?"

She shook her head. Her father was right. When she came right down to it, Eric had not told her very much about himself at all.

Well, winter was coming, and he certainly would not be ready to travel before it settled over the land. There would be many long, long winter days by the fire, plenty of days for him to tell her everything there was.

October, red and gold and rustling, became cold, blue November, which swept suddenly into white December, and on into January 1864. The great cold of winter settled over the Pennsylvania hills, and the comfortable distances of summer grew vast and measureless from horizon to horizon. The Nesterling farmhouse seemed to hunker down against the very cold, and at night, beneath an icy, star-riven sky, there was to be heard the distant booming of blue ice on the rivers and lakes.

But in the farmhouse itself all was warm and safe and dry.

Eric felt strength flowing back to him. He was able to walk now with only a slight limp, and often he would go out with Wilbur Nesterling to tend to the cattle in the barn. Each week he watched from the farmhouse window, waiting for the postman to ride by, and although the paper brought them news of the outside world—Lincoln would run for president again; Chattanooga had fallen to the Union, and Ulysses S. Grant had become general-in-chief —he received letters neither from the army nor from Kristin. At first he was puzzled and hurt by this, but he put things into perspective. Of what use would he be, now, as a fighting man? He was just beginning to walk again. Even if he were fit to travel and rejoin his unit, the roads were impassable. As for Kristin, his heart was with her, hers with him. They had been apart before. He would see her once again, when Time and God arranged it. In the spring. In the summer. When he was hale and fine.

Meantime as the days passed, he told Elaine of his life in Norway, of how he had been cheated out of his land, cast out of his country.

Her outrage was palpable. "How could the Rolfsons *do* that? It is inconceivable. Surely God will wreak a terrible vengeance upon them!"

"He is taking His time to do it, then," responded Eric, in wry dejection. "As far as I know, old Adolphus still masterminds the enterprises from a palace in Oslo, and his disgusting son, upon whose countenance I have twice left my mark, lives a rich and celebrated life in New York with . . ."

He stopped speaking.

Eric and Elaine were sitting in front of the fireplace. A heavy black pot filled with stew for supper hung over the fire, bubbling slowly, sending its delicious aroma all around the house. Elaine was mending one of her father's work coats, ripped on the sleeve by a nail, and Eric worked beside her, sharpening with a whetstone the axes and scythes of the farmstead, so they would be ready for work when spring came. Wilbur had gone off hunting into the woods, seeking deer, "although I'd settle for a reasonably fat rabbit," he'd said. The warmth, their closeness, and Eric's trouble-filled narrative lent to the day a certain contemplative unity, as if Eric and Elaine stood alone against the world. Against the Rolfsons. He had told her much of his life, but—although she had warily waited— never had he mentioned the Kristin of whom he had spoken in his delirium, to whom he had addressed the letter.

But now he had said that young Rolfson was living a great life in New York with . . .

"Kristin?" she asked, so softly he might not have heard her, save that those syllables were resounding in his mind.

He nodded.

"They are . . . the two of them are"—she could hardly ask it—"married?"

"Yes."

Oh, praise God! Elaine thought. "But life goes on," she said, trying not to sound too cheerful.

She did not want him to start talking about this Kristin, whom he had obviously loved very much, and certainly she did not want him to start brooding about her right now.

"I know," she cried, getting up. "Let's do something special. I'm sick to death of needle and thread, and Father won't be back until sundown. Let's get out the cider and pretend it's Christmas again."

Eric agreed. There was no use in sitting here, burdened with gloomy ponderings, when nothing could be done about them anyway. He had seen Elaine's face during his recital of the past. So attuned was she to his own experiences, the expressions on her face made it seem as if she, too, had shared his hardships, his little victories. She laughed with glee when he told her about tailor Leffert and the top hat, cried out in anger when he told of finding the newspaper scraps where his three hundred dollars ought to have been. This was a girl for some very lucky man to have. If, in fact, she were later to marry someone who mistreated her, or played her for a fool, well, Eric would come all the way back to Gettysburg and thrash the wretch himself!

Come back from where?

What fantasy! Again, he was picturing himself a powerful and wealthy man, returning to set aright circumstances that had not developed as he would have wanted them to. Returning in triumph to Norway to reclaim his land, and his name. Returning in triumph to New York to reclaim Kristin and take her away from Rolfson forever. And now, returning to Gettysburg to thrash a man who did not exist for treating Elaine badly in a marriage that did not exist, either!

He might be able to whip that mythical scoundrel, but, in truth, what did he have to offer Kristin, were he to return to New York now?

Nothing.

The equations of life, ambition, desire, and revenge were getting all mixed up in his mind.

Kristin wanted nothing but him, and his love.

Elaine, now pouring the strong cider into mugs, smiling at him, wanted no more than to be loved in return for the love she so freely offered him.

Ah, yes, *he* wanted the other things, dominance and money and power and acclaim. But he did not have them yet, and so he could not give them, even had they meant anything to Kristin or Elaine. Only to a woman like Joan Leeds did they matter.

But Eric did have love to give.

Elaine handed him a mug of cider and sat down beside him. She touched her cup gently to his, and they drank, looking into the fire. The cider was powerful and mellow, aged in an oaken barrel. A few long swallows, a piece of time gone by, and the cares of life were not as burdensome as they had been.

"Before I leave," he said to her, "I will do the spring planting for your father. In return for the care you have given me."

Elaine would usually have suffered inwardly at his mention of leave-taking, but the warmth of the fire, the cider, Eric's proximity had painted her mood in bright colors.

"I know," she said, leaning close to him, "a better way to repay."

There were her lips, soft, smiling, slightly parted, and the perfume of her shining black hair. Had she been an experienced woman, her striking jewellike eyes would have been used enticingly against him. Enticement he might have been strong enough to resist. But Elaine was young, and the desire of her body glowed in her eyes in a manner more playful than provocative, more needful of gentleness and cuddling than of lust. Without thinking, Eric leaned toward her, and their lips met, for the first time in all these months. And, from the instant the kiss began, it was as if they had both been waiting all these months just and exactly and absolutely for this moment.

Eric reached out and put his arms around her, drew her to him. She came willingly, still locked in his kiss, then greedily, wildly, they kissed and clung to each other. He felt her body all along the length of his own, not losing himself gradually in passion, but suddenly, like a flash, a shot, a streak of raw nature not to be denied its due. Elaine said nothing, nor did he, as he carried her to the quilt-covered bed, in which he had suffered and regained his strength, to which now that strength of manhood led him. They were one body, one will, before even they were joined in love, he stripping away some of his clothing, some of hers, she taking the rest from him and herself, too. It was as if there were nothing anywhere: no sun, no snowscaped land, no blasting light; no fire, no house, no anything. Just each other and the other and each other and the two of them again, as they lay down upon the multicolored quilt, which bore so many fragments of designs and patterns, as now it bore the design of their riding bodies and the pattern that their bodies made upon the living fabric of this earth.

"*Iiiiiiii*," she gasped, or something like it, when he opened her, and "*Iiiiiiii!*" she cried, gasping, when he took her for himself. He trembled, shivered, his breath was shuddering as he entered her, full to the end of himself. She writhed beneath him exultant to be taking him, conscious of that exultation, but conscious, too, of a keen and piercing pleasure, never before known, a pleasure so great no one else could ever have experienced it before.

In Elaine's mind, as sensation grew to take her, take her all away, there was nothing but love and desire, desire and more love. To Eric, everything was need and pleasure, and the need of pleasure so long held in abeyance it could barely be recalled. He felt himself inside her, felt her moving beneath him, as if she were drawing his entire self out of the husk of his body. She sobbed into his ear, and her body sobbed against him. He felt within himself the moment pleasure touched her, took her, shook her, and when he felt that, when he felt her enjoying what he had given her, there was no way on earth for him to hold back. Far away along the ephemeral horizons of consciousness, he saw another face, another time, another promise. He tried to grasp at those things, to save himself for a promise made to Kristin long ago. But it was too late. From the base of his spine, up through the curves and moldings of his nature, the blasting force of his need and essence rose, coursing from him to her in throb and ebb and throb. She clutched him with her arms, her body, rising against him as he throbbed, receding as he ebbed, the two of them shaking, shaken, glowing and transfigured. Eric, who had known love both holy and profane, with Kristin and Joan, now knew another kind: simple and pure and very, very good.

Elaine was limp beneath him, and stayed so for a long time. Eric regained his breath, was puzzled that Elaine had not. Then he realized that she was weeping.

"What is it? What's wrong? Did I hurt you?"

"Oh, no." she sobbed. "How could you say that? It was beautiful. I did not know such a feeling existed. But . . ."

"But?"

"But we ought not to have. It wasn't . . . right. . . ."

"It was as right as anything I've ever known. There, don't be troubled."

Outside the farmhouse, not too far away, they heard the blast of a weapon.

"Father!" cried Elaine, leaping from the bed and grabbing up her clothes from the floor.

"Is that it? You're worried about what he might . . . ?"

"What father might think? No," she explained, both agitated and sorrowful at the same time. "Not him so much. It's just that he's tried to teach me the right way in life. And . . . and I know I love you . . . but . . . but it still seems wrong. Now. It seems wrong now. Somehow, it didn't before. Not while we were . . ."

She was trying to fasten her bodice, with trembling fingers. Still naked, he got up from the bed and went to her holding her tightly.

"Don't worry," he said. "You're very young. There is no one right way to love, just as there is no one right way to live life. I am here, as I was here before."

Elaine quieted, letting him hold her. *As you will always be here,* she thought.

They dressed, and went back to the waning fire. Eric added more logs. "Look," cried Elaine, peering out the window. "A storm's coming in from the west."

Eric was used to the snows of Norway, the icy remoteness of his home mountains, but still he was amazed at the progress of this sudden storm. Black clouds boiled to the west, riding the sky, and in moments he and Elaine felt the first rush of bitter wind testing the walls of the house, sucking at the chimney and the eaves. It seemed suddenly colder, in spite of the fire, and outside the darkness deepened even as they watched.

"I wonder where father—?"

"He can't be far. The shot we heard was less than half a mile away."

He had meant to sound encouraging, but in a heavy storm, a half mile might as well have been a hundred. Blinding, swirling clouds of snow came down, hard and sudden as a punch; all landmarks were erased; the very sense of direction was stolen in an instant from man as well as beast. With the snow came freezing, gripping cold, that reached inside a man's shirt, and closed its icicle fingers around his heart. Fear and freezing were companions for a time, but finally a man was alone in the storm.

"I don't know . . ." said Elaine, worrying, watching at the window.

In two minutes the tree line disappeared behind an advancing sheet of snow.

WILD WIND WESTWARD

One minute later the wall of white poured up out of the pasture, and closed on the barn.

Then the barn was gone. And the barn stood only fifty feet from the house.

And then, lastly, all sight itself was shut off, erased, obliterated by the frenzied pelting of icy flakes against the windowpane.

"He must have seen it coming," Eric assured her, not at all certain of the truth in his own words. "He had plenty of time to reach the barn, anyway. He's all right."

"I don't know. I don't know. I seem to feel . . . something."

There was nothing to do about it now. Only a fool would have stepped outside. Eric and Elaine waited. The storm did not subside by nightfall, but rather increased in fury. They supped, with little appetite, on the stew that had smelled so fragrant earlier in the afternoon, and went early to separate beds, but in the night Eric felt Elaine move in next to him, shivering there beside him in fear and uncertainty. In a while he wanted her, and she took him, gladly, and then trembled no more, but lay beside him unsleeping until the dawn.

When they awoke in the morning, the snow had ceased, and the day was cold and clear. The very shape of the earth seemed transformed, newly born, with a sharp sense of expectancy in the air. Drifts in strange shapes swung from the fields into the yard, long arced eddies of ridges and turrets, funnels and peaks. Elaine made coffee, toasted bread. Any minute, it seemed, Wilbur Nesterling would make his way from the barn to the house, grumbling at his ill luck in failing to make it back to the fire the night before.

But he did not return.

By midmorning the task was clear.

"We'd better go look for him," Eric suggested, in a tone so artificially casual he winced upon hearing his own voice.

"I guess we'd better," agreed Elaine brightly.

They bundled up and left the house, stopping at the shed

for snowshoes. It was very cold, but there was no wind. Striking out across the pasture toward the tree line, they made good progress. But what could be found, with blinding, glittering banks of snow bracketing the earth?

"He might have reached the Ordways?" suggested Elaine, hoping.

Hoping against hope. The Ordway farm was at least two miles away through the trees.

"If we could only find some tracks."

They walked into the forest, where the snow was hard and tightly packed. Elaine cried out, fell sprawling face first into the drifts.

"Oh," she cried, laughing when she found herself uninjured.

"What happened?"

"Caught my snowshoe on this branch."

Eric reached down, brushed away a bit of snow, and grabbed the offending twig. It was hard in his hand, and heavy.

The barrel of a gun.

He pulled it from the snowbank, and looked at Elaine. She was staring at the weapon. "It's father's," she said. Then, already screaming, she fell to the snow and began frantically to claw it away.

"Don't," he said. "I'll do it. Maybe you'd better not..."

Better not *look*, he meant to say, but it was too late. Her mittened fingers found a hard, round object buried in the snow, and she brushed away the icy coating within which it was shrouded. Then she stopped screaming, too numbed, too broken, for speech. Eric bent to get a closer look. The blank, icy eyes of Wilbur Nesterling regarded him without expression. His soul had gone to God.

Elaine was never the same after that.

She managed to get through the funeral, two days later, and saw Wilbur's coffin lowered into a grave that had had to be chopped inch by inch out of the frozen churchyard, the same place where she had once kissed boys and let Vance Trumbull caress her. Eric took her back to the farmhouse, hoping that grief would do its work, would

WILD WIND WESTWARD

pass. But she seemed to grow more removed from life, and then she began to get physically sick. He summoned the local doctor.

"Everything's fine," the man concluded rolling down his sleeves after examining Elaine.

"Fine? How can that be?" Eric demanded. "She used to be a vibrant girl. Now she barely moves, hardly speaks . . ."

"Simple melancholy, son. She's lost her father. But she'll soon have a new lease on life."

"I don't understand. How can you be so sure?"

"Son, I'm a liberal man," the doctor told him. "I've seen a lot of life. I know how it goes, and I don't blame nobody. But for Elaine's good name, and yours, too, I suggest you ride up over to see Preacher Tarnower one of these days and make the arrangements."

"What?"

"Son, I hope you turn out to be a better farmer than the mathematician you seem to be right now. One and one make three. Or can you figure that out?"

It was January 1864.

VII

Kristin was looking at herself when the pains began.

She was reclining on a long couch of mauve velvet in the drawing room of the Park Avenue mansion Gustav had purchased, and staring up at her portrait, which Percy Phipps had completed. So stunning was the portrait, so skillful Phipps' work, that it seemed as if her body and soul had been captured by his brush.

Then why did the image on the canvas not feel her pain?

Kristin reached for a small silver bell on a table next to the couch, and shook it twice. A maid appeared.

"Yes, Miz Rolfson?"

"Kathleen, perhaps we'd better summon Dr. Konrad."

"Yes, Miz Rolfson. Oh, Miz Rolfson! Do you mean . . . ?"

"This is my first time. But I think so. Yes."

"And you'll want Mr. Rolfson called from his office too."

That's not necessary, Kristin thought. "If you wish," she managed.

Another wave of pain hit her. The face in the portrait, regarding her across the gloom of this January afternoon, was regal and unperturbed. In October, Phipps had shown the painting for the first time, at a special gathering in the hall at Cooper Union, and after that it seemed everyone in New York wanted to meet her. "I said I would make you famous," Phipps had cried. Indeed, he seemed to have done so. Even Matthew Brady, pioneer in the new art of photography, had come to capture her, time and again, with his camera. "Your picture will be all over the country, my dear," Brady had said. "You will be recognized everywhere, like Helen of Troy. America does not have a goddess yet, but I think we need one."

Kristin smiled, lying there on the couch. If goddesses felt pain when they were having babies, then maybe she was one after all. But she did not smile for long. The contractions, mild at first, came at long intervals, and there was time to recover from the last, to prepare for the next. But by the time Dr. Konrad appeared, just before six in the evening, the pains were less than five minutes apart, and very severe. Konrad was a gruff, peremptory man, but Kristin trusted him, and he brought with him two nurses, older women, who were matter of fact and imperturbable. Mrs. Ratcliff went immediately to the kitchen, ordering the staff there to boil water, fetch towels, sheets, blankets. Mrs. Dentley moved about the bedroom, to which Kristin had withdrawn after the pains began, inspected it with a professional eye, and set about reordering it to her liking.

Dr. Konrad made an examination, and seemed satisfied.

"As I informed you on your last visit to my office," he announced soberly, "I expect a routine birth. You are, how shall I say, somewhat narrow, but that means little, because you are also young and strong."

"Thank you," Kristin said, in a wry tone, as another contraction began.

"Bye the bye, is Mr. Rolfson present?" asked the doctor.

Biting her lip against the pain, Kristin shook her head. The maid may have summoned him, she may not have. Kristin did not care. Why should he be here? It was not his child being born, it was . . .

The pain rose, rose, peaked on a terrible new height.

". . . *Eric* . . ." she groaned.

"What?" asked Mrs. Dentley, slipping another pillow beneath Kristin's head. "What was that you wanted, honey?"

Oh no, Kristin thought. The baby was not even ready to be born, and here she was crying out Eric's name. It had slipped involuntarily from her lips. She would have to fight the impulse to cry out again. Dr. Konrad, moreover, had been chosen because Gustav, to his credit, did not want to see Kristin suffer in childbirth, and Konrad had no aversion to the use of palliatives, if the trial grew acute. Yet, if she took his nostrums, might Kristin not, in dazed half-consciousness, say many things it would be wiser to hold back?

"Don't you worry about a thing," cried Mrs. Ratcliff, coming in with a stack of clean towels and a pan of steaming hot water. "You just relax and let nature take its course."

"Ohhhhhhh!" Kristin writhed as another bolt of pain hit her.

"Everything seems to be progressing just fine," Dr. Konrad reassured her.

Then, at the entrance to the house, Gustav's voice could be heard, calling loudly: "Why was I not summoned immediately? Immediately, you hear! Is my son born yet? *Is he?* You! I'll see that you're discharged!"

One of the maids began to cry and plead for her job.

Kristin tried to sit up. "Tell him it was I . . . who didn't call him. Not the maid's fault. Tell him I thought the pains might be false. Oh . . . tell him anything."

"We can't have that caterwauling out there," Dr. Konrad said to Mrs. Dentley. "It's a disturbance to all of us. Tell Rolfson to come here for a moment."

An instant later Gustav was in the bedroom, his face reddened from anger and drink. He had been at his club. His scar looked white against flushed skin, and his eyes reflected something like greed, as if a child were but another acquisition.

"Why wasn't I called?" he demanded.

"Quiet down," Konrad told him, calmly but emphatically. "I'm in charge here, and everyone must do as I say."

Gustav frowned, but fell silent, his gaze going from the doctor to Kristin.

"My darling!" he cried, rushing to the bed, falling upon

his knees, and grasping her hand. "My darling, give me a fine son!"

The two nurses looked at each other.

Another contraction gripped Kristin, and, without intending to, she squeezed Gustav's hand. He interpreted it as a sign of devotion.

"Darling, I'm here," he proclaimed.

"Please, Mr. Rolfson," said the doctor. "I'm afraid you must withdraw."

"Withdraw? Why? It's my son being born here, heir to a great mercantile dynasty."

"Mr. Rolfson, if you would just—"

"This is my house! This is my wife! This is my son!"

In spite of her pain Kristin found herself only mildly surprised at Gustav's ranting. It was his usual manner, particularly of late when thinking of his child, his son.

"It may be a daughter and it may be a son," pronounced Dr. Konrad, "but if you do not leave and cease your scene, harm may be done."

Kristin sighed again with the pain.

Prideful, doubtful, but wondering, Gustav obeyed. He had, of late, seemed master of all he surveyed. Far to the west, in Ohio, reports had emerged that young Rockefeller was proceeding slowly in the oil business. Gustav's refinery was ready for operation, men had been trained for the work, but as yet only a trickle of crude had been hauled in for processing. "The fool!" Gustav had observed gloating. "He went to all the trouble to fix an arrangement with the railroads, and he can't even get crude to the refinery! I'll bargain that young Godster right out of his trousers!"

But Dr. Konrad was not a business adversary. Neither boasts nor remonstrances were effective against him. Gustav retreated to brandy and cigars in his study, fiddling with the words he would use when he wrote his father, old Adolphus, that an heir to the Rolfson throne had been born. Judging from his last letter Adolphus was aging a little, but still in fine fettle. "If that wife of yours gives you any trouble," he had written, "just give her the

Vanessa Royall

opportunity to remember her family in Lesja. While we know she has been sending them money, she might also be interested to know that Amundsen, the crooked judge, is postmaster. Some letters do get through, but others are lost."

Gustav nodded, thinking about his son. What name to give the boy? He did not wish to burden a son with names already legendary, like Gustav and Adolphus. Harald? The name of a king, true. Lars? Too common, simple; it had not the unique sound these Americans liked. Ah! He had it! Haakon. Haakon Rolfson. Yes, that was what the name would be.

On the bed, birth progressed, and pain increased. Kristin was bathed in sweat. Nurses Dentley and Ratcliff bent over her, kneading, crooning. Dr. Konrad was wet with perspiration himself.

Again, again Kristin cried out. They would have been screams, had she the breath.

"Please, Mrs. Rolfson," he said. "Let me administer a drug to ease your pain somewhat."

Kristin shook her head, bit her lip. Another pain was coming.

"Please, Mrs. Rolfson. For your good and the good of the child . . ."

Kristin looked him straight in the eye, then, with a glance, indicated that the presence of the two nurses troubled her.

"You two take a minute," Konrad said to them. "Have a cup of tea. I'll call you when I need you."

"Yes?" asked Dr. Konrad, when the nurses had gone.

"If you give me the drug, I'm afraid I'll cry out."

"You're already crying out," he said, but then his eyes widened. Kristin had not trusted him for nothing. "A name?" he asked.

She nodded, fighting the pain.

"Not to worry," he said. "My assistants have been at a thousand births. What happens in the room remains in the room, you understand? You need have no fear. Now, do let me administer the drug."

"No, no, it's all right," Kristin told him. "You have given me the surcease I required."

The baby, a boy, was born just after midnight. Kristin was conscious then, but barely. She felt a last sudden spasm, then a series of smaller spasms, diminishing in intensity, and finally a release, an emptiness, and a weariness such as death must be.

She saw Konrad's face—"A boy, it's a boy," he was saying—felt something wet and hot on her hot wet abdomen, saw Dentley and Ratcliff nod in satisfaction. Last, she saw Gustav, exultant, standing above her, with his scar and his smashed nose and his wide sneaky wolf's eyes. She wanted to laugh. She wanted to cry *"Errrrr-iiiic!"* as she had cried with the pain. But she did not. She went to sleep.

In the morning Isabel Van Santen was sitting beside her bed, her long russet-colored hair shining in the January light.

"Well, my dear, I understand that you made quite a fuss."

"I did?" asked Kristin, suspiciously.

"How do you feel?"

"How is the baby?"

"Splendid. Ten pounds two ounces, and with a shock of straw-colored hair. Dr. Konrad is outside. I'll call him."

"No, wait a moment. About a fuss—what did you mean?"

"Just that you were noisy. That's all I know."

"Yes, I remember. I called his name."

"Not Gustav's, certainly."

"No."

Isabel's expression deepened. "Kristin, what will you do now? Eric is dead, and—"

"We don't know that for sure!"

"But, dear—"

"I will go one day at a time, as the child will. He is my child by Eric, not by Gustav. That means . . ."

She fell silent.

"It means what you make of it," said Isabel, sympathetically. "Let me just say one thing before I tell the doctor you're awake. If you ever need my help, right now, this minute, or next month, or next year, just ask. That will be my gift to you."

Kristin reached out with a shaky hand and placed it in Isabel's grasp. "I shall," she said. "Thank you."

Then the doctor came in, followed by a crowing Gustav. The baby was brought in a little later, and placed in Kristin's arms. He was sturdy, and astoundingly well formed. She could not understand how Gustav could not see Eric Starbane in the child's face, the set of his little shoulders, even his strong, steady gaze. But Gustav did not see Eric Starbane.

"To Haakon Rolfson!" he cried, lifting a champagne glass. The entire household staff had gathered in the bedroom, and they, too, raised their glasses in toast. "To Haakon Rolfson!" Gustav cried again. "To the toughest, shrewdest businessman America will ever see!"

Everyone hesitated a moment, watching Kristin. She had a glass, too, with water in it. Now she lifted her glass along with everyone else.

"To my son, Haakon," she said, in a soft voice, cradling the baby, "whatever his destiny be."

"You're not raising that child correctly!" raved Gustav.

Four-month-old Haakon twisted and wailed.

"He is crying," Kristin explained coldly, "because he is tired and hungry. There was absolutely no need to drive down here to the harbor."

"Look at the big boats, Haakon. Look at the big boats," Gustav cried, holding the baby over his head, showing him New York Harbor and the ships in port.

Haakon cried louder.

From the day of the baby's birth Gustav had strutted and crowed, boasting that he would do for his son what his own father, Adolphus, had done for him: turn him into a shrewd, cunning man of maneuver and aggrandizement. No matter that little Haakon was not yet aware that a boat was a boat or a bird a bird, Gustav felt that by exposing the child to certain things, some mysterious vein of knowledge would seep into his pores. The only toys Gustav would allow in the child's nursery were in the shapes of enterprise and industry: railroad cars, ships, cranes, pumps, and hammers. Kristin thought it was ridiculous, and so did everyone else.

"You don't know anything about children," she'd told him in disgust, one evening, when he'd insisted on reading Haakon that day's stock exchange quotations.

"And you do?" he'd responded.

"At least I came from a large family. I learned something." *Never to have a large family with someone you do not love,* she thought.

"And I was an only son," he retorted, "and bested the lot of you."

So he continued his efforts in molding his son, taking him down to the harbor on this fine May afternoon. But Haakon did not know about harbors or ships; he wanted his nap. And he was howling.

"Here, you take him," said the father, in disgust, handing the howling bundle to Kristin. "The day's ruined. We might as well get back. And I took off from the office this afternoon just for this!"

Kristin said nothing. Trying to quiet her son, she got back into the coach. Gustav followed, petulant and brooding.

"And how is business, husband?" she asked.

"Why do you ask?" He looked at her suspiciously, as if she were trying to ease from him information about important matters. In point of fact Gustav was a little worried. The war was not yet over, but everyone agreed that it was only a matter of time. General Sherman was poised for a strike deep into Georgia, possibly all the way south to proud Atlanta, and if that happened, the end could not be far behind. With anticipation of the cessation of hostilities, business was booming. A new era of westward expansion was certain. Hundreds of thousands of people would swarm westward, across the Mississippi, to

Vanessa Royall

establish farms, set up villages, lay out plans for cities. All of American life would be affected, and every category of American business was about to boom.

The carriage moved uptown to the Rolfson's Park Avenue home, its motion making Haakon drowsy. Kristin had given him her breast, and he sucked with languourous greed.

"Why are you so interested in my business affairs?" Gustav asked again.

"I was wondering about Rockefeller, that's all. What more have you heard from him?"

Gustav muttered a curse beneath his breath, and did not answer. Kristin had guessed right. Her husband was worried about his base in the oil business, and about the deal he thought he had struck with the young produce clerk. If, somehow, the young man could pay back his note before 1868, that big new Cleveland refinery would go to him as part of the bargain. Just last year it had seemed an unattainable goal for Rockefeller to achieve by 1868. But, as everyone knew, the war was almost over, the boom ready to begin.

The Rolfson home, or mansion, for a mansion it was, loomed squat and stolid on upper Park, a gray limestone façade with three tiers of windows facing the street. The carriage drew up in front of the house, and Gustav helped his wife and son out. He was surprised. Another coach was sitting at curbside.

"Caller?" he wondered. The coach was hired, and not at all elegant.

They went inside.

"A Mr. Rockefeller to see you, sir," pronounced Clyde, the butler. "He insisted. I asked him to wait in the library."

"Rockefeller?" said Gustav, nervously adjusting his cravat. "I wonder what he wants. Kristin, come with me. Beauty may have charms to soothe the savage beast."

Kristin handed Haakon, now sleeping, to his nurse, and accompanied Gustav into the library.

Rockefeller was sitting upright in a straight-backed chair, although there were many comfortable chairs in the room, as well as a long soft leather couch. He was reading from the Bible, which he set down when the Rolfsons entered. He was the same pallid, self-effacing man they had met in Cleveland, but Kristin noticed a few subtle changes. He wore a neat cheap dark suit, inexpensive but unpatched, and his manner was infinitesimally easier, more assured.

He rose when he saw them, and bowed. He shook Gustav's hand, and bowed again. Kristin was reminded of a snake that has been to charm school.

"Mrs. Rolfson, you look very lovely. I have seen your photograph in Cleveland."

"Cleveland, eh?" said Rolfson, pleased. From the beginning, when first Phipps and then Matthew Brady were taken by Kristin's beauty, Gustav had reasoned that being her husband would bring him added prestige.

"This man, Brady, had an exhibit of the new science, photography. It was not that I went for enjoyment," Rockefeller hastened to explain. "One must keep up with the latest developments. Oil by-products will be a major part of photography, as it develops, if you'll excuse my play on words."

"Oil and photography," said Gustav, frowning and studying the younger man. He was impressed, but he was also discomfited. Never in a hundred years would he have seen the connection.

"Cameras have moving parts," Rockefeller instructed, "and thus require lubrication. Not to mention what is necessary in the preparation of advanced kinds of photographs. . . ."

"Oh, certainly," agreed Gustav, nodding. "One must see all the angles."

"Just as God gives us to understand those angles," affirmed Rockefeller, who patted the Bible he had lain aside, "the Lord helps those who help themselves."

"Well, well," returned Gustav in a booming voice, somehow at ease now, with this mention of God and money. "Let's be seated." He rang the bell, and a maid appeared in the doorway. "Brandy," he ordered.

"None for me thanks," Rockefeller said.

"Tea, then?"

"As you wish."

"Excuse me," Kristin offered, turning to leave.

"No, no, not on my account," said the visitor, using his newly formed supply of charm. "Beauty adds to civility."

Gustav nodded curtly, and Kristin sat down with the men.

"Your call is unexpected, but delightful," said Gustav, after the tea had been served. He was concealing a sharp wariness. "What may I do for you?"

"I need more money," Rockefeller said.

Kristin watched Gustav's face, as he reacted to this announcement. Although it would have been almost impossible, he had been secretly afraid that Rockefeller was here to pay off the loan already. Now, however, with a request for money out in the open, Gustav relaxed. He thought he had Rockefeller at a disadvantage again; he was the sun again, and the other only a planet. Hiding a surge of glee, Gustav pursed his lips and looked judicious.

"How much?" he asked.

"A million point two."

Gustav looked a bit startled, and Kristin knew why. He did not have that much available for loan. He would have to request more from Lord Soames in England and he didn't want to do that. Soames had humiliated Gustav as far as it was possible to humiliate him. Besides which, if Gustav's current contract with Rockefeller came to no good end, Gustav would be ruined and—most likely—Soames would want his head on a golden platter.

But Gustav was a businessman. He nodded and lied. "I've got the money," he said. "But what do you want it for? It seems to me you've already taken on a considerable financial obligation, and—"

"I must have a million point two," interrupted Rockefeller, calm and quiet and implacable.

"Well, why?"

"There is a powerful man in Pittsburgh, by the name of Benjamin Horace. A banker, a politician, and"—Rockefeller gave a brief, descriptive wave of his hand—"he has influence in many areas."

"So do I. So do *we*."

"Buying Horace is important to the Cleveland operation."

Gustav looked puzzled. "What?"

"There is coal and iron ore in southern Pennsylvania, in west Pennsylvania too. There might also be oil."

"Oh, hell, we've—you've—plenty of oil up in Titusville, enough for—"

It was at that moment, listening to the two men spar, that Kristin knew for certain her husband could never beat this strange young man with the pale blue eyes.

"Everything ties together," Rockefeller explained to Gustav, slowly, almost as if he were Gustav trying to explain monetary theory to little Haakon. "Everything in the process must be controlled. *Everything*," he repeated, with fervent emphasis. "No one else must be allowed to control any part of an enterprise, from source to production to distribution to sale."

Gustav appeared startled.

"Except you and me," Rockefeller added.

"And what does this Benjamin Horace control?"

"Horace is a smart man. He has taken vast leases, on the mere chance that oil might be discovered. Southern Pennsylvania is not as promising as the northern part has proven to be, but one never knows. I already have the Titusville field, the railroads, the Great Lakes steamers, and *we* have the refinery. Now I need only a million and two hundred thousand dollars to secure rights to the leases that Benjamin Horace holds."

"The agreement has been made?"

"In principle. I have spoken to Horace."

"What is he like? Can you trust him?"

"No, and that's encouraging. The only person not to trust is someone with an unshakable reputation for trustworthiness."

"How did Horace get all these leases?"

"Much of the land has been homesteaded. Horace was

Vanessa Royall

able to deal with the government before the homesteads were settled. Title to certain mineral rights, if any, that might generally have gone to the homesteader, was held in reserve. A congressman named Creedmore saw to the legal arrangements."

"I see," nodded Gustav, who knew quite a lot about theft of mineral rights. "And so Horace holds a theoretical right, shall we say?"

"It has never been tested in court. And when one is dealing with simple farmers . . ."

"I understand," boomed Gustav, anxious to show that he, too, knew the fine moves of a prime businessman. "The farmers will never take the matter to court."

Kristin was appalled. Those who strove to rule the earth seemed always ignoble, corrupt, snickering among themselves in dark cabals, while the honest and the fine and the brave must ever fight for daily bread. But she remained silent, because she well knew by now that this knowledge being given her, given her unknowingly by two men who ignored her presence, might prove a great weapon one day.

"Horace wants a million two."

"Why can't you get up the money elsewhere?"

"Because I value your . . . cooperation."

Gustav beamed. He tried to hold it back, but he beamed. "Anything about Horace that can be used as leverage against him, if later *we* find oil, and if later he sees that he has been outdone?"

"He is close to invulnerable in Pittsburgh," Rockefeller stated, "because of his money and the men he controls. He married, however"—he glanced toward Kristin—"a woman who was, and who still may be, the operator of the biggest house in Pittsburgh."

"House?" Gustav asked. If this expression were idiomatic, he had not yet learned it.

"A *house*. The madam of a house, and very well connected in her own right."

"Ah," Gustav said.

"She was a New Yorker once. Joan Leeds was her name," Rockefeller said. "Quite attractive. Equally ambitious."

"Well, sir. As you know, you are already indebted to me for a sizable sum. We must agree on terms, *if* I choose to."

Rockefeller was prepared. "I need this money badly," he said. "Everything that comes from this will be blessed a thousandfold. As you know, I agreed to pay back the amount outstanding in 1868, in order to claim the refinery."

Gustav nodded, smug and secure.

"So now," Rockefeller went on, "if you give me the extra money, the one-and-a-fifth millions, I agree to pay everything back one year earlier, by December 31, 1867."

Gustav was dumbfounded. This strange young man was a dreamer and a fool. Appreciation for his own mercantile gifts blossomed again like a new flower in the spring.

"I'll have to contact my English backer, of course," he drawled, "but I'm sure there'll be no problem."

"Very wise of you, husband," said Kristin, at dinner that evening, long after Rockefeller had departed.

He missed the thin cutting edge of her comment. "I knew I was secure all along," Gustav gloated, stuffing his mouth with liver paté on toast, washing it down with Beaujolais. "When he misses the deadline he set, *he* set, the optimistic imbecile, I'll take everything having to do with oil in Pennsylvania and Ohio. And *that's* only the start."

"Anthony Soames must first give you the money."

"He will. He knows what these Americans call a 'sucker' when he sees one."

"Of that, husband, there is no doubt," Kristin said.

Lord Soames transferred the money from England to New York, whence it passed on to Rockefeller in Cleveland. But, for no fathomable reason, Benjamin Horace backed out of the deal. Another summer came. The Rolfsons and the Van Santens and their friends went north along the coast to vacation in Newport, Rhode Island.

"How are you managing?" Isabel Van Santen inquired.

"It is fortunate," said Kristin, "that my younger life was arduous."

"So it is that bad?"

Vanessa Royall

"Haakon is too little now to know, but if he grows up with Gustav, I am afraid he will be ruined. He will become just like Gustav and his execrable old father."

"Have you thought of anything you might do?"

"Yes," replied Kristin, laughing ruefully, "I shall run away. But where shall I go? Gustav has power, money. He will hire men to track me down."

That reminded Isabel of O'Keefe, the Pinkerton man she had hired to find Eric.

"Has there . . . has there been any further . . . news?" she asked tentatively, not wishing to bring up another distressing subject.

Kristin faced it. "No. And if Eric were alive, I am sure he would have contacted me by now. I fear I must accept . . ."

Her resolve failed. She broke down, sobbing quietly. Isabel held her. "It's not for me so much anymore," Kristin managed, between sobs. "I knew him and loved him. But Haakon never will—"

"There, dear. I'm here. I promised you my help once, for whatever it is worth, and that promise still stands. Gustav is insufferable. Even Hector thinks so, and he is a gentle man."

There was nothing to do about it, just then. Kristin recovered, and proceeded stoically with her life. Haakon was a bright light for her, and she found delight and solace in him.

When summer ended and weather cooled along the coast, they returned to their New York home, Gustav to immerse himself once again in business, Kristin to manage the household, to wait, to endure. She enjoyed taking the little boy out in his carriage, but her portrait and the Brady photographs had made her face well known, and many people turned to watch her as she passed. *How wonderful,* she thought to herself, *how far would I have to run in order not to be recognized?*

Returning from a stroll one afternoon in early September, pushing Haakon's carriage before her, she saw a tall, elegantly dressed stranger descending the steps in front of her house. He wore a high silk hat, and a meticulously trimmed vandyke. Momentarily, she was reminded of President Lincoln, but this man's features were more finely drawn. And he seemed to recognize her at once.

"Kristin!" he exclaimed, addressing her in a familiar but not offensive manner, as if he knew her. Perhaps he had seen the portrait, or the photograph, and learned her name. But what was he doing coming out of her house? Then she saw the reason for his oddly syncopated gait: the man had an artificial leg. She had seen them worn by some combat veterans, and they were always apparent, even when camouflaged by expensive trousers, as this one was.

"Yes, I am Kristin Rolfson," she said.

"I have come to fulfill a promise. May I speak with you for a moment?"

"Certainly. Let us go inside."

"No, I don't wish to trouble you. Let me say my piece and depart. My name is Scott Randolph, Colonel Scott Randolph, of the Union army. I was the commanding officer of the New York Twenty-seventh, and one of my junior officers asked me to call on you in case—" He broke off that sentence, and began anew. "A man named Eric Gunnarson asked me to call on you when I came to New York."

Eric! she thought, trembling suddenly. But she had inured herself to the idea that he was dead, and now she held at bay a surge of hope that arose within her. Haakon was growing restless in his carriage, and Kristin did not wish the nurse to hear what Randolph had to say, so she bade the woman carry the child into the house. Randolph's eye was caught by the sturdy healthy fairness of the child.

"A fine boy," he said. "He favors you, I believe."

"Not really," she replied neutrally. "He favors his father."

She looked at him, and he met her eyes. "You were speaking of a Mr. Gunnarson," she said.

"This . . . is difficult to do. . . ."

No, she thought. But she set her heart, and her face, and did not give way.

"Lieutenant Gunnarson asked that I stop and see you

Vanessa Royall

when I came to New York. I had meant to do so sooner but"—he whacked his artificial limb with the heel of his hand—"I was in the Harrisburg hospital for longer than I anticipated."

"Just tell me, please, Colonel Randolph."

"Yes, I'm sorry. Lieutenant Gunnarson was killed during the second day of the battle of Gettysburg, last summer."

Eric Starbane, she heard her voice saying long ago, the words echoing down through time, *I have your image in my hands. I want to have you forever. Will you give me that?*

I grant your wish with joy and with all my heart, she heard him say, across the chasm of mortality.

Now I have your image, he was telling her, *and with your image, you. May I take it inside me forever to keep?*

"You are certain of this?" she asked.

"Yes. When the rolls were taken, he was not accounted for. I myself was with him when he was . . . hit."

"His grave?" she persisted.

"I am afraid . . ." Randolph began. And Kristin recalled what the Pinkerton, O'Keefe, had said about bodies being blown away by explosions, by chained balls. ". . . but let me say this," he decided to tell her, "I attended the dedication of the Gettysburg battleground last November. President Lincoln was there. His speech was brief and entirely inadequate to the occasion, as everyone agrees, but at least there was a consecration of the ground. And Eric Gunnarson's name is on the roll of honor there, for all to see."

His news troubled Kristin the more. Eric had died before he had had a chance to reclaim his ancestral name, Starbane. Somehow it did not seem fair.

"Mr. Randolph," she said. "I appreciate your coming here to see me. I know it was not easy for you. Come inside now, and let me offer you some refreshment."

"No, thank you."

"It is no trouble. I assure you. I owe you a debt for your trouble."

"On the contrary, you owe me nothing. Gunnarson was a good officer and a fine man. We have both lost someone

WILD WIND WESTWARD

valuable and important to us, each in our own way. At any rate, I must be off to Boston. My military career is somewhat hindered now, by this leg."

"What will you do?"

"Return to the family bank in Boston. When I was young, I swore I would never be tied down to a desk. Now it seems I have no where else to go. It ought to be interesting, however. Everyone believes there is much money to be made after the war. That is what Gunnarson and I planned to do. We were going to make great fortunes."

"Perhaps you shall," Kristin said. "It seems a pervasive American ambition."

Randolph smiled, amused. "You are astute, as well as accurate. Perhaps we will meet again."

"Perhaps," replied Kristin. "And thank you once again."

She bade him good-bye, went inside her big house, went up to her room and drew the blinds, telling the servants she wished to see no one. Gustav pushed his way in when he came home from his office, and wondered dully what was troubling her.

"Not you, this time," she told him. "Leave me alone."

"Are you ill?"

"No."

"Have you received some bad news?"

"That is not a proper description."

"If you told me, perhaps I could do something."

"You could leave me alone."

So he did. Gustav shrugged and left the room. Kristin remained there for two days, recapitulating her past life. She examined her life, and where it had led her, and found she could not much longer endure the course on which she was, against her will, directed. She decided to alter that course somehow, very soon.

Two days later, when she came downstairs, perfectly groomed as always, bright and cheerful, no one could see any change in her.

But it was there, inside.

VIII

One year after being wounded on the Gettysburg battlefield, Eric Gunnarson hitched the late Wilbur Nesterling's spotted mare to the charabanc, helped his pregnant wife, Elaine, into the vehicle, and took a drive from the farm over to the battlefield itself, at which he learned that he was dead. Among the great roll of the fallen, there was listed one *Gunnarson, E., 2nd Lt. New York 27th.*

Eric was astounded, and the distress showed on his face.

"What's wrong, darling?" asked Elaine, standing beside him, holding his arm. Her burden was quite heavy already, and she had almost three months remaining to carry it. She looked up at him, blinking against the sun, her eyes dazzled, too, by the new white crosses over the fresh graves that stretched away into the fields.

"How could my unit make such a mistake?" he complained, still incredulous. "I wrote them three times, and I was sure their lack of response meant the matter was at an end, especially when I resigned my commission in the last letter."

Elaine's eyes swung to the roster, on which she saw her husband's name lettered. "Oh, my!" she cried, in a tone more of worry than of surprise.

He did not think much about her reaction at the time, and they spent several hours visiting the graves of men he had commanded in battle only a year earlier. Much had happened in that year. He was now married, expecting a child in the fall, and running the Nesterling farm. It gave him pleasure to be farming again, and he quickly recalled skills he had learned as a boy in Norway. But he wanted more;

WILD WIND WESTWARD

he wanted the great enterprises he and Colonel Randolph had discussed. He could not, however, seek them out now, nor leave Elaine alone just yet. The prospect of a child was doing her good, after her father's shocking death in the January blizzard. A doctor, examining Wilbur Nesterling's body, theorized that the man had stumbled or fallen, in the process setting off the hunting weapon he carried. The blizzard in which he had frozen had only finished the job that the gunshot wound in his chest had begun. For a long time after Wilbur's funeral Elaine had blamed herself, connecting her father's demise, in some process of guilt and retribution, with the afternoon of love she and Eric had spent upon the quilted bed. She had been, at first, immensely fearful that Eric would leave her, too, even after their marriage at the little white Gettysburg church. But over these past few months she had begun to relax.

Now, however, walking slowly with him among the cemetery markers, while Eric searched for the names of soldiers he had known, Elaine grew more and more nervous.

"And here's Private Krantz's grave," said Eric sadly, sinking to one knee. "I wouldn't say that he was a nobleman of nature, but he was one hell of a fighter."

He stood up. "So far, so good. I'm hoping against hope, though. I haven't found any indication that Scott Randolph died. So then why haven't my letters been answered? Unless he's grievously wounded . . ."

Elaine began to cry.

He tried to put his arms around her, thinking that the sadness of the graveyard was disturbing her. She made pathetic attempts to push him away, as if she did not want his comforting.

"Elaine, what's wrong?" he asked, holding her in spite of her efforts.

From the time he'd learned that she was pregnant, Eric knew he must marry her. One did not evade such a responsibility. Then, too, no response had ever come back in reply to his New York letter to Kristin. Besides which, she was the wife of another man. He and Kristin would always belong to each other, but now they were physically separated again, as they had been in the years after he'd left Norway. Some things are meant to be, but others are not. He rejoiced that he and Kristin had been able to consecrate their union by making love in the carriage in New York. And he married Elaine. She loved him utterly, with an intensity that sometimes startled him. But she was a good wife, and seemed to be recovering from the weight of her father's death.

Perhaps, today, these graves were reminding her of another? Perhaps he ought to have come here alone?

"No, no, it's not that," she sobbed. "It's . . . it's your letters. . . ."

"My letters? You mean, to the army? To New York?"

She nodded frantically, her head against his chest, biting her lip and crying.

"What about the letters?" he asked, with a sinking feeling.

"I never . . . I never gave them to the postman. I . . . Eric, I . . . tore them up. They were . . ."

"Never mailed?" he cried, leaning away to look in her face. He felt the astonishment of one who has gone through a part of his life, assuming the world is organized in a particular way, spinning easily upon its axis, only to awake one morning and discover that this presumably predictable earth has torn loose from its orbit and is hurtling directionless through the abyss.

The facts came one upon another.

His unit truly believed him dead.

So must Kristin.

If, at any time during his convalescence, Kristin or the army had contacted him, would he have stayed here in Gettysburg? Would he have married Elaine?

He did not know, because one never knows what might have been. Yet Elaine herself leaped to a conclusion.

"You despise me now, don't you?" she wailed. "You think I trapped you, and you hate me now. But . . . *but I couldn't let you go!*" she cried. "Don't you see? I loved you so much, *and I would have died if you had gone!*"

Then she was sobbing hysterically, and it was only after

Eric had carried her back to the buggy that she regained control.

"Don't worry about it anymore," he told her that night, as they lay in bed. "It's over, you did what you believed to be the right thing, and I'm sure no harm has been done. The Union army has been doing well enough without me, and I wasn't healthy enough to fight anyway."

"But the letter to New York?" mourned Elaine. "To Kristin?"

"Did that trouble you so very much?"

"When I tore up the letter, I didn't know who she was. You didn't tell me until later that she had married this Rolfson man."

"Elaine," he said, after thinking a moment, "I must tell you this. We are husband and wife, and will soon have a child. I know you love me, and I love you. You need not fear for one day, for one *minute,* that I will abandon you. But Kristin must know that I am alive and well. This you have to understand. I must write her, and I must also settle with the army."

Elaine was assured now, and satisfied. "Yes," she agreed, not meekly, but without enthusiasm.

"If you knew that someone was worried about you, concerned that you might have perished, would you not try to contact him, tell him you were all right?"

"I guess so."

"Now go to sleep. The harvest will soon be upon us, and we'll be busy dawn to dark."

She went to sleep beside him, chastened but—in her quiet way—triumphant. Eric lay awake, thinking. If he did write Kristin, as he had last fall, at her first address in New York, would the letter reach her at all? The Madison Hotel could not have been but a temporary stopping place to Gustav Rolfson. No, the best thing would be to telegraph, so that his message would go directly into her hand. He could do so from Gettysburg, and there—also through the telegraph office—he might learn the correct Rolfson address in New York, *if* the Rolfsons still lived there. But

Vanessa Royall

if he telegraphed from Gettysburg, the unusual gossip that a local *married* farmer was cabling a woman in great New York would be bruited about quickly and energetically. No, he would have to go to Harrisburg, but with the harvest coming, he could not spare the time for such a trip just now.

Just as well. Elaine would quiet down, and cease to worry about the matter. He did not want her getting upset, now that the baby's birth was drawing near. And he had another insight: *What if Kristin thinks I am already dead?*

The summer was difficult and long. Elaine caught a chill one rainy day, developed a small fever, and had to take to her bed. She was not actually ill, but neither was she entirely well, and Dr. Cummings of the village assured her that bed rest was just the thing. "Do not worry, though," he added. "The baby is fine, the baby is doing fine."

Still Eric worried, the more so because the same wet weather that sent Elaine to her room also threatened the wheat crop on which he was counting for money. Wilbur Nesterling had left farm and livestock, but little else, and Eric had planned to set aside some money and perhaps open a business in the town. He was not yet certain what it would be: hardware, possibly, because farmers would demand more machinery after the war ended; or maybe he would breed prize cattle; or maybe buy more land. The Harrisburg newspaper, which arrived in the post once a week, was full of stories about new men here in the state who were busy amassing money and influence. Sometimes Eric felt old before his time, as if life had passed him by, chances gone and opportunities lost. It had not been five years since he had fled Lesja, with nothing but a pack on his back, but sometimes it seemed like fifty.

He read about the oilfields in Titusville, to the north, and of John D. Rockefeller, once poor, but now a man of promise.

And he read of Benjamin Horace, called the "Pillar of Pittsburgh" by the Harrisburg reporter. Wasn't that the man Mick Leeds had mentioned just before he died? The man Joan Leeds had taken up with?

Life was unfair. And the newspaper story was effulgent:

> ... Prescient is the word for Mr. Horace. Through commendable, eagle-eyed foresight, and the aid of United States Congressman Angus Creedmore of Pittsburgh, Horace was able to insert a reservations clause in the Pennsylvania application of the Federal Homestead Act, whereby certain leases ...

Lesja! thought Eric, leaning forward to read more astutely. He suspected immediately that Benjamin Horace was, at heart, a kin of the Rolfsons. And he was not far from right in this conclusion. The words, the arrangements, were phrased in complex, legalistic language. But what remained when the dross of lawyer's jargon was stripped away could not but startle Eric, who had known Thorsen and Johanson, Thorvaldsen and Amundsen, the outwardly respectable but thievingly rotten men of his homeland. "For the good of the Commonwealth of Pennsylvania," concluded the article, "and to forestall exploitation by one man of our resources, as has happened in Titusville, potential leasing of mineral rights in the west and south are to be overseen by Benjamin Horace. ..."

Then, Eric asked himself, did not the individual landowner control the rights to minerals that might lie beneath his very feet?

Representative Angus Creedmore asserted that this was not at all the case, due to the special reservation he had inserted into the language of the Pennsylvania Homestead Act, "for the overall benefit of the Commonwealth and her people."

A map accompanied the article, showing areas under the presumptive jurisdiction of this clever Mr. Horace. These areas swept all the way from Pittsburgh east to the Shenandoah Valley.

"Elaine," asked Eric, "did your father acquire this farm through the Homestead Act?"

"No," she answered, knitting baby clothing, sitting up in bed, "no, he bought it outright from the widow of a previous owner. It's not a Homestead farm."

Without really knowing why, Eric breathed a sigh of relief, and went to the window, to watch the rain fall dully, heavily, on the already battered, overripe, unharvestable wheat.

The rain fell that day, and continued to fall through the night, and all through that week. By the time it ceased, and the sun broke through the clouds, tender kernels of wheat had been shaken from their stalks, almost as if the rain itself had been a gigantic threshing flail. There would be no wheat harvest at all, and Eric turned the pigs and the cows into the ruined fields, to forage at will. If the animals grew fat, at least he might sell them for cash money. But not, certainly, cash money sufficient to open a business?

Eric realized, at that moment, how profoundly he had changed. Had he remained in Norway, he would have lived peacefully, happily, from year to year, content in the knowledge that his land gave him a life. Now he saw that he wanted life and the land—although this was not his land, really—and much, much more. In him now, fully matured, was the motivation that fueled and fired the Rolfsons, and everyone like them.

He remembered his vow to Kristin, and to himself:

I will be like the Rolfsons and their kind . . . I will look upon the world as they do, and bend it to my will.

"Don't ever say that!" she had cried.

How naive. They had both been so young then, had had such precious little knowledge of the world and its ways.

"I will get even with the Rolfsons if it is the last thing I do," he had sworn then. And he swore it again now.

But he had no idea exactly how to achieve such an ambition. Soon he would have another mouth to feed, and a corn crop still to harvest in the fall.

According to the custom of the region Dr. Cummings was summoned for births only in the most drastic of circumstances. Mildred Wenthistle, midwife, supervised at all such occasions, assisted by her daughters, Bonnie and Flo, who were being groomed for the calling. Eric was not to worry, they told him in no uncertain terms, but had best mend a fence or curry a horse or perform some other useful task that would keep him out of their way.

"It is going to be complicated enough anyway," Mrs. Wenthistle said. "Your wife is quite frightened, and it's clear for all to see that the baby is large."

She made the remark without inflection, but Eric saw—or thought he saw—a certain tightness, a flicker of concern, around her eyes.

But he obeyed. He sat with Elaine briefly, held her hand, kissed her, and withdrew. Bonnie Wenthistle closed the door behind him.

"Where you gonna be, Eric?" she asked, familiarly. She was a big, bold, lusty girl and he had caught her eye on him many a time. "So I can tell yuh when the baby's born," Bonnie added, with a slow smile. "Why? Was yuh thinkin' of somethin' else?"

"No, Bonnie," he said, disappointing her. "I'll be down beyond the shed, driving pipe for a well. If I can pump water out of the ground, I won't have to carry it from the creek."

"I always said you was a real smart man, Eric. That's what I always say to all my friends. Maybe you can show me one day how to drive that pipe, all right?"

She went back inside the house, and Eric walked down to his prospective well. He had acquired the pipes on credit in Gettysburg early in the summer, before rain destroyed the wheat crop he'd been counting on. The pipe was of good quality, made of lead, one inch in diameter, and he had one hundred feet of it, although he was certain he would strike water long before he went to such a depth. So far, however, he had already driven forty feet into the earth, and had found no trace of water.

He began the task, as always, by pulling up the pipe he had already driven, and inspecting the driving wedge, making certain it had not been damaged on rocky soil.

Above the wedge he affixed a heavy metal cylinder with holes in it, like a sieve. Periodically he would attach a hand pump to the top of the pipe, testing if he had yet found water. If he had, the water would have seeped through the cylinder, found its way into the pipe, and would be drawn to the surface by the suction of the hand pump. But so far this had not occurred; Eric had found no water.

Satisfied that the wedge was in good shape, he sent forty feet of pipe down again, to the depth he had already reached, and screwed on another four-foot length, which protruded above ground. Over the edge of this piece he placed a thick iron cylinder, like a metal sleeve over the pipe. Its wide flat end lay over the top of the pipe, and it was this ram that he began striking with a sledge hammer, driving the pipe increment by increment farther into the earth. When he had driven the protruding piece of pipe down to the level of the ground, he would screw on another length and set to work again.

Fifty feet. No water.

Sixty.

Seventy.

He stopped, mopped his brow, took off his shirt in the bright, warm September sunshine.

In the house poor Elaine was screaming. The sound frightened him, unsettled him. He went to the house, ostensibly for water.

"Everything's all right," said Bonnie Wenthistle, pale.

A curtain of sheets had been strung up, hiding Eric's view of the bed. Elaine was moaning. It did not seem "all right" to him.

"I can get Dr. Cummings. I'll just saddle my horse and ride on over."

Mrs. Wenthistle herself emerged from behind the sheets.

"No cause for alarm," she said, cheerful and hearty.

That was the problem; she was always cheerful and hearty.

"Go back to work," she told him. "Take your mind off it. This is no place for a man, anyway."

Eric obeyed, going back outside. But he saddled his

horse anyway, just in case. He went back to the well, and lost himself in the rhythmic, monotonous slamming of the sledgehammer on the ram. Driving was difficult for a time, as if he were passing through a rocky stratum far below the surface, then suddenly the wedge sank into a soft layer, and each blow of the sledge sent it one or two feet deeper.

Ninety feet.

Ninety five.

He fastened the pump, and tested. Still no water. He had only five feet of pipe remaining, and certainly he could not afford more. Ill luck. He had chosen a bad site. Well, there was nothing to do but drive the last five feet, and, if water did not appear, pull up all of the pipe and try a well at another spot.

In the silence, as he fastened the last section of pipe, he could hear Elaine in pain. The sound tore his heart, and he took up the sledgehammer again, swinging it furiously, slamming it down upon the ram, to blot out the cries he could do nothing about.

Ninety six feet.

Ninety seven.

Ninety eight.

He lifted the hammer to strike again, then paused. An odd sensation. He felt a change in the atmosphere, a subtle alteration in the atoms of the living air. The earth did not shift beneath him; it only seemed that way. Yes, he thought, there is water in the pipe. He removed the ram and picked up the pump, ready to fasten it to the end of the pipe. But as he grasped the pipe, it seemed to quiver in his hand. Eric had time to think *What's this?* when *this* came shooting out of the earth, a thin shining current of bursting black power, rising in the blue air, rising above the trees, curving in a long graceful pattern, catching the wind, spreading out like a beaded black plume against the sun.

Eric fell back, momentarily astounded, unthinking, not realizing what was happening.

"Eric, Eric!" called Bonnie Wenthistle, running out of the house.

Oil, Eric thought, conscious now of what he perceived, but still incredulous.

The black tide continued to shoot out of the earth, falling everywhere like rain, frightening the pigs and chickens.

I should put a cap on the pipe, he thought.

"Eric!" cried Bonnie, rounding the corner of the barn, and gaping at the scene.

What luck, he thought. Oil. This was something he did not need her eyes to see, nor her hardworking mouth to talk about all over the countryside.

"Lord, Eric," she cried, as he struggled to get a cap over the end of the pipe, "Lord Gawd almighty, you sure know how to drive a pipe!"

He struggled with the cap, wet and black and glistening. And ecstatic. In a moment he was happier still.

"Come, see," she told him. "You have a daughter. She's beautiful. And Elaine is fine."

IX

Time, quite suddenly, became an enemy. There was no way, for long, to contain the news that oil had been found. Consequently Eric had to think hard and work fast. He did not know the quality of the substance that had come spurting out of the earth, nor did he know how much of it there was. He did understand from reading, however, that oil was found in pools beneath the earth, and that these pools could cover miles of underground expanse. The pool he had penetrated might just as easily be reached by drilling on the Ordways' farm, or the Renners', or the Fensterwalds'. These were homesteads, and Eric was very mindful of the Creedmore Reservation in the Pennsylvania Homestead Act. He knew another thing, too, with crystal clarity: striking oil was a stroke of fortune that would never come again.

He needed help, and advice. He needed the best of both, and quickly.

Two days after the baby was born—he and Elaine had agreed on the name Elizabeth—Eric Gunnarson sold three cows and five hogs. "I need the cash," he said to the owner of the slaughterhouse. "I have to run up to Harrisburg." The owner nodded sagely, paying out the bills. "Reckon you'll give it a good try, but let me tell you something. There's very little likelihood a poor farmer is a-goin' ta get the better of them bigwigs what knows how to operate. You'll go up there with your hat in your hand, and you'll come sulkin' back here with your tail between your legs."

"Don't bet on that," Eric said.

339

Vanessa Royall

First he stopped at the tailors and ordered a good suit of clothes.

Then he bought a horse, a fine black stallion, and also purchased an expensive saddle. He ordered his initials, E. G., embossed in gold on the saddlebags. The lessons of Colonel Scott Randolph had not been lost on Eric: in order to play the part, one must look the part.

"I must go up to Harrisburg for several days," he told Elaine, as she lay nursing little Elizabeth. The child had dark hair, like her mother, and the same exquisite complexion. But she had Eric's penetrating blue eyes.

"Oh, darling, why?" asked Elaine.

"It's about the oil."

"We don't need the oil. We have the farm."

"I'm afraid we'll be cheated out of both, if I don't find legal help now."

"Must you go?"

"Yes. You'll be all right. I've hired Bonnie to see to you and to keep house. Her brother, Melvin, will see to the rest of the animals."

"Are you sure you ought to have sold the others?"

"If I do what I intend to do about the oil," Eric said, kissing her good-bye, "neither one of us will ever milk a cow or collect an egg or slop a hog again."

"I wonder. I'm worried."

"Don't be."

He gave Melvin Wenthistle instructions regarding the feeding of the stock, and prepared to leave. Melvin was an eager, but somewhat dull-witted boy, needful of caution.

"Whatever you do," Eric told him, "don't take the cap off that pipe in the barnyard."

"Huh? Why not?"

"Because there's money in there."

A slow dumb grin of shrewdness spread across Melvin's wide white face. "G'wan, Eric," he said. "What do you think I am, stupid? Money in a pipe, that's a good one. G'wan. How many pails of slop did you say the hogs get, again?"

* * *

WILD WIND WESTWARD

In Harrisburg, Eric immediately sought the telegraph office, located next to the postal station. Buoyed by the knowledge that he had not found his friend's name on the roster of the Gettysburg dead, mindful, too, of the promise he had made to Scott Randolph, Eric cabled the address he had been given long ago: Randolph Security and Trust, Boston, Massachusetts.

> REQUEST INFORMATION WHEREABOUTS
> COL. RANDOLPH NY 27TH.
> ERIC GUNNARSON

It was ten thirty in the morning. The operator took the notepaper on which Eric had written his message, and tapped it out on the keys. "Will you be waiting for a reply, sir?"

"Yes, I'll just go over to the hotel, and get myself a room for the night, I have business here for a few days."

It was his intention to see a lawyer, to become versed in the things he would need to know in order to protect himself. His newspaper reading, too, had left him aware of how one man, Rockefeller, up north, had managed to gain control of an entire oil field. If one man were also to accomplish this here in the south, Eric wanted to be that man. Briefly he studied a map on the wall of the telegraph office, which showed an amazing network of communications across the country. The world was changing, shrinking. The past was dying. Time was speeding up....

Time. He had too little of it. He started for the door.

"Sir," called the operator, "a reply is coming in."

He took it down and handed Eric the pad.

> RANDOLPH HERE STOP WELCOME BACK
> FROM THE DEAD STOP REPLY.
> S. R.

Eric could not recall ever having been this thrilled, not even as a child. It was as if he could speak to his friend, over this vast distance. But he could not, not exactly. Nor did he wish to put in words exactly what it was he had discovered.

POTENTIAL FOR GREAT ENTERPRISE STOP MUST ACT NEED ADVICE TIME ESSENTIAL

And the reply came clicking and tapping back over the wires:

RETAIN COUNSEL ENTRAIN BOSTON WILL AWAIT.

"When is the next train east?" he asked, while paying the operator for his services.
"Washington or New York?"
"New York. Then Boston."
"That'll pull out at nigh on to six o'clock tonight. You be in Boston bright and early tomorra morning."

Eric considered. He had time to see a lawyer today, and catch the train later. The problem was that he did not know any lawyers. There would be many, doubtless, over at the state capitol, whose handsome dome presided over the city, but he had an instinctive aversion, born of his background and isolated mountain youth, to lawyers making it their business to adorn the place where laws were made. Then he had an idea. In the nearby hotel, which appeared to be quite grand, there must be men of consequence who could recommend some worthy names. After stabling his horse, "for several days, at least," he said, Eric went over to the hotel, entered the lobby, and saw Kristin looking right at him.

He stopped moving, and stood rooted to the floor, transfixed. This was no portrait, but something far more uncanny, that had captured Kristin's face and form, and pressed it whole upon a piece of shiny paper. Then he saw there were more such images, visions.

"Move along there, please, sir," shouted a bellboy, pushing through the lobby with a half-dozen bags. "Ain't you never seen a photograph before?"

Examination of the strange, lifelike pictures revealed that Eric was looking at an exhibit of Matthew Brady's work. There was President Lincoln, and General Sherman, now a great hero since his army had cut the South in half by laying a sixty-mile-wide trail of waste from Atlanta to the sea. There were also photographs of people he did not recognize, but who seemed famous indeed.

And among these was Kristin.

He studied her face lovingly. She seemed not to have aged at all, but there was around her eyes now a hint of remove, a trace of calculation and resolve he had not known before.

The encounter with her image stirred him to increase his own resolve. He was going east! He would see her! And this time he would see her as a man of affairs, of substance, prepared to . . .

Prepared to what?

He had had to sell animals to buy a suit of clothes. He did not yet have train fare. And he was married, the father of a child.

I won't think of it, he thought. *I won't let myself think that she has been waiting for me, and that now I can do nothing about it.*

Eric went to the dining room, ordered breakfast, and watched the businessmen as they came and went. Three well-dressed men, sitting at a nearby table, talked of stocks, investments, the war, and certain items of legislation now before the statehouse. He was just about to ask them if they might recommend good counsel, when a thin young man, ill dressed but spirited, passed by their table.

"Hey, Phil," one of the men called, "get any business out of your shingle yet?"

There was a certain archness in the man's tone, but Phil did not seem to mind.

"Come a day," he said, "when you'll be begging me to split a fee."

The other men found this uproarious, but the younger one seemed not to mind at all. He passed closely to Eric's table.

"Excuse me, sir?"

"Yes?"

There seemed no better way than but to ask: "I'm looking for an attorney. Can you refer me to one?"

The man stopped and looked at Eric, studying him with a dry, wry expression that seemed characteristic. "You don't look like a crook to me," he said.

"I'm not."

"But I am a lawyer. What do you want a lawyer for?"

"I can't talk about it here."

"No one can." This with the hint of a smile.

"Are you . . . that is, when we consider . . ." Eric fumbled.

"You mean to ask if I am any good in the profession, don't you? The answer is that I am the best. I have, and I assure you of this without a shred of modesty, never lost a case."

"Why, that's excellent," said Eric.

"Because I've never *had* a case," said the man, thrusting out his hand. "Phillip Phettle, with a ph, at your service. What seems to be the trouble?"

At first Eric was reluctant. The man had had no cases *at all*.

But that was explainable. "I'm shut out here," Phettle said, without bitterness. "I came here from Vermont, so I'm an outsider. The regular lawyers wish I would move away. But I can't. I'm almost out of money. Now let's talk about your retainer."

Phil Phettle's confidence, his spirit and good humor, appealed to Eric. The man was bright, and spoke well. He seemed to know a great deal about operations in the capital, so Eric decided to test him.

"What do you know of a man named Benjamin Horace?" he asked.

Phettle's eyes narrowed. "What are you up to, sir? I had you pegged for an honest man. Horace is a thief and a half. Possibly two thirds. If you're seeking aid for Ben Horace, you'd best look elsewhere."

He rose from the table.

"Sit down," said Eric. "I think we can find common ground here."

Conscious that time was running, he explained the situation. He had discovered oil—some, he did not know how much—on his farm. No, the farm was not in his name. It belonged to Elaine. No, it was not a Homestead farm. And it was surrounded by Homestead farms. "That means—"

"I know what it means. The Creedmore Reservation Clause."

"Exactly."

"So you are asking what ought to be done to make sure the oil isn't lost to you?"

"Not me alone!" cried Eric, in a voice so sincere it impressed the young lawyer to his base. "No, is that what you think I'm doing here? Absolutely not. Everyone must have his rightful share of whatever profits there are. *That's* why I'm here, and that's why I seek counsel. I have not been in my community too long, but I am getting to know some of the people. They are honest, and that is a hindrance to their well-being—"

"Spoken like a true patriot."

"—and they will be no match for a man like Horace, who has already been able to buy a congressman, and get a powerful law on the books."

"You're fortunate that he did," Phettle said. "A law on the books is a target."

"I don't understand."

Phil Phettle drew his chair nearer the table, finished a cup of coffee, and began speaking rapidly and excitedly. "Does any other state," he asked, "have a law or statute or provision comparable to the Creedmore Reservation? You don't know, I'll tell you. No. So? And does this so-called reservation apply to all of Pennsylvania? Again, no. And was it ever dealt with in the Pennsylvania legislature? No, once more. It is sui generis."

"I don't—"

"A thing unto itself. It's not really a law at all. It's a

pseudolegal maneuver, fashioned to deceive yokels into believing that what belongs to them doesn't. Are you following me?"

"No, I'm right beside you, and maybe running ahead."

"Commendable. There is a course of action that suggests itself immediately. You and your neighbors must petition the state legislature for a hearing on the Creedmore Reservation."

Eric did not have time to respond before the lawyer added:

"But a petition won't work, because your country neighbors are too suspicious to sign it, assuming they can write. Secondly, Horace can afford more legislators than you can, so the petition would be thrown out anyway."

"Afford?"

"Buy. With money. To do his will."

"Here in America, too?"

"Hell, here in America *most!*" Phettle said, vehemently. "No, Gunnarson, don't be deluded. The enemy must always be approached as if it had a preponderance of heavy weaponry. They're sneaky. But so are we."

"We are?"

"I haven't even gotten started yet. No, no, 'I have not yet begun to fight!' That's the way it goes. What are your immediate plans?"

"I have to go to Boston to see a friend."

"This is not the time for a vacation trip."

"He's in banking."

"Traveling is pretty good this time of year."

"I hope to get his help in developing the oil business in southern Pennsylvania."

"Benjamin Horace and Angus Creedmore are not going to like that."

Eric slammed his clenched fist down on the tabletop. A waiter rushed over. "Is everything all right, gentlemen?"

"No," said Eric.

"Yes," said Phil Phettle. "Just bring us some more coffee. Now," he said to Eric, "you say you don't have a Homestead farm. So be it. What we need is a test case.

One of your neighbors, who lives on a Homestead farm, and upon whose land oil is also found, must take Benjamin Horace and the Creedmore Reservation to court. *If* Horace moves in when he learns of the oil strike, which I have no doubt that he will."

"But just *one* . . . ?"

"That's all it takes, legally."

"It would be better if all of us fought together."

"Of course it would. But they're stubborn, independent farmers. Can you get them together to agree on much of anything?"

Eric thought it over. The farmers in his area cooperated splendidly only on matters common to all of them: barn raisings, threshing, wood cutting. Otherwise each individual saw to his business close to the vest, counted his shekels behind a high wall. "Maybe if they knew what it was they were fighting for," he suggested. "Or if *I* bought up the leases myself . . ."

"Then the test case would be yours. And I'd have a client. But where are you going to get that kind of money?"

"Hopefully in Boston," Eric said.

He had to sell the newly purchased stallion to afford train fare, but it didn't seem to matter. Only the future mattered now, and what he could do with it. Everything in the past had been reduced to remote and indecipherable brilliances, like something beautiful he might one time have read.

The train skirted New York at late twilight, striking up through Jersey, across the Hudson, and on up the Atlantic coast. Eric watched from the window, saw the skyline sweeping low and powerful and long against the sky. There, yes, somewhere in that mass of flesh and stone was Kristin. And soon he would see her. Soon, on the return trip from Boston. Elaine and Elizabeth came to his mind, and love filled his heart as well. But still it was Kristin who rose above everything, and he rested content in the hope that somehow life might be put aright.

* * *

Vanessa Royall

He arrived in Boston in the rainy dawn. The black smokestack of the engine belched several last blasts of grime up onto the soot-ridden beams of the cavernous station. Eric walked along the train, looking about.

"Mr. Gunnarson?"

"Yes."

"Follow me, please."

Scott Randolph's coachman, no doubt. Randolph was as good as his word. It was early morning, and the street outside the station was all but deserted, save for a few hackies, disconsolate as their sagging horses, standing in the pale light, dripping rain. A large coach waited there on the street, too. The coachman motioned Eric toward it, swinging up on the seat behind the horses. Eric climbed into the cab, wondering idly why a coachman would not hold the door for his passenger. He soon found out.

Three men waited inside the coach. Two of them grabbed Eric before he had a chance to react, and pressed him back against the seat on one side of the coach. The third man, seated opposite, his face in shadow, got right down to business.

"We know why you're here, Gunnarson."

What was this? Who knew what? "I'm glad you do," he said.

"Don't sass your betters, Sven," grunted one of the men holding him, and twisted Eric's arm behind him.

"I'd advise you to have a nice reunion with your old war crony, and then go back to your farm and your wife and your little girl. You don't want to be meddling in affairs for which you are unsuited."

The oil! Eric thought. And these men were threatening Elaine and Elizabeth. But who were they? Or who did they serve?

"An immigrant boy with no citizenship, who killed him a man in the old country and ran away, no, Sven, that's not the type we like here in America. Why, if that news got out, it could cause you a lot of trouble. Get the point?"

Blackmail. An easy point to get. "But I am a citizen,"

he told them, trying to calculate how these men would know so much about him. "I am also a war veteran."

"Who cares?" grunted the man who held his arm, giving it another twist.

Eric suppressed a groan. He had figured it out. The one person who might use his past against him in this way was Joan Leeds! Now Mrs. Benjamin Horace, wife of the Pillar of Pittsburgh. Of course. But how quickly events were moving. Horace already knew of the oil strike, and was circling to protect his interests. Had he learned of Phil Phettle? Worse, was he ready to hurt Elaine and the child?

"Let me tell you something," Eric told the man, taking a chance. "I know Joan Leeds, too, and if I were she, or her husband, I would not want any diligent inquiry made into the cause of the death of a Mrs. Liz Leeds, Joan's mother, back in New York a few winters ago—"

"Shut up! You ain't here to talk. You're here to listen."

"—and I doubt Mr. Horace's reputation would be well served, in his position as champion of the people of Pennsylvania, to know some of the activities his wife pursued when I knew her in New York. And I knew her *very* well," he added.

"Goddam. These immigrants don't understand nothin' unless you pound it into their thick skulls. Driver!" ordered the man. "Get us out of here, to a place where we can continue this conversation in earnest."

Eric had no desire to endure a beating. Before the coachman had a chance to snap his whip at the horses, Eric kicked out, catching his interlocutor in the solar plexus. The man snapped forward, gulping like a beached fish. The men on either side of Eric, caught off guard, leaned away, getting set to act, but they were too late. Eric drove an elbow into the chin of one, and jerked his arm free of the other. Getting up, he sent a knee into the face of the man who had been talking to him, threw a flurry of punches at the other two, and leaped from the coach just as it began to roll.

"What the hell . . . ?" called the coachman, turning around.

"I changed my mind about the ride," Eric told him, starting back into the station. It seemed unlikely his assailants would pursue him there. He was right. The coach halted momentarily, its occupants deciding what to do, but then moved on.

"There you are, finally. Gunnarson, how are you?"

Scott Randolph. A little older, a bit leaner, but resplendent in morning clothes and cape. "I came down to the platform, but didn't see you."

The men shook hands warmly. "I got off right away, and proceeded to hold a business discussion."

"I don't understand."

"Let us go somewhere and have breakfast and a talk. There are so many things to . . . tell me, did you . . . were you able to stop in New York?"

"Eric, my God, yes. But at the time I thought you were dead, and so I told her . . . your Kristin is exceedingly lovely, I must say—"

"Told her I was dead? Well, I shall stop on my way back to Pennsylvania, and put that aright—"

"—and her son is an adorable blonde child—"

"Son?" asked Eric.

They were in Randolph's coach now, driving to his house. The coach continued to move, the city to pass by outside its windows, the earth to spin, the sun to rise, the ocean to roll against the coast. But for that one fell moment, everything ceased, stopped, caught and frozen in an instant of shimmering time. Kristin had a son by Gustav Rolfson. Now she was as tied to him as he was to Elaine. Oh, there was no way out of the maze life had given them, no way . . .

"Fine boy, too," Randolph was saying. He had noted Eric's moment of consternation, and was not chatting idly filling in time. He guessed at, but did not wish to inquire about, the depth of Eric's feeling for Kristin.

I will not think of it until I see Kristin with my own eyes, resolved Eric, and, with difficulty, put the matter aside.

* * *

Randolph lived in a sprawling house on Beacon Hill. There, over a breakfast of fried haddock, eggs, potatoes, and port, they first discussed what had befallen them since Gettysburg. "I was unconscious or semiconscious in the Harrisburg hospital," Randolph said. "Oh, it must have been for weeks. I was lucky. My leg had been blown away cleanly, and a field doctor cauterized the wound immediately. Save for that, I might have died of gangrene, as did thousands of others. When I finally recovered sufficiently to know what had happened, I tried to learn who among our regiment had survived. Not many. And, do you know, we missed the third and worst day of the battle? Pickett, the Rebel commander, charged right into our lines on Cemetery Ridge."

"Cemetery Ridge? Jubal Early drove us off the Ridge."

"But he wasn't able to hold it. Hours after we were wounded, our men recaptured the area. And when Pickett charged, our men cut him to shreds. Rebs died like flies, the poor bastards."

"It might just as well have been us."

"Hell, Eric, it *was* us. Now, what's on your mind. A great enterprise. That's what you said in your cable. Well, what?"

"Oil. I've found oil."

"Where?"

"On my farm. That is, on the farm Elaine inherited from her father."

"Eric, that's wonderful. Everyone knows that oil is the sine qua non of what the industrial world is to become."

"No, I am afraid it might not be such good fortune at all," Eric demurred, "unless I can keep what is mine."

"Did you retain a lawyer, as I suggested?"

"Yes, and I think he's an honest man."

"As lawyers go."

"As they go."

Eric proceeded to explain the peculiar provision in the Pennsylvania law, spoke of Phettle's advisement that a test case be brought to court, and concluded by telling of Benjamin Horace, and the men who had meant to abduct him at the railroad station.

"That Horace!"

"You know him?"

"Eric, I am an investment banker, and I try to learn as much as I can about every area in business. A man from Cleveland, Rockefeller by name—"

"I've heard of him."

"—has bought the leases to the oil field in northern Pennsylvania. He is now negotiating with Horace to buy these southern leases, the value of which—when the news of your strike gets out—will increase a hundredfold. Horace has been delaying a deal, and now his luck is running high. Setting aside, for the moment, the legality of Horace's claim, he stands in a position to make Rockefeller pay far more than the 1.2 million he had intended."

"But these rights are *not* Horace's to sell!"

"That has not yet been settled in court. The way in which your Pennsylvania situation is now structured puts Benjamin Horace in a crucial position. He can become spectacularly rich, or, if the Creedmore Reservation Clause is found to be without legal validity, he could lose everything."

"How do you—as a businessman—think the court will decide upon the Creedmore Clause?"

"I think it's a laughable provision. Any honest court will throw it out. If it gets to court."

"Phettle wants me and my neighbors to take it to court."

"That," said Randolph, "is one reason why you had that pleasant conversation with Horace's men this morning. If, indeed, they were Horace's men. You, too, are in a crucial position. If you are willing to fight."

"I am."

"Are you really?"

Eric considered his life. Save for Kristin—and Kristin was a miracle the worth of which could not be calculated —discovering oil was the closest thing to wonder that had come to him. At the very least he owed it to Elaine and his new daughter to defend what was theirs. His Gettysburg neighbors, moreover, would not be cheated out of what belonged to them, would not suffer the fate of his former Lesja compatriots.

"Yes, I'll fight. That's why I'm here. I want to get a loan to develop the field, if it really can become an oil field. So I'll need to hire surveyors, and workmen. I'll need a refinery, connections with the Pennsy Road . . ."

"Whoa, there. Slow down a minute." Randolph laughed. "I believe an initial loan will be readily voted by our board of directors, but first you must get your neighbors united behind you. And you had better make haste to do it. The business world is moving forward faster than it ever has. A month, a week, may make all the difference. If Rockefeller wins control, even nominal control, of the southern leases, it will put him in a position to turn a huge profit and pay off his backer Rolfson. If Rockefeller can do this, which is speculative at the moment, he will be so far ahead of anyone else in oil, there will be no catching him."

Eric, his mind already alive with possibility, made the connections. If Horace kept control of the southern leases, Rockefeller's cause would be somewhat hindered. He wouldn't be able to pay his notes to Rolfson on time. This was to the advantage of Gustav Rolfson, who wanted to grasp Rockefeller's base. Should Eric be successful in wresting control of the leases from Horace, he would be in a position of strength, from which he might deal with either Rockefeller or Rolfson, or both of them, as he chose.

And he would also be in a position to profit mightily himself. He would even his ancient score with Gustav from a vantage of wealth and power.

"How much money can you lend me to start with?" he asked Randolph.

New York belonged to the rich. And, returning now, Eric felt like he belonged, too, because he felt rich. His emotional anxiety grew, however, as the moment drew near for him to announce himself at the Gustav Rolfson mansion. It would be best if Gustav were not present, but there was no way to guarantee such a situation. Eric had already steeled himself to the fact that Kristin had Rolfson's child, but, no matter what, he had to see her. He fought and fought again the feeling that, true though their love was, they were destined to live their lives apart.

Realizing that Kristin had no idea he was alive, Eric hired a messenger to take her his card and a brief note of explanation, mentioning Colonel Randolph, and stating his intention to call. He waited at his hotel. The messenger returned to report that Mrs. Rolfson would be happy to receive him at any time that day. Afflicted by a welter of emotions that both elated and troubled him, Eric engaged a coach and drove up Park Avenue.

"Eric Gunnarson," he announced to the butler, entering a vast, glittering foyer. Exactly such a foyer he would have himself, very soon. He believed that only good things were going to happen to him now.

"This way, sir. Mrs. Rolfson awaits you in the drawing room."

Later, Eric barely recalled walking from the entrance, through a great hall, and into the smaller, comfortable drawing room. It seemed he had lost the feeling in his legs, and his head was very light, but exceedingly clear. Kristin was on her feet in the room, and playing in a padded enclosure on the floor was a tow-headed child of less than a year.

"Thank you, Ellison," Kristin said quietly, and the butler withdrew, closing the door.

They looked at each other for a long, long time. Then, scarcely aware of how it happened, they were in each other's arms. Seconds broke down into a thousand parts, one part flowing after the other, so that each portion might be cherished for itself, and eternity beckoned within the circle of their fierce embrace.

"I knew this day would come," she told him, pulling away slightly to gaze into his eyes.

Eric experienced a terrible, sinking sensation; Kristin believed he had come to take her away.

"I am ready," she said. Taking his hand, she drew him near the child. "And so is your son."

Eric's consciousness seemed to waver. Pridefully, bursting with joy, Kristin picked up the child and placed it in his arms. "His name is Haakon," she said. "And he looks like the two of us combined."

The baby gurgled and studied Eric's face. He held the boy, incredulous, and finally put him down again to play. His son, whom he could not yet claim. Eric felt awful.

"One of my most trusted maids has packed a few small bags for me," Kristin was saying, "and so we must make haste . . . why, darling, what is wrong?"

"The time in the carriage on the way to Spuyten Duyvil?" Eric asked, nodding toward Haakon. "He is . . . ?"

Kristin nodded, and put her arms around him again. "What is it, darling? You look so . . . stricken."

"Kristin, what I must tell you is the hardest thing I have ever had to do."

But he did not have to do it. She guessed. "You have found someone else?"

"It was not quite like that, but it amounts to the same thing." And, with his voice close to breaking, he told her of Elaine and Elizabeth.

Wordlessly, they stood apart, considering but unable to alter the chasm of circumstance. Kristin was the first to break the silence. "Then we shall simply have to wait longer," she said.

But Eric had decided otherwise. "Come with me now," he urged. "It makes no difference. I am here, and you are ready to go. In due time I shall make what arrangements I can, and we shall be close if not together. . . ."

Tears pearled upon Kristin's lashes, and she realized, as did Eric, that however much the two of them had been hurt during the course of their love, now it seemed inevitable that their love would hurt others. Uncertain, at that moment, they sought refuge in another long embrace.

"Well, isn't this a cozy scene, though?"

Eric and Kristin separated, whirled toward the door.

Vanessa Royall

It was Gustav, not outraged but rather amused, who regarded them cannily.

"My dear, my dear," he said slowly, addressing Kristin, "I thought you had made certain progress in life. I see, however, that I was mistaken. Still you must sneak about to consort with penniless commoners."

"You will not speak that way," said Eric, advancing.

Gustav lifted a hand. "Hear me out," he said. "I am not about to fight you. Already you have left your marks upon my face. But I am prepared now either to chisel your name upon the tombstone of your life, or on the other hand"—he lifted his hand airily and let it fall—"to offer you an arrangement. You know what it is about, I think?"

Kristin looked astonished, the more so when Eric nodded.

"God damn your soul to hell, Gunnarson," Gustav went on, "but I need you, and you need me."

"I don't need you," Eric proclaimed.

"Don't be absurd."

"What's this all about?" Kristin wondered.

Gustav sat down in a chair, crossed his legs indolently, and motioned the others to sit down as well. They declined. He did not care. "Your commoner lover has married into a vein of potential luck," Gustav drawled. "Oil has been found on his wife's land. As you know, Kristin, darling, if Rockefeller cannot pay back the money I lent him at the time it is due, I shall become a great power in the oil business. But if Benjamin Horace or this son of Gunnar here, whoever might win the rights to the oil lands, were to go into league with Rockefeller . . . well, suffice it to say that my father and Lord Soames would not be pleased. However, I hold all the cards."

"You do?" Kristin asked, surprised.

Eric said nothing.

"Yes, I do. And the reason is because I expect Horace to lose in court."

Eric began to smile. He had deciphered Gustav's ploy.

"You are amused?" scowled Gustav, his face coloring with slow anger. "Why?"

356

Eric laughed now. "You think I need you, isn't that right, Rolfson? If my neighbors and I win in court, Horace will be removed from the equation, and it will be only you and I and Rockefeller still in play. Rockefeller is overextended, and could not loan me money for oil development even if he wanted to. And you—"

"Still have massive English credit," Gustav finished, "and you, Gunnarson, are broke."

"I am backed by Randolph Security and Trust of Boston," Eric told him, with a cold smile.

Gustav was nonplused, but struggled to hide it. "To what paltry extent?" he sneered.

"Two and a half million dollars," Eric said.

Six words from Eric, and everything had changed. The two men stood there facing one another, remembering the first meeting in Lesja, the battle of the riding whip. Eric fleeing his homeland, Gustav apparently triumphant. Those things had happened. They could not be erased. But Eric had money now, and held a strategic business opportunity. He was in a position to hurt Rolfson badly, and it was clear that he would not hesitate to do so. Before, Eric had been a nuisance, an irritating reminder of Gustav's incomplete command over every element in his life. But now Eric was dangerous to Gustav, a true threat to his business empire, especially if he were to gain control of the southern oil.

Everything was changed.

Gustav could not conceal his surprise, nor his chagrin. True, he commanded sums far vaster, and had access to a great deal more. But two and a half million made Eric a power instantly to be reckoned with.

"Let us return to my original proposition," he said. "It is to your benefit to work with me. I shall permit you to develop the southern fields, and use my influence, first, to hold off Benjamin Horace, and second, to bribe the Pennsylvania legislature in the matter of the Creedmore Reservation."

"I have already decided that matter," Eric told him. "The Creedmore Reservation is illegal, and a court of law will so decide. Bribes are not required."

Vanessa Royall

Gustav laughed in his face. "Call it what you will," he said. "John D. Rockefeller makes cash payments to legislators in New York, Pennsylvania, and Ohio. Work with me, Gunnarson. I know the way things go, the 'ropes,' as they say here in America. He who does not know how the rope works is likely to find himself in a noose at the end of one."

"No, thank you."

Gustav gave a slow smile. He was sure Eric had no choice. "You'll be able to make many trips here to New York, Gunnarson. You'll be able to see my wife quite a lot."

"There is no limit to your lack of integrity, is there, husband?" cried Kristin, flaring.

"On the contrary," Gustav snickered, patting Haakon's little golden head. "My integrity is quite well defined by what I have and what Gunnarson, here, has not. My money, and my wife, and my son, who will follow in my footsteps just as I followed in my father's."

Eric stood there, looking down at the other man. Those beady wolf's eyes gleamed up at him, across the ruined nose. The scar, like the bed of a bad river, slanted down over a harsh face. Gustav Rolfson sat easily, with Eric's son on one knee, controlling the fate of that child, and so controlling its mother, Eric's great love.

Eric remembered his vow. "I want nothing from you," he told Rolfson. "I only want what is rightfully mine. And I will have it."

"Bold words," Rolfson laughed. "You don't know what you're up against."

"Good-bye, Rolfson," Eric said, turning toward the door.

"Oh, I do not think it is good-bye. You will be back. You will have to deal with me before you're through. Darling," he added unctuously nodding to Kristin, "you may see our guest to the door. I will spare myself the pain of witnessing your tragic farewell, knowing Gunnarson is now married to a sweet farm girl."

Kristin gave him a glance filled with loathing, and followed Eric into the foyer. He accepted his cape and walking stick from the butler, and then went out onto the steps.

WILD WIND WESTWARD

"It is decided," she told him quietly, hurriedly, "I am ready to go with you. Haakon and I, both."

"Yes," he said. "The time will come. But you must remain here for a little while longer. There will be a great amount of trouble, I am sure, in Pennsylvania. Very bad trouble. Here, at least, you will be physically safe."

"But what of . . . ?"

"Elaine?"

Kristin nodded.

"She is my wife. I must see to her. It is my responsibility. But Haakon is our son, and you are my love. And I shall see to you as well."

"If you need me, I shall come to you. No matter what."

"I do need you."

"Then I shall come."

"I cannot kiss you here."

"It doesn't matter. There is more than a kiss in your eyes. And wherever you go, I am there."

Gustav was in a somewhat fouler mood when Kristin returned to the drawing room.

"In future," he said, handing Haakon to her, "I would strongly advise you against nosing about in my business affairs."

"Yes, husband."

"You are thrilled that your plowboy lover did not have his head blown off at Gettysburg. Is that not so?"

"As you wish, my husband."

"But just because a man is able to escape death in war does not mean he is also able to avoid a surprise bullet in peacetime."

Kristin looked at him in horror.

Gustav grinned. "Terrible times we live in," he drawled, "terrible times."

X

Eric got off the train in Harrisburg, located Phil Phettle, and hired a horse and buggy. The two men immediately started for Gettysburg and the Nesterling farm.

"Honey!" cried Elaine, delighted to see him. "I didn't think you'd be gone so long."

Eric hugged her, and introduced Phil. "He'll be here for supper and a couple of days, at least. It's about the oil," he added, to her puzzled glance.

"Oh, that oil. Why can't we just farm the land and live in peace?"

Baby Elizabeth, in her arms, set up a squall. "Well, before I fry pork chops for you men," Elaine said, "someone else needs to eat first."

Eric paid Melvin and Bonnie Wenthistle for their help, and the two turned to leave. "Hey, wait," Melvin exclaimed, as if remembering something. "I got to tell you. There was a couple men out hunting on your property."

"Hunting?" Eric said. It was only September, hardly hunting time.

"Yep," said Melvin, "an' they was real curious about that pipe out behind your barn."

"What did you do?"

"I told them there was nothing but money in it, yuk yuk yuk."

"Fine Melvin. Anything else happen?"

"Ah . . . nope."

"Horace's men, probably, just as in Boston," observed Eric, when Elaine was out of earshot.

"It's hard to say. It is known that you have financial

WILD WIND WESTWARD

backing from Randolph. So the men could have been working for Horace, or Rockefeller, or even your friend Gustav Rolfson. There is a great deal at stake here now."

Eric nodded in agreement. "And if I don't start right away, I might be lost. Horace has turned down Rockefeller's bid to buy control of the leases in this area . . . as if they were Horace's to buy and sell! We must immediately organize the farmers here, call in men from the north who know how to set up oil rigs, engage barrel makers, begin negotiations with the Pennsylvania Railroad . . ."

"And prepare to face Horace and Representative Creedmore in court."

"And that."

"And the refinery. What will you do? Merely market the crude or try to control the whole process, from production through refining to market, as Rockefeller is attempting to do?"

"I don't know. I don't know. Those are decisions we are going to have to make as we go along. But, riding down here from Harrisburg, I had an idea. Reckless, perhaps. But worth a try."

"What's that?" Phil Phettle asked.

"I'm going to Pittsburgh to see Benjamin Horace. To beard the bear, as it were."

"I doubt it will do much good. He sees vast sums at his fingertips. Nothing you say will move him."

"Yet he thought enough of me to have a delegation meet my train in Boston, didn't he? Hardly the mark of a man who is totally secure."

"But definitely the mark of a man who is dangerous."

Eric took Phil Phettle around to the neighboring farmers, beneath whose land the oil was believed by the surveyors to lie. He introduced the intense but easy-mannered young lawyer to Fritz Renner, Abner Fensterwald, Rupert Ordway, Wilbur Cleanland, and numerous others, and left him to explain the Creedmore Reservation, and the need for unity to fight that clause in court. Eric himself prepared to go out to Pittsburgh.

Vanessa Royall

"Must you?" asked Elaine, as they lay in bed on the night prior to his departure. "First you went away to Harrisburg, then to New York. Now you're off to—"

"Elaine, I have to. Don't you see? It's for you, and Elizabeth. It's for all of us who live in this territory. My whole life has been a struggle to *have* something, to really *achieve* something. And now we are on the verge of it."

"But it seems you'll never be home. A lawyer is here now. There is talk about dangerous men and court battles. Eric, I . . . I don't understand. Why can't we just have had a quiet peaceful life, and love each other?"

"Elaine," he said, taking her into his arms, "Elaine, if one is threatened in life, if what one has is taken away, there can be no peace. Everything is taken away, and nothing remains."

She fought against an impulse to sob. "But all I want is a farm and a husband and children."

"You can have that. And more, too."

"But I don't want more!"

"Come, come."

"Don't touch me. I don't want to be soothed just now."

"Well, let me explain."

"Don't talk. You'll wake the baby. You'll wake your lawyer friend." Phil Phettle was sleeping in a half-loft on one side of the chimney.

"It doesn't matter. This is important. Anything that troubles you is important."

Elaine was quiet for a while, then: "You saw *her* in New York, didn't you?" Before Eric had a chance to answer, she continued. "Oh, I could tell. You were . . . different. Preoccupied. And it wasn't only about this oil business, either, was it?"

Now she began to cry in earnest, and turned away from him. He slid over behind her and tried to put his arms around her shaking shoulders.

"Just tell me the truth. You saw her, didn't you?" sobbed Elaine.

"It was not what you think."

"You love her, and you hate me, don't you? Because I

tore up your letters. Because you think I trapped you with . . . Elizabeth."

"No, of course not. I wanted you. And Elizabeth is so darling."

This was true. Eric could sit holding the child for hours, loving the soft feel of her tiny fist around his finger, watching her eyes as she studied him.

"You must never _think_ those things. I promised I would always love you, and always take care of you, and I always will."

He meant it, and Elaine could not doubt his sincerity, although the existence of another woman, no matter how remote, was not something she thought that she would ever fully accept.

"Why did you see her?" she asked, in a whispery voice.

"To see how she fared. Isn't that natural?"

Elaine wasn't sure that it was. "And how does she fare?"

"Well. She has a child, too."

"Oh?" exclaimed Elaine, pleased. That seemed to make everything more permanent, if not intractable. "Well, at least you don't know anyone in Pittsburgh," she said.

Eric did not answer, thinking of Joan Leeds.

The man upon whom Eric Gunnarson called in Pittsburgh could not recall a time when he had not been fighting for something. He could remember neither mother nor father, but he did recall himself as a small child of not much more than two or three—stumbling alone along the Allegheny River. Where he had come from, with what people he had spent his early days, he did not know. Where he was headed, he did not know, either. Exhausted, he fell into the river, and would have drowned, save for the chance passing of a farm wagon. The farmer, one Ebenezer Horace, jumped in, and pulled the boy out. Since he was sonless, and had land to work, his discovery of an unclaimed but apparently able-bodied child was like the fortuitous bequeathment of a slave. He gave the boy a name, a bed, food, and, over the years, plenty of work to do. Benjamin Horace, however, grew to care little for backbreaking, virtually prof-

Vanessa Royall

itless labor on the soil, even as he grew tall and wiry and steel strong. The discovery of iron ore on the Horace farm outside Pittsburgh seemed to promise a pleasant change. Instead of following the rear end of a horse from one end of a field to another, Benjamin might spend ready money on beer and whiskey and girls in nearby Moon Run, at the saloon old man Horace had forbade him ever to enter, but which he already knew as intimately as he knew some of the girls there. But old man Horace would not sell his eighty acres. He and his wizened old wife, who had bored Benjamin for years by saying rosaries and making novenas and muttering incantations, wanted to live out their days on the farm. That would not have been too bad, except that they wanted Benjamin to do the same. He was only seventeen when the farmhouse caught fire one night, killing the two old Horaces and destroying the rope by which they had been bound to their bed. Benjamin was very fortunate in burning only a couple of fingers on his right hand, with which he had held the torch a little too long.

He got a good price for the farm from the Carnegie people, and moved into Pittsburgh. He had money, ambition, a taste for pleasure and for gaudy accoutrements, whether of clothing or carriage or carnality.

The man Eric Gunnarson asked to see, outside the big bronze double-doors of the executive office in the Monongahela Trust and Holding Company was or had been boss of the Allegheny County Democratic Party, boss of the Allegheny County Republican Party, secretary, treasurer, president and board chairman of Monongahela Trust and Holding, owner and operator of sundry hotels and restaurants, a tool company, a livery, a rendering works, and various temporary businesses not too numerous to mention but too difficult to trace.

"Mr. Horace is not in at the moment," Eric was told, by a brisk, snippy young man in a pince-nez, who was one of the great man's secretaries.

"Then where is he?"

"What's your business?"

"Oil. Near Gettysburg."

The expression of bored superiority disappeared from the secretary's face, and his pince-nez almost fell off.

"You'll find him at the House of the Good Shepherd," offered the man. "He's going over accounts with Mrs. Horace."

"The House of the Good Shepherd?"

"Half-mile down, on your right. Don't let the red lantern over the door put you off. Mr. Horace holds it to be of great sentimental value. In that house he met his wife."

No one answered his knock at the House of the Good Shepherd, a large, elaborate clapboard hotel, surrounded by a wide, pillared porch. It was painted yellow, and Eric recalled that the Leeds house in New York had also been yellow. Knocking again to no reply, he tried the door and found it open. It was quiet inside, and dark, with heavy curtains drawn over the windows. When his eyes adjusted to the gloom, Eric discerned a bar, a piano, and a number of tables around an open floor. The odor of dead cigars hung in the air, along with the sickly-sweet smell of cheap wine.

"Anyone in? Mr. Horace?"

He thought he heard, from some place far back in the house, the sound of voices. Making his slow way across the darkened room, he passed through a curtained doorway, and to his right a wide staircase rose to upper floors.

A young woman wearing nothing but a cotton wrap was coming down those stairs, yawning and stretching. She saw him at the same moment he saw her. He did not cry out, but she did.

After a stunned silence, someone else shrieked. Eric attempted to explain himself. The woman in the cotton wrap scrambled back upstairs. There was the sound of running. Eric felt himself grabbed and slammed against the wall next to the staircase. He looked into a dark, cruel, mustachioed face, and large, angry eyes.

"We're closed, fella. What do you think this is?"

The man readied a fist. Eric got set to fight back. Then, over his assailant's shoulder, he saw another woman approaching, soft and lovely in a green silk robe, her green eyes shining, her oval face as smooth and untroubled as it had been that night in the New York tavern, years ago, and her rich red hair still lustrous as ever.

"Hello, Eric," Joan Leeds Horace smiled. "I always thought we'd meet again. Destiny, don't you think?"

"Hello, Joan."

"Let him go, Ben. I think this is the man you wished to see. He gave me excellent advice once, about oil and money."

Benjamin Horace wanted to see him? What's going on here? Eric wondered.

Joan was smiling that simultaneously enigmatic and omniscient smile of old, as if she not only knew vast portions of Eric's destiny, but controlled them as well. He remembered the last night they had spent together, in the Madison Hotel in New York.

Tomorrow we'll begin planning in earnest, he could hear her whispering, lying beside him in their bed of profane love.

Joan, I cannot, he had said.

He remembered how she had waited before answering, studying him, then: *You will have to learn the hard way that I am right about how life is.*

Was she? Joan was apparently happy, and wealthy, and matched with a powerful man. So was she right about how life is? She thought so.

"So we meet again, Eric," she said, smiling. "You and I and all the time between."

"What the hell is going on here?" Benjamin Horace demanded.

Eric could not help but marvel. Joan was the woman who had once wanted him to pimp for her; now she had her own house, and probably Horace to pimp for her. He looked like a damned tough man, but as Eric measured the stony body, the powerful arms, the cruel, intelligent eyes, he decided: *I can take this man.*

Eric could beat him physically, perhaps. But what about other areas of competition? Arrangements, deals, money, power: other arenas Eric had not yet fully experienced, or not experienced at all?

I can take him there, too, Eric vowed.

"Coffee, Eric? Or a drink? Come, Ben. Let us take our guest into the kitchen and have a nice talk." So saying, she led the two men away toward the back of the house, even as the awakened girls of the Good Shepherd gathered to watch at the railing of the second staircase.

"I understand your precious Kristin is rich and happy in New York," Joan averred, motioning Eric and Ben to chairs next to the table. Ledgers and account books and sheets of paper scribbled full of numbers littered the table. Joan gathered them up and set them aside.

"Kristin is rich," Eric said.

"And you are married to a sweet country girl now. How nice. It must remind you of home."

They certainly know all about me, Eric thought. "There are things worse than home," he said.

"Well, you've come a long way, and here you are." She brought over a pot of coffee, cups, and a bottle of brandy. "And now it's time to deal again."

"If Gunnarson's smart enough to deal," said Horace, who had been silent, taking his measure of Eric.

"Here's to our oil," said Joan, sitting down with the men and pouring a slug of brandy into her steaming coffee.

"It's not your oil," said Eric.

"You son of a bitch." Horace spat. "I could already be the king of oil if it wasn't for you."

"Benjamin . . ." warned Joan.

"You're not the king of anything," Eric shot back, prepared to leap up if the man so much as made a move to attack, "and sending those thugs after me in Boston was an outrage."

"What?" demanded Joan, glancing from Eric to her husband and back again.

In spite of his perpetually cynical smirk, Benjamin Horace looked puzzled. "What the hell are you talking about? Boston thugs? Is this some kind of cheap maneuver to catch me off guard? I know you're getting set up with a lawyer to give me trouble over that Creedmore clause, and I paid a hell of a lot of money to put Representative Angus Creedmore in my pocket, and you're in for the fight of your life over control of the southern oil fields, but Boston . . . ?" Horace shook his head. "You're talking through your hat, my friend."

Joan looked as puzzled at Eric's mention of Boston as Horace had. "What happened there?" she asked.

Eric told them of the men who had threatened him in the carriage outside the Boston railroad station.

"I don't know a son of a bitch east of Philadelphia," Horace declared, genuinely perplexed.

Eric studied the man's hard, flat eyes. Horace seemed to be telling the truth. Joan's eyes were narrow and cool, slits of intelligent green light. "Perhaps I am beginning to understand something. Those men in Boston? You told them you thought I killed my mother in New York, didn't you, Starbane?"

His ancient name. Why did she address him so? Joan noted his surprise and discomfiture.

"You know what always troubled me most about you?" she asked him. "You never seemed to grasp the fact that you are the kind of man who can have anything he wants, a man with the least of desires."

"I don't have my own land yet," Eric said.

Benjamin Horace's eyes went from one to the other. "Your mother? His name? Why don't you clear this up?"

"I received a telegram from New York a few days ago," Joan explained. "It was unsigned, but the message it carried advised us to drop our interest in southern oil, or very shortly it would be rumored that I killed my mother in New York and an investigation might occur."

"I also heard that 'rumor' from Mick, when he was dying at Gettysburg," Eric added.

"Poor Mick," sighed Joan, her eyes softening, "he was so sweet. So sweet and so dumb. No," she said. "Liz died of pneumonia. During the epidemic that year."

Eric looked into her eyes, and tried to gauge the truth,

but he saw nothing therein save his own image. He believed Joan, and he did not believe her. He knew she had taken his three hundred dollars from beneath the floorboards, and he believed she had taken her brother's draft money. But that was all he knew or believed. Nothing else for certain, except the indisputable fact that he could not trust her. He wondered if Benjamin Horace could, or did.

"Why didn't you tell me about that telegram?" Horace demanded of Joan.

"I didn't want it to enrage you," Joan said. "You've got to keep a very cool head until the trial is over."

Horace was calculating. "Then it had to have been either Rolfson or Rockefeller who sent the telegram," he decided, striking the table with the heel of his hand, rattling coffee cups and bouncing the brandy bottle. "Look, Gunnarson, I've had you investigated. Any smart man would, with a big trial coming up over the oil. If you had half a brain, you'd be hip-deep in my past, although spare yourself the effort, 'cause the trail is covered pretty damn good. But we got to see things as they are, and get together here. Somebody is going through a lot of trouble to heat up the differences between us. So I suggest we spite them, strike a bargain, and freeze out both Rockefeller and Rolfson."

"But it is not my oil to bargain away."

"Don't be a dunce. For God's sake . . ."

"I'm sorry, but the oil belongs to my neighbors as well as to me and my wife."

"Oh, Gunnarson, for pity's sake . . ."

"Quite," said Joan. "Eric, you do realize what this means?"

Eric did. Horace wanted the oil fields to himself, all right. But someone else was working hard to spark a mutually destructive war betwen Eric and Horace.

"It's Rockefeller," Benjamin Horace decided. "He's been the shrewdest all along. Rolfson has access to the money supply, but Rockefeller is the fulcrum upon which everything turns, because he controls all the steps in the production process."

Benjamin Horace went on, explaining how he inter-

Vanessa Royall

preted what was happening. Rockefeller, it seemed, needed the claim to the southern fields, and the income to be engendered by them, to pay off the loan Rolfson had given him. If Horace and Eric tied up the matter in court, or any other way, Rockefeller would suffer, and perhaps lose everything.

"No, I think it's Gustav Rolfson," Eric said.

"Well, we know we're both threatened," cooed Joan, "and we know there's more money to be made than we'll ever have time to spend, so let's get down to business here, and strike a bargain with Eric on the rights to that oil he's discovered."

"No," Eric said.

There was a long, long silence.

"You read the son of a bitch wrong again, Joan," Benjamin Horace hissed. "He's the same fool he was when he got off the boat."

"I'm not a son of a bitch," Eric said, rising, "I'm . . ."

"*Still* Gunnarson," Joan Leeds Horace interrupted with a cynical smile. She stood, too, and offered her hand. "We shall see you in Harrisburg Circuit Court, in due course. It seems that is what you desire."

Eric took her hand. There seemed no point in not doing so. From him to her, as of old, flowed the raw attraction. He could not help it. And from her to him flowed in response that demonic allure she had always been able to exert upon him. He pulled his hand away.

"Perhaps we might bargain on different terms." She smiled slowly, conscious of her power.

"No," Eric said, "not anymore."

"Then the end will come in another way," Joan replied. "The two great things in life are love and money. People die for those."

"What about power?" asked Benjamin Horace.

"Power is made up of love and money." Joan smiled again.

XI

Little Haakon had thrived during the winter, and now, in April 1865, at all of fifteen months old, he toddled sturdily, adventurously, all over the Rolfson mansion.

"Hardiness is in the blood," Gustav boasted. "The Rolfson stock prospers always."

"Of course, husband," replied Kristin. "Pray, and how are your business affairs progressing?"

Gustav eyed her suspiciously. "Very well. Very well, indeed," he said, too casually, then turned his attention to Haakon, calling him over for a good-night pat on the head. Gustav believed it a sign of weakness to kiss his son, and believed such kisses would weaken the boy.

"You, there nurse. Get him to bed now. It's quite late."

Kristin hugged and kissed the child, turned him over to Traudl, his governess. Traudl had been hired personally by Gustav. Kristin did not approve of the woman, nor trust her. She was a part of the Rolfson household politics, a politics cold and complicated.

Gustav Rolfson did nothing spontaneously, effected no act or gesture whose potential consequences he had not calculated in advance. Tonight was Friday, and on Friday Gustav always took Kristin to dine at Connaught's, an exclusive restaurant catering to the entrepreneurial rich. But tonight was Good Friday, and Gustav thought it unseemly to be out and about on such a night. He had no religious scruples. He had no religion at all. Staying home was a matter of appearances only.

Now, as he and Kristin sat down at the table in their huge dining room and avoided each other's eyes from opposite sides of the glittering five armed candelabra in the center of the table, he complained.

"You'd think a country like this, which is committed to money, would put aside some of these ridiculous superstitious commemorations."

"Yes, my husband." Kristin motioned the waiters to begin serving. Gustav did not care much for the clam broth, but he attacked with relish the appetizer of pickled pig's feet.

"Business progresses well?" Kristin tried again. All winter, Gustav had been increasingly closed mouthed about his affairs, saying little of his loans to Rockefeller, mentioning only a few times—in considerable agitation— that "your former lover, the Viking plowboy, is bent upon causing a ruckus down there in Pennsylvania. When it comes to a head, no one will be sorrier than he. I ought to have dealt him out of the game long ago. . . ."

Kristin had a feeling that the matter was due to "come to a head" quite soon, but she had no idea when or how.

"Well, the North has won the war, anyway," muttered Gustav. The main course was served, Gustav's favorite, a roasted suckling pig stuffed with barley and brown sugar. Gustav nodded to a servant, who poured him a huge goblet of red wine. As usual, he was served the head of the suckling pig. He loved to dunk the head whole into his goblet, then transfer it, dripping wine, to his plate, whereupon he would devour it carefully, wielding his knife like a scalpel, smacking over each morsel, tongue and eye and brain.

"I feel badly for General Lee," Kristin offered, speaking of Robert E. Lee, who had surrendered to Grant at Appomattox, Virginia, earlier in the week.

Gustav grunted, sucking wine from the snout of the tiny pig. "It is his own fault. Lincoln offered him Union command, way back in 1861. But Lee was loyal to his homeland, and Virginia went with the Confederacy. It's his own fault. No one else to blame."

"What will happen now, do you think, my husband?"

"If I can just get this Pennsylvania oil business settled,"

answered Gustav, pink chunks of pig flesh going round and round in his row of squat molars, "what will happen is that I will make a lot of money and run the oil business in this savage country for the rest of this century. After which Haakon will run it."

"How will you settle the Pennsylvania problem?" asked Kristin, hoping the wine might have loosened his tongue a little.

But he was immediately wary. "What is this?" he demanded, glaring at her. "You haven't enough to keep you amused? That portrait I paid Phipps to do has made you famous. You need but to walk down the street and someone will recognize you. You have a child and a great house, and you sit about with Isabel Van Santen—oh, I know she doesn't care for me, but nor do I for her—and yammer, no doubt, of love and poesy. Haven't you enough to keep you busy? I do."

He reached across to the serving plate, grabbed the pig's rear legs, and ripped off the whole hindquarters.

After she had retired for the night, Kristin did not go to sleep. Gustav was planning something, and Gustav planning was Gustav dangerous. A wise person did not sleep while such a man was spinning webs. The clock in the hallway struck midnight, then one. Still Gustav did not come up to bed. Kristin, afflicted by a gnawing sense of disorder and unease, got out of bed, slipped on her robe, and crept downstairs. All servants had long since retired to their quarters cold in winter, warm in summer, but clean, and better than many of them might ever have afforded elsewhere.

On the lower floor no one stirred, and everything was dark. Quietly, holding her robe to herself, Kristin went through the hall, passed the dining room, moving toward her husband's study. The door, she saw now, was slightly ajar. A long, thin sliver of light, like a gold thread of portent, slipped from the room and fell upon the carpet in the hall.

And Kristin heard voices.

Surprised, because there were no houseguests at this time and because Gustav would not be caught dead chatting with a servant, she pressed herself against the wall, and eased toward the door, peered in.

". . . cannot be a mistake made," Gustav was saying, with eerie emphasis.

From her position Kristin could not see him, but she was able to observe the man Gustav was talking to.

"You need not be concerned," that man assured Gustav coldly. "I am a master at what I do. The men I employ have never seen me, and do not even know my name."

His tone was so icy, his manner so frigid, that Kristin felt a chill shoot up her skeleton, down her spine. The man was almost impossible to describe. He was pale, gray, average. He seemed to have not one distinguishing feature or trait. He was Everyman: undistinguished in coloring, build, height. Strangely, this fact unnerved Kristin all the more. Looking at the man was like regarding the husk of a human being, which looked human, and seemed human, but within which no heart beat, no blood coursed, no feelings or emotions abided, not one.

"I have checked, and you come highly recommended," Gustav said. "I want no trace of my involvement."

The man nodded. "There won't be. I work through a hierarchy of intermediaries."

"No amateurs!" Gustav growled.

"Amateurs always permit their emotions to interfere with the job at hand," the man observed, "and because they do, everything is botched, even if the victim is killed."

Kristin put her hand to her mouth, to stifle a gasp. Gustav was speaking with an assassin!

But who did he have in mind as victim?

"You have, of course, a fee?" he asked.

"Of course," the man replied, without inflection or avarice. He was a businesman, above all. "But the fee depends upon the mission, and the complications attendant on it. We have sufficiently discussed preliminaries. I see that I can work for you, if I choose to. And even if I refuse the job, you have no need to fear that I will ever reveal the details of our conversation."

"Thank you," said Gustav, happy to find a man he could trust. "Next Monday, in Harrisburg, Pennsylvania, a trial is scheduled to begin. It is over the matter of . . . ah . . . mineral rights. Gunnarson, Ordway, Fensterwald, *et al.* versus Horace and Creedmore."

"You want them all killed?" asked the man, with an awful snicker.

"No, just Gunnarson. It is something I ought to have had done years ago. I did not anticipate the threat he would become. I have to act now, right away." He paused, as if he had said too much.

"Why do you want him dead?" asked the man.

"It doesn't concern you."

The man stood and held out his hand.

"What?" exclaimed Gustav.

"Good night. I'm leaving."

"Wait! Why?"

"If you do not tell me your reasons, and all related facts, I will not work for you. You might leave out something important. My men would be surprised. We do not like the unexpected. We plan everything down to the minutest detail."

"All right," agreed Gustav, and the stranger sat down again. "Briefly put, I am in the oil business, having financed the fortunes of a man in northern Pennsylvania. He owes me a great deal of money. I stand to profit if this man cannot pay my money on time."

"Name?"

"Rockefeller. Also, oil has been discovered in southern Pennsylvania by Gunnarson. He and his neighbors, a group of dumb farmers over whom he exercises control, are going to court. Against two men named Horace and Creedmore. It is a complicated matter of mineral rights. I myself want to control and exploit those mineral rights. But Gunnarson has refused to deal with me. If he wins the court case, I lose. Gunnarson and Rockefeller might go into league against me. Or, if the oil strike proves to be a major one, and there are rumors to this effect, Gunnarson may remain independent, in which case I also lose, being, in effect, frozen out of both north and south."

"What if Horace wins in court? Horace and . . . Creedmore, did you say?"

Gustav nodded. "In that case as well I might be frozen out."

"And so?"

"And so I want Gunnarson dead before the trial begins. His death will terrorize those farmers, scare them off. Therefore no court case. I'll go down there personally and make a deal with Horace and the farmers. I'll control the southern fields, thereby depriving that sneaky little Godster, Rockefeller, of half the supply. He'll never be able to pay my notes on time, and thus I'll wind up with northern oil, too, not to mention that big refinery in Cleveland."

"You've got it all figured out, haven't you?"

"My father did not raise a son to win second place."

"Isn't it amazing what one dead man will gain?"

"You should talk. It's what you do for a living."

The stranger did something with his lips—made a fleet, obscure grimace. It was his way of smiling. "Spoken like a born businessman," he said. "And, as businessmen, let us now consider what it will be worth to rid you of Gunnarson."

"I am willing to offer ten thousand dollars," Gustav said.

"Twenty," drawled the stranger.

"Fifteen."

"Twenty, and that's final."

Gustav considered. He had to act fast. The trial was due to get underway early next week. And here was a professional, who claimed to have anonymous lieutenants at his disposal. Part of the fee, at least, would be worth such traceless anonymity. "Ten now and ten upon completion," Gustav said.

The stranger shook his head. "This is our one and only meeting, my friend. I trust you enough to show my face once. You trust me to see that my men do the job you wish."

Gustav capitulated. The way he saw it, he had no choice.

Vanessa Royall

loomed, the hopeful prideful expectation of blood and thunder, cannon and conflict, life and death, for which hardened soldiers live and breathe.

"We march in four hours, so ready your men," the colonel ordered. "Tomorrow, June thirtieth, we ought to be in position along Pipe Creek, covering Meade's right flank. Lee is to our north. So if he can be baited to the attack, we'll see action for certain."

A final burst of cheering ended the staff meeting. Many of these officers, Stonehead of Indiana, Cleveland of Ohio, "Mad Dog" Spaeth of the Minnesota Territorial Irregulars, had served long and bitterly under the timid McClellan. At least Meade would fight, not run, if he got drawn into a battle, although he was still too hesitant for some of the staff.

"The only way to do this," Lieutenant Colonel Spaeth was telling his fellow officers as they left the tent, "is to grab Lee by the throat and kick him in the hind end. That's the way to settle with the fellow. I never liked him anyway."

"Lieutenant Gunnarson," Colonel Randolph called, as Eric waited for the senior officers to exit before he did, "join me for a moment."

Eric was more than happy to do so. Since he'd taken his commission, and been given charge of a company of troops, Colonel Randolph's attention and advice had served him in good stead on many occasions.

Randolph had a steward bring coffee, and the two men sat down at the command table. A large, detailed topographical map was spread upon it, features of the hilly terrain clearly delineated, and the apparent positions of both armies marked by blue and gray flags.

"This is bad," Randolph said, in a voice different from that he had used only moments before to address his staff. "We don't know exactly where their reconnaisance and support units are, nor whether they are quite certain of the location of ours. The whole thing could come to flashpoint by accidental encounter before either side is prepared. And when that happens ..."

WILD WIND WESTWARD

of truce, to discuss negotiations for a peace settlement. There is no hope of such a settlement, as the South will not yield its demand for independence, nor will the North ever accede to such a demand. That is why we are fighting."

"Or not fighting," grumbled Major Stonehead, of the Indiana Regulars, to a chorus of guffaws.

"I repeat," Randolph said, "Lee is entrenched. Meade believes he is not in Pennsylvania to fight, but to give a show of force while Stephens makes his plea for peace to Lincoln."

"Well, let's surprise the old gent," offered Major Stonehead, "and kick his head in."

This suggestion was greeted with considerable enthusiasm, and Colonel Randolph raised his hands for silence. "I was coming to that part," he called. "I said it is Meade's feeling that Lee does not want to fight, and that there will be no battle here *unless we make it ourselves*!"

An outburst of cheering seemed to lift and billow the canvas of the command tent. Second Lieutenant Eric Gunnarson, his gold emblems of rank still bright and new, was surprised to feel a thrill of imminence, and he felt his blood rush faster through his veins. This would be his first battle. If there was a battle.

"General Meade has given me the following orders, which I now pass along to you," Randolph said. "We are going to move to Pipe Creek, and entrench ourselves there. Meade wants Lee to attack *us*. Our reconnaisance parties are scouting the entire Gettysburg area, and so are the Rebel units of Jeb Stuart and A.P. Hill."

"Begging your pardon, sir," asked Major Stonehead, "but we've been up against Hill and Stuart before. If they're along with Lee, I'd say Meade is wrong. Jeb Stuart doesn't come along for a meander in the countryside. I think Lee is getting set to put the fire to our feet once and for all."

"I can only tell you what I have been told," Randolph said, to a mutter of dissent, "but, frankly, Stonehead, I share your view entirely."

The mood of the meeting changed instantly. *Action*

". . . all planning has gone for naught," Eric finished.

During the past few months he had felt himself growing in all respects, coming to terms with command, travail, and his own ambitions. He and Randolph had also grown close, close enough for the colonel to have suggested that they find and exploit some enterprise after the war was over. Eric also told Randolph about Kristin, asking him to call on her if he did not survive, and Randolph made a similar request that Eric contact his own family in Boston, in case of his death.

"The lesson of history," Randolph had told his young student, "is that war advances and multiplies the fields of human activity."

"Isn't that a contradiction?" Eric had wondered. "What of the ruined cities, the devastated countryside, the maimed and the dead?"

"Tragic, indeed. But armed conflict must be regarded also from an objective point of view. All wars finally end. Then cities must be rebuilt, land renewed. The maimed must be cared for. And the dead you have with you always, do you not?"

It had seemed to Eric, at first, a shockingly cold-blooded appraisal, quite at variance with the intelligent, civilized personality he knew Randolph possessed. But when he considered the colonel's words further, he saw the truth they held: Life went on, and had to be served.

"Moreover," Randolph went on, "war is a spur to technology and inventiveness. Consider the expansion of the railroad, the development of communications evidenced by the telegraph, the move to oil as fuel for engines of all sorts. These things do not go away when the battle ends. No, they are platforms from which to build. And that's what I propose. After the war you and I ought to choose an enterprise, and see what we can make of it, see how far we can go."

Eric had agreed, in general terms at first, later with growing enthusiasm. But for now the war itself had to be endured, and survived.

"Get your men into formation," the colonel told him, "for the march to Pipe Creek."

By noon of the following day, June thirtieth, Eric's company was well entrenched along Pipe Creek, and he was proud of them. But by midafternoon they were abandoning the trenches and fortifications forged with so much labor. Because by midafternoon everything had changed.

"What the hell is going on?" grumbled the men, when they were ordered to pack up and prepare to march again. "We just got dug in here, the battle hasn't even begun, and now we're moving out already?"

"Wrong," Eric informed them. "The battle is already on, and it's going to be a lot worse than anyone thought."

It had begun, as Colonel Randolph had feared, because neither army knew exactly where its adversary was located, on those wooded, heavily foliated hills of Pennsylvania. The Confederate cavalry of General A. P. Hill, out on a scouting mission, decided to stop in the little town of Gettysburg. Some of the men needed new boots, and certainly the town would have a bootery. They did not, however, get much of a chance to shop, because in the town itself were Northern troops, riding with the cavalry division of General Buford.

Flashpoint.

Lee abandoned his defensive plans, and went on the attack, so the battle took place not at Cashtown, where he had wanted it, but in and around Gettysburg. Colonel Randolph was ordered west from Pipe Creek to Cemetery Ridge, there to dig in and defend. A forced march across difficult terrain brought Eric and his men to Cemetery Ridge itself, a limestone outcropping shaped like a fishhook, facing Confederate forces to the west and north. There they met the beaten and bedraggled remnants of the Union First Corps, driven from the village of Gettysburg on July first, the first day of battle. Units of General A. P. Hill and General Ewell had slashed the First Corps to pieces, and their retreat to Cemetery Ridge was less a

By a welter of strange events and turnings, his future success in oil seemed dependent on Eric Gunnarson's death. Gustav was not about to become fastidious over a detail he ought to have dispatched long ago. He went to the far wall of the library, and Kristin saw him move aside the Phipps portrait, which was hung there. From a wall safe behind the portrait he withdrew a large leather wallet and from it he removed twenty crisp new bills. Then he closed the safe and slid the portrait back over it.

"I've seen that woman's face before," the stranger observed, nodding toward the painting.

"Many have. Brady, the camera scientist, also captured her image. She is my wife."

The stranger seemed astonished that a man like Gustav should have so lovely a mate.

Gustav handed over the bills, which the man counted and slid inside his breast pocket.

"How will the job be done?" Gustav asked.

"It is up to the man selected for the assignment."

"Well, surely you must have some control over . . ."

The stranger laughed. "I plan to be far from Harrisburg when the deed is done. I suggest the same for you."

"Oh, certainly. But Harrisburg? You are going to kill him there? Why not do it when he is on his farm? In his bed?"

The stranger did not tell Gustav that he sounded like a fool. He did not speak the word. Yet his expression revealed that thought clearly enough.

"Yes," he drawled, "and do you know with what curiosity country folks follow the movements of a stranger in their midst? No, a crowd is the best place, the best cover. The man chosen for the task will know how to blend into such a crowd. He will be the most natural person there, *accepted by all*. He will be *beyond suspicion*—"

Aghast, Kristin listened. How could this be? How could a murderer be beyond notice?

"—and after the deed," the man continued, "the ensuing chaos and confusion facilitate escape. Do you see my point?"

"All right, I leave it to you," Gustav said.

The men moved toward the door. Fleetly, soundlessly, Kristin fled back into the darkness of the hall. While Gustav was seeing the stranger to the door, she made her way back upstairs to the bedroom, and feigned sleep while Gustav slid heavily into bed beside her.

I must leave now, she thought. *This is my last night as Gustav's wife, my last hours in Rolfson's thrall.* She thought, with jittery trepidation, of her family in Norway, still vulnerable to old Adolphus's knoutish vindictiveness. She would have to deal with that matter later. Getting out of here came first.

XII

"Isabel, you must help me," pleaded Kristin on the morrow.

"Why, my dear, you look a fright! Whatever has happened?"

"I must leave New York at once. I do not intend ever to return."

It was early Saturday morning, and Kristin had hastened to the Van Santen home, to ask for the help Isabel had promised so often.

"What about Haakon?" Isabel asked.

"I'm taking him with me."

"To Eric?"

"Yes."

"Why this sudden decision? And you are so agitated! Something *has* happened. What?"

Kristin did not wish to deceive her friend, but neither did she wish to tell of the conversation she had overheard. If Isabel knew that murder was being planned, she might wish to keep Kristin safe in New York, might withhold the aid Kristin needed to travel.

"I have decided I can no longer bear Gustav," she told Isabel. "It is as simple as that."

"I understand, dear. I cannot see how you have stood him this long! What help do you need?"

"A nurse or a maid, to accompany me as far as Harrisburg, Pennsylvania. And a manservant. Valet or coachman doesn't matter, only let him be discreet. I shall send both servants back in two or three days."

"This I can do. When do you wish to leave?"

379

"On the Saturday afternoon train. We shall stop in Philadelphia that night, and go out to Harrisburg on Sunday."

Kristin had planned the trip. She might then take a hotel Sunday night, and find out where the trial would be in time to warn Eric of the planned assassination Monday morning.

"And Eric will meet you in Harrisburg then?"

"Yes," said Kristin, not lying.

"But Gustav is sure to miss you?"

"Gustav has the habit of carousing on Saturday evenings, with people I have never met." She thought of Lord Soames's boys, Rob and Pierre and Vitas; she had often wondered whether Gustav had found similar companions here in New York. In any case he went out without her on Saturday nights. "Sometimes he does not return until late Sunday," she told Isabel.

"Oh my dear, I didn't know *that*."

"It never mattered and now it may be of help. In any event, I cannot use my servants. I do not trust Traudl, our governess, nor any of the others."

"You do not have to. My people are at your beck and call."

The two discussed details and timing, and Kristin returned to her own home to prepare.

Gustav seemed jittery and preoccupied all Saturday morning, and Kristin began to worry that, with the assassination on his mind, he would forsake his regular ritual. But after a lunch of squab hash, he prepared to leave.

"I may be late."

"Yes, husband."

He gave her a sudden, direct look. "I don't believe you have ever understood just how inexorable I am."

"Oh, yes I have, husband. Yes, I have, indeed."

There he stood, feeling so cocksure and mighty. She could not resist an attempt to bring him down a peg.

"Tell me," she asked, "where do you go, and with whom, when you are out on your evenings alone?"

WILD WIND WESTWARD

Gustav colored slightly. "It is my affair, woman," he said.

She saw that he was somewhat discomfited. "I hope you do not partake of sordid delights. It is you who are always guarding your reputation, so precious a thing."

"Quiet! I won't have this!"

"Mr. Rockefeller does not carouse. He reads his Bible and grows ever more and more clever and rich."

"I go," said Gustav, hoping to humiliate her, "to find willingly and skillfully given pleasure I cannot know here at home."

"I have always thought," she said calmly in her turn, "that you took a great liking to Lord Soames's brand of depravity."

Gustav's face purpled, and not only with anger. He averted his eyes as well, and Kristin suspected that she had guessed right. Yet, what did it matter? He could find pleasure with whomsoever he wished. She was leaving and would never come back.

"You'll pay for your smart mouth one day," he promised, storming out of the house and slamming the great door behind him.

Kristin laughed bitterly. She had paid enough already.

"Haakon and I are spending the night at the Van Santens'," she told the servants, ordering up the carriage and bidding that a few pieces of her luggage be packed. She could not take more; the suspicions of the servants would surely be aroused. Kristin herself dressed the little boy, and held his hand as he toddled toward the door, and toward the coach waiting at curbside.

Ellison, the butler, handed her an envelope just as she was about to leave the house.

"What is this?"

"Just delivered, madam. It arrived with the latest ship from Oslo."

Kristin glanced at the envelope. Old Adolphus wrote frequently, communicating to his son new strategies of skullduggery, new twists to the fine art of chicanery he practiced. But the handwriting on the envelope—it was addressed to both herself and Gustav—was not the old man's. She did not wish to delay her departure because of a letter.

"Thank you, Ellison," she said, and helped Haakon down the steps to the carriage.

"And when will you be returning?" Ellison asked.

For a moment Kristin thought he might have become suspicious. She looked into his eyes. No, he was merely inquiring so that the house would be in order when she got back.

"Oh, I don't know," she said lightly. "You know how Mrs. Van Santen is always planning entertainments."

"Indeed," Ellison replied, and helped her and Haakon into the coach.

When the whip cracked and the horses began to move, Kristin tore open the envelope. Glancing first to the bottom of the page, she saw that the letter had been written by Thorsen, once solicitor in her home village of Lesja, now factotum to the Rolfsons in Oslo. A willingness to corruption had won him the prize he sought, although it had not won him Kristin's hand or body. But why was he writing? Her eyes flew over the page.

> ... took sick suddenly ... high fever ... struggled for three nights with the ague ... minister summoned ... profound grief ... last words were "More, more, give me more."

Adolphus Rolfson was dead.

For a moment Kristin was undecided as to what course of action to pursue. She felt neither glee nor pity at the old man's demise; his death meant, however, that her family was immeasurably safer. But if she stopped the carriage and ordered that the letter be delivered now to Gustav, her own plans would almost certainly be ruined. She could not afford that. In any event, given the time it took for a ship to cross the Atlantic, Adolphus had been dead for a long time already. She would leave the letter with Isabel, giving instructions that it be carried to Gustav the following week, with no excess of haste.

Isabel had seen to it that Hector was not at home, and so when Kristin arrived at the Van Santens', all was in readiness.

"I'm sending Sean and Bridget with you," Isabel said, giving Kristin a quick hug as the two servants got into the carriage. "They're excited about the trip, and they're both very reliable. Keep them as long as you like, and telegraph if you need anything. Anything," she repeated.

"I will. But things will be fine now. I know it."

"Oh, I hope so. No one has waited longer than you for happiness."

"I'm sure many have. The dangerous thing is . . ." She had almost spoken of the assassination.

"What?"

"The important thing *is* happiness, in the end," Kristin said. She handed Isabel the letter. "Would you see that this is sent to Gustav? But not until next week."

"Bad news or good?" asked Isabel, glancing at the letter.

"Just inevitable. Gustav should have it, but there is no need that he have it soon."

"I understand."

The servants, Bridget and Sean, were in the carriage. Haakon was crawling all over the maid's lap.

"God be with you," said Isabel, her eyes tearing. The two women embraced.

"Yes," replied Kristin, "and with all of us."

The train arrived in Philadelphia shortly after twilight. Kristin had arranged to stop at the Hotel Constitution, but when she entered the grand lobby there, with its precious wainscoting, three-story windows, and glittering chandeliers, dozens of heads turned her way. The people who stopped at the Constitution were generally knowledgeable and well traveled. They had seen her portrait, or the Brady photos.

"There. Look. Is that not the woman who . . . ?"

"Yes, by Lord, I believe you are right."

"It is that Norwegian woman, whose portrait was—"

Kristin, carrying Haakon, fled upstairs to her designated rooms, leaving Isabel's Sean and Bridget to handle details of baggage and registration.

"Oh, missus, what . . . ?" cried the maid, when she came into the suite minutes later.

"I am tired of people staring at me!" announced Kristin, truthfully.

There she stood, in front of the mirror. She had cut short her lovely hair, worn long since she had been a small child. Now, if she tucked the rest of it up under her hat, she would look quite different.

"Oh, but missus, your pretty hair—"

"Don't fret, Bridget. It will grow back. It always does. How would you like to be stared at all the time?"

"I don't think I should mind," said Bridget, who would never be stared at anyway.

"It's for the best," concluded Kristin. She remembered how Phipps had vowed to make her known by her picture. "Now, Haakon must be fed, bathed, and put to bed. The train ride seems only to have excited him and kept him awake."

On the ride from the train station to the Harrisburg hotel Kristin bade the driver take her past the courthouse, a formidable domed building of red brick and gilt. Once at the hotel she bade Sean to call on all hotels and rooming houses in the city, asking after Eric Gunnarson. He returned, hours later, without news of such a man.

So Eric must be planning on arriving in the city Monday morning.

Was the assassin already here in Harrisburg, waiting?
Accepted by all? Beyond suspicion?
What manner of man was he?

XIII

Elaine woke up screaming, just before dawn.

"What is it? What is it?" cried Eric, holding her close to him. Her shrieks had awakened him from an uneasy sleep. The long, early-morning ride to Harrisburg lay before them, and all night he had dreamed they were riding toward the city for the trial. But though they rode as fast and hard as possible, the hour grew later and later, and the city did not appear on the horizon.

Baby Elizabeth, startled, too, by her mother's cries, began to squall in her crib. Phil Phettle poked his head over the railing of the loft. "Everything all right?" he asked. He had been staying down on the farm, preparing Eric's neighbors for the ordeal of the trial to come.

"Yes, yes, I'm fine," said Elaine. "It was just a dream." But still she shivered in Eric's arms.

"I had a vision," she told him. "Elizabeth and I were walking through the cemetery at Gettysburg—"

"You needn't speak of it."

"But I must. Elizabeth and I were walking there, and I saw my father seated upon a distant tombstone. He beckoned for us to come to him. I hurried toward him, pulling Elizabeth after me, but as I drew nearer, I saw that it was not my father at all, but President Lincoln who beckoned me. I stopped in alarm, but he seemed to want me to come on, so I proceeded. Elizabeth could not keep up with me—in the dream she could walk, but just barely— and started to cry. I looked down to pick her up. We were very near the tombstone now. But when I lifted her and looked again—"

Her voice broke, and she clung to Eric, held him fast.

"—when I looked again, Eric, it was *you* seated on that tombstone!"

Elaine shuddered in Eric's arms, and he suppressed a shiver himself.

"It's nothing. It's only a dream. Things get all mixed up."

"Oh, darling, I hope so. But it was startlingly clear for just a dream. Father, and Gettysburg cemetery, and Lincoln and the tombstone, and—"

"Me?" he finished. He forced a smile. The vision was uncanny in its dark simplicity. "I'm very much alive."

She held him a while more, and said nothing. Finally they rose and washed and dressed. Phil Phettle joined them at the table for coffee, oatmeal, and fried slabs of salt pork.

"You're certain Elaine should attend the trial?" Eric asked the lawyer. He was not worried about leaving little Elizabeth with Bonnie Wenthistle. He was more concerned lest Elaine become excessively agitated by the wear and tear of the trial, which promised to be acrimonious. She had barely recovered from a difficult childbirth, and the constant talk of oil, business plans, and the trial itself vexed and puzzled her.

"I wish I could say no, but I can't," Phil Phettle explained. "You are bringing suit together, and it is her farm, by right of inheritance. What would a jury think if . . ."

"It's all right," Elaine said. "There are some things I don't understand, but my place is beside my husband."

Eric touched her hand, and they ate quickly, in silence. Bonnie Wenthistle arrived, yawning, to take care of the baby. Elaine hugged the little girl tightly, for a long time, then gathered her shawl and stood at the door. Eric kissed the baby, too; she looked up at him with her striking eyes, which seemed to understand him and all that he did. Then they went outside to join Phil Phettle, who was sitting on horseback with the farmers who had gathered there, Ordway, Fensterwald, Cleanland, and Renner. They were ready, but unenthusiastic. Months earlier Eric and Phil Phettle had been able to stir in them an indignation against

Horace and Creedmore, and such indignation had caused them to lend their names to the legal suit. But now, with the time of the actual court case drawn nigh, they regretted their boldness. They were country people, suspicious of legal machinery, resentful now of what they felt Eric was forcing them to do, but too tightly held by the compunctions of their own private sense of honor to renege upon a promise.

"Let's ride and get this thing the hell over with," Ordway grunted.

Eric swung up on his horse, touched its flanks lightly with spurs, and they all galloped off to the north.

Kristin barely slept all night, and awoke long before dawn. Her life, it seemed, had reached a sudden, unexpected climax, the nature of which she could not yet perceive, but whose emotional effect was profound. She felt intensely alive, totally prepared; yet she did not know what is was that she anticipated with such steadfast resolve.

Kristin walked to the window of her suite, and looked out over Harrisburg. Somewhere out there was the man who had been sent to kill Eric. In the newspaper, she had read news of the oil rights trial that was to begin at eleven o'clock that very morning. ". . . Eric Gunnarson, former Union army officer and now a farmer in Adams County, is contesting . . ."

Kristin crossed her arms and hugged herself; it could not have been written in the stars that she and Eric should come all this way, across the ocean, across time and the years, be separated for so long with such pain, only to suffer disaster now.

Kristin breakfasted with Haakon and Bridget in the suite. Sean was solicitous. "Do you wish me to go around to the hotels again, Mrs. Rolfson, and ask after that Gunnarson fellow?"

"Please, Sean, if you would be so kind."

He returned about an hour later. "No luck, I'm sorry to say. I checked all the hotels, and stopped at the courthouse. They are preparing for the trial now, and a bailiff told me Gunnarson was expected to ride up from his farm this morning."

Kristin felt a sudden flash of fear. All along she had imagined the attempted killing would take place in town. What if the assassin lay in ambush along a country road? Then her trip here was all for naught.

"Gunnarson is a popular man," Sean was saying.

"Yes?"

"Several hotel clerks told me other men have been asking for him."

"Other men?"

"At one hotel a man with an eyepatch had inquired. At another it was a fellow with long red sideburns and a stovepipe hat. And at the Penn Inn, it was some dandy with a cape and silver-headed cane."

Kristin was mystified. Was there more than one assassin? She clearly remembered the stranger in her home telling Gustav that his men always made a point to blend in with the surroundings, so as not to appear distinctive. The men described by Sean were definitely distinctive. Disguises?

"Anything wrong, Mrs. Rolfson?" Sean asked, noting the worried look on her face.

"No," she lied. "Sean, I must go out. I'd like you to remain outside the door, in the hotel corridor, and look after Bridget and Haakon."

"Of course, Mrs. Rolfson."

Then, after pinning up her hair and tucking it under her hat, she put on her cape and went out. If Eric was not already here in Harrisburg, he would have to be arriving by eleven o'clock, at which time, according to the newspaper, the trial was to begin. If he were coming by horseback, what approach would he use to the courthouse? Three different roadways led to its main entrance, a convergence of streets already crowded in early morning. By midday the space in front of the courthouse would be a teeming mass of horseflesh, upholstery, leather, haberdashery, humanity. Then Kristin had another thought: Did the assassin know what Eric looked like? Certainly, he would have attempted to learn this, but how could he know for sure?

WILD WIND WESTWARD

She felt a faint surge of optimism. In a sense the assassin might be walking blind, so to speak, until the final moments before he struck. He would be trying to pick Eric out of the crowd, and to do this he would have to get very close, and wait. Kristin determined to get very close to Eric as well. Perhaps she should get a gun . . . but in a crowded area her lack of skill might prove more dangerous than helpful.

Not knowing how or where Eric would arrive in town, Kristin decided to go over to the courthouse. It was not especially large, but constructed in a quasi-Roman, quasi-Greek manner, with pillars and domes and arches scattered about in inappropriate profusion. There was enough marble to give it a formal air, and enough brick to render it American. A few inquiries revealed that the "oil trial" would take place in courtroom three, on the second floor. The courthouse was crowded this morning. Kristin studied everyone, hoping to find behind whiskers, or beneath hat, or even concealed within skirts, the hint of someone who had come here today to kill. But she had no luck, no luck at all, and so, calculating that the assassin would not strike inside the building, she went outside onto the broad steps. Taking a position next to one of the big pillars supporting an insubstantial but pretentious portico, she watched and waited. Scores of people milled about, going up and down the stairs, into the courthouse and out again. Kristin studied every face. *Watch for a disguise that does not look like a disguise*, she told herself, *study the women as well as the men*.

But there were so many people to keep track of! The lawyers were easy enough to spot, generally well-fed men with good clothes and watch chains drooping over swelling girths. The crowd was swelled, too, by citizens trying to get seats in the courtroom for the sheer entertainment of watching a trial. It would be something to talk about, something to have been in on. Then there were the reporters, not only from Harrisburg, but Pittsburgh and Philadelphia, too. The outcome of Gunnarson *et al.* versus Horace and Creedmore would affect the future of the commonwealth for a long time to come, in ways yet incalculable. Kristin recognized the reporters by their notepads and cynical talk. Vendors walked among the crowd, peddling coffee and sandwiches, sausages and chocolates, buttermilk and cheese. A young girl sold fresh biscuits from a basket, and a Union army veteran in uniform, his crutch beside him, sat on the courthouse steps requesting signatures on a petition for pension increases.

Everything seemed perfectly normal.

That was the dangerous thing. The assassin wanted everything to be "perfectly normal."

Then a large carriage pulled to a stop in front of the courthouse steps, and Kristin felt the enhanced excitement of the crowd.

"It's Horace and Creedmore," someone called, and reporters pushed through the crowd to press these luminaries with questions. From her place beside the pillar Kristin saw a fleshy man emerge from the carriage, saw the vehicle bounce several times, as if relieved of his weight.

"Tell us, Congressman Creedmore," a reporter demanded, "what is your view of the outcome of the trial?"

"We shall win!" he boomed pompously, throwing up his fat jaw and hooking his thumbs in his galluses.

Emerging from the carriage after Creedmore was a tall dark-haired man with a rude, peremptory gaze. Horace, Kristin surmised. The man turned to help down one of the loveliest women Kristin had ever seen, a silky redhead with a perfect oval face and cunning green eyes. The woman seemed very calm and sure of herself, yet Kristin's intuition sensed a subdued but constant hunger in the redhead, a grasping need that would never be satisfied, not with men, not with money, not with any of the pleasures of the earth.

The three made their way up the steps through the milling people, with the reporters pushing and darting after them like sparrows attendant upon great hawks. Vexed, Creedmore stopped.

"All right," he said, "clear a little space here, and I'll answer a few questions. There's still time before the trial

WILD WIND WESTWARD

begins, and I understand the plowboys aren't here anyway. Maybe they got scared off, or maybe they haven't scraped the barnyard off their boots yet."

Some of the people laughed, but many others did not. Creedmore frowned, and so did Benjamin Horace. In the hearts of the common people their cause was obviously not pure and worthy. The reporters started peppering the two men with all manner of questions, both technical and trivial. Looking bored, the redhaired woman stepped away from them, saw Kristin standing there, and approached her.

"And whose side are you on?" she asked, politely enough but without prelude.

"I beg your pardon?"

"Are you here as a spectator? Are you . . . ?" She seemed to look at Kristin piercingly, as if she had seen her before, or knew something about her. "Are you in support of Horace and Creedmore, or . . . ?"

"I am for the cause of Eric Starbane!" Kristin stated proudly, having determined that this woman was not.

An expression of veiled alarm showed on the other's face, and she scrutinized Kristin, as if putting together pieces of information and reaching a conclusion. "May I ask who you are?"

Not wishing to use the name Rolfson, Kristin nevertheless saw no harm in offering her Christian name. "Kristin," she said politely, "and you?"

"So. You are the one! I always wanted to have a look at you."

"What? I'm afraid I don't understand."

The woman was smiling coldly. "I always wanted to see exactly what it was in you, that would captivate a man like him."

This woman must know Eric. Kristin was mystified, and even hurt. What dark things had taken place in Eric's life that she did not know about?

"Why do you call him Starbane, though?" the woman asked. "He had some bizarre aversion to using that name."

"You would understand if . . . who *are* you?"

"I am Joan Leeds Horace. Current wife of that dark-haired defendant over there, talking to the reporters. Also former . . . friend . . . of Mr. Starbane, as you call him." Joan smiled darkly. "Once upon a time we were *very* good friends."

She enjoyed the look of pain on Kristin's face.

"Here come the plaintiffs!" yelled a schoolboy, who had somehow gotten on the portico roof.

"I'm sure it will be a sweet reunion for you," Joan was saying, "or did you know he's married now?"

But Kristin wasn't listening anymore. She had no time for Joan's words. Riding toward the courthouse on the middle one of the three roads that led to it, she saw a party of perhaps a half-dozen horsemen. She watched them coming, then turned back to the crowd. It was impossible! The area in front of the court house was jammed, and the wide steps, too. She held to her place at the pillar, looking about, trying to fit together in her mind a picture of the entire scene, trying to evaluate it utterly. If the assassin was here, then something, some tiny little detail, must be amiss. There was the biscuit girl, and the reporters . . .

"See him now?" Joan Leeds was saying sweetly, pointing at the horsemen. "And I do believe that black-haired girl riding beside him is—"

Kristin could see Eric now, as he and his friends rode slowly across the street in front of the courthouse. She saw the woman beside him, who looked shy and lovely and a little afraid.

Don't think, there is no time to think. Look!

Whatever would happen had to happen very soon. Kristin was sure an assassin would not wait until Eric entered the courthouse. Even now he was making his way toward the hitching posts in front of the courthouse. He looked wonderful and strong! His head was high and he sat upon his horse like a . . . like a Viking god. Nothing and no one should strike him down. The girl beside him—oh, she was so young and vulnerable, though—kept scanning the crowd with her eyes, as if seeking among the people some singular terror she might have imagined on a black night.

All right, Kristin thought, *we both love him. And what does that matter now?*

She turned her eyes back to the crowd. Reporters, vendors, biscuit girl, all in their places. Union army veteran . . .

Not where he had been, on the steps with his petitions and his crutch.

Eric and his wife, side by side on their horses, were ready to dismount.

The assassin would not wait until they were down among the crowd. He would shoot now.

Kristin looked wildly about. And she saw him. Partially concealed by the pillar at the farthest end of the portico, he braced against the pillar, the crutch pressed into his shoulder. He was sighting down the length of the crutch, as if it were a weapon. And it was.

"Eric!" shrieked Kristin. *"Eric, look out!"* She did not remember starting to run. All she knew was that she was pushing through the people, trying to reach the soldier with the weapon. She saw his finger tense on a piece of the crutch—it was the trigger and he was firing—and, still running, her head turned toward the street, almost as if she were trying to follow the flight of the bullet. There was a sharp crack, and an explosive aftershock. Kristin saw, magnified a hundred times in her sight and a thousand times in her memory, the fearful, startled eyes of Eric's lovely wife. She saw how Elaine's gaze moved across the courthouse steps, taking in Kristin, moving beyond Kristin to the man behind the pillar and the weapon he held. Kristin would remember to the end of her days the look of instantaneous decision on Elaine's face. And Kristin would remember into eternity how Elaine threw her body sideways from her saddle, flew through the air, interposing her being between Eric and the bullet of a gun.

At a distance the sudden blood between Elaine's breasts seemed a crimson flower pinned to her dress magically, by a magic hand.

PART FOUR

MINNESOTA
1865–1872

I

"We'll go west," Eric had decided, in the awful aftermath of Harrisburg. "We'll go west again, as once we came west from Norway, and have a new life. This time nothing will go wrong."

Heartbreak had visited him, and he no longer wanted a part of the Pennsylvania hills. Heartbreak had called, but victory had trailed in its wake. Still, the earth that held Elaine, the earth made sacred by her sacrifice, was not the place for the new life he and Kristin sought. The east was haunted for them after the funeral and the trial; the west was open and wild and free.

"We'll go west," Eric had decided.

Elaine died in Eric's arms.

"She took the bullet in the heart," Eric told Kristin that night, "just as she took life. There wasn't time for a word. One shot," he said, helpless, angry and incredibly sad, "one deadly shot."

There might have been more. Propelled by desperation, knowing Elaine was shot, seeing the assassin tense to squeeze off another round, Kristin hurled herself at him. His second bullet flew off harmlessly into the air, and she was upon him, there on the stone steps, screaming and pummeling. Not at all crippled, he was also strong, and threw her off with no more than a jerk of his arm, scrambling to his feet. Kristin was on her knees, trying to get up and grab him again, if she could. But when she looked up she saw a small black hole had suddenly appeared between the assassin's eyes. His eyes crossed. Then

Vanessa Royall

he crumpled to the stone. Kristin whirled to find Joan Leeds Horace standing there, holding a tiny derringer, its barrel still smoking, and in her other hand the open purse in which the pistol had been concealed.

Her quick decision and impeccable marksmanship, whatever future deaths they might have averted, were nonetheless disastrous to the fortunes of Creedmore and Horace. True, the assassin was dead, and could do no more harm, but his killing of Elaine exacerbated public temper. Obviously he had been trying to kill Eric. And, just as obviously, had been trying to forestall a fair trial and to intimidate the people on whose land oil had been found.

Who would stand to gain by such a sorry act?

Benjamin Horace and Angus Creedmore.

And so—many reasoned, debated, argued, concluded—Horace's wife had killed her own hired assassin in order to silence him.

"It's not that way at all," Kristin explained to Eric that night. They were talking quietly in the parlor of her hotel suite. Haakon was asleep in a bedroom, with Bridget tending him, and Sean was at his post outside the door, armed with a revolver and a knife. Elaine's body lay in a coffin at the Zapp Funeral Home nearby, awaiting transport to a final resting place in Gettysburg, next to her father's grave. Kristin and Eric were both tired to the marrow of their souls, but this was the first time all day that they had had a chance to talk. There was much to talk about. "It wasn't Horace who ordered the assassination at all," Kristin explained. "It was Gustav."

Fatigued as he was, Eric leaped up from the couch. "Are you sure of this?" he demanded.

"I heard the arrangements made. A man came to our house in New York. Gustav spoke with him in the library. Money changed hands. . . ."

"The stinking scrap of excrement!" Eric cried, striking open palm with balled fist. "I'll—"

"Sir, you may not enter!" they heard Sean warn someone outside the door.

"I jolly well will, by God," a man shot back, "and next

398

time I see Hector Van Santen I'll have your nether parts in a frying pan!"

Eric squared himself and faced the door. Kristin came to his side, and grasped his arm. The door flew open and Gustav Rolfson stormed in.

"So there you are," he said smugly. "I might have known. Get away from that . . . that commoner scum."

"No," she said.

"I am your husband and the father of your child. You obey me, or it will go hard with you, and that I vow."

Eric did not step forward to menace Gustav. He only seemed to. "Sit down, Rolfson," he ordered.

Gustav looked at him. The nature of power is a mysterious thing, its sources often indeterminate and constantly changing. Eric glared into Gustav's eyes, and Gustav glared back just as determinedly. In one sense the conflict between them was as malevolent as it had ever been. But in another way it had changed. If one was not ascendant over the other, now they were evenly matched. That in itself was a vast change, and it meant a shift in the equation of power.

Gustav sat down.

"We are going to have a talk now," Eric said quietly, sitting down in the couch opposite the chair Gustav had taken. Kristin sat down beside him, still holding his arm. "We are going to talk, and you had better listen. Why did you come here?"

"Why . . . why, the evening papers in New York had the news of the . . . the altercation here. I am in the oil business, as you know. This trial might affect me. I ordered up a private railroad car, and came posthaste. Terrible thing," he added, momentarily dropping his vulpine eyes. "About your poor wife, I mean."

"More terrible since you are the cause of it," Kristin said.

His eyes flickered toward her, moved away, came back again, and held. "I beg your pardon?"

"You heard me," she said.

"And you," he accused, trying to change the subject, "you have run away like a slut in the night, with my child. I shall—"

Vanessa Royall

"You shall nothing," Eric told him. "Anyway, Haakon is my son. Mine and Kristin's."

Gustav's eyes flew open wide. It was perhaps the most telling blow he had ever taken in his life. He had no choice but to disbelieve.

"What kind of putrid fabrication is this?" he raved.

"None whatever," said Kristin. "With you, I always used a contraceptive. You never even knew. Do you recall that early time in New York, when Eric was in the coach at the Madison Hotel? That was the day it happened."

"No," he said, breaking into a sweat. "You are only saying this to deceive me!"

"And for more than a month afterward," Kristin went on, "you were too busy with business worries to come to me, weren't you? Never once on that long trip to Cleveland did you lay a hand on me. And then, when we were back in New York, the fear that Rockefeller had outdealt you in the matter of the refinery served to make you impotent."

"I was not impotent!" Gustav railed.

"You hire a man to kill for you," Eric told him, "so why is it not also possible that a man should make love where you cannot?"

Gustav lurched to his feet. Eric stood up to meet him, and shot a fist into Gustav's stomach. The businessman slammed back down into his chair, doubled up, gasped for breath.

"Listen," Eric told him, still in that quiet, implacable voice, "I shall do you a great favor. Once you let me live, and I lived, suffering. I could kill you now, if I wanted. We know that you hired the man who killed my wife, meaning to kill me. But I have already spoken to Phil Phettle, my lawyer, and there is no way we can prove it. Yet what would it mean if I could? You would be hanged. Too short, too sweet for a man like you. So I shall permit you to live."

Gustav gave him a look of fearful inquiry.

"Kristin has always been mine," Eric told him, "and she will be with me from now on. Haakon is our son, and he is going to be with us. And as for you . . ."

Gustav sat there, enraged and desperate, waiting for the blow to fall.

"Eric is going to ruin you," Kristin said quietly.

"Never. He can't do that. He hasn't got the . . ."

"Power? Oh, yes I have. Phettle has asked for a postponement of the trial, until Elaine is laid to rest. If Horace and Creedmore still have a taste for the contest after the funeral, let it be. My neighbors and I shall win. And do you know what we are going to do?"

Gustav shook his head.

"Mr. Rockefeller is right. He has the keys to refining, transportation, and the markets, there in the north. We cannot compete in all those areas. So we are going to combine and lease our oil rights to him. He will be immensely rich, and we will be rich, and you will be . . ."

Eric did not have to finish. Rockefeller's situation would improve immediately, immensely. He would be able to pay back Gustav's loans before they were due, taking permanent control of the refinery as a part of the transaction. Gustav would have enough to meet the notes held by Lord Soames in England, but not much more. Soames would hardly be pleased. He had counted on making huge profits in America. As it was, he would wind up even. It is defeat for a businessman to wind up even. Gustav was defeated, too. He had lost five years, and now he was—figuratively speaking—back in Norway, trying to decide how to found a business empire on the value of the minerals in the Rauma Range.

Gustav saw it all, and his face paled. The scar stood out upon it, mark of sin and desolation. He had no qualms about abandoning his pride, however.

"Perhaps we might make a deal." He leaned forward conspiratorially. "You and I against Rockefeller, eh? What about it, Gunnarson, eh?"

"Call him Starbane," Kristin said.

Gustav bridled, then seemed prepared to speak the ancient name.

"No," Eric said. "Not yet."

"But Eric, you have land now, oil, riches . . ."

Vanessa Royall

"The land was Elaine's. It is mine only by chance and disaster. I am not ready yet. In any case," he said to Gustav, "I will not deal with you. Captain Dubin, master of the *Anandale,* upon which I came to America, always encouraged me to make deals. But I have since learned that there are good deals and bad deals. Your offer is a bad one. Moreover, I do not need it. Get out, Rolfson."

There was a long silence. Knowing he was beaten, Gustav turned peevishly bitter. "I'll never give you a divorce, Kristin," he said. "Don't even bother to ask for one."

"Where we're bound, we won't need one," Eric told him. "We'll never see you again. It won't matter."

Rolfson grinned horribly. "Don't count on that. Don't erase me yet. I'll have my son back, and my wife, too, in due course. Father and I will recoup our fortunes, just you wait."

"By the by," interjected Kristin, "did Isabel Van Santen send over that letter?"

"What letter is that?" asked Gustav, turning to her.

"The one from Thorsen that gives news of your father's recent death," she said.

Gustav sat there for a moment, in stunned disbelief.

"Not now," he muttered. "Not *now*. It's not fair."

"We have had to bear a death this day," said Eric, very quietly, "so it seems passing fair that you bear one, too."

Gustav stood up unsteadily and shambled to the door, all poise lost, all resolve flown.

"But we will meet again," he told them, in a hollow voice, making ready to depart. "Oh, we will, we will."

Then he was gone.

"If I ever meet up with him again, I shall kill him," said Eric, still quietly, but with a ferocity that frightened Kristin.

"No, darling," she told him, touching his face. "Don't be like him. Never be like him. That kind of life destroys one, can't you see?"

* * *

WILD WIND WESTWARD

And so they left Pennsylvania, and headed west. Left Elaine in her grave, and Phil Phettle in supervisory control of the oil leases John D. Rockefeller had purchased. Left with Haakon and little Elizabeth and five million dollars that was Eric's share. Taking the railroad from Harrisburg to Pittsburgh, Eric engaged cabins on the Ohio steamer *Victura,* and aboard her the new family made a slow, stately progress westward, past Cincinnati and Louisville, and on toward Cairo, Illinois, where the Ohio poured into the mighty Mississippi.

"When we reach Cairo, I'll decide where to go," Eric said. He was in no hurry for decision, nor was Kristin. So much had to be talked about, thought about, settled. The children were no problem. Blond, rambunctious Haakon took to Eric right away. For a few weeks he occasionally wanted to know, "Where's Papa? Where did Papa go?"

"I'm your papa now," Eric told him.

Haakon seemed mildly puzzled at first, but gave no sign whatever of missing the severe, fearsome father-man with the scar on his face. Little Elizabeth, for her part, was of a sweet nature, and too young to take notice of much other than faces, bottle, crib, and toys. She regarded everything with calm eyes of depthless blue—Elaine's peerless eyes. Kristin fell in love with her, even as Haakon and his new father grew close.

The war was over now, and as the *Victura* passed down the powerful, slow-moving Ohio, the country itself seemed reborn. On both banks of the river, north and south, country and town alike, agriculture and industry were flourishing. Endless fields were being planted, forests shrieked beneath crosscut saws, buildings were rising in the cities. And river traffic—barges, freighters, passenger craft—plied between the high, solemn banks of the Ohio.

Kristin, who had seen less of the country than Eric, whose image of the world still lay more in Norway than in this savage, beautiful new land, stood at the rail of the steamer, stunned to wonder.

"Does it ever end?" she asked, as they passed Louisville,

heading westward still, westward ever. "How far does it go?"

Eric walked up beside her, and put his arm around her waist. He remembered when he had seen her first in New York, seen her on the *Valkyrie*. Gustav had placed his arm about Kristin then. That was not going to happen again. That was a long time ago.

"It goes on as far as you wish it to," he said quietly, and pressed his lips to her cheek.

"Darling," she said, "let's go someplace where we can be happy and safe. Away from the past, and all the people who made it bitter. Let us go where the air is pure and shining blue, and where the scent of pine perfumes the days and nights. Or does America have a place like that?"

"I'm sure it does," he smiled. "And if it does, we'll find it."

"I want a pool, too," she said. "An icy pool of clear water, like a mirror to see ourselves in, and like nectar to drink."

Together they remembered the holy afternoon at Sonnendahl Fjord, where they had promised themselves for eternity, drinking both image and essence of each other.

"We'll find that, too," Eric said.

They embraced there at the railing of the boat. Dinner was over, the children were in crib and bunk respectively, and in the west the sun was settling over green America. The air was cool, and the riverbanks dark and purple, shadowed by approaching night. It was time.

The lost years, the tragedy of Pennsylvania, had subtly prevented them from lovemaking so far. Consigning hurts and wounds and burdens to the past cannot be done overnight. But time and the land were healing Kristin and Eric; time and the land and love were mysterious springs of inexhaustible wonder. It was time.

"Let's go below," he said, with a breathy, ragged edge to his voice.

Kristin did not demur, but there was something she had to ask.

"That woman," she said. "Joan Leeds. The one who shot

the assassin with her derringer. She said she knew you. Had known you."

"Yes," he admitted. "I am not proud of it. It was a profane thing. I might have acted more honorably, but I did not."

He remembered Joan's last words to him, while the body of the dead assassin was being carted away from Harrisburg court house. "I'm sorry about your wife," Joan had said. "I'm even sorrier that Benjamin and I will not be getting rich on oil. But we'll do all right. I always manage to do all right. And anyway," she added, winking at him with innocence and wickedness combined, "my shot might have saved your life. Or perhaps the life of your sweet Kristin. What do you think? Wasn't such a shot worth three hundred dollars?"

Eric recalled the money stolen from him beneath the floorboard in his room at the Leeds house.

"All right, Joan," he had said. "Thank you. All debts paid, and all claims settled. Good-bye."

"No farewell kiss?" she'd asked, standing there before him, gorgeous as ever, lovely as sin. "Well, if you won't . . ."

And so she had stepped forward quickly, gone on tiptoe, and touched her lips to his.

"You've come a long way, Starbane," she said, "and though you might not know it, you've only just begun. I've learned a few things, too. There are roads I'm not made to travel. Maybe you knew that all along. When you set out upon those trails, think of me once in a while."

"That would be difficult not to do," Eric had told her, truthfully.

Now, with equal honesty, he said to Kristin, "In my heart, there was never anyone but you. And, for my heart and body, never will be, from this moment on."

Kristin clung to him in answer. Arm in arm they went to their cabin.

"Why did you cut your hair?" he asked tenderly, unfastening the catch of her dress, easing the garment down over her shoulders.

Vanessa Royall

"Because everyone knew me." She shivered. "I only want you to know me."

He turned her in his arms, so they were face to face, and drew the dress down over her breasts, which she lifted for his kiss, shuddering with pleasure when the kisses came.

"I know you," he whispered, "have known, and know again."

Kristin unbuttoned his shirt as they kissed, and it slipped away as her dress had. They pressed close to each other, skin to skin, kissing, touching. An aura of pure desire encompassed them, shimmering all about. He took off her dress, and she his breeches, and they lay down in a splendor of ecstasy upon the wide bunk in the cabin. This was the time for which Kristin had been waiting for so long, and now that it had finally come to pass, she could scarcely believe it. Oh, but her body believed it, as she closed her eyes against the world, against the light, to know love not by sight but sensation alone. Wave upon wave of resounding pleasure swelled and broke and flooded upon the shores of her soul, and veiled twilight, suffused in shades of amber, red, rust, flickered and danced behind her eyelids. When he kissed her breasts, she gasped, and when he traced the long, long length of her with kisses, she sighed. She keened in want when he played her softly with his tongue, and when he took her, finally, she cried out as if it were a song from long ago that she had just remembered. She felt him within her, to the depths of her soul itself. Joyously she wrapped herself about him, matching her rhythm to his riding need. No one on the whole wild earth could stop them now. Not man nor mountain nor ocean could keep them apart, nor hold back the tide of pleasure that grew within them, swept toward them, plucked them from vast white beaches of heaven, tossed them spellbound upon an isle of delight. Kristin felt Eric lost within her, not caring, and she was lost herself upon the rolling waves of this enchanted sea. As if she were drowning, fragments of her life passed before her: blue cliffs rising from the fjords, green pastures sweeping to the mountain tops, the faces of her family, safe now upon the ancient lands of home. These things she saw, in a flashing moment. But above them all, beyond them all, was Eric. She felt his body taut and trembling upon her, within her, knew his need as she knew her own, and joined him in the flood of passion, so long held back but now released with such force it seemed all life was washed away before its surging flow.

"We will never be parted again," he whispered to her afterwards, kissing her, cradling her in his arms. "We have had enough suffering and heartbreak for any two lifetimes. All that is ended."

"Oh, I hope so," she said.

"I'll kill anyone who stands in the way of our happiness now."

Kristin said nothing, snuggling close to him, holding him as he passed into sleep. She was happy, tremendously happy. But she was also—way down deep—disturbed. She could not have expected Eric to remain exactly as he had been. He was older, experienced. Years had passed, a war, business battles. But twice recently he had mentioned killing, with a steely hardness he had never possessed before. She, who had lived with Gustav Rolfson, knew the slitty-eyed, clench-jawed look of lawless implacability. Rolfson had known no better; such had been his dismal birthright. And surely Eric had cause for anger and resentment. But there had been something horrible and unyielding in his tone.

No, she told herself. *No. We are free as the wind, westward bound. There are none to touch us now.*

Then she felt a pang that surprised her at first, until she remembered how she had felt after making love with Eric in the old days.

"Darling," she asked, "do you think the galley might still be open? Suddenly I feel famished."

"No, it's closed for the night." He laughed. "But let me see if I can find a way to take your mind off that kind of hunger."

He began to caress her anew, long and lingeringly.

"Oh, I think you are succeeding," she sighed.

And again they knew the passion for which they had been fated and born.

Kristin awoke very late in the night, and kissed Eric once, as he slept. Then she slipped her hand into his, and followed him out upon golden prairies of dreams, beyond which pine trees bowed and dipped in the wind, where deep lakes glinted eerily beneath the cornflower blue of northern sky.

II

Putting behind him a past of poverty, struggle, and want, Eric built one of the first great mansions in St. Paul, on the high, tree-laden east bank of the Mississippi River. Minnesota, which had joined the Union as recently as 1858, was still a wild state. The Sioux had staged what everyone hoped would be their last great uprising in 1862, and many of that nation had moved west into the Dakotas. But the Indian presence was still strong in the land, especially in the far north, where a vast empire of lakes and pine forests had yet to be charted by white men. Central Minnesota was partially forested, a countryside of rolling groves, rich farmland juxtaposed with massive deposits of granite left eons earlier when the glaciers of the Ice Age receded. The southern tier of the North Star State flattened into prairieland that rolled on for a thousand miles across Nebraska and Kansas and Colorado, like a golden sea that finally broke against the vaulting blue Rockies.

When the *Victura* had docked at Cairo, Illinois, Eric was entertaining two choices.

"Kristin," he said, "I cannot see the two of us settling down to ranch on the grasslands. Either we go on to California, or follow the Mississippi to Minnesota. I'm told many Swedes and Norwegians are settling there, even now."

"But what will you do? Is there oil? What? I want you to find peace and reward in whatever enterprise you choose."

"I have been thinking about that. There are many possibilities. Banking, perhaps, or the railroad . . ."

"Somehow I don't think you'd be happy sitting in a bank office."

"And there have been rumors these past few years of astonishingly rich deposits of iron ore, far to the north. I will look into that, for certain."

She heard in his voice a tone of excitement, a desire for adventure, lust for a challenge in which he might pit himself against destiny, a face-to-face confrontation, hand-to-hand combat in the wilderness.

"Well, I guess we can rule out California then, can't we?" she asked, with a smile.

"I've already booked passage on a river steamer north to St. Paul," he told her, looking pleased at his maneuver.

And so they steamed into St. Paul, Minnesota, in the late summer of 1865, prepared for hard work but with every expectation of happiness. St. Paul was a bustling center, although its population was less than ten thousand in that year.

The first person to greet the Gunnarsons in their new base of operations was a canny, cagey-looking man who seemed to be in charge of the river wharves. He stood upon the dock as if it were the deck of a ship, and he the captain, with short, thick legs, broad, powerful torso, and a black patch covering his left eye. His good eye was black, astonishingly large and sharp—from this came the aspect of clever intelligence—and his black hair was glossy and thick.

"J. J. Granger at your service," he said to each of the disembarking passengers, "top of the day to you, I'm sure. And what might your needs be, here in God's country? Perhaps I might be of use to you?"

Kristin was certain this man must be very important in Minnesota, so easily, so commandingly, did he present himself.

"J. J. Granger at your service, sir," said the man to Eric, offering his hand. Eric shook it, found the grip strong and prehensile. J. J. Granger clung to things, as if a handshake were the first step on the way to clutching a man's soul.

WILD WIND WESTWARD

"Perhaps I might be of use to you?" Granger asked, politely enough, but in a manner that suggested what he really meant was *Perhaps you can be of use to me?*

"Perhaps," Eric answered cordially. "What is your business?"

"Just about anything that will turn a dollar," Granger responded good-naturedly, winking.

"Are you in charge here?" Eric asked.

Before Granger could reply, a man in an expensive suit and top hat emerged from the adjacent warehouse office. "Goddammit to hell, J.J.," he yelled, "stop trying to trick the passengers out of their money, and get back to your desk. I hired you to keep track of invoices, not jaw the day away."

A look of steely resentment appeared on Granger's handsome, mobile face.

"You work for me, J.J., and keep that in mind, you hear?" added the man in the top hat, approaching Eric and Kristin.

"For the time being," Granger muttered under his breath, before turning away and going into the warehouse, "for the time being."

"I'm Sylvester Till," said the man, introducing himself to the Gunnarsons. "Head of the Hiawatha River Line. Hope J.J. didn't chew your ears off. He's quite a character." He appraised Eric and Kristin, looked at little Haakon, who was holding Eric's hand, smiled at Elizabeth in Kristin's arms. "Coming to visit or coming to settle?" he asked.

"We plan on settling," Eric said, "especially if I can find the right business opportunity."

Till judged Eric's clothes, manner, appearance. Clearly this big blond Scandihoovian was not looking for a job; he was interested in founding a business of his own. "Well, this is Minnesota," Till said. "We've got just about everything. Lumber, fur trade, shipping, cattle, now the new railroad coming through. Building, if you want to go into that. Thousands of people are going to need homes. Now that the war is over, the rush is on. Homesteaders are buying up land left and right. They're going to need farm machinery. Oh, yes, if you want to go into business, you can pick and choose. You came to the right place, no doubt about it."

"What you say is very encouraging," Eric replied. "But right now I think we ought to find a hotel. Is it possible to hire a buggy?"

"Certainly, certainly," Till assured them. "Just outside the gate. You see it, just to your right. Now, if you'll excuse me, I must be off. I'm sure we'll meet again, soon, after you get settled. St. Paul is a small town, and"—he tipped his hat to Kristin—"and the addition of a lovely lady should certainly be excuse for a gathering."

"He was quite nice," said Kristin, as they took the children over to the gate, while a porter trailed along with their baggage.

"I think we're all going to like it here," Eric agreed.

Several cabs pulled up to the gate, taking on passengers who had been waiting there already. "That damn Granger," muttered Eric. "He delayed us. I hope we find a hotel. I'm going to build us a house as soon as possible. Certainly before winter."

Then, when they were the last passengers waiting, a rattletrap buggy pulled by a sinewy, swaybacked nag emerged from behind the dock warehouse and clopped over to the gate.

"You folks be needin' a ride?" asked the driver solicitously.

It was J. J. Granger.

Eric looked around. No other cabs in sight. "All right," he agreed reluctantly. "Take us to the best hotel in town. What'll you charge for the fare?"

"One dollar even," Granger said.

On the way to the hotel he said what a fine boy Haakon was, what lovely girls Kristin and Elizabeth were, and how it was clear that Eric would go places in Minnesota. He also informed them that the new railroad was missing a trick by not running enough spurs out to the farmland, confided to them that he would soon be in the lumber business, and indicated he had heard a rumor to the effect that the Hudson Bay Fur Trading Company needed an infusion of investment capital. "Might be just the opportunity you're looking for," he told Eric, winking. Then he caught little Haakon staring at his eyepatch, and laughed.

"Never seen one of these, eh, youngster?" He pulled away the patch, showing the discolored crater where his eye had been. Haakon wasn't frightened. He was fascinated. But Kristin turned away.

"Chippewa arry did that," J. J. Granger explained, replacing the patch. "I was up hunting for iron ore in the country north of Lake Superior—"

Eric looked startled, but said nothing.

"—and a bunch of Chippewa didn't seem to care for me poking around. Guess they thought I was a goner when that arry stuck in my eye. Had to pull her out myself, too. Well, here's the hotel. That'll be a dollar and a quarter."

"A dollar," Eric reminded him.

"Oh? Oh, yes. I forget. Sorry about that."

Eric gave him a dollar. J.J. took it, squinted at it, kissed it, and slipped it into his coat pocket.

"Be seeing you," he called happily, driving off.

"If that J.J. isn't the biggest windbag I've ever seen in all my born days," observed Kristin later that evening, after the children were asleep, "then I don't know what."

"I'm not so sure of that," said Eric. He was standing at the hotel window, dressed in his robe, looking out across the Mississippi, where the land rolled away into the west.

"You mean you actually think he made sense, with all that babbling?"

"It was babble, in a way. But things are different here. I sense it. Our experience in America has been mostly in the east, which is older, more settled. More refined, is what I'm trying to say. Who knows but that out here on the frontier it will take men like J. J. Granger to open things up."

"And men like you," said Kristin, coming over to him.

He put his arms around her. "*And* men like me," he agreed.

"Really think Granger knows what he's talking about?"

"Yes. I don't think he has much capital, but he knows where the opportunities lie. And either he's damn intuitive or he's damn smart. I read an article in a St. Louis paper, when we were waiting for boat connections downriver. The article reported that a Chicago geologist had claimed to believe, on the basis of certain magnetic experiments he conducted, that a great range of iron was located in northern Minnesota."

"Maybe J.J. was only telling tall tales?"

"I doubt it. The other two things he mentioned, fur trade and lumber, are major aspects of business in this territory. Now, J.J. could not help but know *that*. But to have his nose cocked for iron, already! My God! Even if the ore is there in quantity, the area is a wilderness. It might take ten years, maybe more, to begin getting money out of it. I do know one thing, though."

"What's that, honey?"

"As soon as we get our house built, I'm going north to see for myself. And I'm also going to write a letter to that Chicago geologist. Sperry was his name. I cut the article out of the paper."

Concentration darkened his face.

"What are you thinking of?"

"I was wondering how many other men must have read that article, or heard about the possibility of iron ore by other avenues. Iron ore is destined to be Minnesota's gold. There are going to be a lot of people who will want it."

Kristin said nothing. She could feel the dark tension of future struggles forming there in the room.

"But I never expected it to be easy," Eric said, cheerfully now. "Of all the potential businessmen in America, J. J. Granger is the one who threatens me least."

"You don't have to worry about it now," she said.

"No," he said, lifting her and carrying her to the bed. "No, I don't have to worry about that now, not at all."

Eric purchased a five-acre lot above the Mississippi, engaged an architect, and began plans for the house and

WILD WIND WESTWARD

grounds. Windward it would be called, a bright, spacious house with light, airy rooms, and sturdy white colonial columns facing the river on one side and the street on the other. From the house a green lawn would fall gently to the trees along the riverbank, and at evening the setting sun would bathe the rooms in radiant colors.

Progress was swift, and by September the architect's plans were complete. It was time to purchase lumber. There were only two sawmills in the immediate area ambitious enough to prepare an order as large as Eric's: one at St. Anthony Falls, a bit north on the river, and the other in South St. Paul. Eric asked for bids, and the St. Anthony Falls plants submitted the lower, guaranteeing shipment before October.

"Very good," Eric said. "The house will be up by winter. It will take years to furnish properly, but at least we'll have our own place."

Three days after he had signed the purchase order, J. J. Granger came to call. He was wearing a top hat now, and a beaverskin coat of obvious style.

"I hear you're lookin' for lumber," J.J. said.

"I was," Eric responded, "but I contracted with the mill at St. Anthony Falls."

"You made a bad mistake."

"I did?"

"Yep. I could have got you that same order of lumber for your house for five hundred dollars less."

"You could have? I didn't know you were in the lumber business."

Granger, who was chewing tobacco, leaned over and shot a gleaming brown swatch of juice onto the sidewalk. The two men were talking in front of the First National Bank in St. Paul. "I'm not *exactly* in the lumber business, but I sometimes act as representative for the sawmill in Anoka."

Anoka was a town north of St. Anthony Falls.

"Are you still working for the Hiawatha Steamship Line?" Eric asked.

"For that idiot, Till?" Granger spat again. "That soft-

Vanessa Royall

handed, stiff-necked pantywaist! He accused me of doctoring accounts, embezzling funds! And not a lick of proof. I ought to have hung him from the statehouse flagpole. Well, look here, Gunnarson, if you need any lumber, that Anoka mill I represent works fast and big. Keep us in mind."

"Certainly will," said Eric idly, sure he would not be needing J. J. Granger's services.

Eric, Kristin, and the children were living comfortably at the St. Paul hotel, and had already met many fine city families. They were sure a good life lay in wait, and were eager for their new house to go up. At last the word came from the sawmill. The shipment of lumber was on its way downriver, to be docked and unloaded at the Hiawatha wharves. A massive flatbarge would be used for transport, and teams of horses waited to haul the lumber from river to building site. Everything was in readiness. Kristin and Eric waited on the riverbank, looking upriver for first sight of the barge. Finally it came into view, a tiny speck on the big, slow-moving river. Then something happened. They did not know what, at first. They saw a puff of smoke, or maybe only dust, form around the barge.

"How odd . . ." Kristin started to say.

Then they heard the explosion. The barge, nearer in the current now, seemed to sink down into the water. The team drivers and stevedores, also waiting there, craned their necks.

"Looks like they got big trouble up there," one of the workmen said.

Now the barge seemed to be wallowing in the water.

"Oh, no!" Kristin cried.

The river moved the barge along, and so everyone on the bank saw it disintegrate, come apart. Lordly twelve-by-twelves floated from the sinking raft, and roofbeams circled like abandoned sticks in the current. Bales of shingles sank without a sound. Windward disappeared in front of Eric and Kristin, and, watching it either sink or float past them, she would have wept. But she was too stunned for tears.

What had happened?

"I just don't know," said the hapless bargemaster, who had managed to swim ashore. "There was an explosion, rather like gunpowder, right along the keel. She started sinking right away. My God, I just don't know."

Who had ever heard the like? Gunpowder on a river barge? Exploding? Any evidence in support of such a claim was on the bottom of the Mississippi, where it remained.

Two days later Eric found J. J. Granger at the Anoka sawmill.

"Hey, Gunnarson. What can I do for you?"

"I expect you've heard. I need lumber for my house."

"Yeah, too bad. What rotten luck about that barge. Lumber. Sure, sure. Just tell me what you need."

Having no choice if he wanted his house built before winter, Eric handed over the order. "Sure we can do this," Granger said, making his calculations. "It'll cost you—"

And he gave a figure nine hundred and twenty-three dollars more than what the mill at St. Anthony Falls would have charged.

"What?" cried Eric. "You told me you could do it for five hundred *less* than they charged!"

"That was then," Granger said. He spat some tobacco juice into a cuspidor next to his battered rolltop desk. "This is now. Take it or leave it."

So Windward went up, on the banks above the Mississippi. The Gunnarsons moved into it in December. It was sparsely furnished, but the big fireplaces warmed it as much as love did, and it was a good place to wait out the long, long Minnesota winter.

In January Eric read in the St. Paul paper that the St. Anthony Falls sawmill had gone into receivership.

In February he heard that J. J. Granger had purchased the mill, had combined it with the plant in Anoka to found Granger Mills.

Vanessa Royall

Eric had learned more than a little from Gustav Rolfson. He recognized the breed.

During the winter Kristin planned her house, ordering the finest of furniture, linens, draperies, china, and silver from New York, Chicago, even New Orleans. Every day, as spring came, so, too, did riverboats, bringing her treasure. Windward was the talk of Minneapolis and St. Paul, and a gala open house was eagerly awaited. Eric corresponded with the Chicago geologist Professor Norman Beauchamp Sperry, who arranged to come north when the school term at the University of Chicago ended. Eric also bought one-third interest in the Hudson Bay Fur Trading Company. The company purchased furs from Indians and French trappers in Canada and northern Minnesota, and transported them south to the Minneapolis-St. Paul railhead by ox-drawn carts made entirely of wood and lubricated, if at all, with bear grease. The endless screech of the carts as they moved along the countryside was strange and eerie. It could be heard for miles before the carts came into sight. And the drivers, rough men in pelts and furs, filthy from weeks on the trail, looked like apparitions out of a lost century. The Hudson Bay Company could not, in fact, handle the entire fur trade. Its president, Norman Kittson, cast about for someone willing to handle the excess trade.

J. J. Granger was able to put up a sufficient amount of capital to win this concession.

J. J. Granger had, during the winter, also consolidated the various sources of coal. Granger Mills and Fuel Company went into operation.

As Eric awaited the arrival of Professor Sperry, and prepared for a surveying trip into the North Woods, Kristin got ready for the open house. She had servants now, to cook and clean, a groomsman for the horses, and a gardener to tend the grounds. Haakon and Elizabeth were tended by a governess who, English by birth, sometimes looked askance at what she considered the rude life of the frontier, but who was bright and very loving to the children. Into this staff, in late spring, came Indian Ned.

A Chippewa, whose tribal name had been Swift Water, he had been captured by French traders during a skirmish and grown up at the Catholic mission on the shores of Lake of the Woods. Renamed Ned, the sullen boy grew into a sullen man, had fled the mission and come south with the oxcarts, with no particular destination in mind and perhaps no thought of any. Eric had come upon him at the Hudson Bay terminal in St. Paul.

"Who are you?"

"Ned. Chippewa."

"How did you get here?"

"With carts. Walk beside oxen."

"Where are you from?"

Ned gestured indeterminately. "Up north."

"Where is your home?"

Ned opened his hands and shrugged.

"Where are you going?"

Ned shrugged again.

"You mean you have no place to stay?"

"Very true," said Ned.

The man's plight touched Eric, who had once been homeless and adrift himself.

"Come along with me," he said.

And so Eric brought the Indian home, intending to give him a meal and put him up for the night. The other servants were outraged at his presence—Indians were killers, everybody knew that—but Ned mollified them somewhat by his perhaps too-eager acceptance of a sleeping place in the stable. He did not care for them any more highly than they regarded him. Paul, the groomsman, was greatly insulted, however.

"Mr. Gunnarson," he declared, "I am a white man. There is a red pagan Indian in my stable, and I will not have it. Get him out of there or I quit."

"Come on, Paul. Be reasonable. The man needs a place to sleep, that's all."

"Absolutely not," Paul said.

"If that's the way you feel ..."

"That's the way I feel."

"Eric," said Kristin, when they had a moment alone, "the party is tomorrow night. We'll have dozens of teams and buggies to take care of. What will we do if Paul leaves?"

"Paul won't leave. Complaining is a way of life with him."

But Paul did leave. On the morning of the open house, when Eric went out to the stable to get his own horse for his usual ride to the Hudson Bay office, Ned was alone in the stable, calmly currying the mounts. Eric had a sudden idea.

"Ned, do you know horses?" he asked.

The Indian did not remove his habitual scowl, but that dour grimace became, for a moment, less severe. "Ned know all animals," he said.

"Do you think . . . that is, how would you like to take care of the stable for me and Mrs. Gunnarson? Do you think you can do that?"

Ned nodded soberly. "Ned do it," he said.

"How did you learn about horses?"

"Spend much time with them. Better to talk to horse than missionary priest. Horse smarter."

There was some comment among the guests that evening as they arrived for the party to see Indian Ned taking and hitching their teams. Everyone knew Indians would not work, and could not do anything right. That was the way they were, and one might as well accept it. But they soon forgot about Ned as they surveyed splendid Windward, and visited with one another. The guest list reflected the most illustrious people in the capital and adjacent Minneapolis, and the guest of honor, Dr. Norman Beauchamp Sperry, proved a learned and informative conversationalist. Perhaps the only man on the Gunnarson's list of acquaintances who was not present was J. J. Granger. Eric saw no reason not to have him, but Kristin was uncharacteristically adamant. While Granger may not exactly have cheated on the price of lumber for Windward, certainly he had not hesitated to turn the Gunnarson's misfortune

WILD WIND WESTWARD

to his own advantage. *If* he had not also engineered that misfortune by sabotaging the river barge!

"It wouldn't be politic, either," she told Eric. "We're having Sylvester Till and his wife, and you know J.J. left the Hiawatha Line under a cloud."

Over a dinner of delicious corn-fed beefsteak, squash, spring peas and turtle soup, the guests marveled at Windward, and sang the praises of host and hostess.

"I doubt we've ever had such a fine young married couple join our society with more élan," cried Mrs. Brubaker, wife of the Hennepin County judge.

She did not notice, nor did anyone else, the brief glance that passed between Kristin and Eric. So normal was their life together, they seldom had cause to remember that Kristin had never been divorced from Gustav Rolfson. But what could that matter? According to an old rumor, reaching Eric via certain stock transactions he was pursuing in the New York market, Rolfson had gone back to Norway.

"Mrs. Brubaker, I could not agree with you more," added Cornelius Bannerly, vice-president of the Northern Pacific Railroad. "And we wish them every happiness here in the magnificent north country that we love so much."

"Hear, hear!" the guests chorused.

"And speaking of the north," prodded Lieutenant Governor Cooper, "I understand Professor Sperry, who comes to us from that incomparable citadel of learning, the University of Chicago, has been studying certain features of our northern regions. Is that so, Professor?"

Sperry, a lean, hungry-looking man with a glint of intellectual zeal in his eyes, seemed to be of two minds regarding discussion of iron in the north. On the one hand his research suggested the possibility of a major vein of ore north of Duluth, and he wanted to talk about it. On the other hand he was here at Eric's request, and was being paid by Eric. So he did not wish to reveal information that other businessmen—and there were many present—might use themselves. But Sperry was glib and courteously evasive, as he described his surmises.

Vanessa Royall

"The land on the north shore of Lake Superior," he said, "is at present all but inaccessible. Yet magnetic studies I have undertaken indicate powerful readings, such as might be gotten only if much metal were present underground. I have gone as far as the source of the Whiteface River to take my findings. Oh, yes, indeed, the pull on the magnet is strong, its action exceedingly bizarre. But to really know for certain if ore is there, and the extent to which it may be, one would have to go much further into the wilderness, into the Mesabi Range itself, and take samples."

"Didn't I hear you say you were planning to do exactly that?" Sylvester Till asked Eric.

"Yes, the professor and I shall go quite soon, and may remain all summer."

"If there is a lot of ore, then what?" demanded Judge Brubaker. "Are fortunes to be made forthwith?"

"Oh, no, no." Sperry laughed. "If the Mesabi does have a lode, it will be years, perhaps a decade, before an area that remote and inaccessible can be profitably mined. But if the vein of ore is as rich as I sometimes believe . . ."

He paused, uncertain as to exactly how much to say.

"Yes?" prodded Heckart Youngdahl, founder of the dry goods emporium that bore his name. "Yes? Then what?"

"Then Duluth may be to iron," said Sperry, "what Cleveland is now to oil, what Pittsburgh is becoming in regard to steel."

"Think of it!" exulted Mrs. Bannerly, a bubbly blond little woman. "Minnesota may yet become the backbone of American empire!"

"If you're traveling north, Gunnarson," said the lieutenant governor, "don't forget mosquito netting. There are mosquitoes up in the north woods big enough to latch on and fly away with you."

The assemblage laughed ruefully at the truth in Cooper's remark. Then, from the front entrance of the house, there was a commotion, followed by a cry.

"I will by God come in if I want!"

And J. J. Granger stood, swaying, in the dining room doorway. His face was flushed and his good eye was blood-

WILD WIND WESTWARD

shot. But it was anger more than the liquor he had drunk that had brought him here, and he regarded the well-dressed guests with a haughty disdain that was almost—almost—convincing.

"Well, there you be, eh?" he roared, pointing his finger at them, each in turn.

"J.J., please . . ." said Eric.

"All of the good, grand people of the state of Minnesota, eh? Think you have everything sewed up, don't you? Everything under your thumbs. Well, I may not have been good enough to get invited here tonight—"

He gave Kristin an angry stare.

"—but I want you all to know, from this night on, that one day J. J. Granger is going to have this whole gopher-ridden chunk of wilderness in his hip pocket!"

He slapped his anatomy in the general area of his hip.

"J.J.," said Eric again, getting up from the table.

"Oh, don't worry, Gunnarson," the other responded. "I'm leaving. I don't usually hold much truck with those that hire a redskin Indian to skulk about the house. You people better look to your scalps, hear?"

He turned to leave, then spun around.

"One more thing. Who's that professor fellow?"

Sperry paled. Tentatively he lifted his hand.

Granger laughed. "Hey, don't be skeered, hear? It's just I never saw me a professor before."

Then he left, banging noisily out of the house, leaving Eric and Kristin to apologize for the ruckus, while the guests, angry and embarrassed, tried to assure Sperry that Granger was certainly not representative of Minnesota's best. Soon Granger's invasion was dismissed, if not forgotten, and the guests settled in the music room to hear a string ensemble that had come all the way from Dubuque. Soft, beguiling strains of violins filled the room, passed out the open windows into the sweet spring air. And there for an hour, at the edge of the frontier, it might have been Paris or Prague or Vienna, not a rude new town on the Mississippi, in a land as wild as young earth.

Made peaceful by music, the guests departed with soft

farewells, and hopes for the future endearingly expressed. Not even Indian Ned's attendance upon their horses and carriages broke the mood.

"I'm just glad," Eric told Kristin, after the guests had left, "that J.J. wasn't here to take in what Professor Sperry had to say about iron in the Mesabi Range. I'm afraid he knows too much about it already."

"How does one go about acquiring the land?" Kristin asked. "Assuming that the minerals beneath it are valuable?"

"It's wild country. Insofar as I've been informed, one goes there and stakes a claim."

"That doesn't seem too difficult."

"The trick is that one must stake a claim on land that holds iron instead of pine trees. Otherwise I might as well plan to go into the lumber business. I think I'll leave that to J. J. Granger."

"Now, if J.J. would only leave the iron to you," Kristin said.

She meant it as a joke, but neither of them laughed.

III

Minnesota was kind to the Gunnarsons. They were readily accepted into the society of the new state, and Eric's enterprise and intelligence saw a constant accumulation of his holdings in the Hudson Bay Company, the railroad, and land acquisitions along the Mississippi and Lake Hennepin. Each summer, too, for three or four months, he would go north with Professor Sperry and a small party of surveyors into the wild woods of the Mesabi Range in northeastern Minnesota. And each summer he would come closer—he was sure—to pinning down the location of ore he had come to call the "mother lode." By the summer of 1871, nearing the sixth anniversary of Eric and Kristin's arrival in St. Paul, he felt confident that the time was nigh. "When I return in the fall," he told her, setting out once again, "I feel sure I'll be ready to nail down the claim and go into business."

"Don't rush, darling. You don't have to. There's plenty of time."

"No, there isn't," he answered. "For the last two years Sperry and I have seen other parties up there. They are hunting, and they are not hunting for elk or moose."

"Granger?" she asked.

"I haven't seen *him* up there, anyway. At least not yet."

"That's because he's everywhere else."

Kristin spoke the truth. If there was an area of business endeavor in Minnesota that had not felt the grasp of the indefatigable, one-eyed entrepreneur, it would have been difficult to name. He had his hands in everything. "Maybe it would have been better," Sylvester Till suggested one day over lunch at the St. Paul Club, "if J.J. had two eyes and only one hand."

Little laughter met this observation. J. J. Granger was no laughing matter, not at all.

Granger was not the only individual on the minds of the Gunnarsons as Eric prepared to leave Windward for the trek north. Professor Sperry was still at breakfast, Indian Ned was readying the packhorses, and Haakon, now seven, frolicked with six-year-old Elizabeth on the wide, sloping lawn. But Kristin and Eric sat on the porch overlooking the lawn and the Mississippi beyond it, in sober conversation.

"I wish Sperry had not brought that Chicago newspaper with him," Kristin said.

But he had, and—after two painful readings—Kristin knew it by heart.

Nordic Businessman Visits Chicago

The great city of Chicago was fortunate this week to play host to Mr. Gustav Rolfson, of Oslo, Norway. Head of Rolfson Worldwide, Ltd., the distinguished foreign visitor charmed many with his story of the fencing duel that left him with a romantic scar. He also excited mercantile enthusiasts with firsthand information regarding his acquaintances in American business, notably Mr. John D. Rockefeller, who recently established Standard Oil of Ohio, thereby becoming America's foremost oilman. "I gave Rockefeller his start, you might say," Rolfson stated. After several years in New York Mr. Rolfson returned to his native country five years ago to mount the financing of what he termed "a new venture into American business. Earlier, I was supported by a British banker," he said. "But you know the British. You Americans have fought them enough! Now I am backed by the Krupps of Germany. I think you shall hear of my adventures in your midst. Naturally, too, there are ties I made during my first sojourn here. And these I will, of course, pursue. . . ."

* * *

"It's almost as if he's thinking of us." Kristin shivered.

"Yes," agreed Eric. "But Haakon is on his mind, too. Whatever one might say of the Rolfsons, they are not quick to give up."

Now Kristin felt true fear. Chicago was but a rail journey from St. Paul. Transportation had made most parts of the country accessible, and the telegraph had speeded communications immensely. The world, as Eric and Kristin had known it only eleven years before in Lesja, was as dead as the brontosaurus. Still, even as they rode the crest of a new age of industrialization, dark entanglements from their past lives would not release them.

"Your family is fine, though," Eric pointed out, "so Gustav did not take revenge when he was back in Norway."

"True," Kristin admitted. She had had a letter from her younger brother, Piet, during the previous month. Mama had passed on. Papa was aging, but still fit. Rolfson had been to the mountains with many Germans. That was all of his news. Except that the family was thinking of emigrating.

"Rolfson sold the minerals in the Rauma Range to the Krupps," Eric explained angrily. "And they used it to build fortifications and forge cannon for war against the French."

"Where Rolfson is concerned," she said bitterly, "everything good is turned either to aggrandizement or destruction."

They were quiet for a moment, watching the children gambol on the lawn.

"Father!" cried Haakon, his blond hair flying. "May I take Liz down to the riverbank?"

"No son. Not without myself or your mother or Ned."

The children had grown attached to the Chippewa, and he to them. When he was not engaged in his duties, he would play with them down in the trees along the river, play all manner of hunting games, stalking games, tracking games. The one they enjoyed most—even though it scared them—was the bear hunt. Haakon, Ned, and Elizabeth would begin in search of the bear. Then Ned would disappear, to become the bear himself. Whether the children found Ned first, or he them, which was usually the case, they loved the excitement.

"Gustav must know we are here," Kristin said. "Do you think he would . . . ?"

"Bring up the divorce again? If he is attempting to set up business in the Middle West, what good would it do for people to know he has been cast aside? Especially by you, who are highly regarded here. But I think he might try to get Haakon back, in some way."

"Never!" cried Kristin, and grabbed Eric's hand.

"Never," he replied, more quietly, but with equal fervor.

Then Professor Sperry, having finished breakfast, joined them on the porch. "Well, well, are you ready, Gunnarson? Let us be on the trail north. I think 1871 will prove to be most fortuitous for us. I feel sure the bulk of the iron lies on the south slope of the Mesabi Range."

After Eric and the professor departed for their long journey north, accompanied by a dozen outriders, hired hands, and a former French trapper called Pesqué, who knew the woods well, time hung heavy on Kristin's hands. The Mississippi Valley, so cold and majestic in winter, became unbearably humid now, the river moving sluggishly, and the green leaves thick and drooping on the trees along the banks. Sweltering days became tossing, sheet-sopping nights. Dispirited residents of St. Paul sat about sipping lemonade, and trying to remember just how it had felt last September when the first wintry blast of Arctic air had howled in the eaves at night.

River traffic was heavy however. So much in the way of supplies had to be moved during the summer months, to make up for the virtual immobility that imposed itself upon the land in winter. Daily, barges and steamers and boats and canoes went up and down the Mississippi. From the porch of Windward there was always something to see. Many times a boat or canoe would pull to the bank, its occupants to take respite briefly in the shade of Windward trees, before rowing or paddling on upriver.

WILD WIND WESTWARD

Indian Ned did not like this. He considered himself the preeminent man present when Eric was gone, and he did not care for the idea of strangers on Windward riverbank.

"It's all right," Kristin assured him, "don't worry about it."

"Give white man inch he take mile," Ned grumbled. "Give him finger, he take hand. Give him . . ."

"Ned!"

And the Indian went off to the stable, or to amuse the children.

Perhaps because his own childhood with his tribe had been so short, or because the mission had failed to succor him, Ned seemed to take real delight in Haakon and Elizabeth. Oh, he would never admit it, and one might not even have been able to tell by the doleful countenance he used in his exchanges with them. But one had only to look at the faces of the two children when he spent time with them. They knew he loved them. They were not fooled by his fearsome visage, his abrupt, cryptic growls.

One afternoon in late July, when Eric had been gone over six weeks, Kristin sat on the hot porch, trying to pretend she'd felt a breeze, and watching the children play with Ned. They were down by the trees along the riverbank, and she was happy to see them there in the shade, rather than out on the baking grass of the lawn. The bear game was imminent, she could tell. Ned had removed the buckskin vest he always wore, had painted his face and torso almost black with the juice of chokeberries, which grew in abundance along the river. Kristin was not terribly enthusiastic about them playing this game now, because it was so hot, and in summer the trees and bushes were so thick she could see neither Ned nor the children for great stretches of time. But what else was there for them to do today? Besides, he took very good care of them. His English was rudimentary, he could neither write nor read, he much preferred the stable to the house. But his soul was good, and Kristin trusted him.

During times like these, watching the children at play and thinking of the years that had passed, Kristin often

Vanessa Royall

said a prayer of thanksgiving to Elaine Nesterling, the sweet farm girl who had given birth to Elizabeth. If there was a heaven, Kristin was sure, Elaine must be in one of the best rooms, or the biggest mansions, or whatever it was that they had there. Her sacrifice, her love, had saved Eric's life, at the expense of her own, and from her to little Elizabeth had gone a gentle, loving nature. While Haakon was verbal, expressive, volatile in his judgments and moods—how like Kristin herself when she had been young!—Elizabeth was a waiter and a watcher. From her earliest years Elizabeth studied her surroundings and the people who occupied them, as if resolutely withholding judgment until satisfied that she knew enough to decide—almost always in their favor. Haakon was mercurial, Elizebeth even-tempered. They were destined to be Starbanes.

"When I make the land claim in the Mesabi Range," Eric had promised, "then I shall take back my ancient name."

Now Indian Ned, dyed to a fearsome hue by chokeberry juice, was ready to play bear. With a long, ululating growl, he shepherded the children into the riverbank trees. Kristin, on the porch, lost sight of them, but she heard the delighted yelps of Haakon and Elizabeth. Those cries meant that Ned had disappeared to play the part of the great bear, at once stalker and stalked. Then for a long time there was silence. Boats and canoes passed up and downriver, their occupants now and then shouting greetings to one another. One of the canoes darted in close, seeking the cool shade of the trees. The sun was beginning to drop now, a hot heavy ball falling in the heat-dazzled sky. Kristin moved her chair slightly, getting into the full shade of a porch pillar. She fought the urge to drop into a doze.

Down among the trees Haakon cried out, and then Elizabeth. There was something about the cries . . .

Then Kristin heard another voice or voices, harsh notes of threat or command. How could that be? She snapped fully awake, staring toward the trees.

Now she heard Ned's voice and fear flooded her being. Because what Ned said was, *"Run! Run!"* with an urgency totally uncharacteristic of him. Sounds of struggle followed, with cries of pain, grunts of effort, and the brittle snapping of broken branches.

Kristin was on her feet now, standing on the porch, undecided as to whether it would be best to go into the house and seek the aid of servants, or to rush down into the trees by herself.

She never had a chance to make the decision. Haakon, his little face a mask of fright and disbelief, came crashing up out of the underbrush, screaming unintelligibly.

Kristin's heart almost stopped in sheer terror. There was blood on his face, and more blood where his little shirt had been slashed. He came running up across the lawn as fast as his legs would carry him, screaming for help. Simultaneously Kristin heard Ned cry "Noooooooo!" in a long wail that ended strangely with an abrupt gargle of despair.

Elizabeth was shrieking, crying, but then fell silent, her voice not so much terminated as merely muffled.

Now Kristin was racing toward the trees, and several of the servants, alerted by Haakon's cries, were out on the porch, then running, too. Kristin reached her son, dropped to her knees, and looked at him. His eyes were clouded with fear, and he seemed confused. The blood on his face was minor, thank God, and seemed to be the result of a scratch. But his shirt had been cut cleanly, not by branch but by knife.

In the trees Indian Ned groaned eerily. There was no sound from Elizabeth. Kristin thought she saw a canoe dart away from the shore, but the moving water and the dappled shadows prevented her from seeing clearly. Giving no thought to her own safety, she plunged into the trees. Light was dim there, the air hot and damp. *Never, they should never have played today.* "Elizabeth?" she called, trying to keep the edge of hysteria from her voice. *Oh, what shall I do if something has happened?* "Ned? Ned?"

She heard a groan of helpless agony down toward the water.

"Ned!"

Scrambling through underbrush, she tripped over a vine,

falling headlong into the damp musk of rotting leaves. Their smell was sickly and sweet, like death. A branch snapped back into her face when she got up, and stung like fire. She cried out.

Again, Ned groaned, as if calling out to her.

Something terrible had happened to him, but he was still alive. What scared Kristin most was that there was no sound from or sign of Elizabeth.

"Elizzie!" she cried, using Haakon's old babytalk name.

Still no answer.

But then she reached the water, and there was Indian Ned. His feet and legs were on the riverbank, but his torso stretched into the current. She saw the butt of a knife protruding from his back, and the blood pouring out of the wound, bright red against his darker red skin, against the blue-black chokeberry stain. He was dipping his head rhythmically into the river, gulping water and spitting it out. The sight mystified Kristin, the more so when she saw that each expectoration of water was colored red like blood.

It was mostly blood.

"Ned!" she cried, and he turned to her. He opened his mouth, and blood pooled behind his lips. Blood from the stub of his tongue, which had been cut out.

"Elizabeth. Where is Elizabeth?" she asked him, aware that he was losing strength rapidly.

Ned could not talk, but he pointed upriver, and made a paddling motion.

Frantically Kristin scanned the river. "Is that it?" she asked, pointing toward a canoe almost around the bend north of Windward.

Ned nodded, and spit more blood. Then he collapsed.

Kristin saw the canoe glide around the bend out of sight. She called for help, and pulled Ned from the river, so that he did not drown. He must have seen the people who took Elizabeth. But he could not talk now. And, she remembered with a sinking heart, even as servants came down into the trees to help her with Ned, he could not write either. Something had to be done. But what? She didn't know. She did know one thing, however. Whatever was to be done, she would have to do it. Eric was in the north woods. It would take a month to get a message to him, assuming he could be found at all.

The kidnappers had chosen their moment with diabolical precision.

"That's just it, Mrs. Gunnarson," observed Ramsey County Sheriff Wayne Bonwit, "I'm not convinced it was an honest-to-God kidnapping."

"What do you mean?" cried Kristin. "Here is the ransom note!"

A week had passed since Elizabeth's abduction, an act surrounded increasingly by mystery. Kristin and the sheriff were seated in the front parlor. Coffee cooled in cups on the small serving tray between them. Neither wanted coffee.

"I want what you want," Bonwit assured her, "the safe return of your daughter. But I didn't like the sound of the note from the beginning. Something about it just didn't jibe with my gut feeling.

"Perhaps if I might see your son again?" he asked.

"Oh, please. He's so tired. He's having nightmares about this."

"But Mrs. Gunnarson, believe me, it may be the only way. Your Indian is dead. He left us nothing but some strange lines on a piece of paper. And I know from experience that, as time goes by, the victim of a crime begins to remember more and more."

Sheriff Bonwit was a sturdy frontiersman, wide, rugged, and hard as nails. But he was also shrewd. Ned was gone forever; Eric not yet returned from the Mesabi. Kristin herself had seen nothing on the afternoon of the crime except the shadow of a canoe on the sun-dappled river. Haakon was the only witness.

"Vera," Kristin asked the governess, "would you ask Haakon to come in here please? Sheriff Bonwit wants to talk to him again."

In a minute the boy edged into the parlor, his great blue eyes wide and appraising. A change had come over him since that afternoon by the river. It was not that he had grown fearful, but he seemed immensely *puzzled,* as if the world he had come to love had suddenly turned on him, revealing itself to have been an impostor all along. His wounded expression tore at Kristin's heart. In time the world breaks almost everyone. Why did it have to happen to Haakon so soon?

"Come on in, son," said Sheriff Bonwit gently, reaching for the ransom note on the table.

The boy edged away from the door, collected himself, and walked forthrightly toward the sheriff, offering his hand.

Gravely, Bonwit shook it. "Sit down, son," he said, motioning to a chair next to Kristin.

Haakon glanced inquiringly at his mother. She nodded and smiled. He sat down.

"Now, son," Bonwit began, "you are probably going to think I'm an old man whose memory is going lickety-split over Minehaha Falls, and I know you told me the story before, but I've got to hear it again. All right?"

Haakon nodded.

"Good. Now what you tell me will help us find your sister, and we *will* find her, make no mistake about that. Take it real slow. You and Elizabeth and Ned went into the trees to play bear. Real slow, now. We've got all afternoon. Tell it just the way you remember it."

Haakon closed his eyes, concentrating. His intense expression reminded Kristin of Eric, when he was lost in thought.

"We went into the trees . . ." Haakon began.

"Don't think too hard," Bonwit said softly, "just let the memory come. Tell me what you saw. Heard."

"I was walking in front of Elizzie. Because she didn't like to trip on the vines. Ned was behind us. Then we turned around and Ned was gone. Just like always when we played the bear game. First Elizabeth and I hid for a little while, because Ned had taught us to be very quiet and wait. If you wait, the prey will give itself away. So we waited, and then we heard a sound."

"What kind of a sound?"

"A long soft scraping sound."

The sheriff glanced at Kristin. They had heard this detail before. The scraping sound would have been the canoe being pulled out of the water and up onto the riverbank.

"So we started down through the trees toward the water. I couldn't see anything at first, then I thought I saw Ned and another man behind some bushes."

"How did you know it was another man? Are you sure you saw a person?"

"Yes," Haakon decided. "I saw the first man then, through the leaves. And I saw Ned's face. He looked surprised."

Now Kristin gave the sheriff a glance. At first Bonwit had reasoned that Ned must have been in cahoots with the kidnappers. What else could one expect from an Indian. But if Ned had been surprised . . .

"Elizabeth and I were going down the slope," Haakon continued. "It's steep and we were going fast. We couldn't stop. Then the man said something foul to Ned. It's a word I'm not supposed to say. And the man pulled out a knife. Then I saw the other man with him."

"Their faces? What did they look like?"

The boy shook his head. "It was shadowy there. It all happened so fast. They had beards, and . . . and they were wearing hats."

"That's a new one," Bonwit cried, excited. "Hats! You didn't say that before. What kind of hats? Fur? Buckskin?"

"No," Haakon cried, pleased to have recalled something that the sheriff considered valuable. "They were . . . they were shiny, like the one Papa wears sometimes when he dresses to go out. But they weren't tall hats. They were . . . round. Roundish."

"Very good, son," said the sheriff. To Kristin he said, "Bowlers or derbies. City men. These fellows knew what they were doing. Had it planned. And, like I said, I doubt it was for ransom, either."

I wish Eric were here, thought Kristin. "Then what happened?" she asked her son.

"Well, Elizabeth and I were running downhill. We couldn't get stopped right away. The man pushed his knife at Ned, and I came through the bushes and the other man had a knife, too. Ned saw me. 'Run! Run!' he said. I grabbed hold of a sapling, and stopped. But Elizabeth, she was going too fast, she couldn't stop. And she ran right into the arms of the second man. He was close to the canoe. Ned and the other man were wrestling. I wish Ned had had a knife. Ned got hurt, but he kept fighting. 'I've got the kid, I've got the kid,' said the man who had Elizabeth. But the man who was fighting Ned said, 'Not her. The other one.' "

Haakon stopped talking and looked at the sheriff.

"You're sure that's what he said? Absolutely honestly sure?"

Tears pearled in the corners of Haakon's eyes. He nodded.

"And then what happened?"

"Then I ran, and the next thing I knew I saw Mama running toward me on the lawn."

He began to cry.

"Hey, now," said the sheriff, getting off his chair and going over to the boy. "It's all over, and we'll get your sister back. What's wrong?"

Haakon sobbed quietly, holding back the full flood of his hurt. "I . . . I was a coward." He choked.

Kristin came to comfort him, but the sheriff's big arm was already around the child.

"What's this coward talk?" he asked with gruff tenderness. "You got in a battle you couldn't do anything about, so you followed orders and got the hell out of there to warn everybody else. Now, that's not cowardice by my book, not by a long shot."

"It isn't?" Haakon asked, doubtfully.

"Not by a hell of a long shot," Bonwit repeated, "and I don't want to be hearing any of this cowardice business anymore. We may be needing you plenty before we find Elizabeth, and I want you to keep your wits about you,

WILD WIND WESTWARD

just like you did down by the river." He gave Haakon a gentle sock in the shoulder. "Can I count on you, now?"

Haakon dried his tears. "Yes," he said, in a small voice. "Yes," he said, louder.

"Good. That's fine. You run along now. Your mother and I have some other things to discuss."

"Damn hard on him," said Bonwit sadly, when Haakon had left the room.

Kristin agreed, then thought of Elizabeth. She was on the verge of tears herself.

Bonwit unfolded the ransom note, written in longhand on a half-sheet of white paper. For perhaps the hundredth time, he read it aloud.

To get the girl back leave five thousand dollars paper money in a waterproof sack in the forked oak behind Rotley's tavern, St. Anthony Falls, on the night of August 10.

"We left the money in that exact tree," Kristin said without spirit. "No one touched it. And we didn't get Elizabeth back, either."

"Just the point I'm trying to make. Point I been trying to make all along. I never thought this was a regular kidnapping. And now, after what your boy told us about those hats, I'm sure I'm right."

"But why do you think that?"

"Stuff doesn't fit together right. Not at all. First, consider the timing. Elizabeth was snatched on the afternoon of the fourth. We don't even *get* the note until the ninth, when it turns up not here but in the mail at your husband's Hudson Bay office. And here it is the eleventh. Know what I think? They didn't want money at all. Only wanted to make it *look* like a kidnapping. Rotley's tavern is the goddamn busiest place in St. Anthony Falls. Them fellows in the derby hats, or whatever they were, didn't *know* any real good places to stash ransom cash, and they didn't know any because they weren't looking for any."

Kristin followed his reasoning, but she didn't accept it. Her daughter was gone, there was a ransom note, so it must have been a kidnapping.

"They didn't even *want* Elizabeth," Bonwit added.

"What?" cried Kristin.

"Just recollect what your boy said. *'Not her. The other one.'* That's what he said. Those bastards in the city hats got more than they bargained for. Probably were figuring on sneaking up into the house, maybe even waiting until night to do it, and taking *Haakon*—"

Rolfson! thought Kristin.

"—but instead they find a fighting Indian, and a whole muddle they couldn't handle. Haakon runs away screaming, they make sure Ned won't talk, but yet they figure they can make some use of the little girl."

"That's why they wanted a ransom!" Kristin declared, still trying to make him see her point.

"Nope," he maintained. "The time factor belies that, it surely does. If they wanted money, we would have got the note right away. But we didn't. I think they were working for somebody. They had to check with him, let him know they'd botched, gotten the girl instead of Haakon. He had to decide what to do. That's when they concocted the ransom bit. It's the time factor, just like I said. Also the money factor."

"Money?"

"Mrs. Gunnarson, not to be blunt, but five thousand dollars is a drop in the bucket to your husband. Either these guys were about the dumbest kidnappers around, or someone who is not so dumb is trying to make us think cattycorners."

"Just to confuse us."

"That's what I said."

"But"—and here Kristin's panic flared again—"but what about Elizabeth?"

The sheriff gave her a hard, straight look, but his eyes were not ungentle. "I figure she's far away from here," he said, "but I don't figure she's harmed or dead. Things didn't work out right, according to their plan. But they're smart, and they hold all the cards—"

Exactly how Gustav always liked it, Kristin raged inwardly.

"—and they got time to wait and see. What the hell do they want? Why, we don't even know. Except they wanted Haakon. Now, you'll forgive me, but I have to ask this."

"Go ahead."

"I understand things are not so good between your husband and J. J. Granger?"

Kristin was startled. Granger and Eric were cool, but unfailingly correct. It was clear that they were competitors in many areas of business, and the iron range loomed as a future bone of contention. But for Granger, who was increasingly powerful, to stoop to kidnapping . . .

"I just don't think so," she told Bonwit. "I have known evil people. J. J. Granger may be hard and ruthless, even a liar and a cheat—"

"Always thought them things you mention was sort of evil," the sheriff drawled.

Kristin smiled, in spite of the circumstances. "J.J. is in the north woods anyway," she said. "He's hunting for iron ore just like Eric."

"My God, iron," observed Bonwit wearily. "What the hell is this country coming to? Used to be you could go out on the prairie with a rifle and a horse and a hoe and, if you got through the winters, live like a king. Or at least a prince. Now, though . . . oh, well. Let me see that stuff the Indian drew before he died."

Poor Ned, Kristin thought, as she went to get the Indian's last message from the top drawer of the desk in the corner of the parlor. It had to be a message, didn't it? What else on earth could it be?

After she had found him wounded and dying on the riverbank, Kristin, two maids, and the gardener had carried him up to the house, putting him down on a makeshift mattress of blankets. He was still bleeding from the mouth, but the dangerous wound had been made by the knife in his back. Dr. Rubleson was immediately summoned, and arrived at a gallop within fifteen minutes. Ned lay on his stomach. Kristin had withdrawn the knife, which seemed only to increase the bleeding. Rubleson took a look, ascertained that Ned could not see his expression, and shook his head gravely at Kristin. *No hope,* his expression said.

"Hey there now, Ned," he drawled encouragingly, "you just relax. You'll be back out currying those horses, no time at all."

Kristin told him what had happened, and that Elizabeth was gone.

Dr. Rubleson's face darkened. "Ned is the only witness?"

"Except for Haakon. And whether he really saw the men who were there is doubtful. He's beside himself, and . . ."

Rubleson dropped his artificially casual manner. "Ned can't talk, obviously," he said. "But we'd best try to communicate with him if we can. There isn't much time," he added, with an emphasis on the word *time* that told Kristin Ned was in his final moments.

She lay down beside him. He was too weak to spit now, but blood continued to leak slowly from his mouth. His eyes were still alert, however, although reflected in them was a knowledge that his life was fading.

"Ned," she asked, "did you recognize the men who took Elizabeth?"

He gave a weak shake of his head.

"Never saw them before?"

Again, a shake.

"Did they say *anything*? Did you overhear anything? While you were in the bushes waiting to surprise the children? Anything that might help us now?"

Ned nodded.

Rubleson was trying to stanch the flow of blood from Ned's back wound, an attempt bound to fail. He motioned to Kristin that there was not much time left.

So, she thought, Ned had heard something. But what? And, without a tongue, how could he tell them?

"Did they say who they worked for?" she asked.
No.
"Why they were doing it?"
No.
"Did they say where they were headed?" she asked, close to hopelessness now. How would she ever communicate with him?
Yes, he nodded.
"Where they were going?" she asked, in disbelief.

He nodded again, and burst into a spate of coughing. Blood poured from his insides out of his mouth.

"It's coming now," Rubleson said, with immense calm. He meant that death was coming.

From some wellspring of reserved strength Ned moved his hand over the blanket, as if writing something. But that made no sense at all. He couldn't read or write. Yet writing was the only means by which he could communicate with them. Had he been able to put down words all along?

"Do you want paper and pen?" she asked.

He gave her a very weak nod, and closed his eyes. Kristin thought for a moment that all was over, but he coughed again. She raced for a tablet and a pen. The inkwell sloshed over onto the rug as she hurried back to where Ned lay, but she didn't care at all. Kneeling down beside him, she laid a sheet of paper beneath his hand, and dipping the pen into the well, placed the quill between his trembling fingers.

"They were talking about their destination," she reminded him, "and you overheard?"

Ned had hung on to his clarity of mind. He grasped the pen and made a line on the paper.

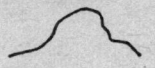

Then he made another line beneath it.

Vanessa Royall

This was followed by a long, looping curve.

Finally, he made another curve, but it ended abruptly. His hand fairly leaped from the page, and his entire body entered upon an intense, terrible spasm. For a full minute he shook and jerked, every muscle throbbing. His eyes were on Kristin the whole time. He knew what was happening to him, right up until the last instant. She did, too, and she was crying. But there was not a shred of fear in Ned's black eyes. Suddenly the convulsions ceased. And his hand fell upon the paper, as if he were giving her a reaffirmation of the importance of the lines he had drawn.

"It's over," Rubleson said, covering Ned with one of the blankets.

Kristin took the piece of paper and stared at it.

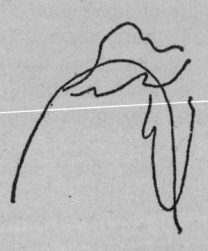

"What do you think it means?" she asked Sheriff Bonwit now, yet again.

He turned the paper in his hand, regarding it from every angle. "You say you asked him where the kidnappers said they were headed, and this is what he drew?"

"Yes."

"Beats me. Aren't any roads or trails in these parts that look like this. Unless it's some sort of Chippewa shorthand.

God, I don't know. These Indians know the lay of the land for a thousand miles in all directions, though. It's in their blood." He studied Ned's final testament awhile longer, intrigued but bewildered. "Got to have something to do with the Minneapolis-St. Paul area, though."

"Why do you say that?"

"Those fellows had on city hats. The ransom note, such as it was, came written on good paper, not cheap foolscap. And the writing was stylish. It was not put down by some half-literate scoundrel looking to pick up some quick money by snatching a rich man's child."

Rolfson, Kristin thought. Even though she knew he was not within five hundred miles of Minnesota, and probably farther away.

"I still think it's Granger behind this somehow," Bonwit reiterated. "Of course there's not a lick of proof to go on."

"What do we do now?" Kristin implored.

"We keep on hunting. We hunt and we wait. You ever done much waiting, Mrs. Gunnarson?"

"Oh, yes," said Kristin. "Oh, yes, I have, indeed!"

IV

"It was Rolfson who did it," Eric raged. "I don't need proof. I know it. He hired men to kidnap Haakon, but they fouled the plan and got Elizabeth instead."

Kristin's messenger had located Eric at his base camp, on the Pike River in the Mesabi Range. Professor Sperry had been wrong. Eighteen seventy-one had not been the year to find a major iron deposit. Eric cut short his stay in the woods, and raced back toward St. Paul, his heart full of rage, terror, and loss. Everything that is special between a father and a child is a little extra special between father and daughter. He returned to Windward bent on blood and revenge. No sooner had his clothing and gear been cleaned than he ordered it packed again.

"Where are you going?" Kristin asked him, fearfully.

"The last word we had put Rolfson in Chicago," he said. "That's where I'm going. If he's not there, I'll find out where he's gone. I'll follow him. And when I find him, I'll kill him on sight."

"Darling, no," she cried.

"No? *No?* If he took her, he deserves to die. Even if he didn't he deserves to die on general principles."

"But you'll just get deeply into trouble, and nothing will be solved."

Kristin was truly worried about him now. His rage, although understandable, made him appear to be what she had always feared: a man like Rolfson himself. No good to tell him, however, that this was what he had promised her he would never become.

"Something is on your mind?" he asked, gently now, studying her expression. "What is it?"

"I, too, thought Rolfson had planned the kidnapping at first," she began.

"But?"

"But I have thought much about it. About nothing else, as you might guess. Haakon was Gustav's pride, true. And I am sure he will eventually try to do something to get him back. But kidnapping?"

"Exactly what he *would* do," Eric declared. "To open up a divorce proceeding, a custody trial, would dirty the air for himself as well as for us. If he is trying to establish himself in business again, he would not want that."

"Nor would he shrink from it if he decided such a course might be successful," Kristin pointed out. "We both know the Rolfson method. They have always maneuvered their adversaries into positions so distasteful that most gave up without a fight. No, he would not first attempt kidnapping. He would threaten to take me before the good people of St. Paul as a wicked woman. I wonder how long the reputation for which you have worked would last, once it were learned that I am still legally married to him?"

Eric came to her and took her into his embrace.

"I'll kill him for that, too," he vowed.

"No. It is natural to want to do so, but such an act would be more disastrous even than finding my name in the public prints. It would seem we have been living a sham all along, when in fact our life here has been the best I've ever known. Until . . ."

"Until Elizabeth was taken."

Kristin nodded morosely. "Sheriff Bonwit was encouraging, though. A city man in a fine hat was observed two weeks ago in St. Cloud." That was a fledgling town, about seventy miles upriver from Minneapolis.

"As if a man of civilized tastes did not once in a while stumble upon St. Cloud," scoffed Eric. "That proves nothing, and Bonwit should know it, too. No, I'm leaving for Chicago tomorrow."

Vanessa Royall

The butler, Sven Engstrom, appeared in the doorway then. "Gentleman to see you, Mr. Gunnarson, Mrs. Gunnarson," he announced. "Dennis Willoughby. He says he is a lawyer from Chicago."

"Chicago?" exclaimed Eric, with a glance at his wife.

"Show the man in," Kristin said.

A lanky, sharp-eyed man in a good woolen suit strode into the room. His manners were impeccable, but he did not seem at all friendly. He studied Kristin with extraordinary interest.

"You are Mrs. Gustav Rolfson, I presume?" he asked.

Eric, his passions already exacerbated by Elizabeth's disappearance, and his hatred of Rolfson, stepped forward, grabbed Willoughby beneath the armpits, and slammed him into the wall. Two paintings came off their hooks and fell, one of them knocking over a kerosene lamp.

Willoughby looked startled, but he did not lose his nerve.

"And you are Gunnarson, no doubt," he said, with a faintly amused tone.

"That I am."

"If you unhand me, sir, I will tell you why I have been sent. You are not, I assure you, aiding anyone by this display."

Eric stared straight into his eyes, and at length the other man averted his gaze.

"My entrance," he said, by way of apology, "was somewhat abrupt. Mr. and *Mrs.* Gunnarson," he stated, "I am here on an important matter which concerns you and a child—"

Kristin noted how he said *a* child.

"—so I ask your leave to speak."

Eric released the man, and he dropped down to the floor, straightening his clothing.

"You are in my home," Eric warned him, "so do not presume too much familiarity." He motioned the man to a chair, and when Willoughby was seated, sat down as well. Kristin came to his side.

"I represent Gustav Rolfson," Willoughby began, nervously now. "I am his lawyer."

He waited. Kristin and Eric looked at him.

"I come in the matter of the child," Willoughby went on, still more shakily now, trying not to look directly into Eric's fiery eyes.

"Which child is that?" asked Kristin, in a hollow voice.

"Why, Haakon, who else?" returned the lawyer, seemingly puzzled. "What other child is there?"

Eric and Kristin exchanged glances again. Did this mean Rolfson had had nothing to do with Elizabeth's disappearance? If so, it meant that some unknown—or even random—enemy had taken the little girl, for reasons equally unknown or random.

Kristin measured the lawyer carefully. Her nerves were taut to the breaking point, but she had, as a result of being in a state of extreme tension, that rare, heightened perception which enhances intuition. She sensed that the lawyer was telling the truth. He knew nothing about Elizabeth.

"State your business," she said.

"Mrs. . . . ah . . . Gunnarson, your husband is suing you for divorce. Or, shall I say, he will institute proceedings unless you agree to his condition."

"Condition?" asked Eric warily, surprised by the singular.

"The boy Haakon is to go immediately to live with his father in Chicago. For now and for always. All you have to do is agree, and a divorce will be handled without"—he made an expansive gesture with his right hand—"undue public attention."

"There is one small matter your client has failed to tell you about," Eric said. "Haakon is my son by Kristin. Rolfson knows this."

The lawyer set his mouth. He was prepared for this particular obstacle.

"Yes, Mr. Rolfson told me you would maintain this argument. And so I shall have to explain a few things to you. The boy was born while his mother was in domicile with Mr. Rolfson, as his legal wife. The boy was christened Haakon Rolfson, and is in the eyes of the law."

"I don't give a damn about the eyes of the law," said Eric, half-rising.

Willoughby shrank back a little, as if he feared an attack.

"Don't worry," Eric told him settling back into his chair, "it's not you I want to get my hands on."

"I regret your attitude, Mr. Gunnarson," said the lawyer piously.

"You'll regret a lot more if you—"

"Tell me, Mr. Willoughby," interrupted Kristin, "what is Rolfson prepared to do if we do not accede to his . . . condition?"

Willoughby shrugged. He glanced at Eric, still fearful of being set upon by the big Norseman. "Rolfson has asked me to inform you that he will bring suit here in St. Paul. Suit for divorce on the grounds of desertion. Suit for custody of the child on grounds that neither of you is a fit parent—"

"What?" cried Eric.

"Listen," Kristen said.

"—that neither of you is a fit parent. You, Mrs. . . ah . . . Gunnarson, by reason of adultery, and you, Mr. Gunnarson, by reason of homicidal criminality."

"Oh, my God!" Kristin exclaimed. The past had come crashing into the present. It seemed that Eric stood here in the room, his Viking axe poised above the squat skull of Subsheriff Johanson.

But Eric held his temper. "It would seem your client has much to prove," he said. "And I expect that he knows how little good a public trial would gain him. He is, as you must know, attempting to set himself up in business. Again," he added.

"Yes, Mr. Gunnarson," rejoined the lawyer, "but bear in mind that the trial will be held here in St. Paul, not in Chicago, where my client resides. To whom, then, would most of the damage accrue? Now, take my advice and give over the child."

"Never!" Kristin declared. *"Never!* You can go back to Chicago and tell Rolfson that—"

448

Eric lifted his hand to cut off her speech, and she desisted.

The lawyer was not especially surprised, but he feigned an exaggerated astonishment. "What?" he cried. "I cannot believe this. Do you realize that you will be branded adulterers. right here in the town you have impressed to such a great extent with your decency and enterprise? Think how you will feel—"

"I know how I would feel if I gave over my son to a monster like Rolfson," Eric told him. "Now, get out of my house."

Willoughby was astute enough to know that any agreement was out of the question. He rose to leave.

"My client is a long-suffering man—" he started to explain.

"Good," said Eric, "then I expect he is prepared to suffer a long time. That is what I guarantee for him, and I trust that you will pass along to him this promise of mine."

"Yes, I shall," said Willoughby, leaving the room. "Yes, I shall certainly tell him, and you may be guaranteed of that, too."

"Adultery and homicide," said Kristin bitterly, after Willoughby had gone. "And both charges true enough, if regarded in the bleakest light."

"That is just it," replied Eric, oddly calm, in spite of the situation. "Perhaps, at long last, I have come to learn something."

"What is that?"

"All along, ever since Lesja, I have regarded things exactly so. Bleak, fraught with ill luck and tribulation. And, true, how much more terrible have things ever been? Our little girl is"—he did not go on—"and now a trial that will surely give many of our new friends pause. But . . . but I am finished being the one who waits for the lightning to strike. Now it is *I* . . . it is we . . . who shall wield the thunderbolt. Rolfson is no god. He is scarcely a man. Sc he chooses to hold *us* up to public contumely in a court of

Vanessa Royall

law, does he? Well, I shall fight him every step of the way, with everything we know about him. Kristin, listen carefully. Recall everything you can about Gustav. Everything. He will never get Haakon, that I promise you, upon the strength of my beating heart! Even if he wins in court, we shall go out to California, or on to Australia, if need be. *Never* will he get our son! And we shall have Elizabeth back as well, wherever she may be."

Eric was standing there, in the room before her, and Kristin saw him not only as the man she loved, but as a person somehow transformed by trial and life. All the past struggles, and the bitterness engendered thereby, seemed suddenly to have flown.

"To find Elizabeth," he was saying, "I am this day going to hire the best detectives in the United States. We have but one clue, a man in a dress hat last seen in St. Cloud. But St. Cloud is no place for a man in a dress hat, so that is a good clue. There must be more, and we will find them, just as we will find Elizabeth."

"Oh, darling," she said, and flew to his arms, his strength.

"I am going to telegraph Phil Phettle in Pennsylvania, and ask him to come here and help us at the trial. He is a good lawyer, and a better man. We will do it." He held her tight, and looked down into her eyes. "We will win." Kristin saw the light shining there, the light of strength and hope and promise, and she fed on it.

"We *will* win," she affirmed. "And I have just now begun to recollect Rolfson's unsavory past. Perhaps I shall have a telegram of my own to send."

V

Phil Phettle arrived from Pennsylvania prepared to do battle against Rolfson.

"So, Gunnarson, you are in hot water again, are you? Well, don't worry. We'll be ready for whatever that fellow throws at us."

But, surprisingly, Rolfson threw nothing whatever. Not at first. It was almost as if he were hesitating or having second thoughts. Willoughby had called at Windward in August of 1871. Phil Phettle arrived there in September. When no legal action had been forthcoming from Willoughby by October, Phil wrote the Chicagoan a formal letter of inquiry, the response to which came with the first snows of the year. Yes, Mr. Rolfson would file suit, Willoughby wrote, but not until the weather lifted.

"What does that mean, do you think?" Kristin wanted to know.

"I'm not sure. I think he hesitated for a reason, but whatever that reason was, he has discounted it. We'll go to court in spring. As to his remark about the weather, just look around you."

The winter of 1871–72 had come down brutally upon the land, creating a trackless empire of ice and blowing snow that stretched from pine forests in the far north to the sandstone cliffs along the Mississippi, hard by Red Wing, where peace pipes once were passed. Snow drifted, too, rock hard and twenty feet deep, out on the southwestern plains, leaving visible only the tops of a few hardy windbreak trees, like stragglers of a ruined army slouching across a wasteland. The same wind that howled triumphantly in the brittle pines roared down upon the fragile huts of settlers, trappers, farmers, icing them and icing, too, the rivers and the fabled ten thousand lakes, and for months on end neither man nor animal strayed far from home or barn. The cold was constant, a bitter, living presence that seemed to freeze the very air, holding the world in thrall. Days were short and pale, and at twilight the sun dogs appeared in the western sky, twin mirages, ghosts of the sun herself, flanking their mother as she sank beneath the dim, ice-crested horizon. When darkness had fallen, the Milky Way exploded across the face of the firmament, and northern lights shot colored fire from star to star, a wild, untamed heaven run riot with eerie, heart-stopping beauty. At the top of the sky reigned the North Star, for which this land was named, the star proud, remote, and pitiless, as if to say: *This empire belongs only to those strong enough to bear it.*

But then, just when it seemed impossible that the sun would ever be warm again, the wind ceased. The wind that had whished down from the northwest all winter long was, suddenly, no more. A man might go out to hitch his team to a wagon upon some shivering morning, and he would smell the hint of change in the air. By noon the wind would have ceased, and icicles melted from eaves in the fleet brave pale sun of noon. The night would be cold again, but the change had begun, and it would not stop. Wind rose now from the east, a wet, warm wind, bringing rain. Drifts melted, almost immeasurably at first, until— incredibly—small brown patches of earth peeked out, harbingers of the land reborn. Ice broke then upon the countless lakes, and finally the rivers flowed again out of the north, and it was spring.

Rolfson struck in the spring.

"Willoughby's in town," called Phil Phettle, rushing into Windward one April afternoon. "He's over at the courthouse now."

Hurriedly, he came striding into the sitting room, to find Eric and Kristin in conversation with a rough-looking

WILD WIND WESTWARD

white man in a business suit, and an even more dangerous-looking Indian in buckskins.

"Excuse me," Phil said, turning to leave.

"No, that's all right," said Eric, standing. "Pierce Trifle, Big Elk, this is my attorney, Mr. Phettle."

The Indian remained seated, glaring darkly at Phil, but Trifle rose to shake hands.

"Pierce and Big Elk have been on the trail of Elizabeth for us," Kristin explained. "Pierce is with the Pinkertons and Big Elk is with Pierce."

"I hope the news is good," observed Phettle. "As I was about to say, Willoughby is filing Rolfson's divorce suit."

"That can wait for a moment," said Kristin. "Mr. Trifle, would you please continue?"

The detective glanced at Phettle, as if he were not entirely to be trusted, but then went on with his report.

"I made several inquiries in and around the town of St. Cloud," he said. "A well-dressed man in a derby hat crossed the Mississippi on the Sauk Rapids ferry, bought supplies, and then returned. He was on horseback, and apparently alone. But he purchased a considerable quantity of foodstuffs, and paid in new bills. Currency of any kind is rare in these parts, as you know. Most of the transactions are handled by trade or barter. But few ask questions in the face of hard cash. The man, however, also bought three blankets."

He looked at the Gunnarsons. There were no questions, so he continued.

"After recrossing the river he rode east. I took that same route myself, stopping at every farm or settlement and asking whether anyone had seen him. It is sparsely settled country. No one had seen any strangers. Then"—he nodded toward the Indian—"I sent Big Elk up into the Indian villages around Mille Lacs Lake. And he hit pay dirt."

Big Elk looked dour and proud.

"It was in late September," Pierce Trifle said, consulting a yellow notepad. "Two white men and a small child were seen camping on the southeastern shore of the lake. They

453

prepared a meal, ate, and bedded down. One of the white men was awake for a while, and then his partner—"

"Was the child boy or girl?" Kristin blurted.

"We have no eyewitness account, but I think it would not be incorrect to surmise that the child was Elizabeth."

"Then what?" Phil Phettle prodded.

"Big Elk and I pushed on. We went north first, but found neither trace of a trail nor anyone, white or red, who had seen the three. Then I made a calculation, which I probably ought to have done from the beginning. Assuming there was some purpose to your daughter's abduction, and operating under the knowledge that she was being taken to a definite destination, I went back to Mille Lacs Lake, and headed toward the only large settlement in that entire region."

"Duluth," he concluded.

"Yes," said Eric. Duluth, a small settlement on the westernmost shore of Lake Superior, was possessed of a fine port. He knew it well. If there were to be any future in iron ore, the metal would have to be shipped from Duluth to manufacturing centers now being built in the east. Superior, Michigan, Huron, Erie, and Ontario: These lakes were the highways of industrial destiny.

"And in Duluth?" Kristin asked.

"Duluth, no luck," Big Elk grunted. "Lose all trail in Duluth."

"Assuming they did go there," Trifle expanded, "there are two probabilities. Either they managed to get a boat east before winter set in, a boat to some unknown destination, or they have managed to stay in the town all winter. That accepted, there are two further probabilities: Either they are still in Duluth, or they are planning to leave. The ice has not yet broken up completely in the north. So Big Elk and I are off for the north again."

"What—" began Kristin.

"Yes?" said Trifle, not ungently.

"What if something has happened to Elizabeth?"

"What we don't know, we won't agonize over, all right?" he advised. "If they took the trouble to get her a blanket, took all the risk of the abduction and the trip itself, we have reason to hope for the best. So do not worry, Mrs. Gunnarson, when there is nothing you can do about it anyway."

"Oh, I hope . . ."

"Hope, yes," Big Elk grunted. "You not worry."

Eric paid the men for their services to date, and showed them out. They were to take the steamer north, again to St. Cloud, and then proceed on horseback to pick up the trail in Duluth. If there was a trail to pick up.

"All right, Phil," Eric said. "You saw Willoughby?"

"Yes. He's filing the suit for divorce and child custody. He is offering one last chance to come to a settlement."

"No," Eric said, and Kristin shook her head.

"The trial will be very distasteful," observed the lawyer. "Forgive me, but it's my job to illustrate this for you, so you will know what to expect. You will be spared nothing. Personal details of your relationship included. And you, Kristin, were in charge of Windward when Elizabeth was taken from your very lawn, right under your eyes. That will be mentioned many times."

"Why," asked Eric, returning to a point that continued to vex him, "did Rolfson not proceed directly last fall? Why did he wait all this time?"

"I don't know," replied the lawyer. "I can only assume that he hoped you would come to your senses and deal with him outside the courtroom. Naturally, he knows that a case of this kind, fraught with emotion, cannot but spill over and harm him a little, too."

"*A little*," scoffed Kristin. "He will get the surprise of his life. Rolfson's winter of indecision, if such it was, may prove to be our salvation."

VI

The case of Gustav Rolfson versus Kristin Rolfson (Eric Gunnarson being named as correspondent) went to court in early May 1872. The particulars, by word of mouth, had been bruited about St. Paul and Minneapolis for several weeks in advance, to the consternation of almost everyone, the sadness of many, and the raw delight of a few. One of the latter, J. J. Granger, was heard to offer his opinion at his table in the St. Paul Club.

"You never know," he drawled. "It goes to show that you never can tell. Who would have thought it? Gunnarson a murderer on the run from his home country? And his wife not his wife at all? No, I just don't know what to think, I surely don't."

"Will the trial have any effect on you?" he was asked.

" 'Course it will," he responded immediately. "Can't help but do me a world of good, no matter which way the outcome is decided. Either way you look at it, the Gunnarsons ain't going to be so high and mighty anymore. And I understand that Rolfson fellow is looking into the Mesabi, too. Well, while they're all tied up here, fighting about who gets a kid, old J.J. will be using his one very good eye looking for a peculiar red streak up there in the big piney woods. Got pretty near last summer, too, I tell you. I could feel it in my bones, and I don't need no University of Chicago professor to tell me where to look, neither. One good Granger eye got to equal at least the brains of a half-dozen professors, right? South shore of the Mesabi, that's where I think the mother lode lies. And soon as I find her, she's my own sweet mama."

His listeners laughed. J.J. was a character, true, but he was bound to become far more powerful than he was already. Never hurts to laugh at the jokes of a powerful man.

"You goin' over to the courthouse to watch the show, J.J.?" he was asked.

"No, no, I got work to do. Besides, I'll be able to read about it in the papers. Should make quite a story."

About that, J. J. Granger was not wrong. Human nature, however lofty its self-perception, contrives many excuses to dwell with perverse delight upon failings, real or imagined. Although there were very few who ceased to treat the Gunnarsons with customary courtesy, many who had been welcome at Windward now found reason to avoid the beleaguered young couple. Innocent until proven guilty, true. But would it not be imprudent to be rash, extending support before the outcome of the trial was definite? Some there were who felt betrayed by Eric and Kristin, as if they had been taken in by false pretenses. The courtroom was packed when Ramsey County Judge Roscoe Bullion banged his gavel and the proceedings got underway.

"Is your client present?" Bullion demanded of counsellor Willoughby.

"I am, your honor," said Gustav Rolfson, standing before the court.

Rolfson had made a quick, last-minute entrance, and now all eyes appraised him. St. Paul was not so sophisticated that newcomers did not create quite a stir, to say nothing of a foreigner who was rumored to be a multimillionaire and, some whispered, a duke or a count.

"Oh, look at his dueling scar!" someone hissed admiringly, at which point Eric shot his tormentor a contemptuous glance. Rolfson reddened in anger.

Phil Phettle affirmed that his clients, too, were in the courtroom, and the preliminary statements were made. Custody of Haakon was preeminent, complicated by the perspectives from which the opposing parties viewed the divorce. Willoughby, speaking for Rolfson, was unyielding:

Vanessa Royall

Kristin must both accede to the divorce and relinquish Haakon. She must admit that she had deserted her husband and, further, accept the judgment that she was, by virtue of adultery, unfit to raise the boy. Phettle pointed out that Kristin had actually *fled* a dangerous and demeaning situation, under intolerable conditions, in Rolfson's New York home. While she most certainly agreed to a divorce, Haakon's future must be considered apart from the Rolfsons' marital fate. Eric was branded an "undesirable immigrant" by Willoughby, until Boris "Mad Dog" Spaeth, Lieutenant Colonel (Retired), Grand Army of the Republic, testified in Eric's behalf, noting that he was not only a citizen, but a contributor to the wealth of the state, and a wounded, decorated army officer as well. At this Willoughby scowled and even Rolfson seemed momentarily subdued. Things were not going to go as smoothly as he had hoped.

"They're just dying to get you on the stand," Phettle told Kristin. "Willoughby doesn't think you're strong enough to withstand the kind of questions he is preparing for you."

"Willoughby is wrong," Kristin told him. "And, by the way, has there been a reply to our telegram yet?"

"No," he said, "but don't worry. The ship was due into New York a few days ago. All will be well."

"I hope so," she responded, less certain now.

When she was called to the stand on the third day of the trial, however, Kristin looked and felt splendid. She wore an ankle-length dress of pearl-white satin, without the customary bustle. Her own figure, she felt, was obscured by that superfluous and silly device, besides which it was uncomfortable. The dress was high at her throat, around which she wore a simple gold choker, and the sleeves were loose and long, but tight at the wrist. Pale gold shoes, buttoned to the calf, completed her ensemble. She had chosen well. The garment set off her high color and golden hair. When she entered the courtroom, there was a hush as people saw her, followed by a long suspiration of admiration and expectancy. If this was, indeed, a stage, Kristin had dressed to play her part.

In one sense, however, her decision to dress brilliantly carried a risk. Old Judge Roscoe Bullion was a hard man, one not inclined to look charitably upon the wiles of the human female. Since no jury attended a divorce proceeding, Judge Bullion's final decision would seal the fate of the parties involved. Bullion looked up and blinked when Kristin took the stand. His eyes widened. His face, with its habitually choleric expression, screwed up a bit more tightly in concentration. A lifelong bachelor, Bullion had found his way into public life by organizing a fiery campaign against indecency and public lewdness in the parks and along the lakeshores of Minneapolis. The holding of hands by unmarried couples he regarded as lewd; mere kissing by married persons bordered on the indecent. Bullion blinked at Kristin once again, and told Willoughby to proceed with his questioning.

The Chicago lawyer, possessed of that same cold politeness he had shown on his visit to Windward, approached Kristin. His voice was deceptively soft, even friendly, but she was not fooled. From his chair next to Phil Phettle, behind the defendants' table, Eric sent her a loving glance of support. She was on her own now.

"I am going to evade nothing," she had told him in bed on the previous night. "Every question Willoughby asks will get a straight answer. It may shock everyone, and certainly Judge Bullion will find his old heart racing, but in the end I am sure that the complete story of our life will win out over Rolfson's inventions and half-truths."

"Would you state your name for the court?" Willoughby asked then. The contest for Haakon's future had begun.

"Kristin Starbane," she told the lawyer, clearly, calmly, looking straight into his eyes.

"What?" he asked, caught off guard.

"My husband's true surname is Starbane," she said. "You see, the name is taken from ancestral lands—"

"Wait, wait," Willoughby protested, nonplused and obviously angry about it. He had barely begun, and already this woman had achieved the upper hand.

"Are you or are you not married to the man here in this court, Gustav Rolfson?"

"I never considered myself so."

The spectators gasped and began to speak among themselves. Judge Bullion banged his gavel, and the courtroom quieted. "Mrs. Rolfson," he said severely, "I will not have this court mocked! I have seen sufficient documentary evidence to indicate that you and the plaintiff are legally bound in matrimony. Now you say—"

"I will explain if permitted," Kristin smiled sweetly.

"I'll do the asking of questions here," declared a thoroughly irritated Willoughby.

"Well, then get on with it," rasped Bullion.

Willoughby collected himself and began again.

"Very well, Mrs. Rolfson. Why do you maintain you are *not* Mrs. Rolfson?"

"Because I feel that I was forced into marriage under duress."

The lawyer laughed tolerantly. "You married *under duress* a rich man who took you from a poor farm in the mountains of Norway and gave you a life of which you could not have dreamed?"

"It is true I could not have dreamed life with him," she shot back, "but nightmares are another thing—"

"Your honor! Admonish the witness to—"

"Hold on a minute," Bullion growled, leaning forward. "This is my court and I'll make the decisions. Now, I want to hear more about this duress business."

Willoughby glanced at his client and Rolfson motioned him to come over to the plaintiff's table. The two engaged in a whispered conversation. When the lawyer returned to the bench, he said: "I wish to withdraw the question regarding duress," he said.

Kristin felt a quiver of triumph. Gustav knew he would look bad in the eyes of the court if his manner of wedding Kristin became known.

WILD WIND WESTWARD

"Overruled," Bullion decided, banging the gavel. "The defendant will speak."

"Mr. Rolfson," said Kristin quietly, "sent men to take over Eric Starbane's farm. One of these men attacked him, and Eric defended himself. The man, whose name was Johanson, died. The judge in our region, one Amundsen, was in the pay of Rolfson and his father. No justice for Eric was possible, so he fled. Rolfson sent every able-bodied man into the mountains, in pursuit of Eric. He also pressed upon me his proposals of marriage. We have a tradition in our village, that when anyone is married, everyone must attend. So I agreed to marry Rolfson, knowing the hunters would come down from the mountains for the ceremony and feast, leaving Eric free to escape."

She spoke matter-of-factly, totally in control of herself. But the effect was powerful. Everyone in the courtroom hushed to listen. When she was through, Rolfson had a hard time keeping his chin up, and Bullion looked enraged.

"A bought judge?" he bellowed. "Is this true?"

"It is not true," Willoughby interjected quickly, "the witness is simply—"

"It *is* true," cried Eric, from his seat. "That is only the beginning of what Rolfson has done."

"You're out of order," said the judge, without much heat.

"Your honor, I must point out," said Willoughby, with a sidelong glare at Kristin, "that we are not deciding the merits of events in Norway over a decade old, but the fitness of this woman and that man"—he gestured toward Eric—"to raise the son produced by my client and Kristin—"

"The child is mine by Eric Starbane, as I have already informed you," Kristin declared.

A gleam of satisfaction showed in Willoughby's dark, canny eyes.

"So you admit to adultery, do you?"

"No," said Kristin.

"What? You say the boy, Haakon, is your child by the

461

Vanessa Royall

man *we* know as Gunnarson. Was he conceived while you were living *in the house of, as the wife of,* Gustav Rolfson?"

"Yes, but—"

"And does that not seem to you to suggest adultery? To suggest wanton, unconscionable lasciviousness?"

"No, it—"

"And now you presume to sit here in your expensive dress and tell this court—"

"If you will just listen to me, sir."

"—that you committed *no* sin, that you are *pure*, and that a child conceived in iniquity, born as a bastard—"

Eric, seated at the table, could bear no more. Phil Phettle's hand was on his arm, as if Phettle knew what might happen, but he did not have a chance to restrain his client. Eric leaped up, did a one-armed vault over the heavy walnut table, and sprang upon Willoughby from behind. Grabbing the hapless counselor by the shoulders, he spun the man around. Wicked words were still forming on Willoughby's tongue, and surprise appeared in his eyes, but he was not yet fully conscious of what was happening to him. "If that is the way you speak to women in Chicago," Eric gritted, readying himself, "then you and Rolfson had best—"

And, with that, he punched the lawyer squarely in the chest, just above the heart. Willoughby flew backwards, struck the table at which Rolfson sat, flipped over the table, and landed on Rolfson himself. Gustav's chair overturned, and both men, lawyer and client, were sprawled on the floor. The spectators were agog, and a few of them were applauding. It took a long time before Judge Bullion got the place back into order. Willoughby came back to consciousness after about ten minutes, but felt unable to continue questioning Kristin that day. He did, however, press charges of assault and battery against Eric, who did not have to put up bail and was released on his own recognizance.

"I wouldn't worry about it," Phil Phettle said. "I doubt

WILD WIND WESTWARD

old Willoughby is going to hang around here very long. You'll never go to trial."

"Then I should have hit him harder," Eric said.

Recommencing on the morrow, Willoughby tried a new tack. He and Rolfson knew they had lost ground, in spite of Eric's enraged attack upon the lawyer. Kristin must not be permitted to speak too much about general issues concerning her life with Rolfson. Instead, she would have to be shown as morally suspect through the most specific of inquiries.

"Mrs. Rolfson, why did you maintain yesterday that you are not, in fact, Mrs. Rolfson?"

"Because I promised myself to Eric Starbane before Mr. Rolfson maneuvered me into a marriage I did not want."

"You say you *promised* yourself to . . . Gunnarson? What do you mean by that?"

"I promised to be his forever, and he promised to be mine."

"Forever?"

"Yes."

"All right. All right, Mrs. Rolfson. You are saying that your promise was, in fact, as powerful as marriage?"

Kristin looked at him hard. "More powerful," she said.

"Hmmmmm. And you had benefit of no clergyman, did you, in the making of this . . . ah . . . *mystical* marriage?"

"No, we did not."

"I see. Are we to assume that you and Mr. Gunnarson also shared certain physical congress, before, during, or after your splendid promise?"

"You may assume whatever you like," Kristin told him.

Willoughby reddened. "I assure you, Mrs. Rolfson, that I am attempting, out of solicitude for you and mindful of the sensibilities of the people in this courtroom, to approach this matter delicately. But if you do not cooperate—"

"You may ask me anything, Mr. Willoughby. There is nothing I have done in my life to be ashamed of."

"What? *What?*" Willoughby was incredulous. "Did you or did you not engage in sexual congress with Eric Gunnarson, without being legally married to him?"

"I did, but—"

"Just answer the question. And did you engage in such congress with Gunnarson prior to your marriage to Mr. Rolfson?"

"I did."

"So do you not admit to immorality on those occasions?"

"No, I do not!" Kristin answered, her head high and her eyes blazing. "One gives oneself to another. *That* is the sacrament! *That* is what makes it holy! The honest promise is more than sufficient to seal the pact. In my heart I have been married to Eric Starbane since we were in Norway, and he to me. We both know it. Rolfson was but a conniving interloper."

"Your honor, the witness must be admonished not to attack my client!"

"Please restrain yourself, Mrs. Rolfson," counseled old Bullion. "I assure you that this court is a fair one, and you will be heard. Mr. Willoughby, you may continue."

"Yes, Your Honor. Now, Mrs. Rolfson, let me see if I understand you correctly. You say you have engaged in sexual congress with Mr. Gunnarson for . . . how long? Over ten years, proximity permitting? And on one occasion you conceived the child who is a subject of this suit. And you maintain further that *not once* were you acting immorally?"

"*Not once,*" replied Kristin, with an emphasis equal to his. She knew what he was trying to do: paint her as a woman whose entire life was a pattern of sexual immorality. Like Rolfson, he was trying to place her in a dilemma, of which immorality was the one horn. Now he painted the other horn: a sanctity of law.

"Are you not placing yourself above the laws of man and God," Willoughby pressed her, "by telling us your love for Gunnarson, made outside the bonds of church or legal court, is greater than the laws of man or God?"

"No," said Kristin.

"No? Let me observe to this court, and the people here gathered, that if one person believes himself to be above law, then of what protection is the law to those who believe in it?"

Kristin caught Rolfson's gloating wolf-eyes on her. He thought Willoughby had her trapped.

"Or," the lawyer continued, "are you not just another guilty, self-indulgent woman who excuses her real immorality on the basis of a totally spurious appeal to 'love'?"

The spectators hushed. They, too, felt that Kristin was trapped now. Phil Phettle kept a very firm grip on Eric this time.

But Kristin was undismayed. "In the Holy Bible," she told Willoughby and the courtroom, "it is written that the highest law *is* love. I believe that, just as I have always believed in the love between Eric and me. If it were known how despicable are the acts and thoughts of Gustav Rolfson, I should be better understood."

"Your Honor!" cried Willoughby. "The defendants will have ample opportunity to examine my client. This is not the time—"

"Sustained," grunted Bullion.

Nevertheless Kristin's defense of her past had led Willoughby to conclude that there was little to be gained by dwelling further on immorality. Now he sought to brand her an unfit mother by dint of gross negligence.

"Tell me, Mrs. Rolfson, did Mr. Gunnarson have a daughter by a previous marriage?"

"Yes, he did."

"And her name was?"

"Elizabeth."

"What became of the child's mother?"

Kristin's eyes narrowed, but she held her composure. "Elaine was killed," she answered.

"Killed? Oh, my goodness. How?"

"There was an assassination attempt on Eric's life. Elaine put herself in the way of a bullet to save him."

Willoughby paused theatrically. "How convenient," he

said cynically. "And who, pray tell, would attempt to—"

Gustav was gesturing from his chair, trying not to appear frantic. Willoughby did not see him.

"—kill such a fine man as Gunnarson?" the lawyer finished.

"Gustav Rolfson," Kristin said, barely able to contain her glee at the sequence of questions.

Once again the courtroom erupted.

"Your Honor," Willoughby was yelling. "Your *Honor!*"

The eyes of mean old Judge Bullion were not so much angry as intensely curious. What had come into his courtroom as a complicated but unremarkable suit was fast becoming the countryman's "plug-in-a-hole," which, once released, brings forth incalculable consequences.

Willoughby sought to regain ground by coming directly to the question he had meant to dramatize slowly, insidiously, through a series of queries.

"Were you not in charge of Windward on the afternoon your child was abducted?" he demanded of Kristin.

"How did you know it was in the afternoon?" Kristin shot back, even as she remembered that Willoughby had been puzzled once by the fact that Haakon was not an only child.

"*It's common knowledge*," Willoughby bellowed. Then, regaining composure, added hastily: "Were you, Mrs. Gunnarson, not in charge of your house and children on the afternoon your daughter was—"

"Not Mrs. *Gunnarson*," corrected Kristin. "Don't you mean Mrs. Starbane?"

Willoughby said nothing, thoroughly exasperated for the moment. The spectators in the courtroom, in whose eyes he has sought to paint Kristin an adulteress, a careless stepmother, and much worse, were not reacting as he had expected. They were having a hard time seeing Kristin and Eric, whom they had known and respected, but who they doubted a little now, as immoral beasts. Something was not right, and they were beginning to suspect that rectitude did not lie in the flat-nosed, wolf-eyed, scar-faced nobleman of Norway. Most of these spectators were themselves from Scandinavia, and they did not perceive a kindred soul in Gustav Rolfson.

"I am Kristin Starbane, born Vendahl," she told Willoughy sweetly. "I told you that at the start."

"I'm asking the questions!" he retorted, with a touch of desperation in his voice.

"Please proceed," she said coldly.

Judge Bullion said nothing. Eric beamed at her. Phil Phettle was smiling, although he tried to hide it. The face of Gustav Rolfson was blank and expressionless. The entire courtroom proceeding was at a crux. If the Starbanes had not yet won, it was equally true that Rolfson was in danger of losing. He and Willoughby knew it.

"Was or was not Elizabeth Gunnarson abducted beneath your very eyes?" the lawyer demanded.

"Yes!" Kristin shouted. "And my first thought was that Rolfson had taken her, in an attempt to seize Haakon."

Her own tension, so well concealed, had broken. She saw Phil Phettle giving her a gesture of restraint. Her intensity had shown through, but only a little. It was enough for Willoughby, who would at this point have grasped almost any straw.

"So," he demanded, "you are not at all what you have tried to appear before this court, are you? You are consumed by hatred for Mr. Rolfson. You see his hand in everything, is that not so? Well, I must hand it to you, Mrs. Rolfson, you certainly sounded convincing for a while. But is not your antipathy to Mr. Rolfson founded upon your own guilt at having been an immoral woman, a faithless wife, and a cruel stepmother, who may have arranged the abduction of Elizabeth, Gunnarson's child by that 'other woman,' who was so conveniently killed?"

The courtroom was deathly quiet, and Kristin fought back tears.

"You accuse my client of kidnapping readily enough," Willoughby went on, boring in, "so why cannot you also be suspected?"

Phil Phettle glanced nervously at Eric, to make sure his passions did not again get the better of him. But Eric, holding himself in check, told Phil: "There's something important in this exchange. Let's not forget it."

"I have no further questions, Your Honor," Willoughby declared obsequiously, quitting on a note, however ambiguous, better than any he had attained thus far.

"What is the matter, Father?" asked Haakon that evening.

He was dressed for bed, and had come down into the parlor to say good night to his parents and Phil Phettle, who sat morosely at the hearth.

"Why, what do you mean?" Eric asked, picking the boy up and placing him on his lap.

"Mama's sad, and you're sad," Haakon said, "and even Uncle Phil is sad. Is Elizabeth dead?"

He asked the question quickly, belying his deepest fears.

"No," Eric told him. "No, she's alive, and safe. We have to believe that. A bad man took her, and we don't know why. He didn't do it to hurt your sister."

"I don't understand."

"It's hard to understand, honey," Kristin told him. "Bad things happen, and this is very bad, but we will see Elizabeth again."

"Come over here, Haakon, and kiss Uncle Phil goodnight," Phettle said.

The boy did so, and was soon taken upstairs to his bedroom.

"What do you think, Phil?" Eric asked.

"I think Rolfson has Elizabeth," the lawyer said shortly. "He meant to have his men snatch Haakon, but they missed. Once they had Elizabeth, what could they do? Kill her? Nothing to be gained from that. No, she is safe somewhere. You see, judging from what has transpired in the trial thus far, Rolfson had many things to lose by instituting proceedings in the first place. That is, perhaps, why he delayed so long. But he had to have Haakon, whom he still regards as his natural son. So he risked damage to his reputation, damage to his future prospects in this country, by pressing the suit."

WILD WIND WESTWARD

"Truthfully, Phil," Eric wanted to know, "what do you think Judge Bullion will decide?"

"Rolfson is shaken now," Phil replied, "but it depends upon how much I can damage him tomorrow."

They all heard a horse canter up to the front entrance of Windward and, in a moment, a loud knocking at the door.

The butler, Sven Engstrom, could be heard answering the knock. Then the door closed and the hoofbeats moved off into the spring night. Engstrom appeared in the doorway.

"Telegram for you, Mr. Phettle," he said. "From Chicago."

Phil seized the envelope and ripped it open. Kristin and Eric watched his face as he read the message. They saw his face light up.

"He's on the train now," Phettle cried, ecstatically. "He's on his way, and he'll be in St. Paul by morning. Haakon is safe!"

VII

"Court's again in session," groaned a bailiff, "Jedge Roscoe F. Bullion presidin'. All rise."

Everyone stood up, and old Bullion trudged in, a bit rheumatically. He banged his gavel. The people sat down. He asked the counselors to come forward.

"You finished?" he asked Willoughby.

"Yes, Judge."

"You ready to go?" he demanded of Phil Phettle.

"I am."

"Then let's get started."

Willoughby sat down next to Gustav Rolfson, who was trying not to fidget or appear nervous. He knew he would be on the stand a long time today.

"Your Honor," began Phettle, "this court has heard many insinuations about the relationship between Eric and Kristin. I say insinuations, although an honest God would know the remarks to be calumnies, pure and simple. The one *fact* that has been alluded to but never stated is that, since 1860, this man and this woman"—he pointed to Eric and Kristin—"have been deeply in love, and have sustained their love where countless others would have given up." He gestured toward Eric, who sat at the defendants' table in rapt attention. "People of the State of Minnesota, here is a man who was forced to flee his homeland, a poor but honest man hounded by the greedy machinations of an unprincipled enemy he neither desired nor provoked. From that homeland, Norway, he came to America penniless, surviving in our midst prejudice and poverty and mistreatment at the hands of those who took advantage of his honesty. Oh, the temptations to bitterness were many and great, but he did not yield to them. Rather, he fought with honor for the Union, he farmed the land, fathered fine children—one who has recently and cruelly been taken from him—and he has founded a fortune by virtue of his own strength and courage."

Phettle paused dramatically, then asked, with theatrical incredulity: "And the plaintiff is maintaining this man, Eric Gunnarson, born Starbane, is *not* a fit father?

"Moreover, at his side, as she has always been, in spirit if not in fact, is the woman he loves and who loves him, a woman strong as he is strong, who gave up her happiness in a forced marriage to a man most cruel, the same man who forced her beloved to leave Norway—"

"Objection!" shouted Willoughby, on his feet now. "Your honor, I object to this maligning of my client."

"Sustained," drawled Bullion. "Counsel is instructed to bring out such points, if any, by questioning the plaintiff."

Gustav Rolfson, certain it was time for him to be called to the stand, tensed a bit and cleared his throat.

Phettle strode back and forth in front of Judge Bullion's bench, waiting a moment, letting the tension mount. Rolfson glared at him. Phettle was smiling. So, too, were Eric and Kristin. Rolfson looked about nervously. Why didn't they call him to the stand? He was ready to denounce that bumptious commoner, and how! Gunnarson would know by nightfall never to cross Gustav Rolfson's path again. If only father could have lived to see this.

But why the delay?

Then Phil Phettle turned to the door that led from the courtroom to the chambers behind it, where witnesses, bailiffs, attorneys, and sundry court personnel often waited. "I call to the stand," he cried, "Lord Anthony Soames of London, England."

The surprise witness strode into this frontier courtroom, looking curiously about, and the spectators studied him with equal interest, craning and straining to see. They had no idea what he was doing here, no explanation whatever why an English nobleman should be attendant upon this divorce and custody trial. But there was a connection, and they knew it for sure when Rolfson himself got up and began to complain. "This is preposterous." He was fuming, red in the face, waving his arms. "This is an outrage."

Willoughby tried to calm him.

"Well, if it is an outrage," Judge Bullion decided, "I want to find out what in hell it's about. Counselor, seat your witness."

Soames took the stand, and was sworn in. He kept looking about, as if somehow he had strolled into a strange world. In a sense, he had. This new building, still smelling of pine, and these rude benches, were removed not only by thousands of miles but by venerable centuries from Queens Bench at Old Bailey. The people in the crowd found him unusual, too, quite exotic in a swallowtailed morning coat with a pink carnation in his lapel. Some of the Minnesota gallants, perhaps with a bit of barnyard still clinging to rude boots, snickered when they saw him. But when Soames regarded them with haughty amusement, they reddened and dropped their eyes.

"Your name is?" Phettle asked.

"Soames," replied the stranger, in a voice passionless yet vastly amused. "Anthony David Westley Winship-Higgins Soames."

Judge Bullion scowled. He regarded Englishmen with only slightly more enthusiasm than he did those who kissed in public.

"Why are you in America, Mr. . . . ah, forgive me . . . *Lord* Soames?" Phettle asked.

"There aren't any lords in Minnesota that I know of," Bullion rasped, "save for the Lord God. This man gets called 'mister' like any of the rest of us."

"I shall be content to conduct myself as a Roman," Soames said, bowing slightly.

"What?" asked the judge, suspiciously.

"I meant that I do not object to being called 'mister,'" Soames explained.

"Oh, oh, all right. Answer the question, then."

"Surely. I am in America because I received a telegram

from Mrs. Gunnarson, or Starbane, who is seated here in the court."

"And what was the nature of her message?" Phettle asked.

"She wished that I would come here to testify in her behalf."

"You know the lady in question?"

Soames smiled slightly at Kristin. "We became acquainted some years ago in England. She accompanied her husband, who sought from me capital funds."

Phettle gestured toward a stricken Gustav Rolfson. "Is that the man you refer to as Kristin's husband?"

"Yes, it is."

"What personal opinion did you reach as to the character of Kristin?"

"I regarded her immediately, and have ever since, as one of the finest women I have ever met. In all respects."

"And what is your opinion of Mr. Rolfson?"

"Considerably less," said Soames coolly.

Now Rolfson could be seen in a panicked conversation with lawyer Willoughby. Was there not some way in which Soames's testimony could be cut off?

"Would you say that Mr. Rolfson is deficient in certain areas? Areas in which Kristin is, by comparison, superior?"

"Of course," Soames said.

"Objection!" thundered Willoughby. "Counsel is leading the witness!"

"Overruled," barked Bullion. "Fitness is the crux of the custody case. I want to hear this."

"How would you judge Mr. Rolfson in the area of business enterprise?" Phettle was asking Soames.

"Mediocre, at best," answered the Englishman. "I extended him virtually limitless credit, and gave him plenty of time to turn a profit. In the end he paid me back, but that is about all. It was . . . how do you Americans put it? It was a 'dry hole.'"

"My client is now making a striking recoupment," Willoughby interrupted.

Vanessa Royall

"When I want to hear about that, I'll ask," old Bullion said. "Mr. Phettle, continue."

"And now," said Phettle, addressing Soames once again, "this is most important, especially since the custody and future life of a child will be decided here. Do you have knowledge as to the character of Mr. Rolfson?"

"I do," answered Soames.

Rolfson was getting to his feet. He was in the process of raising his hands, as if to stop everything, as if to say the entire trial had been a big mistake.

"And do you know anything about Rolfson," Phettle continued, "that might suggest to a normal member of good society that he ought not be entrusted with the raising of a child?"

"I certainly do," Soames said, looking at Gustav with his penetrating, passionless, yet amused eyes. "Once I had occasion, in London's east end, to visit a place of nighttime amusement with Mr. Rolfson—"

"No," Gustav cried.

"—and several friends of mine, in conjunction with Mr. Rolfson, retreated to a back room, there to engage in—"

"No, *please!*" Gustav howled, disrupting the courtroom.

Soames turned to the judge. "Perhaps, Excellency, I might tell you this in your chambers?"

"I ain't any Excellency," Bullion shot back. "But yes, yes I think we ought to retreat to chambers and settle all this. You sure got me curious, I'll tell you that!"

Twenty minutes later it was all over. Livid, Judge Bullion returned to the bench and banged his gavel. He looked upon a trembling Rolfson with outrage and disgust. "Rolfson, I want just a yes or no out of you," he said threateningly, "so I can get to the bottom of this without upsetting the citizenry. Did you ever, in England, know certain individuals named Rob, Pierre, and Vitas?"

Rolfson hesitated, trying to figure a way to wriggle off this hook.

"Be mindful," Bullion went on, "that it is possible to

WILD WIND WESTWARD

have these men summoned here to Minnesota. Lord ... ah, Mr. Soames has indicated that he could arrange it."

"I knew those men," said Gustav, crestfallen, as lawyer Willoughby wiped his face with a handkerchief.

"Well, then, here's the decision," Bullion concluded. "The marriage of Kristin Rolfson, known in these parts as Kristin Gunnarson, to Gustav Rolfson is hereby dissolved." He banged his gavel. "Custody of the child known in these parts as Haakon Gunnarson, goes to Mr. and Mrs. Eric Gunnarson. Or Starbane. Say, why don't you make up your mind on that, Eric?"

VIII

"Eric Starbane," Kristin said, cupping cold pure Lake Superior water in her hands, "here I hold your image, as I would hold your body and soul. May I drink it and have you, forever to keep?"

There were tears in Eric's eyes. "Yes," he said.

Kristin drank, and her eyes were shining, too. Memory. Destiny. The promise of hope.

Then Eric bent and scooped crystal water from the vast, magnificent lake, and held it before her. Sunlight danced in his hands, along with Kristin's image.

"Now I hold you in my hands," he said, "love and desire, yesterday and tomorrow. May I consume them and have them, forever to keep?"

Kristin nodded. Eric drank. They embraced and kissed then, for a long time, at the mouth of the Knife River, where it poured into Lake Superior on the wild rock coast of the north shore.

It was now August 1872. After the trial they had left Windward and come north to look for a place to build a second home in Duluth, so that Eric could be near the Mesabi Range. They bought land on the highest of Duluth's hills, with a view of wilderness to the north and the lake to the east.

The house would be known as Bethland. It would be there, waiting for Elizabeth's return. She would be found. Eric and Kristin were convinced of that. It was only a matter of time and search.

"She was here in Duluth all winter," Pinkerton agent

WILD WIND WESTWARD

Pierce Trifle had reported to Eric. "Big Elk found the house in which she was held. One of the two men who brought her north disappeared, but the other was joined for the winter by a woman. She came to the market regularly, and always paid cash. Seldom conversed, but was always polite. Just before Big Elk and I came to Duluth, the ice broke on Lake Superior. The man, the woman, and Elizabeth disappeared around that time. By boat, most likely. Somewhere east, I suppose."

Somewhere.

But *why*?

Eric and Kristin stood holding one another on a rugged, primeval shore. Behind them rose an empire to be conquered, ranges containing wealth against which the minerals of Lesja, Norway, would seem scraps of metal fallen from a smithy's forge. Haakon was theirs now, and they were each other's. Only two shadows loomed. One was J. J. Granger, and as Eric turned inland, it almost seemed he could see the one-eyed adventurer stalking along the horizon, could almost hear the acquisitive, insinuating *click-click-click* of Granger's pickax as he chipped away at rocks, seeking the red vein that meant fortune. The second shadow was far blacker. Cast by a vanished Elizabeth, it was made of strange fire that tore the hearts of Kristin and Eric. Yet they were full of hope. Big Elk and Pierce Trifle had reported the child always to have been well cared for. There was some meaning, some destiny, for which little Elizabeth, daughter of Eric and Elaine, must have been chosen. She had been taken for a reason, had she not? Or had it been merely an accident? Rolfson's hired hands, surprised by Indian Ned, seizing the wrong child in panic and confusion?

After Judge Bullion had adjourned the trial, Kristin herself had confronted Rolfson. He was a beaten man, but undefeated. He had lost a major battle, but not a war. That perfervid Rolfson *meanness* still burned there, far back in his eyes.

"No, I don't have Elizabeth," he had told her, looking

straight into her eyes. "You could come to my home in Chicago right now, if you wished. You would see she is not there."

"You are lying," she had accused, even though she sensed, at that moment, he was not.

"What does it matter to you?" he had asked, with his old insensitivity. "She was Gunnarson's daughter by the farm girl. You have Haakon."

"Yes, I have Haakon."

Then she had seen it: genuine, visceral pain, not to be eradicated, in Gustav's eyes, expression, even in his bearing. He was barely able to form the words, but he did.

"Haakon is truly not mine?"

"No," she told him.

He was silent for a moment. When he spoke again, it was the hard, abrupt Rolfson she had always known.

"Well, I will always have something of yours, too, my darling."

"What's that?"

He gave an indeterminate gesture. "Your memory, my love," he replied cynically.

"Could it have been Gustav all the while?" Kristin asked Eric now, on the north shore. "Maybe we were right at first. He had to get Haakon, and tried to do that by kidnapping. It failed. The only other means available to him was a trial, which he knew would be risky. That was why he delayed so long in filing the suit. But could he have Elizabeth, somehow?"

"Trifle and Big Elk will find her," Eric said soothingly. He was still looking inland, toward the range.

"What are you thinking of?" she asked.

"How best to transport the iron ore out of the wilderness and to the harbor in Duluth."

"You haven't found the iron yet." She laughed lightly, teasing him.

"But I will. And then I'll load it onto freighters, and . . . here," he said, bending to the narrow strip of sand on the beach. He made a line with his finger. "This is the north shore of Lake Superior . . ." he said,

"... and here is the south shore..."

"... and this is how she flows into Lake Michigan..."

"*Eric!*" Kristin cried.
But he was busy drawing, and with a swing of his hand, he showed her where Chicago was, a burgeoning industrial city at the base of Lake Michigan.

"*Eric!*" she cried again, her heart in her throat. "It's like the lines Ned drew before he died!"
Together they stared at Eric's diagram in the sand.
"Chicago!" Eric gasped. "Rolfson has Elizabeth! What was it that we asked Ned? '*Did the men say where they were going?*' Indians know the lay of the land for a thousand miles. Ned was trying to tell us what the men had said. And since they would have been spotted on the railroad, and did not want to cross all the distance between St. Paul and Chicago on horseback, they came to Duluth and waited for the ice to break up before taking Elizabeth on to Chicago by boat."
"And that's why Gustav sounded sincere at the trial," said Kristin, "when he said she was not at his home. She was not at his home *then*. But she is *now*."

Vanessa Royall

Her heart was in a tumult of hope and certainty.

"And he also said," Eric added, "he would always have *something of yours*."

They clung to each other, clinging also to the very real possibility that they were right.

"We have not come all this way to be flouted now by that wolf-eyed animal," Eric said then. "This shall be the end of him."

He was angry, but his anger was contained, controlled. He would go at once to Chicago. He and Kristin belonged to each other now, and would never be parted again. That union, so long in coming, had brought with it a mature strength, which was as hard as the iron Eric sought, and as tensile as past struggles had made him. Kristin was still in his embrace, and he looked down at her, kissed her. Sonnendahl Fjord glimmered in memory, and the ocean they had crossed, and this great continent into whose western regions destiny had led them. "Here we are," Eric said. "Here we stand. Here we shall triumph. You and I and Haakon, and Elizabeth, too."